THE
FORGOTTEN
PROPHECY

RAY LeCARA JR

SYNER-G PUBLISHING

SEATTLE

Published in the U.S. by Syner-G Publishing, Seattle.

Publisher's Cataloging-in-Publication Data
Names: LeCara, Ray Jr, author.
Title: *The Forgotten Prophecy* / Ray LeCara Jr.
Description: Seattle, WA: Syner-G Publishing, 2022. | Summary: When strange events in town start appearing in Simon's dreams, his journey to uncover what is really happening leads him to a conspiracy of buried secrets and a prophecy that he may somehow be a part of. But evil forces, both human and supernatural, are determined to keep him from confirming if there is a forgotten prophecy underway. And what, if anything, he's supposed to do next.
Identifiers: LCCN: 2022914848 | ISBN: 978-1737939467
Subjects: LCSH Nightmares—Fiction. | Prophecies—Fiction. | Catholic Church—Fiction. | Good and evil—Fiction. | Horror. | BISAC FICTION / Horror | FICTION / Thrillers / Supernatural
Classification: PS3612.E222 F67 2022 | DDC 813.6—dc23

Book Jacket Design © SGP | Front/Back Cover Image: Pixabay/Ria Sopala | All interior images licensed under Creative Commons Zero 1.0 Public Domain License

Printed in the United States of America

Syner-GPublishing.com

Third Edition

To Jenny—

PROOF THAT ANGELS DO EXIST AND
WALK AMONG US MERE MORTALS

ii

"The world is a dangerous place to live, not because of the people who are evil, but because of the people who don't do anything about it."

Albert Einstein, Theoretical Physicist

"The belief in a supernatural source of evil is not necessary; men alone are quite capable of every wickedness."

Joseph Conrad, Novelist

"Just as no man can enter any place without the help of him who has the keys, so no one is admitted to Heaven unless its gates be unlocked by the priests to whose custody the Lord gave the keys."

from **Catechism of Trent** *by Michael Malone*

iv

PROLOGUE
MONDAY
DECEMBER 25, 1967

THE VATICAN
ROME, ITALY

Quietly entering the pontiff's private study, the monsignor left silent impressions in the plush carpet.

"Sanctissimus Pater?" The monsignor's voice was reverent. A whisper.

Before him, the newly installed eighty-year-old pontiff stood silently praying at the window overlooking St. Peter's Square. Trembling hands worked the beads of the rosary behind his back.

Frail. Hunched over. This new head of the church was an unimposing figure. Age and the weight of humanity upon his round-backed shoulders had taken their toll.

He was dressed in his formal papal vestments—a robe of white complemented by a sleeveless cape that came to his waist. Around his neck an ornate gold crucifix, signifying his devotion as a follower of Christ. It lay across his chest about three inches above the white sash surrounding his waist. Further accentuating his attire was the white zucchetto. A skullcap.

The Most Holy Father stood in contemplation of tonight's homily at sunset—a service in honor of the Christ King's birth. It was early afternoon, but he was still fatigued from Midnight Mass. His first as pontiff.

Born Helmutt Venderhoff in 1887 to potato farmers in Southern Westphalia, Germany, his family was part of the largest emigration cycle in the history of the German state. Persecuted by the Imperial Chancellor of the German Empire, Otto Van

Bismarck, during his anti-Catholic campaign known as the Kulturkampf, Catholics made up the majority of over a million German citizens who emigrated between 1880 and 1890.

Bismarck saw the Mother Church of Rome and Pope Pius IX as wielding too much political power. A threat to his grand plans of uniting Germany. Though only one-third of the population was of the Catholic faith, the instituting of certain anti-Catholic laws severely limited religious activity and education within the country, eventually leading to the mass expulsion of all Jesuits from the country in 1872. While these laws would be rescinded by the early 1880s, the distrust and harassment continued for many years after. So embittered was the Catholic population, they continued their exodus until the 1890s.

Helmutt's own journey west would come at great cost. The youngest of six children, his mother died shortly after giving birth to him. His father, wrongly identified as a Catholic conspirator wanted for crimes against the German Empire, was one day picked up for questioning with Helmutt's older brother never to be seen again. Too young to remember, Helmutt and his other siblings would make the voyage to America in the latter part of 1888 to join several family members who braved the journey years earlier. Of the two brothers and two sisters who accompanied him, only one of each survived the grueling passage over. It was difficult to recall whether his siblings had fallen ill during the trip over or shortly after arriving in America. Either way, he would learn that it was not an uncommon occurrence for immigrants in those days.

Settling in a strong German Catholic community in Baltimore, Maryland, his earliest memories are those of a nurturing family steadfast in their faith. His faith would give him strength even in the worst of times and why he heeded the call to become a priest — a calling that saw him return to the Mother Country during World War II. There, under the guise of his collar, he helped German-Jews escape while praying over the sick, wounded, and dying. Each predicament more jarring than the first. Each testing and affirming his faith that much more. And while he felt for Mother Country, he could not side with the brutal nature of leadership that ruled Germany.

Years of service and ecclesiastical accomplishments brought him here to Vatican City. Following in the footsteps of the First Pontiff, the Apostle and Saint, Peter, Helmutt was humbled but resolute with the enormous responsibility he recently inherited. Such were the times that saw the new Bishop of Rome and Leader of the Holy See not only shepherding Church doctrine, but also ensuring the financial stability of Mother Church whose investments were widely dispersed throughout the world and influential enough to impact financial markets globally. His predecessors concluded that if the Church was to survive in this new era of emerging economies and growing capitalist regimes, it would have to be run as a business.

But this did not interest Helmutt. As Holy Leader of the Church, he was more concerned with trying to carry out the new, albeit unpopular, reforms in church practices dictated by the Second Vatican Council — a council convened by leaders of the Orthodox Churches to reform practices and Canon Law in a modern world. Completed prior to Helmutt's installation, he would have to bear the burden of officially seeing these changes through while also balancing his role as peacemaker in yet another tumultuous period in history.

His was a view of optimism, though. Discomforted by the pomp and circumstance of certain Church practices, such as his own coronation, he saw his position more as a chance—perhaps the last — to engage humankind in global unity before it was lost to a real "war to end all wars". Humanity was at an impasse. The proof came in the form of chaos and destruction. Two global wars, the second of the two unleashing Hell's fury in the form of atomic weapons dropped in Japan, changed nothing. Man had learned nothing in this modern age. Continuing conflicts in Korea, Vietnam, and the Middle East made that crystal clear. War protocol, though now governed by a set of international humanitarian guidelines like the Geneva Conventions, did little to curb the slaughter of innocent lives at the hands of zealots and despots looking to further their ideological causes as World War II demonstrated.

Still, the papacy made every possible effort to be involved in the reshaping of Europe, its most influential sphere. Embedded in NATO and the United Nations, representatives from the Vatican kept the Church informed and engaged. Most recently, with the aftermath of the Arab-Israeli War in June and the escalation in Vietnam — the West's futile attempt to stave off the growing threat of Communism — the new pontiff shouldered the responsibility of seeing that God's light was brought to all corners of the globe. Helmutt's only hope was that people would heed that call because now, more than ever, there was a need for it. The evil one's influence was spreading like a cancer, poisoning the world as it did so. It seemed his dominion would soon overtake this sacred earth. And with it, God's greatest achievement: Mankind.

Sweet incense, thick and overpowering, threatened the monsignor's tear ducts. His nostrils flared in response as he waited for the older man in the room to acknowledge his entrance.

Deep in thought, the pontiff hadn't heard the monsignor's gentle rap on the door. Nor did he hear him enter.

In absolute veneration, the monsignor's eyes circled the room to ensure everything was in order, the monsignor silently stood behind waiting.

The red wall-to-wall plush carpet was undisturbed, save for the vacuum marks. Much of the leather furniture and wood tables shined from recent polishing. Two oil paintings placed above shelves of canonical and ecumenical texts — one from the sixteenth century, the other eighteenth century — adorned the walls in richly carved gold frames. The most antiquated of the two was of Jesus standing amidst a crowd of children, the other of the Apostles watching Jesus ascend into the heavens. The statues in the room, one of Mary crushing the serpent beneath her feet and a smaller statue of Saint Peter, very much like the one greeting the public in the Vatican courtyard, were specifically requested. On the 1740 mahogany pedestal desk was a Bible and some reference texts neatly arranged near the pontiff's notes for this evening's Mass.

It was in this room that Pope Pius Paul came to compose his homilies and conduct meetings with private visitors, from foreign dignitaries to specially selected couples preparing for marriage. Arranged through the Prefect of Prefecture of the Papal

Household, the prefect coordinated the pontiff's meetings and schedule, as well as the internal affairs of the household within the Vatican. A cherished and envied appointment, the prefect was the closest aide to the pope in the Vatican. Since it was only through the monsignor that people could schedule an appointment with the Holy Leader, it was up to the prefect, as Papal Secretary, to screen those individuals.

A small movement out of the corner of the pontiff's eye drew him away from the window. Except for the bleached white Roman collar around his neck, the towering figure in the doorway was dressed in a cassock of black with purple piping.

"Si," the pontiff murmured in Italian.

"There is a woman here to speak with you. Forgive me, but..."

"Yes?" the elder asked as he rolled the beads shakily between his thumb, fore, and middle fingers.

"I don't know how she made it in. And a scene is certainly something we wish to avoid."

Resigned to the moment, his peace disturbed, the pontiff slowly shifted in place to face the monsignor. "Come now, Benjamin. Who is she? Why all the fuss?"

"Her name, Holy Father..." The monsignor swallowed hard, finding it difficult to reveal the vistor's name. "Her name is Sister Maria de Jesus."

The pontiff's eyebrows rose at the mention of the name. He had heard of this woman from Adánia, Columbia. Labeled a heretic and dismissed by many within the Church community, she was denied a papal audience by other popes before him. Visited as a child by the Virgin Mary, it was rumored she long held a vision of the future more cryptic and haunting than even Bernadette or Lucia's.

The monsignor studied the pope's face. Watched him process the news.

"She is indeed the one," the monsignor confirmed. "And she refuses to leave quietly. There is something very important she claims she must speak to you about. Something about the Weeping Age that is upon us."

Helmutt Venderhoff took in a deep breath, exhaling through quivering lips before murmuring something inaudible.

"Pater?" the monsignor asked, straining to hear the pontiff.

The pope shifted his gaze, catching the custom-made rosary beads suspended from his prefect's fascia. Making the sign of the cross over his forehead, pursed lips, and heart, he then nodded to the monsignor to send in the nun.

Exiting the room, the prefect heard the pontiff utter four words before kissing the crucifix at the end of the beads:

"And so it begins..."

MONDAY

MARCH 31, 1980

1

With legs pumping, the scrawny boy feverishly peddled his 1975 Huffy Thunder Road 4. Swaying left and right in perfect synchronicity under him, he made his way through the woods surrounding the outskirts of town. Gaining traction on the thawing path, the boy used every ounce of energy to push the bicycle as fast as it could go. He was determined to make it to the Stanton home in time to meet his friend off the bus.

Clearing the nearly frozen marshes near Gutterman Lake, he came alongside tracks of the Boston, Hartford and Erie Railroad Line. What was once an integral part of the town's lifeblood, it was eventually overtaken by New England Railroad. Its tracks since abandoned eleven years ago.

Pivoting the bike, the boy slid to a stop. Catching his breath, he wiped the hair from his eyes with the back of a dirty hand. Sweating under his green winter coat, the boy hardly noticed how cold it was.

Feeling fearless, he faced the train tracks, grinning from ear-to-ear. His mother would beat him senseless if she knew what he was up to. Using the wooded shortcut to Philip Junior's house was forbidden alone. Especially summertime when the foliage grew so thick it was nearly impassable. But it wasn't summertime.

Do it!

What had always been in the back of his mind finally grew into a bonafide dare as he challenged himself to one of the greatest jumps of his life.

Backing up some fifteen feet, the boy studied his target as he had many times before with his less daring best friend.

Yes... you can make it.

Awash in confidence on this auspicious day and fueled with the adrenaline of his rebellious act, the boy began his advance.

Yes...

A chilly March wind blew about him as he primed the pedals. The bike — a hand-me-down from his brother, a sophomore at Nazara High — was alive under him once again.

An eternity to reach the tracks, he coasted for an instant. When they suddenly appeared before him, he anticipated the next move carefully. At this point, with seconds to spare, calculations were crucial.

Feeling the faint contact of rubber to iron before pulling back hard on the handlebars, he was airborne. And free.

Soaring over barren ground, the nine-year-old boy straightened himself into a standing position while fighting the impulse to throw his hands up in triumph.

Then, just as quickly, gravity's strong arms pulled tiny Icarus back to terra firma. As the rear tire made contact, he expertly leaned left, using his leg to pivot the bike to a skidding stop. His small chest rose and fell rapidly as he took in his nearly flawless execution. It was such a feat that he temporarily forgot that Susie Green kissed him, little Johnny Pahana, on the bus earlier.

If only the kids at school could see him now. If only Susie Green were here to witness his accomplishment.

Excited to share the news with his bestest friend and classmate since kindergarten, the boy made off again, unaware of the small puncture in his rear tire.

He was even less aware of a set of eyes watching from the woods.

2

Electric and full of energy, the room was alive. Crowded. It was a wonder anyone could move. All around young people were jumping and moving to the "Macho Man" by the Village People. Standing at an angle where he could see the whole floor, one young man, Simon, watched the glittering disco balls bask everyone in prisms of light.

Glancing over at Larry, Simon's former college roomie from freshman year, eyes closed and hands raised high as he swayed to the beats, he couldn't help but feel like he was missing out on something. He terribly missed the scene.

But things had been hard lately. Between finishing up school and dealing with his wife's pregnancy, life was stressful. And with his wife out of work, money was tight. Living on a budget. No job. No future job prospects yet. It knotted his stomach even more when he thought of his student loans.

Then there was his uncle's passing. Five years on and it still left him empty. This loss was made raw once more by the recent and sudden death of the university's English Department secretary. By far the friendliest person on campus. She made him laugh one day with her comments and eyerolls while he waited for his advisor. Returning to the English Department without her there was difficult.

Simon ran his fingers through his hair, anxious to remove any thoughts of death from his mind. Yeah, getting out tonight was something he needed to do, he rationalized. Too bad he felt so damn guilty about it.

A young girl, probably a freshman, wearing tight blue short shorts and a bright orange tube top three sizes too small, rolled up beside him on roller skates. She handed him a flyer while flashing him a toothy smile in between snaps of gum.

He had seen her on campus before. Easy on the eyes, she wasn't easily forgettable. But he couldn't remember where or when he saw her last. Then again, he wasn't one to hang around campus much being married and all.

Skimming the flyer, he saw it was a list of activities for the university's rather late Spring Break week. Classes were wrapping up in little over a month. Tonight's dance, put together by one of the university's student organizations, was the kick-off for the week of events.

Simon was surprised by the number in attendance since most everyone he knew headed down to Fort Lauderdale or Daytona.

Watching the roller-skating bubble-gum snapper make her way through the crowd, sexy and carefree, Simon secretly longed to be single again. Single and free of all responsibilities.

Out of the single scene for over four years now, he married his high school sweetheart, Sarah Burnett, two years into college. After meeting in Art class, their relationship wouldn't blossom until the following year. Shortly before she graduated.

Simon tilted his neck until he heard it pop in relief. Anxious, he was feeling a little old — even though he was the same age as everyone around him — and out of place. He needed to relax.

Observing couples dancing with amusement, he waited for his friend to acquire some drinks. A couple of beers would be wonderful for his nerves right about now. Then again, a couple always led to more. Especially in this environment. Sinking into an alcohol-induced stupor was not going to make recent events any easier to deal with. Yet Sarah did encourage him — though with some indifference — to get out. And it *was* a campus-sponsored event. Such evening events usually began and ended at a decent time.

Earlier in the day Simon visited his uncle's gravesite. Going to the cemetery made him feel closer to his uncle. It was as if the gravestone was the physical embodiment of the person he terribly missed.

Though raised Roman Catholic, over the years since his uncle's death, Simon found he strayed farther and farther from any type of organized religion. Following his uncle's murder, Simon cursed God and all the Church stood for. He refused to speak any prayers or blessings, be they during holiday gatherings or bedside. But what thickened the saliva in Simon's mouth into bitter bile even more than his uncle's unsolved murder was that his uncle was a priest.

"I don't care if I do go to Hell. I will never forgive God for allowing this to happen to one of his own," he confessed to his wife — in a controlled rage — during their first Christmas together. "He took my parents and then he took my uncle. A priest! He allowed this to happen to a priest!"

He even refused to wear a keepsake his uncle had given him when he was a boy: a yellow gold cross necklace.

The first beer Larry brought him went down like water. As much as he tried to decline the offer for the one — and the others to follow — Larry was insistent. But instead of washing away his anxiety, the alcohol only left him hyper focused on his uncle.

Perhaps it was the timing, so close to the anniversary of his uncle's passing. But he found himself visiting the gravesite more often since the dreams started getting worse. These dreams, though difficult to recall, left lasting impressions — *echoes?* — well after he woke.

He shuddered at the thought of them now. A sobering shudder. Vaguely recalling the strangeness of his dreams to his wife a few weeks earlier, she expressed skepticism. And with good reason. For the last two years she's been supporting them both while he finishes school — an unspoken source of brewing contention. There was no way, he concluded, his wife was ever going to understand what it was he was experiencing.

From what Simon could tell, Sarah seemed to attribute his odd behavior to the dark cloud of uncertainty over his future following graduation. Maybe he *was* unsettled about life after school. But more than that, with no job prospects in his field of study, the enormity of responsibility that came with marrying early coupled with impending fatherhood, he was left paralyzed by the thought of bringing a child into this world unprepared.

With the baby due any time now, it would no longer be the two of them. As husband and father, he would need to step up and support the family — a tremendous responsibility for a twenty-two-year-old without a steady income and medical insurance that comes with steady employment.

Simon thought they were always careful. But birth control isn't always one hundred percent foolproof.

An existential crisis notwithstanding, it was, after all, only natural given the circumstances. His child was about to enter the world with a daddy beset with emotional baggage. And that bothered him. Knotted his stomach with the painful realization that this baggage even threatened his relationship with his wife at a time when they both needed to be on the same page.

Simon was beside himself, feeling lost with no one to turn to. And if Simon could not go to his wife, whom could he go to then? His friends? Larry was perhaps his closest friend. But marriage and living off campus these last two years changed everything. Single and without a care in the world, Larry, and those Simon hung with, were all at very different places in their lives.

Three quarters into a second beer and a shot of Jose Cuervo Especial, Simon was finally feeling more relaxed. A third beer—and second tequila—helped relegate thoughts of his uncle and Sarah to the outer periphery of his consciousness. Bunched up close, he and his friends claimed their small area on the dance floor. Anita Ward's "Ring My Bell" followed a set of songs from the Bee Gees, encouraging any remaining onlookers to get in on the fun.

Larry flanked Simon with a female friend, Jackie. The two were on the make, each having just gotten out of relationships. Jackie's former boyfriend was a pot addict while Larry's former girlfriend wasn't happy keeping with a monogamous relationship.

Larry backslapped Simon's shoulder before tipping his left hand to his lips to give his signature *I'm-going-for-more-beer* gesture. Then he was off, disappearing into the crowd. Tall and gangly, his super-sized perm the only part of Larry still visible in the dimly lit room as he navigated his way to the makeshift bar.

It was then that Jackie moved in a little closer for a dance.

Simon looked a wreck. The first two buttons of his sweat-drenched shirt were unfastened and clung to his skin. His head and neck were drenched under a layer of perspiration. But under the disco lights, under the alcoholic stupor that dulled some senses and heightened others, it didn't matter.

Jackie's advance took him a little off guard. But then everyone was falling in love with the newly released "Lost in Love" by Air Supply. Resting her head on Simon's sweaty chest, he held her close. His cheek atop her head, he briefly felt at peace. The alcohol and music helped to wash away his responsibilities in short melodic waves. When the song ended, he was about to give her a hug when her lips found his.

Standing six inches taller, Simon had to lean into Jackie's five two petite frame for the hug. A gorgeous girl with feathered, shoulder-length brown hair, Jackie was blessed with full pouty lips and big, bright hazel eyes. Well endowed, her tight v-neck tee provided proof that teased the senses. A sheen of sweat glistening from her unavoidable assets as Simon lowered his head to face her. Then his hands confirmed what his eyes knew to be true: she wore her tight, bell-bottom jeans very well.

Simon knew of Jackie. Knew of her reputation. It was rare to find her single. But this night found her lonely, too. Her tongue quickly found Simon's.

Another song started up. A Rod Stewart single. Simon felt eyes on him. But he surprised himself with how much he welcomed Jackie's lusty lips. He readily met her hungry mouth. Cupped in his hands, he held her face, wet with perspiration. Returning the intensity of her kiss, he tasted lingering toasted almond shots and the saltiness of sweat on her upper lip. Drawing closer, her knee moved between his legs, stirring him even more.

Sarah's difficult pregnancy limited their intimate time. But it wasn't all Sarah. Simon's worries about school and the baby left him nearly void of any intimate feelings. He wondered where those feelings had been all these months. Right now, those feelings had him feeling like a teen virgin on his first date.

"Kenny's got his van with him tonight," Jackie enticed in between mouthfuls of tongue.

Simon's head spun. The alcohol clouded his thoughts. Tempered his worries. But it threatened to return.

He wanted out of his clothes. Out of this place with the loud music. Away from the crowd.

He wanted to touch her. Feel her warmth. Be in her.

To Jackie's moans, Simon breathed into her ear. "Oh, Sarah, I've missed you so much."

Jackie abruptly pulled away. Eyes rapidly welling up. "You... you're an asshole." Shoving him aside with both hands, she pushed her way through the crowd in sobs. Leaving him on the dance floor embarrassed and confused.

"What the hell was that all about," Larry asked, greeting Simon with another beer.

"I'm not sure. She got pissed at me all of a sudden." Simon rubbed his temples. Which were beginning to throb. Did he call her Sarah?

He swallowed back some beer before eyeing the exit. The waves of responsibility, of life, were crashing back into shore.

"Forget that, man. What were you doin' gettin' it on with her?"

Simon didn't really want to address Larry's questions right now. Clarity suddenly thrust upon him, the previous alcoholic haze seemed to instantly dissipate. The music blared. Worsening his sudden headache with each pulsating beat. Part of him wished he was in Fort Lauderdale. Anywhere, really. Anywhere but here.

"Hey man," Larry again prodded, getting into Simon's face. "What the hell was up with you swappin' spit with Jackie when you have a wife at home?"

Waves of guilt washing away what little alcohol remained in his system. "Larry, don't sweat it. I screwed up. I know, man. It just... I don't know. It just happened."

Larry glowered as he watched Simon put down his beer to grab his denim jacket, a crumpled heap on the floor, from behind a chair against the wall. "You know," he said, grabbing Simon's arm with some force to make sure his point was made, "some of us should be lucky enough to have someone like Sarah."

Simon jerked his arm out of Larry's grip and quickly into the sleeves of his jacket. He did not need to hear this. Not now. "Hey, what can I say, Larry? I ain't no saint."

And with that, Simon was out the door and into the chilly last night of March.

3

Little Johnny Pahana made his way back home from his friend's house the same way he came, knowing full well it would anger his mother. She didn't like him taking that path even in daylight. even more than taking this path in daylight. But so caught up in sharing his tale — and suggesting he and Philip Junior should try it again on Saturday together — he innocently lost track of time. Of course part of that time was spent trying to convince his friend that he *actually* made the jump.

The little boy didn't fear racing home in the twilight; the dark never scared him. Even the sound of a freight train in the distance, a rare occasion, didn't faze him as he toyed with the idea of attempting the jump again.

Johnny veered left, following the railroad tracks up to the abandoned general store. As young as he was, he was smart enough to decide against going past the lake again this late in the day. It didn't help that his brother kept trying to frighten him with stories of the upcoming *Friday, the 13th* movie. Johnny wasn't about to chance going anywhere near the lake at night, lest there be a Jason of its own lurking nearby.

Making his way along the tracks near the boarded-up structure, he was distracted by a whimpering cry emanating from somewhere within the underbrush. Though there was but a hint of light permeating the shadows surrounding the woods, it was difficult to see anything clearly. Johnny was lucky to know the path by heart.

Then he heard the whimpering cry again.

Followed by his mother's voice. "You need to leave those stray animals alone. They could have rabies."

Even though his mother scolded him whenever he brought home a stray, punctuating her warnings by forcing him to read Disney's *Old Yeller*, he hated knowing an abandoned pet could be hurt. Alone.

Catching movement of something in the brush, he set his bike down, preparing to venture deeper into the dark shadows.

In the distance, a freight train's whistle blew a warning that woke the little boy up to the reality of the situation.

It was late. It was dark. And he was in for a whole lotta hurtin' when he got home.

Swatting at whatever annoying pest flew about his face, he hopped back onto the bike to make his way past the dilapidated building. He would come back tomorrow. Connecting once more with the original path, he proceeded to the crossing point over the tracks.

The bike, however, was moving slower under Johnny's weight no matter how hard he peddled. Crossing the tracks, it was evident something was wrong. Determined to press on, he stood to give his peddling more power.

But as Johnny crossed the tracks, the bike came to a jerking halt, sending the boy careening off to the side. He hit the cold ground, the handlebars jabbing forcefully into his stomach as the bike collapsed over him.

Uprighting the bike, he discovered the rear wheel had become lodged. With every effort, it would not budge. His small fingers felt along the rim of the tire down to the tracks to locate the catch without much success. Even worse, the tire, as much as he could tell without seeing it, was nearly deflated.

Mounting the bike once more, the boy rocked it under him frantically, trying to free the wheel. Still the wheel would not budge.

Forgotten, in the distance, another whistle blew from the oncoming train.

Surrounding the tiny young boy, among the shadows, a larger shadow moved in. Hovering near the tracks, it closely observed the desperate child. Delighting in the scent of the little one's rising frustration.

And fear.

Tears streamed the boy's puffy red cheeks. Spittle flew from his small mouth as he mimicked grown up words often heard by his parents when angry.

Another whistle. The boy snapped his head in the direction of the oncoming railway vehicle. Squinting for a line of sight in the darkness, the boy was so preoccupied with trying to dislodge the stuck wheel that he completely disregarded the proximity of the train.

He needed to get home. And now. Even if it meant leaving the bike.

The tracks were vibrating; their intensity quickly escalating as the boy tried to clear himself from the bike.

With a half-hop in the dark, he caught the leg of his pants on the special grip pedals he received as a gift for his good grades. The thumping in his heaving chest matched the tracks' vibration, culminating with his rising fear. Unable to see anything before him, Johnny became trapped-up once again in the falling bike's frame, hitting his head on one of the iron rails.

Emerging from the darkness, a shadowy figure readied its assault on the boy to complete its evil task. After weeks of watching and waiting, it knew the child's every move. The deflated wheel was simply a stroke of luck the shadow hadn't anticipated. It was all too easy. And under the cover of nightfall this overcast March evening, there would be no witnesses.

The train came upon the youth with a loud, thundering roar. At once there was an ear-piercing shriek of metal-on-metal as the train crushed the boy's bike. Shards of twisted metal flew into the air in all directions.

Too dark now to distinguish anything except for the single headlight of the engine at the nose of the train, endless boxcars followed, rattling past the shadowy figure. As the last of the cars finally squealed by, the figure inspected the tracks with a feeling of elatedness.

That the train destroyed the bike was certain. But there was no body. The figure contemplated this development. Without further explanation, it felt certain the boy was dead.

Assuming the deed done, the figure set off in the direction from which the train had come. Until it felt something grab at its insides. Forcing it onto the loose stones. The smell of tar and metal overwhelming to the senses.

Someone — or something — was approaching from behind. The figure froze in fear of having been caught in its earlier villainous act.

Enveloped in the blackness, what drew near was an even darker silhouette. A swarm of buzzing of insects accompanied him. It was the same incorporeal presence who taunted him endlessly, delighting whenever there was misery. Its demeanor could be warm and inviting, turning icy cool without warning or provocation. Hard to please was this presence, this creature, who approached.

"My Lord..."

Still on hands and knees, the subservient figure beckoned from his position of compliance.

From behind — no, around — the dark silhouette, a crimson light began to burn. It revealed the presence to be wearing a desert robe and sandals. Kneeling, it drew itself ever closer to the sniveling figure on the ground. When it spoke, its voice seemed to prick the ear drums with sharp icy daggers. "You have failed me. And for that failure, you will pay."

The punishment wasn't just directed at the human form still inhabiting the shadowy figure, but the many beasts within. Most especially Asmodeus. The demon delegated to destroy the child.

On the ground, the figure's insides began to burn. The many demons inhabiting its mortal shell laughed at the images filling the human's mind. Images of mutilated corpses devoured by hordes of deformed demonic creatures writhing over one another. A taste of what was to come if he did not carry out the requests of the robed one before him.

Violently thrust into the air, its body was forced like a rag doll onto the loose stones. Over and over again. "No... My Lord..." it shrieked. "Please don't! It wasn't... me! I always do as you command!"

4

Simon returned home late, even though it was only around 9:00 PM when he exited the campus dance. He probably would have stayed a little later if he hadn't pissed Larry off. Simon was certain it was more about Larry not getting laid than anything else, though. Jackie had, after all, stormed out minutes earlier killing any chance of a hook-up.

The entire ride home a blur, once in the door, Simon turned on the tube before fixing a honey ham sandwich. He hoped some food and aspirin would quell the throbbing in his head.

About a month ago he figured if there was no change he would have to speak with a doctor. Putting the cheese and ham back into the fridge, he then grabbed a Schlitz. Popping the tab, he read the message Sarah left for him on the freezer door while swallowing down a couple of Bufferin with a gulp of beer. The psychologist called earlier in the evening. It was to confirm tomorrow's appointment to assess some tests Simon underwent a week earlier for his migraines. Perhaps the doctor could prescribe something for him. Yet Simon wasn't going because of his migraines. He wanted to talk to someone about the dreams.

No sooner had Simon finished his sandwich and beer did he hear the chimes from the clock behind him on the paneled living room wall. It was already 2:00. Up off the sofa, he stretched before shutting off the television set. Time to get some sleep. There was nothing on but old *Benny Hill* reruns anyway.

In the dark from the living room, Simon made his

way past the bathroom on his left, then entered the kitchen-dining area before descending three steps to the sunken, green shag-carpeted room that currently served as a multipurpose room. It was here that he kept his small desk with typewriter. And dresser, too. It didn't fit in the small bedroom off to the right. Currently under renovations, it wouldn't be long before the room ceased its function as a makeshift office to ultimately become the baby's room. He nearly stubbed his toe on the crib haphazardly placed in the center of the room.

Entering the room to the right, Simon shed his clothes and sought cover under the blankets next to his wife.

Simon was remembering his time in college. A psychology class taken freshman year. He was recalling the professor explaining how, contrary to what most people believe, sleep does not occur gradually. It is instantaneous. This notion was fascinating to him. He always perceived dreams as a mysterious thing. The mind in total control as the eyes and ears were shut off to the world.

"Kinda like automatic pilot," Sarah breathed into his ear one night after a spontaneous spurt of lovemaking. Bodies naked and exposed, they clung to each other in the dark under the covers as much for love as warmth.

Sated and content, it took no more than a few heartbeats before she was out herself. Her steady breath on Simon's chest.

To Simon, dreams were always an escape from reality. A place where he could be free when he felt constricted. It was also a place where he could find answers to questions that plagued him when he was awake. But as of late his sleep was anything but an escape.

Lying awake thinking, words in his mind harder to concentrate on, there was no mistaking the part of him looking forward to at least a few minutes of sleep. Dreams or no dreams. And no sooner did he think this was he there.

Flying.

Simon was suddenly aware of flight. Some nights it was limited to only a few feet above the ground. Tonight he was soaring.

But by the time he fully registered this, he was lying face down on the ground. Brushing himself off, he observed a dilapidated wooden building before him. It appeared long since abandoned. It was nighttime. Dark, except for an ominous moon obscured by overhanging trees. From afar there came to his ears a faint train whistle.

Ahead were tracks. Train tracks interlaced with large, dark shadows. Simon recognized blurred city lights visible from the outlying area.

Overlooking the tracks from the front porch of the wooden structure where he found himself, a youth in high-top Converse sneakers was having great difficulty crossing on his bike.

A train whistle wailed alarmingly closer this time.

Simon watched the boy entangle himself trying to hop over the bike. Unable to balance, he fell hard onto the rails.

Simon winced. No sooner had the boy fallen did the train charge out of nowhere.

Simon's surroundings shifted in a blur. He was suddenly track side hovering over the kid. The deafening sound of metal-on-metal engulfed them both as the screeching wheels of the train connected with the boy's bicycle.

But the sound came from behind Simon, not in

front of him. Simon cuffed his ears, glancing over his shoulder in time to see parts of the boy's bike sent in various directions. Holding his breath, Simon heard a whimper that was not his own. Safely, at his feet, was the boy. Then, once more, Simon was on the front porch of the boarded wooden structure.

"WHAT HAVE YOU DONE?" Something from the surrounding wall of thickets, with an icy guttural shriek, screamed at him. Foul smelling saliva showered him.

Simon instinctively squatted to protect the boy. But the boy was no longer there. Feeling something grab hold of his neck, Simon was forced to the ground. Knocking his head on something hard, his breath shallowed as he struggled to remain alert.

As consciousness faded, Simon's last memory was of a shadowy figure hovering over him with a large object.

Nothingness. No thoughts. No sounds. No images. There wasn't even any pain.

Simon's eyes slowly fluttered open. He cautiously surveyed his new surroundings. It was a place he was quite familiar with. A place where he often played when his parents were alive. He was standing in the backyard of his youth.

Before him was a garden statue of the Blessed Mother. The Immaculate Virgin Mary. Her arms outstretched and welcoming. Simon was around seven years old when his mother received the two-foot statue as a gift from his great uncle. To his younger self, the stature was large. Life-like.

The statue began to transform. No longer two feet, it grew to three. To four. No longer in the corner of the yard near the flowerbed as he always remembered it, it was now in the middle of the yard.

Continuing to grow, it began ascending.

Becoming flesh. Radiant, warm beams of light emitted from all around the statue made flesh.

In her eyes were the origins of the Holy Light surrounding her. At once he understood everything in the universe. He understood why he was here. His purpose in life. How the actions of any one individual can irreparably alter the future.

For good. For bad.

Simon watched the woman — the mother of Jesus — continue to rise. No longer wearing a blue shawl, she was now dressed all in white. Her lips were moving. He strained to hear her voice. Increasing in resplendence, the light eclipsing her forced him to shield his eyes.

Then he heard it.

"Go in the name of God. You know what it is that you must do..."

As everything was engulfed in the white of the light, Simon became vaguely aware of having had this dream before. But he was most bewildered by her parting words.

"For you are the *kefa*."

TUESDAY

APRIL 01, 1980

5

Pope Pontius I watched the crowd from his cathedra.

"Of all the temptations and forces surrounding us," Archbishop Avarassi said, speaking from the lectern of Saint John's Cathedral, "the responsibilities to honor and heed the call to our faith is the greatest of all mortal burdens."

The cathedra is the altar chair reserved for the leader of the Church. In this case it was the archbishop. But as was custom, he acceded the symbolic seat when receiving notable dignitaries as a gesture of respect. None was more deserving than the leader of the Church himself, the visiting pope.

The term cathedral, though technically assigned to any church that serves as a bishop's headquarters and not necessarily any type of architectural design, couldn't help but embody the grandeur that came with the design of most cathedrals. This one, constructed of mostly granite and sandstone, was an homage to the medieval cathedrals of Europe. And one of the most cherished structures in Boston, Massachusetts. Nearly two hundred years old, St. John's combined the elements of both English and French designs, with an accent on gothic architecture. It was a marvel to behold.

Partially destroyed by a fire in the late 1800s, it stretched over three hundred feet from the entrance doors to the sanctuary with a maximum width of one hundred, thirty feet at the transepts. Following the aisle to the foyer of the church, the choir and organist sang and played from above on a balcony illuminated by the brilliance that shined through a large Renaissance stained-glass rose window. The rose window, a design of French influence, was flanked on the outside by two spires reaching upwards of two hundred and fifty feet.

With its maximum interior measuring at a height of one hundred and four feet, the cathedral had a floor area of forty-three thousand square feet and a seating capacity of nearly two thousand. From the center of the ceiling hung a massive three-tiered crystal chandelier consisting of twenty-five arms and twenty-five bulbs. It was surrounded by a series of arches supported by Corinthian columns. Between the columns, three on either side of the nave, hung large tapestries of the apostles. Illuminating the interior in prisms of colored light, three large stained-glass windows reminded the congregation of Christ's sacrifice. Signifying Saint John, the Apostle's role in church dogma were frescoes behind the altar and set within — and above — the apse.

Between the pope's chair and the one to his right belonging today to the archbishop was the tabernacle, the holding place for the Eucharist—the embodiment of the transfer of bread into the body of Christ. Set slightly inside the apse, or alcove, it was shrouded in white linen beneath a small white cross signifying its holy connection. On either side were ornate candelabras with burning candles of white. Seated at this center point of the altar area the outlying floor plan was in the shape of a cross, referred to as the transept, with both the left and right sides extending outward between the altar area and congregation.

On one side stood a statue of the Virgin Mary holding baby Jesus. A statue of Joseph on the other. Closer to the altar, on the outer rim of the sanctuary, stood statues of heralding angels with trumpets in hand.

Before the pope was a crowd of religious and political dignitaries in what was his first visit to the United States since his installation less than a year earlier following the death of Helmutt Venderhoff, Pope Pius Paul. Sitting before the congregation of politicians, diocesan priests, sisters, bishops, and faithful followers, the pope maintained a penitent expression as the archbishop spoke about maintaining faith in a world wrought with temptation.

"It is we," the archbishop said over the pope's thoughts, "who must continue to be the beacons of light in this time of darkness, rekindling the spirit our Lord made flesh nineteen hundred and eighty years past."

Pope Pontius agreed. Yet his vision of being a "beacon of light" was slightly different than the one envisioned by his colleague at the lectern. His eyes keenly surveyed the throngs of people in the pews. As he caught the glances of parishioners eyeing him, he met their stares only to watch them turn away.

God's fallen and misled sheep is how he saw them all. No longer regarded as the instrument necessary for guiding individuals to lives of decent, moral behavior, the Church had been reduced to provider of empty words and meaningless messages.

The mystery, as he long suspected, was lost. Society's downward spiral attested to that. Especially in the western world. Since de-mystifying the Mysteries of the Church and welcoming the masses with open arms, this pope's predecessor sought to aggressively promote the edicts of the Second Vatican Council. Established in 1965, it was supposed to be a move towards making the Church more accessible by, among other things, changing the official language of the Mass from Latin to English. All it succeeded in doing, as Pontius saw it, was absolving its members of shouldering any accountability for living philistine lives. Furthermore, Venderhoff's plans, in support of the Vatican Council's changes, backfired. While it seemed that populations in diocesan parishes increased over the last thirteen years, with church membership peaking approximately five years ago, fewer parishioners were attending the regular celebrations. Empty of its weekly attendees, Rome's satellite churches were falling farther into the red. Parish priests were now lucky to see their fellowship on the holiest of holidays like Christmas and Easter. In western societies, more individuals were becoming "free thinkers" as fewer parishioners took their baptismal commitments seriously.

Archbishop Avarassi motioned to Pope Pontius as he spoke his closing words. "Together with our newly installed leader, we can hope, as the new millennium approaches, to one day achieve world-wide peace and unity."

Nodding in assent to the archbishop's reference, the pope silently reflected on the amount of work to be done. And just how much there was left to prepare for.

6

The burly fry cook was barking from behind the counter. "Dammit JJ, can't you shake that tush any faster." His unshaven face red from leaning over the grill all morning.

"Ya know, Ed," Jenny's transplanted west coast accent apparent as she handed him another order, "you are super lucky I love ya. Otherwise I'd tell ya to kiss my damn grits." Giving him a wink and a lick of her chops, she picked up two dishes — one a turkey club order, the other a fish sandwich — before returning to the floor.

Ed grabbed the ticket with a half-smirk noting how college girls were all sass these days. How he wished he were a few years younger. But hey, it made him feel young and alive to be surrounded by them.

His diner was bustling today. And that made Ed happy. He assumed the additional traffic coincided with the pope's visit. Even if the additional patrons were no more than passers-by on their way to Boston. While not an overly religious guy, he was fine with the church boss visiting nearby if it meant more green paper and coin in his registers.

The failure of Vietnam and the Watergate scandal notwithstanding, the recession of the '70s still impacted the economy. Rampant unemployment and gas shortages affected every small business owner, like Ed, who worked damn hard to make a decent living on his own terms. This was especially so here in Connecticut, where the growing tax burden on property owners alone was enough to set one back. With the exception of Bridgeport, Ed always thought Litchfield and Fairfield counties were close enough to the New York border to become a separate state of their own. Compared to the rest of the state with cities like New Galilee, Hartford, New Haven, Bristol, and Nazara, it was as if towns like Jordan were worlds apart anyway. If the state's cost of living were to ever reflect the working class, the entire western part of the state would have to be removed from the equation.

"Damn that Carter," Ed mumbled, cracking eggs over the griddle. Squinting through a cloud of grease smoke, he flipped over several strips of bacon.

It still angered him every time he thought of the American hostages held in Iran. He hated politics. But he hoped the Republican candidate, despite his being a former actor, would be able to free them.

Ten years earlier Ed entertained the idea of opening a second place. Back when business was brisk every day of the week. Then the economy tanked. In fact, it seemed as if the entire world was spiraling. So, it came as no surprise that his business was too. Lucky for the advice of friends and family, he never broke ground on a second diner. If he had, he'd be even deeper in the hole than he was now.

Flipping the sizzling eggs with one hand, he attended to his sweaty brow with a forearm wipe. At least he still had his health, he chuckled as looked down at his extended stomach. Retirement, for anyone else his age, should by now be but an arm's length away. These days, though, it never seemed any closer.

"Freida!" Ed yelled to his wife of seventeen years, wiping his hands on his apron. She was working the register at the front. He then went about placing slices of crisp bacon onto the sourdough bread he prepared minutes earlier. "Freida! BLT.

Table 12."

He placed the plate in the window, swatting at a curious fly. Though flies would occasionally sneak in during summer months, it was rare to see them in April.

Freida was still working on getting a customer settled with a bill and out the door when Ed yelled again. "Jesus, Freida! Drop everything and get this out there or Marty will have a fit."

Ed flashed Freida one of those *you-know-what-I-mean* smiles as Freida finished up at the register. That smile became the signature of their working relationship. A tough-lovin' working relationship they always joked about because it wasn't easy working with a spouse. "Come on, girl. You know how those high-powered important people are. And since good ol' Marty is an attorney..."

"I know, I know. Time is money," Freida replied when she came for the order. This was after filling two cups of coffee on her way. To survive in this business, one had to learn the art of multitasking. Still, she didn't pay much mind to Ed. Even if he was a little more agitated than usual today.

Jamie, a twenty-something redhead going through a subtle punk-rock phase, rushed behind the counter. Though Freida reminded her countless times about the dress code, her studded collar was visible around her neck.

Regardless of her dress code defiance, there were few girls who hustled as fast as her. In the time that she filled three sodas from the fountain, poured a coffee and hot water for tea, she also gave Ed two other orders. Two number two lunch specials and one number seven with mayo. Hold the tomatoes. Add hot peppers. No pickle. One of the five sitting at table three wanted a slice of apple pie. The other a salad with house dressing. She would get those herself.

Ed acknowledged the order with a mumble as his three tossed patties were met with a greasy hiss.

"Hey, Kathy," Jamie exclaimed, passing another older waitress as she went out onto the floor. She hadn't seen much of her all morning. It was *that* busy.

Kathy smiled. "Lookin' good, Jamesie." The young woman reminded her of her own daughter who was estranged and living in some other state with a hippie boyfriend who never could seem to hold down a job. "Big Ed, is number six ready yet?" Kathy checked on her order while replacing the coffee filter and adding fresh grounds to urn number three.

"Just a minute, babe."

"Kat!" Jenny motioned to Kathy as she came around the corner stuffing her tips into the jar behind the counter.

"Hi, JJ! Ready for Easter? Getting together with your folks?" Kathy finished pouring the rest of the water into the reservoir and flipped the switch for it to begin dripping.

The girl rolled her eyes and scoffed. "I don't think so. My boyfriend invited me to spend it with his family. Besides, he lives in Manhattan. I've never been to Manhattan. He says he's even going to bring me to see a Broadway show in New York City."

"Wow," Kathy gushed, wishing she were young again. Things were much less complicated then. It was easy to get lost in reverie when around these girls.

"Yeah, well, you only live once. Right?" Jenny said cashing out a customer and giving Kathy a wink. "God, I could use a smoke right now!"

"Forget Broadway," Jamie said as she came

behind the counter to grab paper placemats, utensils, and menus. "I'd much rather see that Richard Gere guy in... What's that movie that just came out?"

Kathy took a guess laughing. "*American Gigolo*?"

"Yeah! What a dreamboat that guy is," Jamie cooed as she went back out onto the floor.

"I'd let him do me," Jenny added as she passed a flushing Kathy on her way to have a smoke in the backroom. "Fer sure!"

Ed was looking over at Kathy's order suspended in front of him with squinty eyes. "Yo, Kath! You sure this guy wants his burger pink?"

"Yep," she replied, preparing a bowl of ice cream for table eight. "About as pink as my cheeks right now."

"JJ!" Ed yelled. "Your six is ready for pickup."

Kathy noted the odd coincidence silently to herself: Number six for table six. A first for today. Then it occurred to her this was about the fifth or sixth time that order came in so far.

Sometimes the waitresses would bet on how many customers might order lunches or dinners that matched their table numbers. But as she made her way back out onto the floor with her bowl of ice cream, a commotion interrupted her thoughts. Several people were up from their tables, congregating around someone on the floor.

Then a woman started screaming and all Ed wanted to do was knock her one. Maybe then he could at least think straight. Her shrill screaming was enough to make his ears bleed. Or shatter glassware.

Throwing down his spatula, he ran from behind the grill, through the swinging double doors and out into the dining area.

"Someone help him. Please! Oh, God! He's choking!"

Ed observed a few of his older female customers cover their eyes. Others were watching like it was a freak show at a circus, chewing their food in slow motion.

Muttering a string of expletives under his breath, Ed navigated his bulky frame through onlookers surrounding the patron on the floor. "C'mon people. 'Scuze me. Move, huh!"

With his luck, Ed couldn't help but fear the end of his business. All because, he surmised, dopes like this guy can't chew food properly. And with very little money saved up for his retirement, he could only imagine the worst.

Yet, for all he knew, with the pope in town, if he didn't help the guy, he wouldn't only lose the biz. He'd guarantee himself a one-way ticket to the nasty man downstairs.

Noticing Freida to his left, frozen in place with a look of sheer horror on her face, he yelled her into action. "Freida, call a friggin' ambulance, will ya! Hurry, girl!"

Then something truly curious happened. And though he would forget this after everything calmed down, what happened so quickly, with each blink of his eyes, seemed to play out like frames on an old reel of black and white film.

Blink.

One of his waitresses was trying to help people back to their seats.

Blink.

A woman was jumping up and down hysterically. Her tongue flapping wildly along with the slack flesh under her chin.

Blink.

One person was leaving the diner. Even in the commotion, Ed wondered if he paid his bill yet.

Blink.

Patrons surrounding the gentleman on the floor were keeping his head raised as he gasped and tried to breathe. Or swallow. Ed couldn't tell which.

Blink.

Kathy's cheeks were wet with cascading tears. It was her table. Ed knew she was going to blame herself. She was that kind of person.

Blink.

In all of the madness, a young man emerged from the back hallway leading to the restrooms. Ed watched in astonishment as the men and women surrounding the man on the floor moved aside to allow this young man through.

Blink.

The man on the floor, who was writhing and gasping, calmed suddenly as the young man knelt beside him.

Blink.

His view suddenly obstructed, the more Ed tried to maneuver in closer to the incapacitated man, the more he found himself somehow farther away.

A paramedic crew made their way through the front doors, drawing his attention. Beyond the paramedics Ed noticed a gentleman outside the diner. It was the same guy who promptly exited when the commotion began. Though he seemed in a hurry earlier, he now stood facing the entrance. But he wasn't watching the commotion. He was looking right through the doors at Ed.

Fresh air, Ed speculated. While he waits for the commotion to settle. Or maybe he was the one responsible for calling the paramedics. After all, they arrived awfully fast.

What was puzzling, though, was the smile that seemed to play on the man's lips. And the growing cloud of swarming insects about his head. Flies?

Ed squinted.

Berith.

Maybe it wasn't a smile. Perhaps it was the glare of the sun on the door's glass that caused him to see things that weren't there. Ed was squinting after all.

Ed made for the door. Unsure of what he would say, he knew he could at least ask the guy if he had paid. As the proprietor, that wouldn't be too untoward. All some patrons needed was an excuse not to pay their bill. He'd seen it all before. Maybe he'd ask the guy if he was the one who called for the paramedics. Then he could thank him rather than think the worst.

As Ed neared the door, however, the stranger's eyes widened. A stack of wrinkled brown papers he was holding fell from his hands. And though Ed and the man were separated by some distance, one inside and one outside, in the time it took for Ed to lower his eyes to the papers on the ground then back up to the man's face, he experienced something he'd never be able to explain. Ed felt the stranger from outside directly in front of his face — an impossibility.

We. Are. Legion.

Overpowering his senses, a fetid odor penetrated Ed's nostrils. It seized his throat, causing him to gag.

Witness the power of Berith.

Then as the corners of this stranger's mouth spread into a hideously evil grin, Ed felt a cold hand grip his heart. Squeezing his eyes shut, Ed slumped to the floor clutching his chest.

7

Rising in unison, the congregation applauded the archbishop's closing remarks.

They then settled back into their benches as he made his way to the front of the altar. He bowed before returning to the chair he occupied near the visiting pope.

A tall man of six feet five inches, Pope Pontius I was a regal and stately figure. The members in attendance were humbled by the holy figure's presence alone. But his stature accentuated the revered position that much more. Surrounded by his party of traveling cardinals and the newly reinstated Swiss Guard, to be anywhere near him was very intimidating. Even more intimidating was his reputation as a candid speaker who preferred not to mince words.

Dressed in an ornate chasuble of white and gold, the sleeveless vestment of the finest cloth hid his arms until they came up from his sides. He paused after the archbishop returned to his seat before rising from his own chair behind the altar. Wearing the three-tiered one hundred and two-year-old papal tiara of gold, his stature now towered at just over seven feet. Signifying his reign as the highest priest in the Church, the tiara was topped with a gold cross and decorated with precious gemstones.

Approaching the front of the alabaster high-altar, he faced the alcove that held the tabernacle and took a bow — customary procedure per the ecclesiastical rubrics determining liturgical practice.

"My dear lambs of God," the pope began once he

was at the ambo, pausing to look to the heavens for what one would assume was divine inspiration. He took a few breaths before he again eyed the throngs of people who filled the cathedral. "Behold, the world we live and breathe is at a turning point. Arab nations continue warring with each other. The global economy, long held ransom to the uncertainties of capitalism, is at a standstill due to high petrol prices and fuel shortages. The threat of Communism continues to rear its ugly head. Leaders of third world countries are forced into defensive postures as first world countries plunder their resources. Install puppet regimes. Invade sovereign territories. Proof, my brothers and sisters, that colonialism still exists. Even in the twentieth century.

"After two world wars and countless other conflicts that have since taken fathers from their children, husbands from their wives, and sons from their mothers, the reigning superpowers continue to divide the world up amongst themselves. And, I might add, under the pretense of peace and democracy.

"What is overlooked is that peace can only be achieved through a symbiotic relationship with other nations — other peoples — with coordinated trade efforts, for example, rather than with acts of violence, terrorism, or duplicity.

"In a world of unpredictable events, we can look back through the history of civilization and find one constant — the love of our Lord, Jesus Christ. It is through Him that the Church remains a living testament to faith and a higher code for living — a code that transcends barbarism, slavery, and imperialism. In its lifetime, Mother Church has outlived monarchies, dynasties, and countless governments. In the name of the Church, many of our ancestors have died to see that the mystery, the ever-living grace, continues. And just what does that say about mankind?

"My dear brothers and sisters, the Lord God is *with* you. But are *you* with our Lord God? Ask yourselves: Are you truly welcoming God's presence into your lives? Do you seek Him out only in times of misery, ignoring the Sabbath, or your allegiance to Mother Church?

"It would seem in these modern times in which we live, people are distracted more than ever from the Holy Word. Unwilling to wait for the bread of Heaven, they would instead take of earthly bread, engaging in immediate fulfillment and gratification without regard to the laws brought before us by Moses."

His steely eyes scoured the congregation. Many had their eyes focused on him. But their blank, inexpressive faces revealed a lack of understanding. He wondered if any of them were even listening. Truly listening. Were they present or merely occupying space so that they could then use today to further their own agendas within their own communities? With their constituents? Pope Pontius watched the politicians nod their smug-faced heads, deaf to the pope's words. Others flipped through their missalettes and songbooks.

"Let me assure you that the day of reckoning is here — Judgment Day, my friends, *is* close at hand. And you will be punished," the pope warned, narrowing his eyes as a heat began to arise within him.

Pointing a bony finger in the direction of the congregation, he held back nothing, feeling enraged the more he looked upon the indifferent crowd. "Before the Christ King, our Lord, you will be punished for your transgressions. For your sins. For your lack of morals. For your infidelities... your inability to repress your animalism. For defying the cherished commandments you claim to follow!"

In stark contrast to his normally pallid skin, his cheeks flushed a reddish hue as the heat of anger consumed him. "The Lord will NOT be merciful! He has been that while you have enjoyed your brief time here on earth. No, he will PUNISH you on this Day of Reckoning because *you* failed to search him out and keep him close."

Pope Pontius, true to his reputation, was direct in his message. Some of the faithful seated in the back rocked in their seats, holding up their hands to feel the pope's words mumbling "Amens" to bookend his message. The majority, much to his chagrin, continued their dispassionate stares. Shifting uncomfortably.

Especially angered by the local prelate and political representatives — their attendance more political than religious — it was their apathy that disgusted and fueled his rage. It made a mockery of the apostolic faith they were supposed to be practicing. But he knew the cure. It was time to stop sugarcoating Church doctrine. He was determined to incite fear back into their hearts. Fear that was too long absent. If people feared once again that what they did on earth would ultimately determine their passage into Heaven, then they would think twice about living lives of sin and filth.

It's not entirely their fault, the pope concluded. People were like cattle. They needed direction. Rules. And something to be fearful of.

Unlike his predecessor, Pope Pius Paul, who ignored the knowledge of the future that was bestowed unto him, Pope Pontius would make mystery a part of the Church once more. He would insist sinners be accountable for their misdeeds. He would bring meaning back to those who lived meaningless lives, providing them the "bread" for which they yearned. For the fall from grace and lack of mystery not only came from the misdirected and absent leadership of two millennia in the Church, but from Christ himself. Because He couldn't bring Himself to prove Satan — the imitator of miracles — wrong, mankind has been denied the truest miracle of all.

If only Christ jumped when Satan dared him, the pope mused silently. He would have saved mankind the trouble of suffering a lifetime with the promise of a glorious afterlife in Heaven. Any truly moral, hard-working man cannot sustain his family on ideals and promises alone.

Nor should he have to.

"So," the pope began, his earlier tone of anger all but absent from his voice, "what can you possibly do to gain Heavenly access? Look around you. The day has come to repent. The Church has always been here. It always will be. Come. Give to the Church. 'Suffer unto thee,' the Lord said. Suffer unto the Church, for *we* have suffered unto you. Cease your senseless indulgence in material goods. Repress those desires to cheat. Steal. Speak falsehoods. To lie with thy neighbor's spouse. Instead, look to God's most divine graces. Do not be deceived by heretics or false preachers who claim they know God and the ways to Heaven. Repress yourselves from depravity and debauchery, for it will be your undoing. Attend services regularly. Absolve yourselves of sin regularly. Receive Christ regularly. Offer up your heart, soul and, yes, even your financial support to Christ.

"Do this and I promise you," he beseeched, pausing for effect to better retain the attention of those in attendance awaiting his finish, "I will see to it that the leaders of the world see the light. For I, as caretaker of Saint Peter's Church, will provide you the Heavenly bread you seek."

Long held a secret within the hallowed halls of the Vatican, and thought to have died along with Pope Pius Paul, Pope Pontius also knew of the future.

And of a forgotten prophecy.

Because of this, it would be through him that mankind would find salvation. And he told those assembled at St. John's all they needed to know. "For it is then, and only then, in Christ's name, will you be saved."

8

The special Mass in celebration of the pope's visit some hours earlier concluded with the pope pressing the flesh with a long line of faithful in the foyer. His stark warning already waning in the minds of most who attended — many of whom could not even look him in the eyes when they shook his hand.

A buffet luncheon followed for the visiting pontiff and the prelate guests, proving an opportunity for him to engage in light discussion with various leaders political and religious on a variety of initiatives as they pertained predominately to Mother Church. But in the absence of a planned meeting with the American President — a meeting postponed due to the president's busy election-year schedule and the state of affairs between Iran and Iraq, in addition to the Soviet's occupation of Afghanistan — the pope *was* able to have a brief conversation with the United States' Secretary of State since even the vice-president was unable to attend. Currently in Europe, he was encouraging European pressure on Iran with regards to American hostages.

Having talked his mouth dry and pressed palms till they were red, Pope Pontius retired to his room to rest before the evening's special dinner in his honor. From here the pope's plan was to return to Rome in time for Easter. Only five days away.

Accessed through a small sitting room, the pope's guestroom was an adjoined room off to the right. Paneled with mahogany, the sitting room contained only three pieces of furniture. Abutting the two oriel windows overlooking the grounds between the rectory and the church were two 1860 antique Victorian mahogany armchairs plush with green cushions. Against the partition wall was a nineteenth century antique oak library table. Atop the table was a pewter tray with glasses and two crystal decanters.

The sleeping quarters, unlike the ornate style of the sitting room, was furnished with a floor of white carpet, a double-sized bed, nightstand, and modest-sized bureau. Directly across from the doorway was a washroom. Though rather small and tight in space, it did contain an old claw-footed tub. Unlike the paneled walls of the sitting room, this room's décor was done in beige and white. The windows, same as in the adjoining room, were without curtains. Privacy was instead assured by blinds.

While there were no other decorations, a crucifix hung above the bed. Above the bureau was a photo of the previous pope, Pope Pius Paul. As was customary, photos of the current pontiff were usually displayed in both public and private rooms. Seemingly forgotten, this one still awaited replacing.

Luggage bags neatly placed in the corner of the room, the pope's clothes were already unpacked and meticulously placed in the drawers. As much as he wanted to wash up, he couldn't take his eyes off the photo of Pope Pius Paul. Removing the framed photo from the wall, his inspection found it layered with dust. Forgotten. An appropriate metaphor for what had become of the Catholic faith. Judging by Helmutt's appearance, it was taken shortly after his installation. Pope Pontius marveled at how his predecessor looked much healthier than he did in his last days.

Monsignor Benjamin Postillio, Pope Pius Paul's prefect, exited the Vatican residence with members of the Papal Family and Papal Chapel following a brief meeting. To the director of the Holy See Press Office he handed a prepared statement to be disseminated regarding the pope's condition of health. Later he would see to it that documents usually meant for the pope's consideration would be looked after. Regardless of the pope's condition, the Church was expected to continue with its normal operations. The pope's true condition concealed for as long as possible.

Pope Pius Paul lay in his papal apartment. A nondescript dwelling in off-white, it was without the accoutrements one would expect from someone in his position. Helmutt Venderhoff would have it no other way. He lived his life and led the Church by the same principles he preached. He would die the same way.

But time had a way of passing too fast. His nearly ninety-two years of mortal existence came and went in what seemed a mere heartbeat. How it troubled him deeply when he ruminated over whether he sufficiently used Mother Church in his later years as the means with which to prepare mankind for what was about to befall it. With the dawn of the third millennium twenty years away, the greatest challenge mankind would ever face lay before him. Before them all.

But he was only mortal. His time on earth was finite. This fact was punctuated by his current condition. Having been administered the sacrament of Anointing the Sick, it wouldn't be long before he received Last Rites.

Debilitated by the advanced stages of Parkinson's Disease, a series of strokes over the last three years left him immobilized. He was well aware there were those within the Vatican who saw him as weak and impotent. Making matters worse, he suffered from an onset of dementia and Alzheimer's.

Or did he?

Mind still sharp, controlling his motor functions was nearly impossible. Yet it was as if his approaching death blessed him with extrasensory perception of the soul — a spiritual perception only available to those acutely aware the cessation of their mortal existence was close at hand.

Most recently he was discovered talking to apparitions that were surely not in the room, for only *he* was able to see them. Were the angelic visitors who came to comfort him only in his mind? A figment of imagination conceived of his faith and convocation? Or were they truly celestial beings?

It was difficult to be sure these days.

His prefect reentered the room. Though in the last couple of months he had seen to the day-to-day operations, he spent a considerable amount of time in Helmutt's presence. While others would come to pray at Helmutt's bedside, the monsignor opted to sit and read silently from his prayer book in a corner of the room. At times he would sit with his hands clasped in silent meditation. Whether this meditation was prayer or not, Helmutt couldn't be sure. But the behavior struck him as remarkably different than that of the other prelates who knelt at his bedside reciting prayers. Or held his hand while he tried desperately to communicate with them. Too often, the most he could do in response was place a palsied hand over theirs and force what he hoped looked like anything but a grimace.

Whatever the reasons for the monsignor's relative distance, his watchful eye over Helmutt could not be denied. Whatever was needed, the monsignor was attentive enough to see it through, from doctor appointments to prayer services to regularly scheduled meals. Helmutt even witnessed a rare occurrence when a meal arrived late. Though the action took place in the hallway far enough from the pope's earshot, parts of the monsignor's scolding was heard nonetheless. While occasional rumors of the monsignor's mercurial behavior reached Helmutt in the eleven-plus years the younger man served under him, it wasn't until most recently he saw, or heard, anything close to what he *suspected* was only rumor.

And yet, even in his debilitated state, it occurred to Helmutt that the monsignor was perhaps always *too* attentive. Fastidious in his ways, the position of prefect did bring with it a level of expectation. After all, as prefect, overseeing the Papal Household was a distinguished responsibility not to be taken lightly. And from what Helmutt gathered, the monsignor clearly knew his place and position. He operated from a level that elevated the expectation of others around him even more.

It was because of all this that the dying pontiff motioned for his prefect to remain in his chambers the second time — the last time — Sister Maria de Jesus called on him.

9

Saint John's Rectory was less active than earlier. Some local politicians lingered, as did a few reporters looking to interview the pope — which the archbishop's aides quietly took care of. Besides the caterers, there remained a handful of religious officials, most of whom were from abroad and wouldn't be staying for the banquet. Since the special evening reception held in his honor wasn't until later in the evening, it afforded the pope a chance to rest. Hence the reason he was currently sequestered upstairs at the other end of the building

Navigating the caterers busy breaking down the luncheon, two priests managed to sneak refills before the portable bar was disassembled.

Like the rest of the Queen Anne-style rectory, the room the men stood in was a marvel to behold. Wall-to-wall plush carpeting. Paneled walls. Polished oak floors in the hallways. The place was lavishly decorated. But it was the fireplace in the very room they were in that was the most impressive of all. On either side of the richly carved mahogany mantel were the sculpted faces of Saint John, the Apostle.

The bishop reminded himself to ask the archbishop if the sculptures were custom-made. If not, and they were actually found somewhere, he would be very interested in knowing where.

"Bless you," the older man said to the young bartender as he accepted his glass of wine.

Though there were many priests in attendance today, fewer in number were of the Church's upper echelon. Not a practicing Catholic, the bartender knew the man before him was important because he stood out from his companion and the other similarly dressed attendees.

Wearing a cassock of black, buttons of purple ran the length of his gown to his feet. His pellegrina — shoulder length cape — was also accented with purple piping, matching his sash and zucchetto. As mandated by Canon Law, the color offsetting the black was based on the office held by the cleric. A large gold cross, steadied by a heavy gold chain, lay across his chest.

Similar in style, the papal white dress signifies His Holiness. Cardinal dress is accented with red piping. Archbishops, like Avarassi, dressed in colors of violet.

Raising his glass, the bishop toasted the younger. His usual go-to beverage a bit stronger, the bishop realized the luck in getting a decent Pinot Grigio at an event such as this. At least he wasn't drinking Zinfandel. "Congratulations, Father, on your recent success."

"Thank you, Bishop Reibold, sir," the younger priest said appreciatively. He was fully aware of the religious elder whose name and reputation preceded him.

"And welcome back. I heard you went away for a year of spiritual enlightenment."

The younger priest held up his glass as he studied the bishop. Tall, he was a burly man for his age. Still an imposing figure, the younger priest reckoned how striking the bishop must have been in his prime. Equally impressive was seeing him today in his official church attire to celebrate the pope's visit. "It's good to be back where I can serve to the best of my abilities."

"You've certainly created quite a name for yourself. Your writings on the subject of Christology are fascinating," the bishop complimented as he straightened his sash.

According to periodic Vatican newsletters sent out to church officials that included information about up-and-coming prelates, as well as matters pertaining to doctrine and practice, the young, fit priest who stood before the bishop was one of the Vatican's fastest rising stars. And among the most popular at the moment.

Sipping the blood red port from his glass, the young man smiled. "My work has afforded me some perks. Like my temporary assignment in Connecticut, for example."

Bishop Reibold raised his eyebrows. "Oh? Back in the states again, eh? And where in Connecticut might that be?"

The priest answered with a bewildered expression. "Surely you have received a letter informing you of my arrival?"

"Dear me, my boy, I have not."

"Sipping too much sacramental wine, have we, Bishop?"

The bishop chuckled reflexively at the young cleric's attempt at humor, finding such haughtiness when addressing a prelate unbecoming. It would seem the young cleric's national attention came at the expense of any humility.

But Saint Catherine's *was* currently understaffed, however unlikely it was for the bishop to overlook such matters. Assigned to a diocese in the Constitution State some two years prior, he was finding the task was indeed overwhelming despite his best efforts. He could certainly use all the help he could get.

Reminiscing back twenty years to his very first assignment as bishop, he recalled the small village in the South American country of Columbia. It was there that he cemented his faith and calling. For many years he continued his work in third world countries only to return stateside some five years ago following the death of a fellow pastor and good friend. Local once more, he set out to help rebuild diocesan parishes in urban areas. But the emotional toll of dealing with such socially and economically depressed areas was beginning to eat away at him. Though no less of a challenge, taking on a regional diocese in the town of New Galilee, Connecticut, he reasoned with himself at the time, would be a welcome and refreshing change.

After watching the last of the dawdlers disperse, the bishop swallowed his pride. Refocusing his attention, he placed a big, liver-spotted hand on the young priest's shoulder as the younger headed into the hall. "So, what else was in this letter that I should know about?"

"I have a degree in accounting..."

"Wonderful! I could use someone like you. I've got a little old biddy working the books now. Sister Anita McAffrey. My goodness, I think she's been doing them since Christ was born. Once I was installed, I didn't have the heart to replace her. I guess it's about time we had someone like you down there."

"...and I'm to report to Saint Catherine's tomorrow, as a matter of fact."

There was no poker face hiding the bishop's response. But he recovered quickly. "No time like the present, eh?"

Amazing how things worked in the world. The Church was no different than the corporate environment. Most everyone always had an angle. Maneuvering was only part of the chess play.

"It's not like that," the younger priest said from behind a mischievous grin, as if reading the bishop's thoughts. "I hear you've done wonders for the New Galilee community. But you've been shorthanded for some time now."

Continuing to follow the priest stiffly down the hall, the bishop couldn't disagree. "That's no lie. It's hard to run the diocese, counsel, and administer to the sick when resources are difficult to come by. I don't know. I've been everywhere and I can't believe what I see in our own country. And in Connecticut, nonetheless."

The bishop downed the last of his wine, pleased with its effects. Carrying tables, the catering clean-up crew made their way by as the two men flattened themselves against a wall. It was the younger priest who broke the momentary silence.

"I grew up in Goshen and it's even changed there. One has to wonder, though, how much progress can be made when the events of the world impact the local economies like they do."

"That's right. I forgot you said you were originally from Connecticut," the bishop said. Adding with a snort, "At least Connecticut is the insurance capital of the world!"

"Don't forget the subs," the younger added, in reference to its shipyard, Electric Boat.

"Hear! Hear!"

The bishop and priest clinked their empty glasses in salutation. Secretly, though, the bishop wished big business, like the insurance companies, did more for their communities to service the less fortunate. Electric Boat, on the other hand, was unionized. As he saw it, that was one way to look out for the little guy.

"Say, I've got a great idea," the bishop said, brightening up. He long ago shed any egoism, choosing instead to approach even the most difficult and awkward situations from a reflective perspective. This was his way of reaching out to the newest member of his parish. "How would you like to drive back with me to New Galilee? Unless, of course, you have other plans."

"I would be honored, sir. One of Saint John's clergy was going to bring me. Surely, I could spare him the trouble."

"That would also give us a chance to talk and get to know each other." The bishop paused, sizing up his new colleague who stood no more than a few inches shorter than he. "You'll love New Galilee. And I know New Galilee will love you."

Placing their glasses on a tray of dirty dishes held by yet another passing caterer, the two made their way down the hall towards the staircase.

10

Both bishop and priest came to rest outside the pope's door. Blocking the door was a member of the elite branch of the Swiss Guard who easily stood upwards of seven feet. Seeing one of the new and imposing Guardia Divino up close was both terrifying and exciting. Besides the tight collar of white, the members of the Special Forces wore uniforms of blue topped with berets of the same color. Brandishing a SIG-Sauer P225, the broadsword was replaced by a 9mm double-action pistol of Swiss design. For tradition, two ceremonial Swiss Guards in Renaissance costumes — complete with puffed sleeves and striped knickerbockers of red, blue and yellow — stood at the end of the hall and at the bottom of the stairwell, leaving the very lean, very broad, and very solid Special Forces soldier to personally protect the pontiff.

Serving as sentries, the Swiss Guards under the former pope maintained a mostly ceremonial presence. That changed after the installation of the new pontiff. The Swiss Guard was currently on its way from being a band of one hundred soldiers to a small army of three hundred, with three quarters of the Guardia Divino currently trained in Special Forces.

The bishop felt like a little kid about to meet Santa Clause. Having the popular pope here in the states meant a lot to him because he and the pope had a history. Friends, they attended the same French seminary in the late 1940s. But as is most common with friends who live busy lives far apart from each other, life got in the way. No matter the many years since their last exchange, the bishop always followed his friend's successes with interest. And pride.

Turning to the young man beside him, the bishop enlightened him on his past friendship with the pope. "Pontius and I have known each other since we were in our early twenties. He and I met in France studying the priesthood. Goodness, he's lived all over the place. His father was an Italian Magistrate and his mother was an interpreter for the United Nations for years. She later transferred to the Italian Government."

The bishop may have been looking in the priest's direction, but it was clear from the far-away look in his eyes that he didn't really see him at all. He was recalling memories long since passed. "Good ol' Ben. I always knew he'd go far. I just never knew how far. Over the years we kind of lost touch with one another, you know. Oh, he was a magnificent scholar, too. Like you, his writings impressed many leaders of Mother Church. They took notice and sought him out for his comprehensive studies of sin and End Times.

"Then there's his two recently published books: *Key Holder to the Church of the Future* and *A Calling to Greater Faith for All of God's Followers*. Both are selling in such large numbers all over the world, it is rumored that the publisher can't keep up with the demand."

The younger priest attempted to speak. But the bishop was not done.

"Did you know he was an *In Pectore*?"

The other priest nodded. He was well aware that the bishop's friend was Cardinal Roberto Benjamin Postillio, secretly given the title by Pope John XXIII. However, Ben was more widely known for his role as prefect for the previous pope, Pope Pius Paul.

"It wasn't a secret that he always had his sights set on the throne of Saint Peter. He always believed he could make a difference in the world. We all did in those days. You should have heard him when we studied Ecclesiology. He could debate for hours about the Church as an institution and its practices. I'll never forget when he became prefect for the Vatican. Though he sure must have been at odds with Helmutt Venderhoff's ideology."

11

At first sight, the bishop could not believe how young his friend looked considering they were both in their late 50s.

"My wits! Peter Ludwig Reibold! How long has it been?"

But Ben's rather cold and ceremonial greeting gave him pause. Next to him, the young priest was already on his knees kissing the oversized Fisherman's Ring on the pope's finger. The Bishop was left foolishly standing, expecting instead to embrace his old friend.

Arm extended, Ben coolly smiled at his old classmate. He patiently awaited Peter's formal acknowledgment. Bishop Peter Reibold slowly, stiffly, dropped to his knees before kissing the outstretched hand. Exactly as ceremony dictated.

Satisfied, Ben dropped his hand and took a step back as the two visitors rose. He clasped his hands before him, extending the index fingers to form a southern-pointing steeple. "So, Peter, at least twenty years. No?"

"At least," the bishop answered, feeling uncomfortable with the awkwardness suddenly overshadowing what he assumed would be an auspicious occasion. It wasn't every day one was able to get an audience with the pope. Even if they were a member of the Church. Rarer still was having a past friend ascend to the highest position of the most powerful church in the world.

"Yes." Ben answered, seemingly unaffected — or unaware — of the bishop's discomfiture. He then rubbed his chin as he looked past his old friend, focusing his attention on the younger priest. One eyebrow raised.

"Forgive me, B-Ben," the bishop stuttered. "Where are my manners?" Moving aside, the bishop motioned to the younger man. "Ben, this is..."

"Father Jacob Uzziel Dawz," the pope finished, extending his hand from his chin.

"Your Eminence," Jacob acknowledged, bowing his head.

Bishop Reibold also bowed his head. Again caught up in a moment of overwhelming awkwardness. Feeling oddly out of place, he couldn't help but wonder if the two already somehow knew each other. Then the bishop rationalized his feelings: The priest was making a name for himself. It would only be natural that he would be on the holy leader's radar.

"A pleasure, indeed," the pope said, tightly grasping Father Jacob's hand between his own two.

Embarrassed by his own behavior, the bishop could hold himself no longer. After a pregnant pause, he yearned to speak. To somehow salvage what was left of his dignity. Here before him was not only the leader of the highest office in the Church, but a former friend from his youth. As awkward as he felt, there truly was no greater excitement than to stand beside someone with whom he attended seminary. Someone who had achieved a lifelong dream.

"What a small world! Would you believe I was moments ago telling Father Jacob how you and I attended the same seminary in France together? Remember those days, Ben?"

Clearing his throat, the pope released Father Jacob's hand. "Peter. May I have a moment with you alone."

It was not a question.

"Certainly. Jacob?"

"Oh, don't mind me," Jacob said, dismissing himself. "You two probably have much to catch up on."

"Nonsense, Father," the pope smiled. And placing a hand on Jacob's back, he added: "This will take but a few minutes."

Jacob left the room, closing the door behind him. The Special Forces guard stood to the right of the doorway. Jacob made his way past him only to be stopped with a hand nearly the size of his torso.

"I just need to use the head," Jacob said. Growing impatient when there was no response, he explained: "I'm supposed to wait for His Holiness to finish his meeting with the bishop. Now I need to drop a deuce. Sure wouldn't be proper for me to use his toilet. Would it?"

The guard frowned before moving the priest's hands up over his head. After patting Jacob down, the guard motioned him forward.

"Make it quick," he demanded with a heavy Swedish accent.

Jacob entered the bathroom, locking the door behind him. After noisily rustling his belt and lifting the toilet seat for the guard's benefit, he tiptoed to the tub to place his ear against the wall, straining to hear the conversation in the adjacent room.

The bishop watched the young priest leave before turning to face his old friend after the door closed.

"Jesus, Peter, don't you have any respect," the pope charged.

"Don't I have any what?" The bishop was at once caught off guard by his peer's sudden change in demeanor.

Anger evident in his voice, the pope was direct.

"I, Peter, am the Pontifex Maximus! That's Supreme Pontiff in case you weren't sure. How about addressing me as such. Young Father Jacob certainly seemed well educated on the etiquette of displaying proper respect."

"Ben..."

"I did *earn* this, you know."

"I... I don't understand. I *did* show you the proper respect. Did I not kneel and kiss the Fisherman's Ring?"

Thoughts of his earlier actions upset him greatly. Instead of a sign of respect, he felt the forcing of the ring kissing was capitulation. Submission. Humiliation.

Perplexed by the awkwardness and tension that now pervaded the room like a stoked fire with no ventilation, the bishop felt the thick air was toxic. Lacking oxygen.

He realized he was perspiring. His breath shallow. Yet nothing could have prepared the bishop for the pope's coming outburst.

"As Pope Pontius, I am the Keeper of the Keys. To the multitudes of people who claim themselves Catholics and Christians alike, I *am* God. And whatever the Keeper of the Throne of Saint Peter says on earth, so shall it be said in Heaven." Ben then snorted, having extinguished his anger. After making his way to the antique table against the wall, he poured some brown liquid into a crystal chaser. "I am the true rock, dear bishop! Whatever the Keeper of the Throne does on earth, so shall it be done in Heaven. You remember that from the Bible, don't you? Scotch?"

Raising a trembling hand, the bishop politely declined the offer.

Knowing his former classmate would most likely

decline anyway, the figure in papal clothes didn't bother turning around. Much less acknowledge his subordinate. Once poured, he downed the scotch with one gulp. "All these many years and you haven't changed at all, Peter."

The man the bishop once knew as Ben wiped his mouth with the back of his hand.

"Still weak. Feeble. A disgrace to the priesthood."

"I'm sorry to disappoint you," Peter offered. Embarrassed. Further humiliated.

It was true that the years had been kinder to Ben than to Peter. Ben, as the bishop began to recall, always enjoyed holding a certain degree of power over others. It didn't matter if it was athletics or academics, he appeared to get a perverse thrill carrying an advantage over another individual. With this and his lineage, Ben, even early on, felt he was above everyone else.

Though Peter recognized these characteristics when they were young men studying at seminary, he thought nothing of it because of the many acclamations Ben received. First in school. Then in subsequent years, rising quickly in his prelate status. In those earlier days, Peter dismissed his observations, casting them aside as possible pangs of an unconscious envy. Surely even a man about to enter a lifetime of servitude in the Church was capable of such emotion. He was, after all, only human and would confess this as a sin. But he saw now it wasn't a sin. It was an apt observation.

"Your Eminence," the bishop began, his tone one of formality. He would defend himself. He deserved that much. Then he would get the hell out of this room. "I've given myself to the Lord. I have done His work since I was ordained over thirty years ago. I've had no desire to become anything more. I am above no one. I serve God. Same as you."

Ben poured himself another drink, swishing the scotch in the chaser before taking another sip. "C'mon. You know you've been jealous of me ever since we were young."

"I—" Peter protested, but was interrupted.

"But I do believe you are correct about being disinclined to become anything more. Your work in New Galilee affirms it. Sure, you're affecting the lives of a few families. But you do this at the expense of failing your mission."

"Which is?"

"Why raising money for Mother Church, of course. You barely cover diocesan expenses, leaving very little for Rome. Yes, I've seen your financial sheets, Peter. You've made a mess of the New Galilee Diocese."

The pope rotated in place. Leaning against the table, chaser in hand, he eyed his despondent friend of the past with loathing. "Oh, I know all about your work as the good and faithful foot-soldier. The Good Samaritan. Always working with the poor. The elderly. The downtrodden. And the children. Yes, especially the children. Still trying to beat down those memories of the orphanage, eh?"

It was a dig at the bishop's own childhood, spent for the most part, in an orphanage. The driving force behind Bishop Peter Reibold's foray into ecclesiastical life, it was also the very reason why he dedicated his life to helping society's youth.

"Meanwhile, New Galilee is only becoming more economically depressed as more minorities transition in. Feeding off the government's teat, they also love to suck what they can from the Church."

"That's not true. My God, what have you become?"

"And since most of them are illegals, the racial divide in your area only burdens local resources, making matters worse by creating a deeper chasm between the haves and the have-nots. I am fully aware of this, even if you are not. Oh, and it's not completely endemic to Connecticut. Or even the Northeast, for that matter. However the socioeconomics are, your job extends *beyond* the counseling and administering. The Church, as you have failed to realize, is a business."

"You can't be serious. Times are tough. It's the nature of the economy, Ben. These are the very times the Church must provide strength and bring people, especially those of varying races and socio-economic backgrounds, back in the pews. Why, those in need are among the most faithful I've ever known. No matter how difficult things get, they remain steadfast in their faith. Besides, things will change once—"

"Ever the naïve one. Look around you. No one gives a damn about God anymore. The vagrants use religion to excuse their insignificant lives. Breeding like rodents, they go on to have ten children and become burdens on society. For the others, besides a place to go on the weekend for show, Mass also serves as an excuse. An excuse, that is, to act like hedonists and yet still feel comforted because they can be saved by simply asking for forgiveness!"

The pope chuckled at Peter's horrified expression. "Open your eyes. In this country, like most other depraved western societies, it's all about greed and status. Not God. It's certainly not about helping the common man. Born. Raised. Condemned to a life of servitude, capitalist societies prosper by keeping him poor and uneducated. Furthermore, this current melee the United States is in, it has brought unto them the wrath of the Arab nations with their oil obsession. They could have been rid of this dependence years ago. Imagine the wealth and resources this country could be generating for its people right now. However, as is always the case, someone's coffers are surely being filled."

The pope swallowed back the last of the scotch in his glass. But slower this time. Savoring the rich, intense malt flavor. And the burn in the back of the throat as it went down. Closing his eyes, he relished a hint of caramel in the aftertaste before continuing.

"The American ethos of decadence, vanity, and hubris will continue to spread like an untreated infection. It already has. The U.S. is far too young and proud to learn from centuries of missteps made by the British, the Spanish... hell, much of Europe. Lest we forget the legalizing of abortion or the prevailing attitudes regarding what your fellow countrymen call sexual freedom. Such laissez-faire attitudes disgust me in ways I cannot even begin to articulate. Liberalism at its finest, no?

"The Church, dear Peter, used to be good at keeping these things in check. Governments and religions — two things that could always be counted on to keep its people indoctrinated with purpose despite their suffering existence. Governments call it patriotism or even solidarity; religions call it faith."

Peter stood aghast. "You're the leader of the most powerful church in the world and you sound... you sound atheist. I've questioned my own faith, too. But dear weeping Jesus, this belies centuries of work by millions of believers. In which direction can you lead Mother Church if you don't even believe in your own cause? This is not what God intended when he left the Church to Apostle Peter."

A smirk played about the corner of the pope's

lips as he placed his glass back onto the tray. "Well, my friend, since you seem to know so much... Just what did God intend? Because with all that I've seen over the years, it certainly makes one wonder if there even is a God."

While Ben's disdain for those he deemed inferior had, without question, influenced his ambitions, there once existed in him a strong belief in the divine and the Holy Trinity. Yet now it seemed his years of consorting with the elite as a prefect, and in his most recent position of absolute power, he no longer looked down on those whom he deemed beneath him. His conceit also solidified his belief that only *he* possessed the power to one day bring about the change necessary to usher in a new age for the Church. He wasn't kidding when he said that he was God. A view, the bishop speculated, Ben must have held long before becoming pope.

"How can you say such things?"

"Because I had an epiphany, Peter. I realized we are standing upon a precipice." The pope dismissively waved his hand in the air. "There are things in the works your feeble mind cannot possibly fathom. It is with this knowledge that I finally realized my purpose in life. And I've spent the last twenty years putting the pieces in place to ensure I would one day be in this position."

The pope strolled towards the window, placing a hand on the back of one of the two sitting chairs. "Explain to me why we have so many wars in the name of religion? The Arabs, for example, fighting with Israel and amongst themselves. All of them in lands once holy, warring in the names of Mohammed, Allah, Jehovah. David. Explain to me what the Muslims, Protestants, Baptists, Catholics, and Jews truly argue over that could not have been resolved if not for centuries of animosity? At the very core, there is a shared belief that none wish to acknowledge. Their histories, their stories all interconnect. But they would rather not have the mindless faithful acknowledge such a reality. Instead, they work hardest to get them frothing at the mouth. They prosper pitting one faith against the other.

"And let me ask you, Peter: Where was God when the Olympic athletes were killed in Munich eight years ago?"

He did an about face, waiting for an answer. But the bishop could only stand slack-jawed, absent of a response.

"Perhaps Helmutt is partly to blame," the pope noted, moving his crosier — his papal scepter — to the other chair so he could sit. "But I think we've done a poor job spreading His word in the past millennia. If we'd done a better job laying the groundwork, would the focus of this so-called life be simply centered on a global economy of capitalism and the acquisition of material wealth? Thrown away is what used to be a focus of living a life of morality, no?

"Corrupt as they are, the United States is well on its way to becoming possibly the greatest and only superpower. Though they were founded on religious principles, that they've abandoned them doesn't bode very well for the long-term. It's because of this that their future hegemony is uncertain.

"Helmutt," the pope said as he crossed his legs and looked about the room, remembering the photo he found earlier today, "was such an idealistic codger. Yet his greatest weakness was his failure to truly see the big picture. That's where he failed, you know. He had so much time, too. And he blew it.

"You see, I, Peter... I see the whole picture. I always could see the bigger scheme of things. I knew it when I studied Ecclesiology and End Times at seminary. Something clicked. I knew it when that crazy ass nun came to see the old fool. I've always known what is good for Mother Church. And trust me, I'm going to see to it that the Church and all its truly faithful are rightfully served. I will guarantee them that which they seek. Much more than even Christ ever has."

Narrowing his eyes, the pope lowered his head to peer into the distressed bishop's watering eyes. "I will even create a Church that will stand up to such imperialist states as the American one if I have to."

Paralyzed. Speechless. The bishop could only blink in response to what Ben was proposing. Silent protests crawled their way down his cheeks.

The pope smiled a wide, toothy grin. Unlike the cool, forced smile earlier, this one was quite authentic. It elongated the wrinkles alongside his mouth into a pair of pronounced parentheses. The smile made his chin seem longer and thinner than it was. "Oh, come now, Peter. Don't you agree that the mystery has long been gone from the Church?"

Awaiting a response, he looked impatiently at the quivering man before him.

"I... I don't know. What do you care anyway? You don't even believe in God."

The pope leaned back and laughed heartily. "I'm inclined to believe there isn't one because if he does exist, he is a pretty goddamn sadistic bastard. Wouldn't you agree?"

Peter didn't answer.

"Let's talk seriously. Real talk. What if I told you the root of our problems with the world, mankind, and our own religion, lie with Christ?"

Peter's terrified stance in the middle of the room was slowly beginning to annoy the pope. Deviating momentarily from his message, he implored Peter to sit instead of cowering like a frightened animal. "Do come and sit down. Please, I beg of you. I mean, Christ Jesus, really now."

Peter refused to move a muscle, much less acknowledge the pope's request.

Bereft of patience, the pope continued. "Do you know what the Great Mystery of the Church is?" He caught himself and laughed again. "I mean do you know what the Great Mystery of the Church *was*? We were all taught it is related to the Sacraments, namely Baptism and Eucharist. Right? Yet, isn't it also the belief in the miraculous? Isn't that the true mystery? And is there anything more miraculous than Man? Isn't that why there was a sect of angels who were jealous? I mean, why would one devote to living piously on earth if there wasn't a place in Heaven guaranteed? Right? That one's existence is *worth* something? So, wouldn't you agree, then, that Christ should have jumped from that damn temple when Satan confronted Him following His baptism?"

The bishop's bursitis flared from his rigid posture. He needed to sit down. More than that, he needed to get out of the room and away from this heretic. "I do not," he said cautiously, stiffly retreating to the wall nearest the door, "agree."

Unconvinced, Ben asked: "How is that even possible? Think beyond what you were taught. Instead, think about what you know to be true borne of experience. It would have clearly demonstrated that Jesus Christ was who He said He was. Irrefutable proof that He indeed existed. By not jumping, He's become nothing more than a character in a book whose name incites violence and conflict. The world, according to the Bible, wasn't even supposed to last this long. And yet, it has. What does that prove? Why, lack of His existence is what it proves.

"Like the cryptic writings with messages that we now call Gospels. Written far too long after Christ had come and gone, can they truly serve as an accurate account of *who* and *what* He was? The man was nothing more than a propagandist in preacher's clothing selling an image to people suffering under Roman authority anyway.

"Sure, He gave people hope. Ripe for the times, His target audience was really the poor and uneducated. Pissing off a bunch of Jewish rabbis and the Roman government does not a messiah make. Sorry. But it is true. A mortal, mythologized by the Acts, He is at best responsible for transforming the Roman belief system in polytheism to that of one god."

The pope then sighed. "Nothing more than an opportunist, if you ask me." Picking lint from his frock, the last statement was more of an aside to himself than for Peter's benefit.

Weakly, from his spot across the room, the bishop denounced his long-time friend. "You... you're not the man... I used to know. I don't know you anymore." But the bishop's legs betrayed his courage to finally speak the truth. Giving way under him, it left him vulnerable. He crouched in prayer.

Never in his life was he so frightened. So paralyzed with fear.

Deep in prayer, the bishop recalled his past spent in Columbia. There he brought the hope and light of God to a ragtag community of peasants ravaged by civil war. Enduring countless beatings, he was threatened with death several times over whenever he implored the guerrilla soldiers to cease their drunken pillaging. Beaten and bloodied, he relied on his faith to protect him as he fought to protect women and girls from rape or a life of servitude. Every day was a day lived in fear.

But that fear paled in comparison to what he felt today. At this very moment.

Regarding Peter's cowering as a sign of weakness, it enraged the pope so much that he was tempted to use his scepter to bash in the spineless skull of the weakling before him. "So feeble. So pathetic you are. Soon you will understand my vision. As will everyone the world over. And they will thank me. And it won't be long before they beg for my forgiveness. My blessings."

Long since gone from the Church, Ben was determined to bring back the true mystery. And the miraculous. To mankind, he was determined to give that which Christ denied nearly two thousand years earlier. He was the rock of the Church, the real savior born to lead the flock.

The bishop's eyes were tightly closed in prayer. He witnessed a side of the pope he hoped others never would have to. He was sure that someone as nefarious as Ben could very well bring about the end of Christianity.

Maybe even mankind.

Bishop Peter Reibold swallowed hard at the thought.

"C'mon, now. Get up," the pope insisted.

The bishop remained unmoved, even at Ben's urging, continuing to whisper prayers. But Ben's patience had long since expired. "Peter, I said stand up! Damn you."

Even if he could, he wasn't about to. The entire ordeal numbed his senses; he felt betrayed by his own body. And by the man who was once his friend. The man who now oversaw the very institution he pledged his life to. In an instant, everything that once gave his life purpose had been shattered.

"Oh, admit it. You would never stand a chance if your god ever appeared before you," the pope mused, rubbing his temples, reveling in the intimidation he commanded.

But Peter remained steadfast in prayer.

"Prayers and more prayers. Words, you blathering idiot. Just meaningless words." Knowing how much he intimidated the bishop only fueled his power trip. He *was* God. Here on earth, no matter what anyone said, Roberto Benjamin Postillio was more than the rock of the Church and the Savior. He *was* God.

Struggling to stand without something to grab on to, the bishop crawled to the door. Using the knob for support, he slowly and painfully came to an upright position.

The pope cocked his head to one side. "Since it appears we're done here, why don't you go fetch me your new friend. I would love to continue conversing with him."

Back to the door, the bishop dared to open his eyes once more. With a shaky, sweaty hand he turned the knob about to exit while speaking the final words he would ever say to his former friend. The only words necessary after this traumatic encounter. "May God have mercy on your soul."

The pope rose with a start. Grabbing his scepter, and with a gesture unexpectedly nimble for a man of his age, he propelled himself forward.

Extending the Papal Scepter before him, he slammed the door shut behind the bishop. Then, like a serpent, the pope drew himself threateningly close. His acrid, malted breath hot on the bishop's face.

"Haven't you been listening to a word I've said? Since it appears you're either too stupid or too senile to read between the lines, I'm going to fill you in on a little secret for old time's sake."

Ben clutched the bishop's jaw in his bony hand as his icy blue-gray eyes bore into Peter's. Perspiration made the skin clammy to the touch. And the pope silently noted the stink of the bishop's cowardice as he thrust his head aside to scream directly into his ear.

"There is NO God!"

12

J acob, with his ear against the shower wall, listened in on the bishop and pope's conversation — catching very little of what was said — until he heard a door open and close. Peering from the ajar door, he could make out the bishop retreating down the hall. Once more before the Special Forces Swiss Guard, Father Jacob waited for the guard to allow him re-entry.

Inside, Jacob attempted to speak first. But the pope put a finger to his lips. Only after the door was shut did he address the younger priest. "Long have I waited for this moment."

"You have received my letters, then."

"Of course. They have never left my side in anticipation of this day. And the days to come." He patted a lump under his robe, falsely alluding to the possession of Jacob's letters. "You have some additional documents of importance for me. Do you not?"

"I do, Holy One," Jacob said, his voice cracking before he fell to his knees clutching the pope's hand. Overcome with emotion, he broke down sobbing. "I was afraid no one would understand what I was going through."

"There is nothing to fear now. The divine works in mysterious ways. Ways we may not understand. But for good reason. Such is the way of the Lord," the pope feigned.

Licking his lips, the pope inhaled deeply. He needed Jacob. Needed to retain Jacob's services. Therefore, indulging him was essential. That Jacob reached out to him some years back was no coincidence. The pontiff knew the part he had to play if he was to keep Jacob focused on his mission.

"Timing, Jacob. Timing is everything. I was meant to receive your letters just as I was meant to be the leader, the rock, of the most powerful church in the world. Now, the documents..."

"And the bishop?"

The pope snapped in response. Impatience present in his voice. "What about the doddering fool?"

"You do know I will be working with him."

"Of course..." the pope said, unaware. How did he miss this? He considered the ironies and coincidences of past events. Things truly did have a way of falling into place. "It would seem," he whispered under his breath as he briefly turned his back to his younger counterpart, "that our dear Maria wasn't that crazy after all."

While the pope was turned, Jacob quickly wiped his nose and cheeks with the back of his hands. Embarrassed for his earlier lack of composure, he sought to appear calm. Confident. In control of his faculties before the pontiff. Jacob hoped he was allowed a bit of latitude when it came to his highly emotional response. Only natural when standing before the leader of the most powerful institution on earth. Appropriate or not.

Brushing aside thoughts of Sister Maria, the pope chose his words carefully. "You must go with the bishop," he said turning to face Jacob once more. "I seriously doubt Peter Reibold will have any inclination to speak with me ever again. Especially after our last conversation. However, that doesn't mean you shouldn't contact Rome regarding affairs pertinent to the parish." Winking, he added:

"Especially those relating to finance."

From under the sash surrounding his waist he pulled out a small envelope of parchment wrapped with a ribbon of red. It was sealed with the papal crest. Handing the item over to Jacob he explained: "We do not want to arouse suspicion." Jerking his hand to discourage an erratic fly, the pope explained: "You will know when it is time to contact me. I shouldn't have to emphasize the significance of these times."

"No, sir," the priest replied, accepting the pope's offering and solemnly vowing his allegiance. "I'll not fail you, Holy Father."

"Now, the documents. Where are the documents? I *need* those documents. Time is short."

The priest nodded, removing a wad of wrinkled, folded papers from inside his blazer.

The pope placed the papers underneath his sash. "You've done well. But so as not to draw any attention this evening at dinner, it is best you keep your distance."

Jacob nodded before turning to leave, pausing with his hand on the knob.

"What is it now?" the pope asked, fatigue and mild annoyance threatening. The talk with Bishop Reibold and this morning's Mass left him exhausted. He needed to rest before putting on his holiest face for the evening's banquet.

Head down in solemnity, the priest turned round slowly. He was hesitant to ask a second time. "I'm sorry, your Eminence. When did you say I'd know to contact you?"

"Be it today. Be it tomorrow. Be it ten years from now. Should my suspicions regarding these documents prove to be correct," the pope said softly, walking over to the door to usher Jacob out, "we will all know."

Father Jacob left the room unaware that he was nothing more than a pawn in a game that had yet to be played out.

And while he would go on to work with the bishop, he and the bishop would never speak of this day.

13

Requesting that he not be disturbed in order to meditate in prayer before dinner, the pope instructed his prefect to inform the archbishop of his wishes. And his Guardia Divino saw to it that no one entered the room.

The pope, however, had no intention of praying. He only wanted to rest before having to put on the façade of the all-faithful leader. Removing his zucchetto, he propped up two pillows and sat on the bed in the adjoining room. Closing his eyes, he padded the part of the sash hiding the documents Jacob brought him as he drifted off. So much to do, so little time.

The monsignor entered the Cappella Sistina, the small chapel once known as the Papal Palace. Measuring one hundred, thirty feet long, it was forty-four feet wide and sixty-seven feet high. Precisely as the dimensions of the Temple of Solomon were described in the Old Testament. It was originally built between 1475 and 1483, in the time of Pope Sixtus IV della Rovere. Decorated with frescoes of various parts of the Old and New Testaments painted in the 1480s and early 1500s, its floor was a mosaic of geometric patterns of Byzantium design using colored and semiprecious stones. Today, on this first day of June 1979, less than twenty days since the passing of Pope Pius Paul, it was serving as the meeting place for the College of Cardinals. The purpose of their meeting: selecting a new pontiff.

Having spent the morning celebrating the Votive Mass Pro Eligendo Papa, the afternoon was set aside for voting. That is, once lots were drawn to select three members to collect ballots, three to count them, and three to review the results. Completed, the electors were then to write their choice of pontiff on square blank ballots imprinted with *Eligo in Summum Pontificern*. Or *I elect as Supreme Pontiff*. Folded in half, the ballots are then placed into a twenty-five-inch chalice on the altar.

To be elected, the chosen one must receive a two-thirds majority vote. If this does not occur, another vote needs to take place; two votes in the morning and two in the afternoon are allowed each day. Each time a voting session occurs, the ballots are burned; the smoke signaling what decision, if any, has been made to the outside world — black for no decision, white for an elected pontiff. Such procedures, mysterious and guarded, were of a tradition mostly unchanged since the 1500s. Prior to that time, villagers, priests — nearly anyone who came out wanting to participate — often had the pleasure of helping to select popes.

Monsignor Roberto Benjamin Postillio sized up the crowd: one hundred and ten cardinals between the ages of 50 and 80 from six continents and nearly fifty-two countries. Shut off from the world and provided comforts at the Apostolic Palace, they were sure to drag out the procedure. Due to an imposed press blackout, the press — like the rest of the outside world — would have to wait for the white smoke.

Little did the cardinals realize, as they hugged and shook hands with one another, just how quickly their decision would be made.

Having addressed the convocation on occasion

over the years, and some individually, they knew the monsignor quite well. None of them, however, expected his presence today. Rather enjoying the surprise, the monsignor fought a devilish smirk.

Listening to them all engage in conversations of many languages, it was like visiting the United Nations. Slamming the wooden door shut, he waited in silence for their attention with his hands folded behind his back. Startled into attentiveness, the conversations soon died down as the cardinals settled into their seats one by one.

Oh, yes. They knew the monsignor. So well did they know him and his rage that they quickly fell silent.

"For several years I have served as our Holy Father's prefect. I have also served as your humble guardian in keeping the now prostrate leader at arm's length from your most interesting cabal.

"Gentlemen, we all know the harm brought unto the Church by the Second Vatican Council and made worse by that damn dinosaur who now lies buried in the crypt beneath St. Peter's Basilica. Leaving nothing sacred, he opened doors best left closed and sought to remove nearly all traces of mystery from the Church."

The monsignor methodically paced the floor, massaging his chin with his left hand.

"Over the years, I have seen to it that your amoral whims have been satisfied at the peril of my own position. I have steered the old man for the last ten years in the directions you shamefully requested and included your unprincipled agendas in his every decision concerning you or the countries you represent. I have sat back while you bilked Mother Church of her financial resources. And I've helped quiet scandals from erupting, saving you the embarrassment of public disgrace."

It was here that the monsignor stopped pacing. Pausing to look out over the crowd of elderly cardinals, he added his most cunning diatribe. "But it has come at a high price. Take heed, my brothers. The Church currently faces a debt that will reduce it to nothing more than a monastic shrine by the end of this millennium thanks to your selfish whims. A restructuring of the Church is in order to ensure its survival. The time has come for someone with forward thinking to lead. To bring the mystery back. And to put an end to the squandering of financial resources. Between your recklessness and the fool's attempts to change the world, Mother Church has been greatly burdened."

The monsignor lowered his voice. A slow rage simmered from deep within. "While it may be true that Helmutt has given many of you a membership of more patrons than you could ever hope for, consider the cost. He has permitted radical changes to take place, such as inviting homosexuals into the Church, allowing marriage of its pastors in the western hemisphere, and condoning the use of birth control. Most egregious was his position on abortion before he passed. A position basically excusing immoral behavior. And women priests? Really? Sacrilege! The disbanding of the Swiss Guard, the long-standing protection provided for pontiffs? Highly dangerous and irresponsible.

"For centuries, the Church has suffered persecution. Only since 1929 have we truly come unto our own once again. Dammit, we own Rome! The World!"

The monsignor's face flushed a deep red at this as he branded a fist in the direction of the cardinals. "With nearly two hundred million acres in the

Church's possession, we are among the largest of the world's landholders. Properly administered, our influences in financial and political matters throughout the globe could make us a supreme power rivaling that of a first world country.

"Helmutt was *obsessed* with living piously," the monsignor noted after somewhat composing himself. "If he only—"

A voice from the corner of the room interrupted him. "He was a good man, Ben. Brought faith back."

"We may be guilty for raiding the cookie jar," someone else said, "but it's been a long time since someone took that office determined to do more than *act* like a Christian."

A third noted that the previous pontiff was uncomfortable with the pageantry connected to the papacy.

Murmuring voices seemed to echo the sentiments of the cardinals who dared to voice their opinions.

"He wanted to accept people for their differences. To bring them into the Church. He wasn't trying to embrace the decadence of the West. He was trying to deal with it head-on. No, Helmutt was trying to deal with the West and its influence on the world," another cardinal, off to the center right, clarified.

A sea of whispers rose from the gathered group.

How interesting, the monsignor mused inwardly. That the lot of them would audaciously defend the old man was downright ludicrous considering they were guilty of embezzling vast amounts of money from the Church.

In the previous decade, the Church fared well in financial matters under Helmutt's reign while Christianity enjoyed a robust, albeit brief, resurgence. People once more crowded into churches and flocked to join religious orders. But there was a price to all of this success. Because many members of the Papal Conclave took advantage of the resurgence by lining their own pockets, their greed never adjusted to the decline of wealth within their own parishes — their major source of revenue — when the world economy began to contract in more recent years.

The monsignor knew all this. It was he who assisted in fabricating the true extent of their revenue streams using church programs and papal office dictums centered on community outreach as cover for their pilfering in parishes wealthy and poor. Once those circumvented revenue streams dried up and pyramid investment schemes backfired, it was he who once again devised plans to keep hidden the misappropriation of funds.

Hungry as ever, their greed never diminished. "Charlatans," the monsignor reflected while scanning the sea of scarlet skullcaps for the dissenters. "Charlatans all."

He knew it would take some convincing for the fat swindlers to acknowledge the reality of the situation. Since they would never change, he would have to collect on all his past favors to serve his own personal agenda. Part of his plan all along. And why he made sure to keep meticulous records. He'd blackmail them all if necessary.

Speaking slowly, he addressed them from a position of false righteousness. "Do you not see what has become of Mother Church?"

The monsignor knew full well that on some level they understood, however stubborn and inflexible they were, for this was the new reality. Scandals within Mother Church had been ongoing for decades, with the popes doing much of the pillaging themselves. Living lavishly. Like kings. Only a few, like Helmutt, were the exception. Since the turn of the century, beginning with the World Wars — most especially the Second World War and the Vatican's secret relationship with the Nazis — nothing was off limits. As unholy as the Holocaust was, most within the Church, especially the pope at the time, looked at it as an event that did not directly involve them. As they profited from the relationship with Nazi Germany, it was then a question of how to maintain its secrecy.

Only a few, even when faced with the temptation of riches and power, chose to follow a model of morality.

Cardinals and bishops were no different. Each operated within a very profitable sphere of influence, no matter their base of operations.

The irony of it all, chuckled the monsignor.

It was also much of this group who vehemently disapproved of Helmutt's vision of restoring respect to the papal throne, fearing a disruption to the status quo. That was where the monsignor came in, operating from a position of power from inside the pope's inner circle as prefect.

The monsignor continued his argument before his group of peers. "The Church, thanks to Helmutt, has seen fit to allow in every wicked person, every vagrant, and every sinner. And to what end? To bring the Church back to the people?

"At the same time, he welcomed the riff-raff with open arms, Helmutt lost the Church's long-standing traditional patrons *specifically* because of these new policies. And while new members flooded the churches and the orders, the number of *traditional followers* not regularly attending Mass, withdrawing from the orders, and/or no longer interested in strengthening their faith, are on the rise once again.

"And why not? There's nothing to prevent them from ever getting into Heaven. Thanks to Helmutt, whatever perverted, heinous, or depraved act a person feels justified committing is covered. All one needs to do in their hour of desperation is ask for forgiveness. Understand me when I tell you, because of what he set in motion, the rights and responsibilities of the faithful — keeping holy the Sabbath, fulfilling the commandments of the Church, coming to share as a community in the sacrifice and celebration that is Mass — is negated.

"We must face the truth. God's children wrongly assume there are no reasons for regularly attending the celebration anymore."

There was a murmuring among the gathered until another cardinal brazenly broached what was also on everyone's mind. "What of the prophecy, then?"

The noise level rose. Unable to identify the speaker, the monsignor leered over the assembly. As depraved as their flock, they were all too happy to bleed dry the last Bishop of Rome. Sensing they were about to be strong-armed, it was only natural that they attempt to deflect the conversation. Bringing up the unspoken prophecy uttered from the lips of a crazy nun was akin to a poker player betting on an empty hand.

The monsignor assured himself of their capitulation, holding back his once-more simmering anger. They were unaware of the hell they'd pay otherwise. His nostrils flared as he inhaled sharply. Tempering his response, the monsignor put on a very confident and convincing face.

"Prophecy? You speak of Mother Maria, no

doubt. And the fabled secret that has haunted these hallowed halls. Gentlemen, you speak of another injustice brought unto the Church."

"You know what it is..." a cardinal in the crowd accused.

Once more, the cardinals erupted into a clamoring row.

"True. This much is true, gentlemen. But since Helmut refused to divulge any information, even while on his own deathbed. And Maria is..." It was here that the monsignor was unable to conceal a toothy grin. "Well, she is, of course, nowhere to be found. What can I say other than all is now lost but to the lips of the dead. Where it belongs."

He was lying. And many in attendance assumed as much. Their indignation only grew louder. Bolder. Riled by what they were hearing, they were becoming more vocal. Sensing an end to their order was at hand, a cacophony of voices demanded they be told the truth about the prophecy.

"SILENCE!" Enough was enough. Their disgraceful participation in one of the most lucrative corruption scandals entitled them to nothing.

Clenching his white-knuckled fists behind his back, rage coursed rapidly through his veins. "You imbeciles! There is NO prophecy. The woman was bewitched."

A wicked scowl formed over Ben's face as he eyed the assemblage of cardinals, irritated by their pettiness. He was determined to refocus the conversation. "Enough of this madness," he said, feeling his last ounce of patience slip away. Infuriated, he made his intentions known. Into the air he thrust his forefinger. "Know this my brothers and hear me well. I am your choice for the next pontiff. Do you hear?"

Some cardinals stood. Others shouted out in protest. One cardinal, a Spaniard, even made for the door. Spanish accent thick in his speech as he addressed the conclave before leaving. "I don't care who you all decide to become the next pontiff, but you will do it without me. No mas! I am removing myself from this conclave."

Daring to face Ben, he further stressed his view by pointing at the tall prefect. "And I'll be damned if I ever agree to you."

A hush fell on the gathered. They witnessed in unison Ben's face become a series of red and purple blotches. Eyes wide before narrowing into slits.

Exasperated beyond control, the monsignor charged the cardinal, catching him completely off guard. Surpassing the Spaniard in both strength and height, the monsignor pushed him violently up against a concrete wall. "Then, dear friend, that is exactly what you shall be."

Striking a blow to the sixty-eight-year-old cardinal's stomach, the monsignor demonstrated to the others present his willingness to do whatever necessary to prove a point.

Collapsing to his knees, the elder Spaniard gulped in futility for air.

Reaching for the crucifix on the custom-made Rosary hung over his sash, the monsignor growled through clenched teeth. Twisting it, he lifted the handle at the head to unsheathe a slender three-inch blade.

Gasping in horror, the room of holy church leaders watched the defecting cardinal on his knees panting. Oblivious to what was about to happen next.

"I. WILL. BE. THE NEXT. PONTIFF."

Intent on making certain everyone in the room understood, each word was punctuated by the thrust of the blade into the fallen cardinal's neck. Blood spurted in messy splashes everywhere.

The cardinal's body slumped to the stone floor in a pool of crimson every bit as rich in color as the crimson in Michelangelo's frescoes.

The monsignor looked out over the mortified crowd before reiterating his demands. "Trust me when I tell you. I will be the next pontiff. Even if I have to kill every one of you!"

Squatting before the body, the monsignor swiped the dead cardinal's skullcap to wipe clean his blade. Quite chafed with the lot of them, the present situation was slightly more complicated now that the cardinals provoked his tantrum. No matter, it would no longer be business as usual. He was destined for Saint Peter's throne. And he was going to have it. Regardless of anyone. Or anything.

Rising, he discarded the bloody cap. "Have I made myself clear?"

Terrified by the monsignor's sheer barbarism, the men in the room were dumbstruck. When no one answered, with the dagger still held tightly in his hand, the monsignor repeated himself. "I said, 'have I made myself clear'?"

In the hopes of avoiding the monsignor's wrath, there was a chorus of acknowledgment.

"Excellent. Then I trust your decision will be wisely made. And completed ever so expeditiously."

The room fell silent once more after the monsignor left. With a mix of revulsion and guilt, the old men watched as the pool of blood beneath Cardinal Garcia continued to deepen.

As did their own shame.

14

S imon was being summoned from somewhere far away. Somewhere beyond. "Simon?"
Like in his sleep, whenever he wanted to wake up, he found himself immersed in a body of water swimming to reach the surface. Breaking the surface, he felt the release and tried to raise his heavy lids.

"Simon. There now. Very good. Welcome back."

A penlight blinded Simon's eyesight as the doctor checked each of his pupils. The scent of pipe tobacco heavy on his breath.

"Aw, could you possibly get that thing out of my eyes," Simon grumbled, holding up a hand to shield his eyes from the annoyingly bright light. "What time is it, anyhow?"

The man in front of him obliged. "It's after five."

As Simon's vision adjusted, he watched the doctor's short portly frame waddle towards a large wooden desk. Standing all of four feet, five inches, only with Simon seated could the two face each other eye-to-eye.

Beyond the doctor, the familiar cozy office adorned with leather furniture and lit in a soft, warm light, once more came into focus. Taking in the antique Oriental rug covering a wooden floor, Simon ran his eyes around the room admiring, as he had in the past, the wooden shelves overstuffed with books that would never make sense to him.

No different than in the past, he always wondered what all the books were about. Much of what was in the office reminded him of his childhood. Not much changed since Simon started coming here nearly ten years ago. Certificates and diplomas decorated the walls, as did pictures of the doctor with various people. Simon's eyes rested on an award that was presented for service in 1978.

To Dr. Victor Luke Samuels, it read, for *Exemplary Work in the Field of Psychology.*

The doctor distracted Simon before he could finish reading the finer print on the plaque. "Well?"

"Well, what?"

"How do you feel? You've been under hypnosis for nearly an hour."

Simon focused his sleepy gaze on the doctor. "Tired. Maybe a little better, I guess. My headache is gone. I suppose that's a good sign."

The doctor responded with a hairy closed-mouth grin. Nearly impossible to see his lips, it was like much of his facial features: all hidden under a big bush of brown hair.

"Please tell me you found something."

"First, tell me what you remember," the diminutive doctor replied. He was now seated on the edge of a large leather chair that he maneuvered in front of Simon.

At such a proximity to the doctor, Simon observed how Samuels' Beethoven-style coif hid his features. His eyes would also surely be hidden behind hair and large, round cheeks if it weren't for the wire-framed spectacles he wore all too often on the tip of his nose.

"Can you recall anything? Anything at all?"

Simon tried his best to, sucking on his bottom lip. "Am I supposed to?"

"Well, I ended your session with a hypnotic suggestion leaving it up to you to make yourself aware of your dreams." Scratching away at his beard, the doctor explained his perception of the session. "I don't think you're going crazy, if that's what you're worried about. As for the dreams you've been having, you recalled a couple of instances where you flew about visiting sights familiar to you. These places seemed to be either visited or inhabited as a child. Rest assured these things are common."

The doctor paused, thumbing through notes written during the session. Simon waited anxiously for the *but* comment.

Pushing his glasses back up over the bridge of his nose, Samuels leaned back against the decorative pillow serving as a back cushion before delivering Simon's expected *but* statement. "But I did come across something interesting on my second attempt to reach deeper into your subconscious."

What Simon always liked about Samuels, even though he stopped coming to him as frequently as he did when he was younger, was that he never held anything back. He would usually tell it like it was. Most always in a manner that made sense of things. It was why this current exchange was becoming somewhat awkward. It wasn't like Doctor Samuels to skirt around an issue.

Simon wondered if he was misreading Samuels on account of being more sensitive to things lately. "What is it?" he finally asked when the doctor still hadn't followed through.

Reaching to the table on his right, the doctor lifted a small tape recorder. Carefully watching the counter, he rewound it to a specific spot before pressing play. "There is something I want you to listen to."

"What? What is it?"

"Just listen," the doctor said turning up the

volume.

"...*nine... ten. Simon, can you hear me?*"

It was the doctor's voice on tape followed by Simon's.

"*Yes.*"

A long pause was then followed by a cough and clearing of the throat. Samuels held up his hand to Simon's puzzled expression, silently encouraging patience. Seconds later, the doctor's voice was heard once again.

"*Simon, do you know why you are here,*" the doctor asked.

Following another pregnant pause, Simon responded with "...*second chance...*"

"*Second chance? Okay. Now, Simon, what second chance?*"

"...*second chance,*" Simon repeated.

"*Explain what you mean by second chance.*"

"*I... know... him.... I know who he is.*"

"*Okay, good. Know who? Whom do you know?*"

"*Father, I am here.*"

"*Are your parents with you now? Can you see them?*"

"*Coming,*" Simon said. It sounded like fear in his elevated voice.

"*Okay, focus on my voice. I'm going to count to three and then you will feel a protective shield around you. This will protect you and keep you safe. You can freely describe where it is you are right now. Okay, Simon?*"

"*Yes.*"

"*One. Two. Three.*"

What Simon did not know is that the doctor, at this point, placed the palm of his hand on Simon's chest. He then followed with a loud vocalization, removing his hand as he shouted "*Bam!*"

Under hypnosis, Simon reacted as if shocked by electricity. It was all part of the hypnotic process that combined voice with touch.

Once more, Doctor Samuels was heard on the recorder. *"You are now protected from whatever you feared. Whatever you do fear. A protective shield now surrounds you. You can describe and explore your surroundings feeling safe. There is no pain. Do you understand?"*

"Yes."

"Now describe your surroundings for me."

Silence.

"Simon, where are you now?"

Silence.

"Where are you going? It is safe to tell me."

Silence.

"Are you going to visit your father? Your uncle, perhaps?"

"Dreams." Simon finally answered, his voice a whisper from far away.

"Good. Yes, dreams. What about your dreams? Can you explain them to me?"

"Visions."

"What visions are those? Visions of what? What is it you see?"

The silence that followed was longer than before. In between nonchalantly scanning the room for the time, Simon stole sheepish glances at the doctor. As far as he was concerned, it was taking forever and getting them nowhere. Simon was still waiting to understand the point.

"Simon? Simon, are you still with me?"

"I... am here."

"Let's begin again, shall we? Remember, you are in a safe place. What can you tell me about your dreams?"

"Keys. Must... keep..."

That Simon was unable to answer coherently seemed to alarm Samuels. Simon intently focused on the doctor's reaction.

"*Have you lost your keys?*"

"*NO!*"

Simon's voice, angry and defiant, resonated from the crackling speaker of the recorder.

"*Okay, Simon. Take a deep breath and we'll begin agai—*"

"*I... KEFA!*" Simon broke in, suddenly breathless.

"*KEFA,*" he hollered. "*MUST PREPARE...*"

Simon repeated the phrase several times before the doctor shut off the recorder.

The two sat in silence before the doctor addressed the young man.

"That was it. Aside from the steps to bring you into a state of hypnosis and some work prior to reaching this point, I couldn't get another word out of you after that. It would appear your dreams are more real to you than they are to most others. You may possess a heightened sense of awareness buried deep within your subconscious. And that, in turn, resonates more deeply with you in your dream state. I don't think it necessarily portends anything other than a manifestation of worries and burdens. Things very real and dramatic in nature given your current circumstances. You are about to become, in the true sense of the word, an adult after all."

The doctor patted Simon's knee before rolling the chair back to his desk. "Wrapping up four years of college. An expectant father. Tremendously stressful events in one's life. There's a great deal of responsibility ahead for you." He paused to look at Simon. "Then there's the fact that your parents died when you were younger. And here you are now about to become a parent yourself. This, Simon, can be very heavy stuff on all levels of the subconscious."

Doctor Samuels smoothed the hair surrounding his lips. An absent-minded tic of his. "One can feel a personal abandon in losing someone close and at the same time be very conscious about not wanting to pass that same sense of abandonment onto one's own kin. Your uncle, for example, took care of you. His untimely passing is surely still a great source of trauma because it compounds the loss and trauma already manifested in your response to the death of your parents."

"I'm aware of all of this." Simon sat picking at a hole in his jeans. He heard much of this before. He wasn't very interested in analyzing his losses or the past. Especially the emotional side of it. Not anymore.

"Things okay with Sarah? I wouldn't be doing my job if I didn't ask how the married life was going."

Simon wasn't entirely truthful. "It's going fine. Well, as well as can be expected. You know, the pregnancy and all."

"Forgive me for asking, but you're not trying to deal with these responsibilities by taking any recreational drugs or through heavy imbibing?"

"Huh?"

"Drinking."

"Oh," Simon laughed. "No, Doc. Believe me, I have too much to do to escape from reality that way."

Doctor Samuels prepared his pipe. Once packed and lit, he puffed away while watching Simon stare at the floor picking away at his pants.

When Simon did sneak a peek up, Simon was sure the doctor was falling asleep. His heavy lids appeared partially closed.

Then the little man suddenly came alive, startling

Simon. "Um, I am curious, though."

"About?"

"Are you familiar with the word *kefa*? I think it may either be Latin or Hebrew."

Feeling the doctor's eyes on him, Simon could only shrug his shoulders. He wasn't remembering any of his dreams with any clarity. Even after the doctor supposedly gave him the suggestion to remember.

"I'm sorry. I'm not really sure. Why?"

"I could check it out for you."

"I don't... Is it really necessary? I'm beginning to think I may have been studying a little too much. Lately, anyway. All that reading for school could very well be influencing what I think and how I dream. That, and all the stuff you mentioned earlier. So, I'm really not sure."

"Young man, now is not the time to deflect."

"I'm not. I just think it's like you said. Maybe it's all beginning to catch up with me."

"This could very well be true. We all have quite certainly had something akin to apparitions in our dreams — visitations, if you will. Or they could be interpreted as such. Know what I am suggesting when I say that: *interpreted as such.* Because, well, however you'd like to believe, it has been researched that much of what we see in our dreams are the faces and voices of those whom we have met in our past lives."

Simon made a face. To which Samuels reiterated his earlier statement. "Yes, lives. Plural."

"Really? Come on now, Doc."

"I'm simply communicating a belief system found in nearly all cultures and religions that within our dreams lie the connections, the links, mind you, to those past lives that we have led."

"I'm not sure I understand why."

"Perhaps to assist us in making wiser choices. At the very least, maybe to keep us from repeating the same mistakes." After a few successive puffs on his pipe, the doctor continued. "The brain, you know, is a fascinating part of the body. Take for example... rather, it could be argued, that everything that's been on your mind has easily influenced the activity in your subconscious, thereby engaging, or stimulating if you will, your neurons into a flurry of unconscious REM activity.

"Consider what you've been through in the last five, ten years. The mental strain and toll isn't given as much due as the emotional part. Yet, we replay memories and recreate scenarios when we're awake as much as when we're asleep. If you haven't' processed those events, the mind will try to do it for you.

"Then there's your studies and what you've been reading. Connections made to memories. Thoughts. Feelings. Aspirations.

"Add to this the external stimuli of movies and television..." The doctor scratched away at his beard.

Simon wondered what the doctor would look like hairless.

"I mean you grew up with an uncle who was a priest. Religion has a profound effect on the subconscious. The mind may be trying to work out your inner emotional conflict, attempting to process, maybe even compartmentalize, all your experiences in a way that will help you cope. Understand. Process. Accept. Heal. Maybe that's the key to understanding your dreams."

There really wasn't much more to say. All of Simon's medical tests from the previous week revealed nothing out of the ordinary. Simon expected the doctor to prescribe meds for the migraines and recommend restarting a regular regimen of therapy sessions.

Glancing through Simon's file, the doctor came across a note he wrote to himself some years ago. He leaned back in his oversized leather chair which in turn caused his short legs to dangle inches above the floor. "You know, you came to me when you were younger at the behest of your uncle after the death of your parents."

Doctor Samuels had always been a friend of the family — more a friend to Simon's uncle. Echoes of forgotten memories in the form of images flashed somewhere just out of reach. "Yeah, I was in middle school. Sixth grade, I think."

"You were beside yourself, no matter how much you denied it. I think somewhere in the recesses of your mind, losing your parents *and* your uncle... I think it has been more devastating than you ever wanted to acknowledge. And if I may be truthful with you, I don't think you've ever given yourself time to grieve your losses... especially the loss of your uncle."

Simon's nostrils flared, ready for the doctor to throw the "D-word" at him. He looked everywhere but at the doctor in a futile attempt to hold back pooling tears. A few hours ago he had again been to his uncle's grave. The stone, marked to show the site of his uncle's resting place read: *Faithful Follower. In God's Hands He Rests. Father Matthew Jason Free. April 6, 1933 – March 30, 1975.*

Pursing his lips, Simon tried to ignore an errant tear that came to rest on his upper lip. "I'm well aware of the pain, Doctor Samuels. But while the death of my parents in a car accident appeared to be a matter of chance, my uncle's murder has always been, by far, the most difficult to accept."

The doctor nodded in agreement, scooping up fresh sweet-smelling tobacco into his pipe. He padded it down into the warm hole with a tamper. "When you were younger you admitted that you were never really close to your parents. The loss of a parent, however, can still be a very traumatic experience at any age. Especially if one is still in school. Suddenly it becomes difficult during those formative years to associate with classmates who have... have their parents present for functions, for example. It can, over time wear a person down. I think it has worn you down. I think perhaps you haven't given yourself a chance to truly grieve for them. And why you may be..."

"Depressed?" Simon asked, finishing the doctor's sentence in anticipation of what he was sure the doctor was hinting at.

Samuels didn't miss a beat. "Are you depressed, Simon?"

Simon inhaled sharply, fighting the impulse to go on the defensive. He wondered if in his next life *he* could be the shrink.

"Because if you are, that takes us into a different direction in terms of how we help you process this. Work through this. Now there are signs, I won't deny that. But I think it's more a case of repressed anger, guilt, and some other stuff that you never fully released. Stuff that cannot be resolved in one session."

Through his nose, Simon exhaled slowly. If there was such a thing as multiple lives, he hoped his future self would be spared what he had already lived through.

"Feeling suicidal?"

"No." Life was hard. But not yet to that extent.

Samuels pressed the young man before him. "No thoughts of 'They would be better without me' running through your head?"

"No."

"Okay. Good. I mean, look at your most recent accomplishments: a baby on the way. A lovely wife. An education. Yet, there's no one to share them with. It's understandable that you would be bothered by this. But if you're depressed..."

"My parents were always gone anyway. When they died, it wasn't any different than when they were alive. So I don't feel that it has come to bother me as much as you say. You and I already discussed this far too much during my sessions as a kid. My father, who worked for a pharmaceutical company, traveled the world. Preoccupied with an adopted child..."

"Because she could not conceive a sibling for you," Samuels reminded Simon.

"Maybe, but..."

"And you rarely refer to him by name. Still. To this day."

"I didn't really know Samael, okay. And it wasn't long after they adopted him that he fell ill with Multiple Sclerosis. From that point on, I was a nonentity. My mother rarely left his side. When Sam died a year before their accident, she went into a depression she never quite recovered from. That child was her life. She couldn't bear to see him suffer. It was my uncle who took me under his wing. Even when they were still alive."

The doctor sucked away on his pipe. Suspended above them both, trails of smoke curled and looped in slow motion. "Consider the pain and guilt your mother was feeling. They could not conceive another child. The guilt she must have felt. Her *and* your father. And then with the child's illness taking much of their time away from the child she *did* conceive."

Simon clicked his tongue, refusing to look up at the doctor.

"From your experience as a father, you will develop a deeper understanding of these events and your parents' response to it all. You will come to know the pain. The fear. The all-consuming, overwhelming desire to protect another life at all costs. But you will also discover the incredible joys.

"I want you to know that your uncle's death was hard for me, too. Hard to believe that was only five years ago. Death... death can be a difficult concept to accept. To grasp."

"I'm not disagreeing with you on that one," Simon said quietly before rubbing his hands over his face.

The doctor took the hint that maybe enough was discussed for the day. "Would you like to continue at another time? If you want my opinion, I think you should never have stopped coming for counseling. I think you wanted to ignore the whole thing, hoping it would simply fade away. We could begin our sessions again."

"Nah," Simon said waving his hand, ultimately dismissing the subject. "Maybe after graduation. If the headaches haven't ended by then."

He stood to leave, offering the doctor his hand after a stretch and a yawn. "I do thank you for all that you've done for me. You've always been there for my uncle and me. I really appreciate that."

Taking the young man's hand, the doctor thoughtfully reflected on his feelings for the boy. "I want you to know how pleased I am that you continued with school. And that you've done so well in your personal life. Your uncle would have been very proud of you. Please call me again if you need anything. But don't be surprised if I check in on you in a month or so."

Simon nodded.

"And do give my best to that lovely wife of yours. Tell her I will be thinking of her and the baby. Oh, and Simon?"

Simon pivoted to face the doctor on his way out of the office.

"Yeah?"

"Happy Birthday."

Simon left the doctor's office without a concrete explanation for the headaches, the dreams, or the things he said while under hypnosis. Given the doctor's long-standing relationship with his uncle, Simon couldn't bring himself to completely confide in the doctor. At least not as he could when he was younger. There were things he didn't want to get into. Stuff he was embarrassed to revisit. Stuff he was afraid would alarm the doctor.

So he wasn't completely honest with the doctor about his most recent episodes. And he left out his memory lapsed blackouts. Twice in as many days. He feared a tumor. But nothing showed up on the hospital scans.

Could the doctor be right? Did he just not want to accept that he was indeed suffering from a form of depression? Should he consider antidepressants? Something for anxiety maybe?

Or was it something worse? Worse than a tumor that could be removed. Worse than depression that could be treated. Or anxiety. Maybe he was experiencing some kind of psychosis. Symptoms tied to some form of dementia. Schizophrenia, perhaps.

Shrugging off thoughts that were growing more troubling with each chest pounding beat of his heart, he concentrated more on first getting home as he made his way through the lobby and out to the parking lot.

Sliding into the orange Ford Pinto, its tan plastic seats icy cold and hard to the touch, Simon closed his eyes and paced his breathing. Just in the short distance from the doctor's office to the car he had worked himself up pretty good. Sweaty and short of breath, the frosty air helped.

It was time to explore what was most likely his last option. Though he had cursed the Church since his uncle's passing, going so far as to avoid stepping foot in one for years, visiting a priest was perhaps the next best logical step.

As the engine turned over, Simon took the doctor's words to heart. The time had come. After all these years. There was no reason to put it off any longer.

WEDNESDAY
APRIL 02, 1980

15

Father Jacob Dawz held the host representing the body of Jesus Christ before a very ancient Sister Mary Harrison during the Early Morning Prayer service in the small third floor chamber.

"The body of Christ."

Catching a whiff of Ben-gay, it occurred to him that of the earthly pleasures the common man are drawn to, much is due to scent. There was nothing pleasurable, however, about Sister Mary's odor. Nor was the Ben-gay the strongest odor to violate his nostrils.

Pheromones, he reminded himself, recalling the delicious fragrance of the young. Too long had it been since he enjoyed the intimacy of a female. The musky scent. The taste of...

"Amen," Sister Mary repeated. She once more opened her wrinkled mouth to reveal a white pasty covered tongue.

Sister Mary's breath jolted Father Jacob back from his erotic musings. Reflexively nodding, he placed the wafer gently onto her expectant tongue.

He closed his eyes. Why did the shape of her closed mouth have to resemble a puckered anus? When he opened them again, Sister Mary was on her way to her seat, the image of her ugly wrinkled mouth already fading from the priest's memory almost as fast as the growing guilt he felt for such thoughts.

Early Morning Prayers, part of the Liturgy of the Hours — a canonical blueprint of times and worship practice for Church officials — was a ritual as natural as breathing since much of their time was dedicated to prayer, whether privately or in public. Parish priests and nuns often agreed to celebrate the earliest prayers together, especially around important religious holidays or when in the company of prominent visitors. Unabashed in each other's presence, they stood before one another in sickness and in health because of such devotion to their faith.

Wiping the golden chalice holding the Sacrament, Father Jacob marveled at the necessity of such ceremony. Though the sharing of the Eucharist wasn't part of the prayer service, it was something this parish incorporated because of the Easter holiday prayers. Archbishop Avarassi, the one who would normally lead the prayer session, was praying at a church near Boston's Logan Airport. Late the night before, after the banquet in the pope's honor, the archbishop accompanied the pope on an unscheduled trip to another parish closer to the airport. There they remained to visit and pray with some local priests this morning.

Presiding over today's service in the Saint John Convent before a group of twelve was the long-winded bishop from Connecticut, Peter Reibold.

Fatigued from the previous day's euphoric meeting with the pope, Jacob's only energy came from the nervous excitement he derived from the secrecy of recent affairs. Regarding everyone in prayer, he couldn't help but feel sorry for them.

A chosen one, none were as special as he. Unlike him, they were pathetic. He alone was secretly helping the most powerful man in the Church. In the world.

And nothing thrilled him more.

After smoothing his frock, he interlocked his fingers and bowed his head in simulated prayer. Unlike a church service, these prayer sessions did not require an altar server. That didn't prevent Jacob from recalling a young boy from a previous parish where he was in residence. But that was over three years ago.

Another place. Another time.

"What is this?"

Aberthol North, a second-grade altar boy of Saint Rafael's, stood in the backroom sacristy behind the altar. Perplexed, he was unsure of what he found.

"Nothing." Father Jacob was fully aware of what the boy discovered. But it was getting late. Things still needed to get done before visiting with some elderly members early in the evening. He encouraged the boy to leave what wasn't his alone. "We still have much to do, Bert. Leave it and come here."

When the boy failed to come to him, Jacob harshly warned the boy. "You are testing my patience, Mr. North."

The two were cleaning up after the weekend Masses. Two weddings and three baptisms were also scheduled. Tomorrow there was a funeral. Saint Rafael's was a small parish church, but with a very devout following. This could be attributed to its ethnicity and socioeconomics. Made up of a growing African American and Puerto Rican population, the congregation saw a significant increase as more people moved to the area to work in one of the mills. While not exactly an easy life, it was a chance for a better one.

This was Father Jacob's second assignment in less than six months due to the shortage of pastors in the area. Further complicating things was his intent to study abroad.

Jacob didn't mind. It thrust him into service, immediately forcing familiarity with ceremony and protocol. With much to do, in addition to tending to the parish's finances, his work here made him feel important. Needed. Necessary.

Almost immediately he established a good reputation by quickly gaining the acceptance of the stiff fossil, Father Marshall Miller. Not long after Miller learned of Jacob's involvement in the Vietnam War, he shared his own experiences from World War II. Thus, his icy demeanor soon thawed.

"Father, what is this?" The boy's question was followed by the presentation of a beat-up leather-bound journal found in the back. It was unlike anything he had ever seen before.

Standing beside the boy, Jacob noted how the boy's chocolate skin starkly contrasted with the white altar boy vestments he wore.

And North, Jacob's inner monologue needled. What kind of family name is North? The boy's last name certainly didn't sound very ethnic.

Confused by what he saw on the brittle parchment pages, the boy innocently sought an explanation. Appearing to contain a collection of images and writings, some entries were splattered with reddish brown colors. Most curious, several hinges and latches were fastened into both its front and back covers.

Bert happened upon the item in the candle cabinet while trying to kill some pestering flies. He was intrigued, as any young child would be. That Father Jacob might be the owner of the book was inconceivable to the youth. It was also irrelevant.

"My mom has a diary."

The priest hastily grabbed the book from the boy's grasp with one hand. Seizing the boy by the shirt collar with the other, he effortlessly lifted the youth's small frame into the air several feet from the floor. "Trust me, boy, it is none of your business."

Growing bluish-green veins prominently displayed themselves on either side of the priest's perspiring forehead. "If you know what is good for you, you will forget this and what you found." Visible on the priest's forearm were odd-colored patches that appeared to be multiplying.

"Father! Your arm!" the boy gulped feverishly.

Father Jacob chuckled at the boy's expression. Mesmerized, Bert couldn't remove his eyes from the patches of skin bubbling along the priest's arm.

"If you only knew the truth," Jacob muttered, recalling all he endured over the years. As quickly as his anger flared, he composed himself while putting the boy down.

He was a monster. That much was true. Yet he still had control over his faculties. Over the evil spirits within. Or so he hoped. For now, anyway. "Speak word of this to no one. Understand?"

Fond of the boy, he was content to let the boy be. At about the same age when he first ran away from home, Jacob was certain Bert had a much better chance at succeeding in life than he ever did. He knew Bert's family. They were a good family of good people.

But the boy, returned to the floor, remained motionless in a state of shock by what he saw. The priest heard the boy's imploring thoughts. Asking. Begging for an explanation.

"Bert, it's none of your business. Let's get back to work. Forget about what you found. What you saw. Forget about what just happened here."

Jacob tried to shut out the boy's thoughts. It was important they move past the current awkwardness.

Ignoring the boy, the priest began tending to the items on the altar once more.

Father Jacob did his best to work around the traumatized child. If the boy thought what he saw was scary, Jacob hoped he would never have to witness the demons who feverishly beckoned for *him* in the dark of night. Certain in the beginning they were Heaven sent, only later did he realize he was seduced by the dark angel, Lucifer. And from there, into him entered multiple demons to exact the dark one's bidding. For what purpose and to what end had yet to become clear.

Bert, even in his youth, knew full well what he witnessed was evil. He also knew it wasn't truly Jacob. With a tiny trembling hand, he reached out for the priest. The *man* behind the collar. "That wasn't you..." Shaken by what he saw, his lips paled. "Maybe Father Miller can help you."

For but a heartbeat the human side of the priest *was* swayed, summoned by the boy's courage and faith. It was the kind that came with innocence before exposure to the evils and sins of the real world tainted it all.

But the evil within awoke at the mention of Father Miller. Something inside Jacob stirred. Snapped.

This time it was stronger than ever. And he convulsed under its power, trying to fight it with his mortal soul every step of the way.

As much as he denied it, Jacob knew full well what the demons were capable of. He feared what they *could* do. What they *would* do.

Then everything about Father Jacob's physical appearance changed. With each act of his soulful defiance, the wickedness within responded that much more violently. It overtook him, mutating his features and expanding his skin beyond known human limits. "Bert. Run!"

Collapsing to the floor, he tried to warn the little boy. But his voice, low and hoarse, was nearly inaudible. Convulsing several times, it was a struggle — a struggle over command of his soul — he endured before. Many times before.

Cracking under the strain, his chest lurched forward. What was the human shell known as Jacob suddenly took flight. Upwards he went. Rising through the air. Accelerating as he neared the cathedral ceiling. About to collide, Jacob reflexively raised his arms before him for protection only to descend as rapidly as his ascent. Arms flailing.

One of the internal entities within played with Jacob. Played with him as a cat might play — *torment* — a mouse before finishing it off. It was a reminder, a reminder of the power it — *they* — commanded over their mortal host.

Jacob was airborne several more times. Each time close to crushing his body either against the ceiling or the floor before being whipped more violently in the opposite direction.

Bert fearfully withdrew to the altar, scuttling backwards away from the scene before him.

The devils incarnate rose Jacob's body from the floor in one erect motion, forcing the priest over to the young boy.

"Not you... I know it's not you." Sobbing, the boy repeated what he knew to be true as Jacob's transformed hands seized the boy's throat. Bert watched as thick yellow secretions oozed from eyes that were once black beads.

Taking in the scent of the innocent, the demon-priest, in an act of desecration, tossed the boy onto the altar. The action knocked over the small crystal ewers filled with water and wine. Hitting the floor, they shattered into several little pieces. The Host, about to be separated and placed into the tabernacle, spilled over the altar and onto the floor in scattered pieces.

The world around the boy closed in as blackness engulfed him. Sensing what was to happen next, he knew he didn't have much longer to live. That's when he reached out one last time to what was once Father Jacob. "I... I forgive you."

A violent spasm rippled through the priest's body. The devilish creature hovering above Bert responded in a low, deep growl. "What. Did. You. Say?"

"I forgive you, Father Jacob."

The beasts controlling Jacob Dawz retreated slightly as his human side momentarily gained control. "Dear sweet boy. I had such... fondness for you."

"See... Not you."

"I am so sorry, Bert."

"I forgive you. God forgives you."

The altar, adequately lit on most days from the winter's afternoon sun through four surrounding ornate stained-glass windows of the gospel writers Matthew, Mark, Luke, and John, now darkened a scarlet black as threatening clouds rolled overhead.

"Bert, I c-can't hold him back..." What was left of Jacob's humanity disappeared in one final contraction.

Powerless, Jacob watched as the force possessing his body punctured the child's chest plate, splintering the altar beneath the boy's frail frame. In its hand, parts of Bert's shredded spinal cord caught on pieces of broken bone as his heart was savagely seized.

Everything within yards of the church ceased to

move at that very instant. Even the trees stopped swaying. It was as if earth's soul, in that one singularly defining moment, died along with the boy.

Outside the clouds released a hard, driving rain as the unholy figure turned to face the large cross against the back wall above the presider's chair. If rain were the tears of angels, then choirs of angels sobbed for Bert's soul.

Heart and spine parts in hand, bloody entrails ran the length of the desecrator's discolored arm. His defiling act one of outright defiance against Jesus Christ. The Messiah. The one who everyone believes will rise again. The one who will return — in glory — to judge the living. And the dead. The one whose kingdom shall have no end.

A strong wind picked up outside the church, slamming against the windows and rattling the doors as if trying to enter. Lights flickered before giving up, leaving only the few lit candles to cast an ominous glow on the macabre scene.

All around the desecrated boy's body flies descended.

"Magnificent, isn't it? The power! It is THIS that I, Carreau, Prince of Powers, possess! I too can command all things." Mockingly the demon scorned the blessed eight-foot plaster reminder of the Christ King's sacrifice.

With bloody clenched fists, he uttered a blasphemous declaration that was interrupted by the many within. "I will capture... WE. We will capture... YOUR SOUL, Savior," came the voices of the legion within the transformed priest.

The lifeless plaster statue of Christ suddenly came to life, opening its eyes to the abomination that was the demon-priest.

"Yes!" the demon-priest squealed in delight. He

would not be here if He did not fear what their master had planned. "You will soon attest to the power of a true god. Believe us, Christ," the mutating villain warned, his fingers squeezing the spurting blood free from the heart of the innocent he held tight in his grasp. "Suffer you and your precious mortals will before all of mankind is wiped from existence! Slaughtered like animals before your very eyes."

16

The bishop stole glances between the road and his passenger with a worried expression. Driving for nearly an hour, it would be close to another two hours or so before they reached New Galilee. Jacob didn't seem himself all morning, quickly falling asleep when they got underway.

"You okay, Jacob?"

After Bishop Reibold's humiliating reunion yesterday with his old friend, it took nearly every ounce of strength he had to fight the urge to immediately return to Connecticut. Even if he did promise Jacob a ride.

Quiet during morning prayers and breakfast, neither man was truly in the mood to talk this morning. Still, the bishop couldn't help but sense something strange, even wrong, with Jacob.

"Jacob?"

Jacob shot up in his seat, startling himself and the driver. "Huh?"

"Dear me, Father! I didn't mean to wake you. Just wanted to make sure you were feeling okay."

Jacob rubbed his eyes and yawned as color returned to his face. "Yeah, I don't know what's going on." He squeezed his eyes shut before shaking his head to clear it.

"We're almost there. Less than a couple of hours. It's not really that far."

"Of course." A former Connecticut resident, Jacob was familiar with traveling to the surrounding New England states. "I haven't been sleeping all that well lately."

Jacob returned to the spotted window of the brown '74 Oldsmobile Toronado. Trees encircled with yellow ribbons littered the landscape — a grim reminder of the Iranian hostage crisis.

The bishop noticed Jacob looking at them. "It's awful about those sixty-six hostages, isn't it? We must keep them in our prayers. Continue praying for a peaceful solution."

Jacob didn't register the bishop's words. With each blink, the world before him changed. The last time he blinked, he was no longer in Connecticut. But back in Vietnam.

17

Swatting at a swarm of annoying flying insects, the marine opened his eyes to an overhead canopy of mature tree crowns. It reminded him of his childhood. Hiding in the woods, he would spend hours at a time looking up and dreaming about all the exotic places under the same sky.

Then the smells overwhelmed his senses. Sweat. Body odor. Shit. The scent of something putrefying. Constant reminders of life in the booby-trapped terrain northwest of Saigon where the smell of death was never far away.

Stifling a yawn, he realized he nodded off while writing his latest journal entry. Humping through the humid jungles of Vietnam loaded down with eighty pounds of weight like a sweaty pack mule had that effect.

Patrolling near the Ong Thanh Stream, he was part of the Second Battalion, Twenty Eighth Regiment Delta Company. The Black Lions. From their NDP — night defense perimeter — they were preparing to follow Alpha Company on a return trip to yesterday's surprise find: a large-scale bunker and tunnel network.

Thick drops of perspiration blotted the tiny pages of his pocket journal as he struggled to scribble down the date on damp paper: Tuesday, October 17, 1967.

Writing the date after each entry instead of at the beginning gave each day he lived that much more meaning. Not that he really had anything to live for. But surviving against the odds was something he was familiar with. It's why he was eager to enter the military. It's why he kept a journal of observations and thoughts.

Removing his M1 helmet, he used his military issued green towel to wipe his face and head before securing the journal under the stretchy band around the steel pot.

The muggy, damp air consumed him. Dirty fatigues clung thickly to his body. The sensation of a million things crawling all over a constant that never ceased. This is what it was like to serve as an infantryman in the foreign jungles of Vietnam. And while it may have been, by far, the shittiest place he could find himself, joining the Marines offered a way out of his miserable home life back in the states. Even if it meant trading one shithole for another, where middle and high school years were spent floating between a drunk aunt's place and friends willing to offer their couch. So long as it meant never returning home, he didn't care where he was.

All was quiet for now — well, what passed for quiet — as the grunt's company awaited orders to begin advancing. Right now they were waiting on Alpha Company.

Time in the jungle — day or night — took some getting used to. But the longer one was here the better it became to read the signs. To listen for the clues its many vocal inhabitants communicated. If ever too quiet, chances were they were not alone.

The marine closed his eyes against the backdrop of familiar jungle sounds. Intermixed with the ambient noise — a symphony of animals and birds — he heard his fellow jarheads commiserating. One of them was again going on and on about his girlfriend back home.

Sleep, never much of a luxury, descended on him

like a warm blanket on a cool night.

Sleep. Yeah. Maybe a few minutes.

Frowning, the teacher disapprovingly eyed the boy's journal from over his shoulder. "Mr. Dawz, what are all those marks over your book?"

Sister Anne stood behind Jacob tense as the snapper arm of a mouse trap. All she needed was a trigger and she was ready to destroy any child who got in her way.

Jacob did not move. But his grip tightened round the pencil.

The stern nun needled him, discontent with the moody seventh grader. These days in her career, they all usually rubbed her the wrong way. This Dawz kid was no exception. If anything, he epitomized what was wrong with today's youth.

"Mr. Dawz, you have these unholy markings and drawings all over your notebook and journal. It's bad enough you don't even take the notes down that I write on the board. And since your frequent absences have resulted in few completed assignments..."

White knuckling the writing implement, Jacob's left leg unconsciously bounced up and down in response to his growing anxiety. "I made it in today, Sister Anne. *I'm here*," he said, demonstrating restraint.

"Young man, don't interrupt! And don't expect to be complimented for doing something everyone in this class is required to do. Now, about that writing of yours stuffed away in your desk."

Humiliated by the discovery, Jacob was at once overwhelmed with an intense wave of heat that pulsated with every beat of his heart. The more he tried to ignore the layer of perspiration forming on his forehead, the worse it became.

"Such dark, violent stories," the teacher continued. "Why are you writing such disturbing stories about your parents? Especially your father. Where is your faith, young man? This is unacceptable here at Saint James. I think it best we contact your parents."

In his seat, the boy came alive. His abrupt movement startled the short, frail nun who stood barely at five feet. "Do not call my house. Please!"

It was bad enough he had to deal with his parents' perpetual arguing. His father's drunken nights. The beatings as he tried to protect his mother. If his father even caught wind of what he was writing.

"Then perhaps we should continue this after class with the principal."

In her words. Her tone. Her demeanor. There was nothing but disinterest. It wasn't as if she and the other adults at the school were dumb to his situation. But for a woman who was supposed to be of faith, a religious sister, she lacked compassion. Empathy.

Getting here today was a struggle. Up nearly all night, he had fallen asleep in time to miss the bus. Yet his teacher could care less. Feeling defeated, Jacob shrugged his shoulders, resigning himself to the fact that he was never going to win her approval. No matter what he did. Just like his relationship with his father.

"Whatever," he mumbled.

"Excuse me?"

Flushing with annoyance, reddish hues erupted across the teacher's ivory blotched skin. Her raspy voice shook more than usual — an indication the senior was all-too ready to pounce.

"Now class, if you all recall," she began, addressing the class but peering at him over horn-rimmed glasses perched atop the bridge of her nose. It was a routine of hers. An ill-intent to motivate others. To embarrass students by reiterating her task at the expense of signaling out those who misunderstood. "I mentioned this already to you several times..."

With hands on her hips, she sharply turned her nose down at Jacob, pursing her shriveled, wrinkled lips. "What do you think you are doing?"

Jacob eyed the chain around her neck attached to her spectacles. There were times Jacob thought about choking Sister Anne with that chain.

Having snapped the pencil, he realized all eyes were on him. As they always were. Judging him. He was the anomaly. The freak with the terrible home life. The charity case.

But even if no one in the school cared, most of all his teacher, they were living in a fantasy world if they thought all families were like those portrayed on television. Not everything resembled the *Andy Griffith Show*.

Let the nun before him try one day in his shoes. One day with the bastard that was his father. Yeah, maybe he wrote stories. But the crap he dealt with daily was real. Even if the resolutions in his stories were not. He was angry that his father should be allowed to treat them such as he did.

He was certain one day his father was going to go too far. And it would be the death of his mother — or him — at the hands of his father.

In his stories, his father paid for his crimes. Usually with his life. As it should be.

It's not like any of his prayers have ever been answered anyway. How many nights did he fall asleep clenching his fists? The pillow moist with his tears. Dreaming up ways to kill the man who was supposed to be his dad.

Unlike the stories they were forced to read in class, at least his stories reflected his own reality. They even gave him a sense of control. Of which he had none outside his fiction.

Television wasn't any better. *Leave It to Beaver*? He hated the show for its insincere depiction of family life, once remarking to a classmate that he identified more with Eddie Haskell's character. Unlike Eddie, he wouldn't have just picked on Beaver, he would have likely kicked the snot out of him.

But Jacob was most resentful of shows like *My Three Sons*. If he couldn't have a father like Andy Griffith, why couldn't he have a father like Fred MacMurray?

Standing beside Jacob, the teacher was relentless in her pursuit. A ploy to motivate Jacob into meeting his academic objectives? *Hardly*. This was purely personal.

"I swear, young man, I don't even know why you are here. You are going to end up exactly like that no-good father of yours. If you cannot handle the schoolwork, how will you ever be able to handle a job?"

Set in her very rigid, structured ways, she had grown tired of excusing the folly of her adolescent students. With each generation, more godless than those that came before, they were more distracted. More rude. And much less focused on their education. Their faith.

So very close to retirement, she was not going to let this one hellion ruin her final year at Saint James Catholic School. Let the principal handle such an ignorant, belligerent degenerate.

"Probably even need an exorcism to rid yourself of the vileness that is you," she spewed while angrily gathering pieces of the broken pencil.

Jacob's leg bounced more wildly now. In his clenched fist, dirty fingernails pierced the flesh of his palm. "Stop. Riding. Me!"

Though Jacob spoke in a low, controlled voice, the boy's entire body trembled with the rage of having been singled out. Embarrassed. Belittled. One too many times.

But even filled with rage, Jacob acknowledged he wasn't entirely innocent. But he was no more mischievous than those his age when he was present. This, however, was lost on his teacher who took it all personally. She turned a blind eye to the true reasons for his acts of defiance. Had she, or anyone, been receptive enough to dig a bit deeper, they might have been able to work with the troubled boy. Maybe even save him.

The sister didn't like the boy; she didn't like most boys. Furthermore, she was void of any patience or compassion when it came to his home situation. Marriage was sacred. If the boy's parents were experiencing problems, perhaps it was because they failed to include God in their lives. Rarely ever at church, they were also always late with tuition payments. Always enough money for drink. The mother seemingly pregnant every time she'd see her.

Devil's seed. There was a reason why the mother could not keep any of her other babies. There was a reason why the father couldn't hold down a job and was enamored with the drink. But since they refused to seek out Christ for forgiveness — to enlighten their path to salvation — their child didn't have a chance.

The apple never falls far from the tree, Sister

Anne thought to herself through smoldering eyes. Oh, yes, she remembered the boy's father from his own days of school.

That is why she welcomed any excuse to kick the boy out of her classroom. At least it would give her the opportunity to work with those who were here to learn.

Jacob felt the teacher move up behind. But before registering her actions, he felt the painful pinching of his ear. Sister Anne tightly gripped the lobe. Pulling on it, she led him out of his seat and walked him to the door. "That's it. Off to the principal young man. NOW!"

The boy waited until he reached the door before pivoting. His expression one of such malevolence that it made the teacher shudder.

No one in the room moved. They all waited to see what Jacob would do next.

Jacob grinned before salaciously licking his lips, delighting in the response his next action would produce. Drawing his fore and middle fingers up to his lips in a V-shape, he grunted loudly as he darted his tongue in and out between them.

Right on cue, the teacher lost control. Feeling violated from the offensive gesture, she screamed for him to leave in an elevated voice not used in years. Clutching the edge of the closest student desk, she fought to maintain her composure. More than any time during her forty-three years of teaching she wanted to strike a child — this evil seed, this burden on society — with all her might.

"Get out of here, now! You rotten, evil, son-of-a..."

That's when he took one last look around the room. Removing his green clip-on tie, he threw it on the floor at her feet before flipping her off. While some of his classmates looked mortified, and rightfully so, some of the boys were smirking. Jacob wasn't sure if witnessing the bony teacher lose control was behind the smirking. Maybe it was the nervous awkwardness created by seeing a fellow classmate get booted from class.

Then again, they may have been smirking because only he had the balls to pull something like that off. He guessed it was probably a bit of all three. It didn't matter, though. He was done.

Striding from the room, he didn't walk to the Principal's Office. Instead he walked straight out the front doors of the school as its *Congratulations to the Class of 1962* banner was being hoisted up for the upcoming eighth-grade graduation.

Destination unknown to him at the time, he was sure of one thing. Wherever he went, so long as it wasn't here, he would be fine.

Or so he thought.

Mortar shots startled Jacob into action. He scrambled for his M14 while attempting to assess the situation. Some klicks from their location was the Lai Khê town garrison. According to the maps, a few smaller villages lay several klicks in opposite directions.

If only he could right himself in order to know which direction he should...

Brilliant colors lit up the not-yet-dusk cloudy sky smudged with smoke. It occurred to Jacob that at no time since his arrival in Vietnam was the sky ever clear.

He listened for orders over the bombardment's thunderous roar within the theater that would later be known as the Battle of Ong Thanh.

A group of FNGs — new recruits fresh from boot camp and cherries in the field — were overwhelmed by the ambush. Multiple explosions disoriented them all because they appeared to be coming from everywhere at once. Soon the place would be overrun with V-Cs.

Cocking his rifle, Jacob hit the dirt. Fire was coming from all directions. And because some of his own company was shooting blindly, they were all twice as likely to get picked off.

"Friendly fire, my ass," he remarked under his breath. "Lousy freakin' euphemism, if there ever was one."

There was no way to communicate. Not with the cacophony of this latest round of explosions. It was difficult to even see one another, much less the enemy. All there was left to do was shoot in the direction of the oncoming gunfire.

He thought he heard his sergeant yelling something about reinforcements. It was too late for that now. Certainly not when your enemy hid in plain sight. And not when you can't tell enemy from ally.

Scores of bullets pelted the ground nearby as Jacob dropped his ruck for better maneuverability.

He set off crawling over to an 18-year-old black boy from Georgia he befriended. Lean, he was a two-hundred-pound high school football hero everyone called Rusty. Even though his name was Russel. Jacob wanted to yell to Rusty that if he didn't make it, he'd do him a solid and marry that high school sweetheart of his he was always bragging about.

Rusty took to parading pictures of his hottie every chance he had. Growing annoyed with all the damn bragging, not many believed he even had a girlfriend. Until her letters arrived.

Then it was clear why Rusty bragged about her.

And much like everyone else stuck out here, one's ability to survive came from knowing there was someone to come back home to. Or something.

Jacob had neither.

"INCOMING," someone yelled.

Another explosion. This one rocked the ground, feeling too damn close to where Jacob lay. Streams of rain soaked his face. But something deep within sensed it wasn't rain. Jacob screamed as parts of Rusty's body covered him.

Scuffling along the ground on his elbows with a mixture of fear and discipline, Jacob made his way into the thick brush, passing over — and through — Rusty's remains. He crawled for several minutes at a time. Pausing only to catch his breath, he used the lighting of mortar and gunfire to illuminate the growing duskiness. Zigzagging to the right, he slipped down a muddy embankment.

A burst of pain suddenly erupted in his lower right leg. Jacob swore aloud. Then immediately regretted it, catching three advancing silhouettes.

Rifle raised, he set his M14 on automatic, emptying an entire mag of twenty rounds in a spattering of shots. Cocked on his elbow, he replaced the mag with another from his belt. Eyes blurred with grime and sweat, he took no chances. Keeping his finger pulled back on the trigger, the rifle vibrated in his hands. He took down two of the three soldiers closest to him. Dropping inches away, they gasped and gulped for air as death approached.

Gurgling sounds erupted from their throats as Jacob extracted his M6 bayonet to finish the job.

Illuminated before the incandescence of weapon fire, Jacob spotted the third V-C drawing stealthily nearer. Grabbing one of his frag grenades, he pulled the pin out with his teeth and tossed it forward before scurrying backward to find cover.

The explosion accomplished its mission. But also alerted more of the enemy. Voices and sounds continued advancing as Jacob became aware of more bullets humming past his ears. It hit the nearby foliage with a series of popping sounds.

A barrage scattered debris over on the hill where he dozed off earlier. Overhead the sky lit up to reveal the jungle teeming with still more oncoming enemy soldiers. They kept coming, one after another like... Like ants... Like ants swarming in on the flesh of a newborn.

Ants in this part of the world were unlike anything Jacob had ever known. Recalling the gut churning sight of hundreds — if not thousands — of ravenous insects consuming a discarded baby some klicks from a local village, the flesh-eating army ants of Vietnam were ferocious and unrelenting.

In horror, he witnessed what he prayed he'd never have to ever see again. Placed in a haphazardly dug hole, it took no time at all for the silent killers to become alerted to their next meal. Seconds later, the Mongol horde of carnivores overtook a villager's unwanted baby. Their large, sharp mandibles tearing at the rejected writhing newborn's tender flesh — flesh disintegrated with acid spewed from tiny mouths digesting it as they tore it apart. What it left behind was too much for Jacob to...

Jacob took to crawling again, the pain in his leg ignored as he dragged it uselessly behind. Sliding off balance down a slight slope, he found himself near a tree with its base partly hollowed out. Desperately feeling his way in the dark, Jacob took refuge inside.

Surprisingly, the hole was larger than he estimated. It provided just enough cover. He pulled brush that was within reach up to the opening. But not before another V-C came dangerously close to discovering Jacob's hideaway.

Using the flashes of light overhead to place himself, Jacob managed to creep from his spot, coming to stand directly behind the enemy. Sweat — or was it tears? — trickled over his cheeks and into his mouth as he grit his teeth.

Then the sky lit up again exposing Jacob's intended target. Fighting the pain in his leg, the marine relied purely on adrenaline and training. His adversary, having neither the chance to use his weapon nor shout out as Jacob's bayonet was wedged into his throat, remained silent during his execution. As the serrated blade exited the back of the victim's neck, Jacob listened to the crack of the spine and crunch of the collapsing esophagus.

Falling against the tree, Jacob was exhausted but alert with pain and fear. Slowly sliding into a seated position, he took the dead, bleeding enemy combatant with him. Like a tapped keg, the blood flowed freely.

Jacob concealed the body using as much brush as was in reach. He'd be safe as long as he could get through the night.

Back within the protection of the tree's cavity, he remained obscured while explosions continued to bring the night sky to life like a violent lightning storm.

Rifle ready, Jacob sat alert to the sounds of his unit's slaughter. In waves it came to him from somewhere in the distance. Soldiers — many not long out of high school — screamed in reflexive response to the insanity that overwhelmed them as death closed in. They yelled for their girlfriends. Their mothers.

Even God.

But no God exists here in these jungles. Revulsed, he wiped roughly at the tears mixed in with the sweat covering his cheeks. With no special girl in his life or family worth caring for, he wondered what his frame of mind would be like in his final moments.

The carnage continued throughout much of the night. The screaming until dawn. A mixture of gunpowder, spent fuel, and burning flesh heavily saturated the humid air. Especially following the napalming that took place northwest of his location. The Viet Cong overtook Jacob's unit in fighting that lasted for several hours, leaving many of the more seriously wounded alive to die in agony.

Jacob gagged back the threatening acid in his stomach. Didn't anyone realize the armies of the United States were defeated the very instant they set foot in these jungles? Victor Charlie was one with every valley, rise, plateau, rice field, and swamp. Many were conceived, born, and raised in these jungles. They knew it was inhabited with flesh-eating fire ants. Leeches. Monkeys. Tigers. They knew where the booby traps were hidden. Knew where the more than thirty thousand miles of tunnels were. It was all used to their advantage to deceive, fatigue, and ultimately conquer any foreign invader.

No matter how strong the airpower or number of targets destroyed, it never seemed to deter the Viet Cong resistance.

They knew it. The grunts on the ground knew it. It was the politicians in Washington who didn't.

Jacob waited before giving himself a chance to fully breathe. Though the remaining V-Cs scoured the area thoroughly, they somehow bypassed him.

Opening his pants enough to allow himself some room, he went about relieving himself. He wasn't as afraid. So long as he remained in the tree and out of sight.

Morning became afternoon. Afternoon became evening. At times Jacob couldn't ascertain his state of consciousness. Was he the only one alive out of his unit? Was he dreaming? Awake?

It was difficult to tell. At one point, he found himself walking among the dead. Rifle in hand.

Then he felt the weight of his load bearing equipment lessen. He, too, became lighter. He became so light that he began rising into the air. Lush jungles blurred into shades of greens and spotted browns as a vast desert appeared under him.

Jacob closed his eyes. Not one for heights, nothing about the experience was comforting. And he wished it away.

When he finally mustered the courage to lift his lids once more, he found himself back on terra firma face-to-face with a vaguely familiar bearded man.

The man was dressed in sandals and a simple Middle Eastern wool tunic. Atop his head was a cotton or wool headdress that was also wrapped around his face and neck. Though it was difficult to discern his features, it appeared he was smiling at Jacob. He seemed to be sizing him up. Very much intrigued by him. Guiding Jacob by the elbow, the stranger motioned him to the edge of the promontory on which they stood overlooking the desert.

Swatting a fly buzzing about his face, Jacob swore he had been here before in his dreams. Yet everything around him appeared much sharper than any dream. Hyper-realistic.

"*I understand you've experienced a pretty hard life.*"

Jacob heard the stranger beside him speak. But he spoke with unmoving lips. The voice strangely came from within Jacob's head.

Wiping the sweat from his face with the back of

his hand, Jacob caught sight of the blood. Dried to a brown color now, it was caked on his fatigues and skin. Rusty's blood? His own?

Looking up from his hands to the stranger, he observed the stranger's lips move. "You've always had to work so much harder than anyone else. But with so little respect in return."

Jacob squinted. The sun was very bright. Strangely enough, though he should have been sweating profusely in the bright, burning sun, he wasn't. Yet whenever the stranger spoke, it was difficult to concentrate on his words. As if he was caught in some sort of haze. Or heat stroke.

"You were forced to make do when no one gave you anything, much less a chance."

"Pretty much." Taking in the barren desert, Jacob habitually felt for his pack of smokes from his steel pot. But he wasn't wearing his helmet.

"Looking for this?" the stranger asked. In his hands, he held what Jacob was looking for.

Scrutinizing the figure before him, Jacob fetched his pack of smokes from their place behind the stretchy band surrounding the helmet. It was also where he kept his journal, among other things. But it was nowhere to be found. Only the cigarettes.

Pulling the last stick from the foil, the marine tossed the crinkled pack and fished his fatigues for matches. Lighting his cigarette, he felt out his new desert friend, continuing to regard him with extreme caution. Sucking in hard, he welcomed the nicotine.

"What's your point?"

"What if I told you I could give you all the riches of the world and free you from the worthless life you have now?" This aged man of the desert smiled. But it was a black fly that darted across the man's stubbled cheek that drew Jacob's attention. Taking flight, the fly zigzagged in the air before coming to land on the man's broadening lips. Lips that revealed rows of rotted teeth.

Ooh, that's not good, Jacob thought to himself. Then again, he was used to seeing many Vietnamese with teeth equally as bad. But just as he decided not to hold it against this stranger, the teeth appeared less decayed. Or were they?

The desert stranger motioned towards the barren land before them. It extended as far as the eyes could see. Then the desert transformed. Materialized. Into cities. No. Kingdoms. Before him were kingdoms of shining yellow metal. A Mirage? A dream?

Exhaling, the marine returned the unfiltered end to his lips. Something wasn't right.

Eyeing Jacob with intense curiosity, the robed man's eyes never left his as he spoke. "No more troubles. Imagine that. The world. At your feet. A way out of your misery."

Jacob once more sucked in the smoke deeply, listening intently. No one ever offered him anything at all. Much less the world. But as with all things, there was always a catch. A price to pay. Even in this dream-like state, Jacob knew that to be true.

After one last drag, the marine flicked the butt off the precipice. For all he knew, this was more than a dream or hallucination. The caked-up blood on his skin and fatigues was his own. He was dead. Screaming out into the void like the rest of them.

He decided to humor the stranger. Since he was already dead, what would it matter? "Fine. What's the catch?"

The stranger appeared bewildered. "Catch? Why, all I ask is that you follow me. Then anything you dare dream shall be yours."

The man's arms opened once more to the vastness that lay before him. In the distance, a world of gold shimmered in the intense sunlight.

Jacob, moving his hand before his face to deflect a couple of annoying insects, grinned at the absurdity of it all. What the hell did he need with a kingdom?

The stranger spoke again, as if reading his thoughts. "Perhaps the beautiful slices of life that men of your youthful age desire?"

Before him materialized beautiful long-haired women. Young. Nubile. Sexually hungry. Open mouthed, their sexualized rhythm was hypnotic. Beguiling. Jacob couldn't remember the last time he was with a woman.

Eying pert nipples beneath crop tops that hardly covered their full, round breasts, the hedonist in Jacob was at once stimulated and at attention. Barely dressed, the material stretched enticingly against the forbidden fruit that lay underneath. Atop such long sexy legs, the girls danced about, playfully touching each other. And themselves.

Oohrah!

"Pleased?" Jacob's tempter asked.

There was no denying that even Farrah Fawcett had nothing on these future Playboy bunnies. But he played it cool by shrugging off the images of carnal pleasure.

The desert solicitor switched tactics. "A family, then? That which has eluded you... someone to love and watch over you."

Before Jacob, the girls dissolved into an image of domesticity replete with a family in the back of a house. This time he was there, too — well, a mirror image of himself — surrounded by laughing children and a pretty woman. A retriever barked as one of the kids threw a ball. Jacob watched the dog bound playfully after it.

Surrounded by the kids and dog, Jacob's doppelganger embraced the pretty female that was his wife before shifting his head in Jacob's direction. And waving. Jacob reflexively waved back as the visage faded at the sound of the stranger's voice.

"You already know who I am."

Jacob couldn't tell if that was a statement. Or a threat.

"Follow me."

Not a very religious person, it did seem he was being offered salvation — a chance to redeem himself. Start anew. Rise up from the misery that was his life. Be someone. Be something. Find God.

Now that he thought about it, the figure seemed — did seem — familiar. Very familiar.

"Family. Power over your destiny. Freedom from worries. Eternal life. All you must do is follow me. And I will give you the life you have long suffered for."

The figure's promise was seductive. Buying into the robed man's covenant, Jacob closed his eyes to hold fast to the quickly fading images. His thoughts vacillating between the girls with their sexual energy and the more stable visage of a wife and family.

Then his sanguine thoughts were interrupted. A threat to all that he was promised.

"Fail to follow me," the desert man warned, his whisper an unmistakable hiss against the background buzz of swarming flies, "and pay the price."

The surroundings dissolved to reveal once more the Vietnamese jungle littered with decaying corpses.

"For an eternity."

18

Father David Anjelo Tomassi waited in silence for his final confessant to exit the confessional. Listening for the familiar creak of the floor and bench of the pew, it was his usual practice to run down a to-do list or use the solitude to talk with his deceased sister.

With his small black leather-bound prayer book in hand, he bowed his head and went about reciting his closing prayers after hearing the thud of the kneeler against the floor.

David Tomassi found God late in his life. It was not an initial calling that drew him to holy convocation. Never quite able to overcome the death of his sister, he also sought to reconcile the distress suffered during his time served in Korea. Drafted into the Army, he saw heavy combat during his fourteen months overseas and experienced firsthand the toll war takes on those involved.

It was perhaps worst for those who first fought in World War II. American exceptionalism distorted the narrative very early on, leading to the incorrect assumption that the United States came in and won the war single handedly. The U.S. may have been indispensable to her allies, but it was a collective effort that led to victory over the Axis powers. Regardless of America's use of atomic weapons.

The arrogance of the military in the years after the "good" war bred incompetence. Especially on the ground where troops went up against North Korean and Chinese military. This was a different war. And what U.S. troops would see and experience left long-lasting scars both physical and mental.

Brutal combat. Starvation. Extreme weather elements. Rats. An inability to identify the enemy because they blended in with the peasant civilian population. Sometimes brazenly changing out of their military uniforms in plain sight of U.S. gunners.

Though of age, Tomassi missed the opportunity to serve during World War II. Graduating high school only a couple of years after his sister's death, with the country still in the throes of the Great Depression, his immediate responsibility was to step up and support the family. His best and most readily available option: farm hand.

As much as he enjoyed working outdoors, working full-time as a farm hand was hard labor. It was also an unreliable source of income. Work was often seasonal and fiercely competitive with others who were also seeking employment. Erratic New England weather patterns affected crop yields and ultimately the amount of work available. Winter months in the northeast were the worst. To supplement his income, Tomassi sold papers before trying his hand at writing articles himself.

At the time of the attack on Pearl Harbor, Tomassi was working in upstate New York. Under General Electric's National Defense Program in Schenectady, he worked as part of the civilian war effort. Along with the American Locomotive Company, and both the Army and Navy Depots, nearly sixty thousand people were responsible for contributing to the nation's military needs. They worked round the clock on engines, propulsion systems, communications, and top-secret advanced weaponry. Since Tomassi's job was deemed critical, he couldn't be drafted even if he wanted to enlist.

Twelve years after starting at G.E., Tomassi

would get his chance to serve in the military as a rifleman in the Korean War. By this time, he was already in his early thirties. But that afforded a distinct perspective. The first of which was sacrifice. As much as he grappled with his sister's death, he was awash in guilt over not doing his part in the previous conflict. Regardless of his contribution as a civilian, he was never comfortable knowing his peers — friends and former classmates — were being shipped into harm's way while he remained safely stateside. It was even more difficult when some of them never made it back home alive.

His age also affected how he perceived the horrors of war. Maybe if he had served during the "good" war, he would have been hardened to what he witnessed during the "forgotten" one. Not even a decade after the second world war ended, new tech made the effects of war ever more devastating — as if that was even possible in the wake of the Holocaust. Never in his lifetime did Tomassi imagine he would witness such inhumane barbarism. Worst of all: U.S. complicity in the slaughter of innocents.

Wounded three times during his tour, he considered himself lucky. Trench warfare was dirty. Dangerous. And that danger didn't always come from the enemy. His first injury: shrapnel on the arm of his right side. Then, while in a fox hole, he caught shrapnel fire to his neck and shoulders. The third occasion he was fortunate enough the phosphorous burns he sustained were only to his back and legs.

Unlike his father, David Tomassi was never emotionally strong enough to swallow life's hardships and move on. Especially when he was younger. Like many other families at the time, the Great Depression did not leave the Tomassi family unscathed. Money his parents had saved — all their dreams — gone over the course of only a few years. And while his father was lucky enough to have work when nearly everyone else didn't, there was no coming back from what was lost once his mother stopped working.

Tomassi wasn't an only child. His parents also had a daughter. Laura Angioletta died at age thirteen from polio when Tomassi was fifteen. Her death profoundly affected the entire family, not just her older brother who was her best friend and protector. After his sister, he was closest to his mother. Because of this, her misery and sadness paralyzed him. As did the suffering of others around him. Family. Friends. Strangers. It got to the point that it no longer mattered who it was.

Several times his parents tried to fill the void left by Laura's death. But while their efforts succeeded in his mother's three pregnancies, each time was met with bitter disappointment. She hemorrhaged so badly during her final pregnancy that she bled to death.

It was a mishap that might have been avoided. But Tomassi's father, distrusting of medicine and science, refused to bring his mother to a hospital. A mill worker whose own father emigrated to the United States from Greece, Tomassi's father was a strict solitary man who believed in the law of the belt. When it came to marriage and child rearing, he was a firm believer in the old ways.

A few years after his mother's death, Tomassi's old man lost his hand threading one of the drums in the textile mill where he worked. It was modern medicine of the time that kept him from bleeding out. True to form, he continued working even with one hand.

For all his father's imperfections, Tomassi never

saw him cry. Not after Laura died. Not even after his mother died. As stone cold as his father may have been, he persisted through one crisis after another with an air of resolve and steely determination. It was only years later, upon reflection, that Tomassi realized his father had become more withdrawn following Laura's death. And with each failed pregnancy. Work, and hard drinking in his later years, were his only escape. Perhaps that's what contributed to his death. The elder Tomassi died of a massive heart attack while Tomassi was overseas fighting.

Going to fight in Korea Tomassi hoped he'd be able to make a difference regardless of how and where he was deployed. The death of his sister. Witnessing his mother become a shadow of her former self. His father's distance. His family's financial instability. All of it left him feeling powerless. And his war experience was no different, despite his motivation. This time it was on an even greater scale. Furthermore, it solidified his apprehension about death. If it hadn't been for the religious personnel who reached out to him during his time overseas, especially when he was recovering from his wounds at the Mobile Army Surgical Hospital, he might not be alive today. He found his conversations with chaplains comforting. Inspiring even. So much so that after his tour he decided to explore religion more thoroughly.

With help from the GI Bill, Tomassi attended college and earned a counseling degree before entering seminary. A test of his faith came shortly after he was ordained. Serving his first clerical assignment in Columbia, it followed a barbarous clash of political parties that left many dead and many more wounded. Their country, void of resources, lacked a stable government and, above all, a belief in God. But Tomassi's faith was surprisingly strong. After all he endured, the power of prayer gave him strength when he was weak. Rekindled his faith when he doubted. It was this that he brought to others.

Feeling aged by the memories, the priest sighed heavily. He recalled a quote by English author Thomas Browne: "It is a brave act to despise death; but where life is more terrible than death, it is then the truest valor to dare to live." Though never able to fully escape it, through religion, he came to better accept the suffering that surrounded him. Even if death still frightened him. It was faith in Jesus Christ that provided him with the courage to live and serve.

Before kissing the crucifix attached to the chain around his neck, Father Tomassi closed his own prayers by making the sign of the cross. It was time to head back to the rectory. He had a long night ahead of him.

His last act before concluding this time set aside for the Sacrament of Penance and Reconciliation was signing his breviary. He gently ran his thumb the length of the book's cover before moving up midway to complete the sweep: a left to right motion. This he did while whispering his sister's name and asking her to keep him in her prayers.

Exiting the booth, Father Tomassi failed to notice the young man sitting in the first pew until he was almost on top of him. "I am sorry, son. Were you here to confess your sins?"

Father Tomassi hoped he was done for the evening. Not that he minded another confessant. Confession for many patrons of the church were recently becoming less about penance and more about obligation. Worse yet, many were blatantly sugarcoating their sins. Or outright lying.

Parishioners had taken to skipping services more often these days, remaining out of sight until their sons or daughters married. Or until a relative died. Father Tomassi wished more people attended the Sunday celebration. He always looked forward to seeing members of the community and he yearned for a little good news every now and then. Or some good cheer.

That's how it used to be. It saddened him to acknowledge how much things change.

The young man rose to face the pastor. "Father Gordon?"

"No, I'm sorry. Father Gordon is currently indisposed."

"Oh."

"He's quite ill, actually. I'm Father David Tomassi."

The young man embraced the priest's outstretched hand and introduced himself. "Simon. Simon Free."

"Now that we have that out of the way, did you speak with him often?"

"Not really, no. Father..."

"Tomassi."

"Yes, Father Tomassi. I was wondering if I could trouble you, then, for some of your time?"

"It is not a confession you seek?"

"No. I just need to talk to someone. I don't have anyone else to turn to."

Giving the young man his trained, reflexive smile, the priest nodded in consent before beelining to the altar.

Back in the pew, Simon watched Father Tomassi step up into the sanctuary. Bowing before the altar, a sign of respect before entering the holy area, he disappeared to the sacristy in the rear to put away his penitential stole.

Waiting for the priest to return, Simon rose and genuflected before approaching the rows of white candles lining the walls off to the side. Though years since he last visited a house of prayer, he lit four candles out of respect: one for each of his parents. One for his uncle. And one for his unborn.

The priest emerged from behind the altar dressed in traditional black. Confessional stole removed. Coat in hand.

Bowing before the altar one last time for the day, the priest dismissed himself from the Lord's house. He turned to Simon. "Let's go next door, shall we?"

19

An early 1900s Colonial-style structure, the three-story rectory was built mostly of red brick and sat across the street from the church. Home to five parish priests, it was enough room for both living and attending to the ministry of the parish.

Quaint in appearance, the rooms smelled musty. Yet the scent — a mixture of stagnant cigarette smoke and incense — was vaguely familiar to Simon. And comforting. A collection of vinyl and cloth outdated by twenty years, the furniture was neatly assembled in a room of faded, once colorful, wallpaper. A dim lamp in the corner cast shadows that were good at hiding years of collected smoke and dust.

After preparing some coffee and setting aside some baklava on a small plate, the priest led Simon to a small room. A parlor, Father Tomassi explained it was what everyone else referred to as the sitting room.

"I never know what to call things anymore," he said chuckling. "I know the kitchen is the kitchen. The bedroom is the bedroom. I remember when one did their business in the washroom. Anyway, I'd just as soon call this room a parlor."

Sipping his coffee slowly, the priest savored the warm liquid. The walk from the church, though a short distance, had chilled him.

Simon guessed the priest to be in his late fifties. Maybe early sixties. Underneath thinning silver-colored hair, a twinkle in watery blue eyes that leaked when he smiled revealed Michelangelo-drawn wrinkles. Simon was sure they were formed from whispering prayers all his years as a church servant. Of an average build, Father Tomassi looked to be roughly short of six feet with slightly hunched shoulders.

Crossing his legs, the priest leaned back. "Now, my son, what brings you here? It seems I have been talking your ear off. And if I understood you right, you came here so that I may listen to you. Not the other way around."

He was happy to have someone to talk to. Even if the All Hallows Rectory was full of priests, having a young man to talk to was a welcome change.

Simon struggled with how to begin. Placing his cup on the floor at his feet, he leaned forward trying to disregard the throbbing headache that threatened since arriving.

"My parents passed away a little more than ten years ago. I was raised by my uncle who, coincidentally, was a priest. A graduate of Nazara High School, I spent my elementary years in parochial schools."

Simon paused, unsure how to continue without sounding like he needed a weekend in a rubber room. But taking Doctor Samuels's advice, he felt it important to start here. To provide a context for the stranger before him with whom he didn't have a history.

"The death of my parents... was difficult." Still pained by the loss after all these years, Simon lowered his head. "But it was the death of my uncle that was the most painful."

"Of course. Go on." Father Tomassi urged Simon using his counselor's voice. Confounded by the young man's familiar features, he assumed it was from the times he performed Mass over the town line in Nazara. He'd certainly know and remember if Simon were a member of All Hallows here in Bethlehem.

"His death was perhaps the most painful because of how close I was to him. And because he was..." Simon paused before speaking the word. "Murdered."

"I see." Thoughts of the nearly forty thousand U.S. troops who died during the Korean War suddenly came to mind. Remnants of Father Tomassi's earlier thoughts back at the church. He swallowed hard as the statistic also brought to mind the roughly 100,000 others who were wounded, many having lost arms or legs. Left out of statistics were the thousands mentally affected. Then there were those veterans who were never found.

The priest shifted in his seat, pushing thoughts that never quite went away from his mind to focus on the young man.

"Once my uncle was killed, I found myself rejecting the Church. I'm ashamed to admit it. But I was hurt. And angry. Angry that my uncle was taken from me. Especially at a time when I needed him most. Making it sting that much more was... Whoever killed him was never found." Simon withdrew into the large sitting chair. "Would you believe I even thought of becoming a priest at one time?"

"And what changed your mind, besides what is probably the most obvious?"

"I found it difficult being around so many sinning men in collars with little or no faith, unlike my uncle. I've seen it in their body language. Heard it in their words."

Tomassi nodded to indicate he was intently listening.

"Men who have used the collar to abuse their positions... This *also* caused me to lose all faith in the

Church. In priests. Even in God."

"Or so you thought." Priest or no priest, Father Tomassi recognized Simon's frustration and even shared some of the young man's concerns. The subject of faith was, after all, a serious one for Father David Tomassi. And those who would abuse their religious positions were not men of faith.

But Simon had revealed something very important. "My son, I understand your concerns. But you would not be here if you truly lost all your hope in God."

"Yeah, but..."

"It is easy to lose hope in men. Their hearts, minds... their faith can be turned. They are fallible, if you will. And that seems to be where your true disappointment originates." Father Tomassi smiled warmly. "Tell me about yourself. Are you in school?"

Simon struggled to find the right moment to address his dreams. "Yes. I'll be graduating next month."

"Congratulations. That's quite an accomplishment."

"Thanks. I've been pursuing a degree in humanities. Thinking about maybe getting into teaching."

"A noble profession. One certainly doesn't pursue that field for the money."

Simon chuckled. "No, I guess you're right. But I'm fortunate to have another income."

"Oh?"

"I'm married."

"So young, too."

"Yes, but we didn't get pregnant until *after* we got married."

The priest nodded. His look more of approval than disappointment. Or misplaced concern.

"I owe much of my success to her, actually. Sarah is not just my wife. She is also my very best friend."

Here Tomassi's smile broadened in response to the young man's sincerity. "How did you both meet?"

"High school sweethearts. We met before she graduated. She was a senior and I was a sophomore at the time."

"Wow. And to stay together during those years you were still in high school. That can be difficult."

"Not if you find the right one."

"Touché," Tomassi said with a wink and nod. After a pause, the priest then asked: "Does your wife work?"

"She's an entry level associate for a marketing firm in Nazara. We got married after she earned her Business Associate's and went to work. She's been the one supporting us while I've been in school."

"That's quite a sacrifice."

Simon swallowed hard. It was always understood that Sarah would work while he focused on his four-year degree. What created tension was his inability at times to focus. Especially once the anniversaries of his parents' and his uncle's death came around. Then there were the dreams. Never quite able to enjoy and appreciate the positive things — positive people — in his life, Simon always felt unsettled. Out of place. Estranged from the world.

Then Sarah got pregnant.

"How many months along is your wife?" the priest asked.

"She's due at any time."

"No kidding! Exciting, isn't it?"

"Yes and no," Simon confessed. "Money's tight with her on maternity leave. I still don't have a job lined up. I mean, we kind of saved up for this, but... You can't begin to imagine the pressure I am under."

Father Tomassi nodded. Initially the young man came in blaming his woes on the Church. This concerned Tomassi. But much of it, he concluded, comes from Simon's pain. Pain that ties back to the relationship he had with his uncle. A brother. A man of the cloth. Like Tomassi's own life, the young lad before him experienced death at a tender age. All the wounds of his youth clearly haven't yet healed.

What was promising was what Simon chose to surround himself with in the present. A supportive wife. The start of a family. An education. The completion of a degree. All excellent signs. No matter how much pressure the boy felt he was under, he had a lot going for him. He was on the right track whether he believed it or not.

"Excuse me, Father Tomassi." A young priest hesitantly approached the parlor.

Father Tomassi shifted in his chair to face his colleague and housemate. "Yes. What is it, Joseph?"

"It's Father Gordon. Can you come upstairs?"

Father Joseph Carpenter moved about nervously in place waiting for Father Tomassi. He relied heavily on his revered mentor for support. Even the older priests in the rectory looked to Tomassi for direction, especially recently with Father Jonathan Gordon's ill health.

"I'll be right there. Tell Francis and Daniel to stay with him. I also need you to call Liz. Tell her we'll need her husband."

Father Tomassi was standing now as Joseph disappeared into the kitchen to make the requested phone call. He turned his attention to Simon.

Coffee finished for quite some time now, crumbs were all that remained of the baklava. Regardless of Tomassi's requested presence upstairs, it was late.

"I apologize for rambling," Simon said, certainly

not blind to the obvious. "I didn't mean to take up so much of your time. The time... I didn't realize how late it was."

"It's quite okay, son," the priest assured, rubbing his eyes before running a hand over his face. "You weren't rambling at all. These are miserable circumstances. And this will probably be a very long evening. Please stop by again. Perhaps we can finish our conversation sometime in the near future."

Simon reached out to the pastor's extended hand. "Sorry for the trouble," Simon apologized again. He hoped they would have a chance to speak again. Perhaps he'll be able to bring up his dreams at that time.

"Nonsense," the priest said. "This may sound strange, but there is something about you that... something special I cannot yet make clear."

Simon accompanied Tomassi into the hallway.

"Then again, I may be prejudiced when it comes to families. Especially young ones. You have much going for you. Don't let the most precious of moments pass you by. Enjoy them." Holding Simon's shoulders before turning to take the stairs, he added: "They are what give our lives meaning. God bless, my son."

As Simon headed in the opposite direction to see himself out, he heard Tomassi shout from the stairs.

"Whatever you do, Simon," he heard him say, "give up on the Church, if you must. But don't ever give up on Jesus Christ."

20

Everyone in the rectory was in a miserable state. Upstairs lay an elderly priest seventy years old suffering from emphysema and a recent bout with bronchitis. Having endured several strokes over the last few months, the latest slurred his speech. Nevertheless, he kept going. Celebrating Masses. Visiting the elderly. Vowing to slow down only when the "good Lord" decided to take him.

"S'long I'm live," he told Tomassi, speech slurred, "I'll 'tinue to Lord's work. Mens likes us cannot serve the Lord from hospal beds."

When chronic bronchitis confined him to his bed, he refused hospital care. Instead he relied on a local parishioner. A nurse. When she wasn't there, Father Joseph tended to him. The bronchitis, however, only worsened due to Gordon's weakened state. All residing clergymen in the rectory were sure pneumonia wasn't far off.

Father Joseph paced the entire length of the house, running his hands through a thick mop of hair. Into one room he'd walk, sit for a beat, then rise again to enter the next. With these men since he was ordained a little over a year ago, he had grown very close to them. It worried him to see the priests upset. He often wondered who would take charge of things if anything were to ever happen to Father Tomassi. He descended the stairs to get some water.

In the vestibule, Simon's hand was on the doorknob ready to leave when he felt something flow over him. Through him.

Propelled by the warm feeling emanating from

within, Simon made his way through the house. Through the hall. Past an open-jawed Joseph. Ascending the stairs, he proceeded to where the commotion was taking place.

Reaching the top of the stairs, Gordon's bedroom — formerly a guest bedroom — was to the left. He lay in a fluorescent-lit room surrounded by Fathers Tomassi, Francis, and Daniel. Gasping and coughing, he labored to communicate his final words.

Father Francis erupted when he saw Simon in the doorway. To him, this outsider's presence violated the sanctity of the moment. They were in mourning. A friend and confidant was about to pass from this world.

"My God, in all that's holy, what is he doing here?"

"Simon, my son, this is an inappropriate time to..." Father Tomassi attempted polite intervention only to be silenced by Simon's raised right hand. Taken aback, he would have been offended by the gesture if it wasn't so curiously familiar. Distinct.

Then it hit struck him. And he prayed he was right. The gesture appeared to be one often depicted in Christian iconography. A Classical Greco-Roman gesture encouraging patience. With his closed hand raised, only the thumb and index fingers were extended. Pointing upwards.

Under duress, the others didn't seem to notice.

Approaching the infirmed priest, Simon spoke in a voice that was strangely not his own. "Dear Jonathan Gordon."

Tomassi silently watched with wary fascination. Cheeks moistened by a fresh stream of tears, Father Daniel was also taken aback by the surreal scene before him. "What magic is this?"

Distorting Gordon's already gaunt and colorless

features, the stale ceiling light and dullness of the faded beige walls cast an even greater pall on the situation.

But as Simon entered, the others in the room were witness to a visible and undeniable change in their ailing companion. Though still shallow of breath, he at once calmed as his eyes locked with the young visitor's.

"D'ciple... cometo... prepare me, hashe... not?" Gordon's grip tightened around Francis' hand as Gordon turned to him. "Do not... be afraid," he whispered, suddenly absent of any previous impediment.

Tightening his grip around Daniel's hand, he assured him as well. "There is nothing to fear. We are among friends. This is what I have been waiting for."

Overcome with grief and blind to the wonder appearing before their very eyes, Father Francis lashed out. Jerking his hand free of Gordon's grip, he moved to block Simon. He was determined to keep the concealed devil from advancing the bed-ridden priest. "This is madness. Who the hell are you? Who do you think you are coming in here like this?"

Against his better judgment, Father Tomassi intervened. He silently prayed that what was unfolding before them all was indeed an act of divinity. "It's okay, Francis. It's okay."

Wide-eyed with real fear, the other priest disagreed. "No, it's not. Something's wrong. We have to help Jonathan."

Father Tomassi eased the seventy-three-year-old's feeble frame into a chair. "Something is wrong, Dave," Francis repeated, his red eyes puffy and moist. He pleadingly searched Tomassi's own for an explanation to the too-difficult-to-comprehend scene.

David cupped the elder priest's face with his right hand. With his thumb he wiped away some of the tears. "All will be well, Francis. I'm scared, too."

Father Tomassi wasn't kidding. And yet, he inwardly acknowledged waiting all his life for this. Or something *like* it. He was, after all, a priest. As such, there were miraculous events to accept, along with the belief in the mystery of the Lord. He taught others to believe. Why was it so difficult for him — for any of them — to believe an encounter such as this? After witnessing so much misery and death in his lifetime, was it possible to witness the miraculous?

As if reading Father Tomassi's mind, Father Gordon addressed his friend. And the others in the room. "There is no need to be frightened. This is the day I've been waiting for. Just as this is the day *you* have been waiting for. But this is no miracle. Our host has come for me, not to cure me."

Father Francis pleaded once more with his colleague. "He's delusional. He's HAPPY to see the grim reaper. If this was someone sent from God, there would be no way he would let Jon die."

Father Tomassi's retort erupted with unintentional fierceness. "You're forgetting all that we've ever been taught to believe in. What we preach to our congregation. Look at us! Even if Jesus Christ were to ever appear again, we would never know it. We'd crucify anyone who'd dare to claim to be Him.

"I get it. I do. I struggle with my faith every damn day. But too blind and skeptical have we all become these days to believe overt miracles exist. And if they do, they must be the work of the devil. We're old. So old. And we've become too jaded by false prophets like the shysters claiming to be ministers soliciting money on television."

Daniel shot back. He was as superstitious as Francis. He waved a shaky finger at Simon. "He's no Christ, David!"

Father Tomassi swallowed bitterly. This was not the time to engage in a heated, passionate ecclesiastical debate. There would be plenty of time for theological discussions on Divine Providence later. This was an experience he didn't want to recall with feelings of skepticism or anger. Especially towards his friends. And even if Jon was going to die, this was not the end according to their faith. To bear witness to whatever miracle allowed Jon to speak so clearly was enough to make a believer out of him. For the moment.

Simon held Father Gordon's hands in his own as the elder priest spoke. "An angel told me you would come."

A radiant light, visible only to Father Gordon, emanated from behind the younger man. "It is time, Jonathan Gordon."

"Yes, I know. I am all yours. You may commit my soul to God, the Almighty."

Taking Gordon's right hand, Simon placed his other hand gently over Father Gordon's chest.

Father Daniel moved over to where Father Francis sat. Together they held Father Gordon's left hand.

Flanking Simon, Father Tomassi tenderly caressed his good friend's forehead, pushing hair from his eyes.

Before surrendering himself to Simon, Gordon beckoned him closer. "You really are the one. *Kefa*," he whispered. "It's not too late. There is still time."

Then, as Simon made the sign of the cross, Father Jonathan Mark Gordon exhaled for the last time.

21

Simon was in the backyard of his childhood where he had one of his first dreams of the Immaculate Mother. It was something he never confided to his uncle when he was alive. Buried in Simon's subconscious for years, parts of it now began to replay itself over again in his dreams these last few nights.

Or were these new visions? New dreams? Remembrances like Doctor Samuels said his hypnotic suggestion would reveal. If Simon was ready, he couldn't be sure.

Surrounded by his parents, he strained to look see their blurred, featureless faces. Disoriented in the enveloping mist, he fell into a welcoming embrace. It was his uncle hugging him in the foyer of his high school, Nazara High. Startled and overcome with the grief he felt as a boy following his uncle's passing, he began to cry.

Cupping the boy's face in big hands, his uncle comforted the boy. "Don't weep for me, Simon. I'll never be far. I will always be with you."

Simon hugged him harder this time. But once their embrace ended, he was now facing someone else. Another priest. Older. Older than even Father Tomassi.

"Simon, God is with you. As is your uncle," he said. "Your mission has only just begun. Be strong. Open your heart and you will see what it is that you must do."

Blinking, Simon was back at the All Hallows Rectory. The elderly priest lay in his bed holding

Simon's hand. His features betrayed any pain. But Simon knew otherwise.

From his position on the bed, he spoke to Simon. "Father Tomassi will realize that he is right about you. Soon he will remember just as you are beginning to remember. There is something special about you. A reason why you were chosen. The Lord always knew that in the end you would serve him like no other."

Simon's surroundings blurred in a rushing wind that swept about him. Finding himself in the cramped college dorm room he used to visit as a college freshman, he sat before a Ouija board. The boy across from him in a tie-dye shirt was talking wildly.

"Man, that's it. We're done."

"What? Why?"

"The board says that you're too holy."

"That's insane," Simon argued. They had already been through this multiple times.

"Look, these things shouldn't be toyed with anyway."

The other boy, who was initially into experimenting with the board was now visibly uncomfortable. Shaken. He rose to open the shades darkening the room. They were spending the evening attempting to contact dead spirits.

"You're saying this now? Then why are *you* able to use it?"

"It's different. Look, man, there's something different about you. It gives me the creeps, okay. See how the eye goes all over the board like that when you touch it. *I* don't even have to be touching it with you. To work, it's supposed to take *two* people. Two!" Visibly shaken, the boy then swatted Simon's hand off the planchette. "Hey, that's enough."

"Geez. You sure are superstitious," Simon said,

getting up to leave.

"Yeah? Well, you're too damn holy."

Simon then felt the feeling of flight. Soaring high, he was rising above the dorm room. Above the hall. The college. Then high above the state.

He rose through the clouds, watching them pass beneath him. Above he marveled at the Milky Way's expanse. Much of it usually obscured by the artificial light of cities and towns. Visible before him now were brilliant points of light set against gaseous clouds of lavender and pink. Part of him wished to continue his ascent. To reach out as far as he could to the stars. The heavens.

He wondered where such a journey would take him. But as sudden was his ascension, so was his fall. Descending to the apartment he shared with his wife, the stars above would have to wait.

From outside the window, he observed two people lying in bed. One was himself.

Any other time this would have been very awkward. But in the last few days he was growing accustomed to such dreams that tested his sense of reality. His gaze shifted to his pregnant wife. Her face hidden under her chestnut brown hair.

Mesmerized by the way the early morning sunlight shined off her brown, smooth skin, he at once felt a wave of love. For her. For their life shared together.

Covers half-off, she lay with one arm supporting her face on the pillow. Her nightgown, bunched up at the knee, exposed her left leg to the early morning sun's rays.

She twitched subtly. Brought on by the movement of the unborn in her belly. The twitch caused her to stir. Then slowly finding herself awake, she sat up.

THURSDAY
APRIL 03, 1980

22

Simon opened his eyes as he rolled over.

"You all right?"

Already awake, her eyes took in her husband, and she smiled before answering. "Yes, thank you."

She brushed aside a lock of Simon's hair before kissing his temple.

"What time is it?"

"Half past seven."

"Been up long?"

"A while."

"I'm sorry."

"Don't be. It is what it is. It's okay." Sarah shifted in her spot to get comfortable.

"Still, you need your rest for the baby."

"What about you? It's a good thing you have this week off from school. You haven't been sleeping well at all. What time did you get home last night?"

Simon warmed out of embarrassment. He couldn't remember much. "I'm not sure."

"I know. I know." Simon stole a glance at his wife's large belly while she lit up a cigarette. The look was not lost on his pregnant partner. "I know I shouldn't but it's been almost six months. I can't hold out much longer. Besides, the doctor says the baby is healthy."

Turning away from Simon, she exhaled some smoke before returning to her husband's silent, concerned look. When his expression remained unchanged, she guiltily extinguished the cigarette.

"Fine. But you try carrying all this weight

around. Always nauseous. Always sick. Always hungry. It's a good thing I'm going to have this baby soon. I've about had it."

"You forgot irritable."

Sarah's moods transitioned quickly these days because of the pregnancy. It didn't take much to make her cry, either. Simon made light of the situation in an attempt to get her to smile.

"What?"

"Always sick. Always hungry. AND always irritable. Oh, and gassy, too!"

Sarah playfully pushed her husband aside as he moved in to kiss her lips and pat her belly. "That's quite enough, Bill Murray."

Sarah placed a hand over her husband's. Palming her stomach, she could feel the heat from his hand. "You're so warm. I'm sure the baby can feel that."

"Kickin' much?" Simon asked.

"The baby's been pretty active this... Ooh! Did you feel that?"

No matter how many times they felt any movement, it never got old. For either of them. They exchanged smiles. Proud parents already.

Simon kissed her belly before giving her another kiss.

"Any luck figuring out what it is you're going through?"

Simon rolled onto his back, his left hand behind his head. He stared up at the ceiling. If there was a perfect way to kill the moment, this was it. "I haven't found the answers that I think I need. I really don't know what to do. Truth is I've been very confused lately. And everything around me seems to be getting increasingly weirder."

"How do you mean?" Sarah posed her question while attempting to pull the covers up to shut out the coolness of the room. Though it was the first week of April, it was still cold yet.

With Easter around the corner, she reminded herself, so too was Simon's birthday. Like when he was born, it was again falling on the Easter holiday. She contemplated whether to give him his gift now or wait. It was always hard waiting. Rubbing her belly, she smiled at the thought of the baby possibly sharing Daddy's birthday.

Stroking her left arm, Simon studied Sarah's face for understanding. "I wish I could make you understand what the hell is going on. I wish you could witness firsthand everything I..."

"I've been seeing something, I'll tell you." Her tone turned serious. "You waking up in the middle of the night soaking wet. Your face so white I could swear you've died or something. And you mumble and ramble on and on while you sleep. Did you know that?"

Simon propped himself up on his elbows. "You never mentioned any of that before."

"Is it that important? You're restless. What's the big deal? This is the first week off you've had since your semester began."

"Sarah?"

"The pressure is overwhelming. I remember it all too well myself. Look, you're turning 22 on Sunday. I'm due at any time. And you're graduating in a month. Cut yourself some slack. There are a lot of things going on in your life right now. It *is* normal to feel the way you do. That's why I haven't said anything about you being out late this week."

Guilt rushed in on Simon like a tsunami. "Sarah, I haven't..."

"I know what you're about to say. I know you haven't been doing anything that would violate my trust or the sanctity of our marriage. I trust you. I have always trusted you. But I also know this is something you need to work out for yourself. It's not that I haven't wanted you to be a more engaged partner with this pregnancy. But if you need your privacy, I know I have to give it to you."

Sarah wasn't finished. She took Simon's left hand in hers. "I also know not having your uncle around to see this baby is eating away at you."

Simon got out of bed, brushing aside Sarah's last statement. He was grateful to her for letting him search this out on his own. He'd be divorced right now if he were with anyone else but her. How he wished he could properly express just how excited he was about their future. About the baby. Prior to his recent dreams, he was often dreaming about the two of them raising their child.

Simon recalled bits and pieces of his current dreams, far from the blissful ones of him, Sarah, and the baby. The images coming to him over the last few nights were unlike anything he ever experienced. At least, not since he was a child.

It left him exhausted. Perplexed. Scared. His posture stiffened as the throbbing in his head returned.

"Can you recall anything specific that I've been saying in my sleep? Is there anything else you maybe haven't told me that I should know about?"

Sarah adjusted her position in the bed before quietly admitting a major detail. "Well, you were levitating the other night."

Simon turned from the window in panic. "What?"

Sarah was unable to contain the giggles bubbling in her throat. "No, silly. I'm kidding."

Simon politely smiled at Sarah's attempt at levity.

But for the last few days he was having strange dreams of flying, the Blessed Mother, his deceased uncle, and playing with a Ouija board. Levitation wouldn't surprise him at this point.

Then there were the blackouts — periods of time that were nothing more than a blur to him. He scolded himself for not pursuing this problem more seriously with Doc Samuels. Or Father Tomassi.

Simon knelt beside the bed.

Sarah, having moments earlier removed the covers, sat against the headboard rubbing her exposed big, brown-skinned belly. Getting comfortable never really seemed possible these days.

"Sarah?"

"Hmm?"

"Did you happen to catch the local news yesterday?"

"I caught some of it. Yeah. Why?"

"Did you hear what happened to a kid out on the outskirts of town?"

"The abandoned part?"

"Yeah."

"That the story about the kid who was almost hit by a train?"

"That's the one. He was nearly killed. But he was saved."

"Saved?"

"According to the news, the engineer of the freight line running that night thought he hit a kid on a bike. Everyone is in an uproar about it. The bike was destroyed. But the kid who was on the bike claimed some stranger came out of nowhere before the train hit him."

"Out of nowhere?"

"Yeah..."

"To what? Grab him? Kidnap him?"

"No. To rescue him, if you believe it."

"What time was this?"

"I'm not sure. In the evening, I think. Anyway, his parents are hoping to find who it was. But nobody has come forward."

"Witnesses?"

"Not according to police."

"Simon, what's new about strangers doing creepy things in Nazara? The crime rate has always been pretty high here. You know that. Let's hope someone comes forward with information cause who's to say this person who 'saved' the boy really was trying to be a Good Samaritan."

Simon choked on his words as he expressed what he hoped wasn't true. "I think I was there."

Trying her best to listen and take all of it seriously, Sarah was also very much aware that her hormones were responsible for occasional rollercoaster mood swings. But right now, like an ignited flame, there was a flare making its way up along her spine. With it, perspiration. And a growing fear. The baby kicked in response.

"Why do you think you were there? What reason, Simon, would you have to be involved?"

Simon stood, reading his wife's nonverbal cues. "I don't know. It was Monday night. I visited Uncle Matt's grave. Stopped off at the dance. Then I was home. In between is... is nothing but a blur to me. But I had this dream..."

"A dream?"

"Yeah, look, I know this all sounds preposterous. But I swear I dreamt about the boy Monday night."

"I see."

"Look, something's up. I don't know. And I find it odd the local news didn't even feature anything on it until yesterday."

Close to erupting in hysterics with frustration, Simon felt his heart beat rapidly in his chest. Dropping to his knees aside the bed, he turned to rest his back against the mattress.

Sarah played with the hair atop his head. "So you dreamt about something that was on the news a day later. A coincidence. You could have heard it in the car or heard someone talking about it without even realizing it."

"No. I—"

"Well, it will pass," she said quietly. Assuredly.

"I don't think so... because there is more."

Simon felt Sarah stiffen behind him. "What more is there? Jesus, Simon, you have the nerve to tell me I shouldn't be keeping anything from you. That if there is anything I might have seen you do or say at night that I should tell you. Why? You haven't even told *me* everything. Why are you keeping me in the dark?"

"I don't know. I'm just..."

"What Simon? Were you there as a witness? Did you protect the boy? Maybe there's a side of you that I don't know. That you're hiding from me. Are you some sort of stalker that—"

"God, no. It's nothing like that."

But Sarah wasn't done. Though somewhat relieved, she was only getting started. "Well, we're supposed to be in this together. No matter what it is. For better or worse. We're just starting out here. And with the baby coming along, I need to know that I can count on you. That you'll always be honest with me."

"...scared."

"I am, too, hon." She was scared more than she was comfortable admitting. This was supposed to be the beginning of their lives together. Sure, things were bound to improve once Simon graduated, and both were working. But with the emotional acid churning inside them both, she silently feared their chances of making it once the baby came. Things change when there's another life to care for. As an independent woman, Sarah knew that if Simon couldn't provide for her, she'd always be able to survive on her own. Her father taught her that. What she never counted on was getting abandoned with a baby to care for. Bringing another life into this world changed everything.

Simon pivoted to face her. "Here it is, then. On Tuesday, I went to the hospital to pick up the results of some tests on the headaches."

"I know that already. You told me *that* morning how you couldn't bring me in for my doctor's appointment because of it. I *am* the pregnant one, remember."

"I'm sorry, Sarah. Christ, I already told you I was sorry."

Sarah visibly recoiled. Not that they fought a lot. But given her emotional state, she was much more sensitive to any expression of anger. Especially when the volume of the voice matched the tone.

"Listen," Simon said after giving himself a moment to calm down, "after I was done... or sometime from when I finished later that morning until later that day... the evening, possibly. Oh, I... I don't remember." Simon searched his memory. Again, he found it difficult to recall with clarity what he did during the day. Yet when he got home Tuesday night, he had another dream. This time he was sure that what he dreamt was real because the headlines in the next morning's paper read: *Man Chokes to Death in Jordan Diner: Investigation Underway.*

"Does this still have something to do with the boy?"

"No."

"Something else then?"

"Yes."

"Let me guess: another news-breaking event?"

Sarah's sarcasm was frighteningly on-point. And biting. He was sure she was still cross that he raised his voice.

Getting up, Simon crossed the room to sit in the corner on a rocking chair they received as a wedding gift from Sarah's grandparents in Canada.

"Simon, please. I didn't mean..."

Frustrated, she reached out to understand her husband as best she could. More than ever she needed him here. In the now. Not distant. With the baby so close, she couldn't afford to be isolated.

"I haven't really understood any of what you've told me. At first, I didn't really expect all this to continue. I was hoping somehow it was nerves, you know? That gradually it would improve as we got on with our lives."

She put her face into her hands. After a few awkward moments, she adjusted her hair from her eyes. "Please let me in. Tell me what you think is going on, okay? No matter how strange it sounds. You have to tell me it all because you're really scaring me. You say you're worried about me. Worried about me smoking. But this is worse, isn't it? You missed the last doctor's appointment. How am I supposed to count on you if you can't be here physically or mentally?"

Simon saw tears wet against her cheek.

"This really upsets me. I want the best for our baby. And that means I want... I *need*... Daddy to be well."

From a shaded corner of the room, the heat of embarrassment — of shame, of guilt — was overpowering. Simon's voice, quiet and shaky, summoned the words to put the series of events from these last few days into perspective. As difficult as it was for him, accepting one odd event as another one occurred, it was all lost on Sarah. And he cursed himself for putting their unborn at risk. Her worrying all the time was not healthy for the baby.

"I saw another person in my dreams. Presumably the same man who died in Big Ed's Diner. It was in yesterday's paper."

Elbows on knees, Simon held his forehead in his hands. He didn't dare look at Sarah. And from her there came no immediate response. "In my dream, I was there for lunch. I had nearly the entire day before my appointment with the shrink."

Thinking hard, he tried to recall the sequence of events. "I had come out of the restroom where I went to wash my hands. Funny thing is, though it makes little sense, I washed my hands twice. Not only did I take my time to lather both hands thoroughly, I rinsed them with such care. In retrospect, the whole process seems oddly painstaking. Then I remember going to dry them. But there were no towels left.

"Weird looking back on it now. How I didn't wipe my hands on my pants. It's almost instinctive to wipe wet hands on your pants, you know? I didn't even touch the door as I exited because someone was coming in as I was leaving. And there, after I stepped out of the restroom, a few feet in front of me, was a man on the floor.

"People were all around him. I mean, it was quite a commotion. Yet, from where I was standing, there was... there was a gap. He saw me through it."

"Who did?"

"The man... the man on the floor. He motioned me to him. But that seems impossible because when I reached him people were trying to remove food or something from his mouth. Or throat. I don't know. Maybe even resuscitate him. Then I was kneeling beside him with my dripping hands while he looked straight at me."

Sarah crawled across the bed and made her way down to the floor beside Simon's chair as he spoke. He was sweating and his hands shook. His glossy eyes were lost in his tale.

"The man grabbed my arm. And hard. All while looking into my eyes. Into my soul. I think he was smiling... or trying to smile. Or speak. It looked like he was trying to say something before his eyes bulged..."

"Bulged?"

"Yeah. They went huge! Like they were going to pop out of his head. It was gross. It was scary. These bulging eyes. And then his eyeballs rolled to the back of his head."

Tears mixed with beads of perspiration collected on Simon's upper lip. "He... he was having a fit of some kind. At that instant, with my wet hands, this urge overcame me to... to bless him. And that's what I did. I made the sign of the cross on his forehead. Then... then his body... it relaxed."

"Relaxed?"

"Yeah. It went limp. Lifeless. He... he died. At least I think he did."

"Nobody said anything to you in your dream?"

Simon sniffed hard and wiped at his eyes. "See, now that's what I don't get. No one registered me. Then everyone cleared out of the way as the paramedics moved about the man's body."

"And you believe this occurred in real life, too?

Like with the boy?" Sarah was trying to get the story straight. Trying to understand.

"Well, no. I mean, I... I don't know what I mean."

"There's been no mention, hon, of a stranger baptizing a dying man in a restaurant."

"I know, but..."

"The only queer thing I see out of the whole situation in the restaurant, from the article not your dream, is that the person who died was a preacher. Did you know that?"

"No, I didn't."

"I don't know. *That* sounds kind of odd, I think. It sounds odd because..."

Simon slid off the chair down to his wife, resting his sweat glistening forehead on her chest. "I know. My uncle."

"Yes, your uncle."

"Do you even believe me?"

"I believe there is something that we need to get to the bottom of. I don't like seeing you like this. I don't like seeing you hurting inside."

Sarah ran her fingers through Simon's hair, holding him as she would soon hold her own child.

A chill ran through his body making her shiver as well. He put a hand on her belly. "You believe me, then?"

Head on her swollen breasts, Simon felt her chest rise and fall with every breath. Beneath his hand, the child within her full-term belly kicked.

After a long, deep breath, she answered him. Answered him with the answer he needed to hear. "Yes, Simon..."

She silently prayed he couldn't detect the distress in her voice as her eyes fell on the photograph of Simon's Uncle Matthew taped to the closet mirror.

"I believe you."

23

T he third day of April brought with it unusually warm weather to Nazara, Connecticut. A continuous breeze blew through the partially open windows and into Simon's bedroom. Sarah and Simon returned to the comfort of their bed, sleeping — albeit fitfully — until almost noon. Simon awoke to the sound of dishes clanging in the kitchen.

Before the full-length mirror attached to the closet door, Simon pulled a bright green pair of polyester knit *adidas* running shorts over his Fruit of the Looms. He may not have always played first string, but he was a high school athlete. Because of this, his post high school body was still pretty firm. He was lucky his youthful metabolism allowed him to remain fit. Even if he wasn't as active anymore. Then again, the stress associated with school and a baby on the way was certainly enough to do it.

Shirtless, he patted his belly while noting how his brown-sable colored hair hung past his ears and onto his neck. He needed a haircut. And a shave. About to turn twenty-two in a few days, the stubble covering his cheeks and lining his cut jawline gave him an older, more mature appearance.

He wondered how his child would look? Be it boy or girl, would it have his hair? His features? Sarah's?

Something sparkling over on Sarah's dresser distracted Simon from the mirror. It was Sarah's gold cross necklace. He had one somewhere, too. From his uncle. Angry at the world. His faith. God... He may have thrown it out. He couldn't recall.

Sarah's cross reminded him of a little gold angel pin he bought her shortly after they began dating. That was something the two of them were in need of right now — angels. About to reach for the necklace, he heard the heavy steps of his pregnant wife.

Sarah was descending the few stairs of the room adjacent to the bedroom. Moments later, up came her arms from under his. She glided her palms over his chest, placing her cool cheek to his warm back. At five feet, five inches, she stood just a few inches shorter than Simon. Soft, feminine hands danced around his abdomen. Her mocha-colored skin a contrast to his lighter tone. Simon found her eyes in the reflection. But not before stealing one last glance at the necklace on her dresser.

When they first began dating they worried about the reaction people would have to them as a couple. Born to a white mother and a black father, Sarah was, as she eloquently put it one day when they were in high school, "permanently tan." But race was of no concern to Simon. Immediately enamored by her radiant personality, he also found Sarah to be one of the most beautiful girls to ever give him the light of day.

Her exotic brown eyes, big and expressive, were most alluring when reduced to half-moons to accommodate a smile that was both genuine and sincere. Lips full. Thick. Luscious. He was lost looking at her smile as much as he was into her eyes.

And in those early days of high school, it was rare to see her vulnerable. Exposed. When emerged from her bashfulness, her guardedness, her smile was at its biggest. Nearly as bright and warm as her presence.

Even now, as Simon admired her peeking out from behind him in the mirror, face swollen and round, she was as captivating as the first time he set eyes on her.

"I love you, Simon Free," Sarah said from behind, her breath hot on his right ear.

He pivoted in place so he could hug her. "I know, baby." Fighting the earlier headache that threatened to surface along with a fear he could not readily define, he forced a smile before squeezing her close. "I love you, too."

24

The day had come and gone too fast. Together, Simon and Sarah ventured to A&P to stock up on munchies for the expectant mother. Then to Barker's Department Store to purchase the last of the paint to continue working on the baby's room.

"Do you think we'll finish this before we have to go to Lamaze class tonight?"

They were in their former multi-purpose room, music playing from the AM radio in their bedroom. With a due date not more than a week or so, they were trying to finish preparations for the coming baby.

"Most of it, anyway. I'm almost done." Stepping back from the last of the stenciled Muppet characters on the wall, he took in their recent work. "Um, not to change the subject, but this whole process might have been a lot easier if we knew the sex of the baby. You know, for the colors and all."

Sarah rubbed her belly admiring the room. "I know. But I still think it's special." She held the stencils in one hand while Simon finished coloring in the picture. "The room is perfect for either a boy or a girl."

Following a Muppet theme, the room was done with the cast of Muppet characters. Kermit and Miss Piggy adorned the wall planned for the baby's crib. The wall to the left of the crib: Gonzo and his hens; on the wall separating this room from theirs was Fozzie and Animal.

Between the two of them, they spent the last couple of months working on the room painting.

Repainting. And stenciling. It wasn't much. But it was the best they could do. The room would still have to house one of their dressers since the apartment was so small.

Simon handed Sarah the paintbrush before returning the lid onto the paint can. "I'll touch up the parts we missed or screwed up sometime this weekend. Okay?"

She acknowledged him with a smile, pleased with their progress. Though invisible to him, the smile also reflected an appreciated day of normalcy. It was a while since they spent some quality time together. Moments like these strengthened their bond. And she loved him all the more for it.

Wrapping the paintbrushes in paper towels, Simon couldn't help but laugh.

"What?"

Looking from the walls to the rug, he mused at the color scheme. "The colors sure don't match this tacky bright green shag rug."

"Don't laugh," she countered playfully. "With what we can afford, it's all a work in progress."

Leaving the room to put paint supplies away, he yelled back to her. "I wasn't saying it's a bad thing, ya know?"

"Yeah, yeah. I know what you're thinking. But I think we've managed to pull this marriage-school-pregnancy thing off quite well so far."

Simon returned grinning. Plopping on the floor beside the chair his wife sat in, he rubbed her swollen feet as they talked.

"My aunt wants to give us a rug she doesn't use anymore. It'd be a great replacement. But I fear we'll move before we get it," Sarah said, adjusting herself on the chair.

Earlier today the multi-purpose room housed a

desk and typewriter, which Simon finally moved to their large living room. He put it against one of the paneled walls. Out of the way. That left a dresser against the wall that was flush to the kitchen. No matter how they managed it, it would be tight for a bit accommodating a crib, changing table, and dresser.

"Anyway, whatever the gender of the baby may be, I really think she'll..."

Simon caught the sparkle in her eye. An expression of a child caught revealing a secret she promised never to tell.

Sarah bit her lower lip before involuntarily bringing her hand up to her mouth. Ready to correct herself. "What I meant to say was..."

"Yeah, what was it that you *meant* to say?"

Sarah laughed, slightly embarrassed. But also giddy with excitement. "I think he *or* she will be very happy here."

"Nice save."

Simon chuckled at her smooth attempt to include both genders in her corrected statement.

It was clear from the beginning that Sarah wanted a little girl to dress up in bonnets and Sunday dresses. More than the cliché, she also wanted to raise a daughter strong enough for the world around her. She saw society changing and was comforted in knowing that with the dawn of the '80s more women were certain to enter the work force in greater numbers. The feminism movement, along with stronger, more empowered female roles in television and cinema serving as role models, almost ensured a greater breakdown of barriers that long kept women from receiving the same opportunities as men.

Sarah was determined to raise a girl who would be independent. And damn proud of her gender and her heritage. Because not only would her child have to make it in the world as a woman, she would also have the burden of trying to make it as a woman of color.

"You don't know that," Simon said to her when they found out she was pregnant. "You and your siblings are the product of an interracial relationship. Because of this, you and your brothers don't even look related. We don't know what color our child is going to be. What we do know is that the child will have French Canadian blood. French West Indie blood. Some Italian. Some Greek. This we definitely know. So, black or white, boy or girl... Who cares?"

Sarah did. And that was the point. She often spoke passionately about the sexism and racism she witnessed and experienced growing up. It was only natural considering her upbringing.

"You okay?" Simon asked after finishing her feet.

"I dunno," she said grimacing. "I'm not sure if it's the paint getting to me or if I have to go potty again."

"Well, here, let's get out of here for a while."

"Yeah. And I think I'll head into the bathroom for a bit."

25

After returning from the bathroom, Sarah grabbed from the bedroom closet the photo album of her family. While Simon prepared something light for them to eat, she sat in the living room thumbing through old photos.

In recent weeks, she found herself thinking more about her father. How she wished he were still alive. He would have loved having a grandchild and playing the doting grandfather.

When Sarah was younger her father was her world. Seeking work and a new life, her father's family emigrated from Martinique, a territory of the French Antilles. Seeing the Statue of Liberty was the greatest moment in all their lives, Sarah's father used to say of his parents. To them it truly was a symbol of hope and opportunity.

As a youth growing up in Canaan, Sarah's father avidly pursued education. A voracious reader, languages fascinated him. By the time he entered college he was fluent in English, French, and Spanish. To Montgomery Franklin Burnett, education and the written word were necessary crucial elements if America ever hoped to rise from the trenches of racism.

In his thirties, he began following Dr. Martin Luther King. King's message and activism began to awaken something deep within him. He even spent several days in Chicago to hear King speak a year before his assassination. The experience moved Sarah's father. And he yearned to pass along King's message to others. Especially his children.

Referred to by his middle name, Frank was fifteen when his parents came to the United States. Only one of a few black students in an otherwise all-white high school, it wasn't nearly as difficult as the persecution he suffered by the local black population. Though black himself, he was a darker, richer shade. But a prejudice existed within the community and extended beyond shades. He and his family soon discovered an animosity deeply rooted in ignorance.

Yet Sarah's father established himself early on as an intelligent child, maintaining grades at honor level as he worked on his English and practiced his speech to sound more like his classmates and less like his own family. It was an act he would later regret. But to overcome one of the many hurdles necessary to succeed in a white America, he felt the assimilation was the only way to move forward.

By joining the school's athletic teams, coaches were more than happy to harness his natural athletic abilities. He would go on to lead his basketball team to the state finals his junior year, where they placed a win for the first time in school history. His talents also helped the school's baseball team win their division in his junior and senior years. Through his athletic efforts, he earned scholarships to continue his academics.

Not that this exempted him from racism. In fact, it reared its ugly head more times than he often admitted. He — along with the other black players — couldn't change into or out of their uniforms with white teammates. Since he would have to walk home after most games, it was not uncommon to find students waiting for him. Jealous of the attention he received, they sought to take out their resentment physically. Fighting back was often rewarded with retribution that was far worse. And while school officials, parents, and kids loved that their team was winning, losses often fell on his shoulders more than any well-deserved credit for wins.

Racism was even embedded in his nickname. Affectionately called Monk, it was a derivative of an offensive title someone had given him earlier in his high school career: the "Montgomery Monkey". But many people, even the coaches, were unaware of his nickname's history.

Once in college, everything changed. Transplanted from one of the most rural parts of Connecticut, Eaton Somers College in Hartford offered Frank the opportunity to interact with people of various races and ethnic backgrounds. Amidst the fierce academic competition, his was a challenge extending beyond merely proving to others he was as capable as any of his white counterparts. He had to prove it to himself.

One of life's great hurdles was accomplished when he met Sarah's mom. Though only social friends at first, over time they found each other sharing similar ideas about life. And love. Once graduated, they married before Frank went on to further his schooling. Sarah's mom went on to work for a dry-cleaning business.

Earning a Master's and a Doctorate Degree, Sarah's father eventually became a full-time Professor of Literary Studies at Northeastern Connecticut State University. He also became Head of Curriculum, working towards integrating cultural literature into the university's curriculum. Though it would take nearly twenty years to accomplish, Dr. Burnett would be responsible for broadening curriculum to acknowledge racial diversity at the university. Even then, it was offered only as a series of electives before he died. However, his faith in education, and in God, never wavered.

"Always trust in God, for all things happen for a reason," Sarah often recalled her father saying to her more than once on their return from Sunday Mass. Sundays the family attended Mass, no matter the weather. If any of the kids were sick, Sarah's mom would stay home with them while Sarah accompanied her father without question or complaint.

Her small frame embraced by his big arms, Sarah, as a young child, would often lay with her head against his chest. The scent of Old Spice strong on his wool cardigans.

"Mon petit ange," he'd whisper to her. His wired spectacles resting on the tip of his nose as he gazed upon his daughter adoringly.

Sarah always looked up to her father. A respected scholar, she also admired his wisdom, too — wisdom gained not only from books but also his many experiences. It was no surprise, then, that her own choices in life often reflected her father's approach.

Late at night, after spending some time preparing for a class or writing in his journal, he'd check in on her before retiring. They would often talk for hours about *Mary Tyler Moore*, women's rights, and feminism. Black sitcoms, racism, and episodes of *All in the Family* also figured into their discussions, as would news of crushes and suitors. No subject was off limits. Sarah's father was not just her father. He was her very best friend.

Ever observant, he could always sense his daughter's feelings. Attuned to her moods, more so than he was to her younger brothers, he could tell if she was upset about something at school: whether it was questioning a teacher's comment, teasing from classmates who were supposed to be her friends, or dealing with white boys too intimidated to seriously want friendship, much less a relationship.

Because of Sarah's skin tone, she found it difficult over the years to relate to the black community as much as the white one. Much like her own father during his adolescence. This, she learned, was why her father was so insistent on being an integral part of her life. He sought to pass all he knew on to his daughter, much more than to his sons. As black males, his sons would go on to fight the world in a different way. Sarah's father knew that for a woman, a woman of color — however light or dark, it was going to be a different struggle.

"You have to be strong, Sarah Marie. The Lord is going to challenge you in many ways as you grow up. It is a test of strength. Of character. You must remain ever faithful. You must be the best that you can be with the God-given talents you possess."

At this point he would always use his fingers to guide her chin upwards to meet his wise eyes. Eyes deep brown in color.

"There is nothing standing in your way but yourself. Don't ever let anyone tell you differently. Your color and your gender make you who you are. They don't change what is inside you."

"I'm not like them, Dad. I don't even look like you or Mom."

"That is for a reason only God knows, angel. We, your mom and I, were hesitant at first to become involved. It was only because we thought of how everyone else sees things. Not how *we* see things. What truly matters is our love. And our faith. We knew that when it came time for a child. Boy or girl, she would grow up to be the best that she could be, facing the world as we did. Perhaps stronger. Wiser."

"How am I supposed to do that?" she would often ask herself alone in her room, hating on her lighter shade. Hating on her nappy hair. Her big nose. Hating on her thick pubescent figure.

Reflected in the mirror she'd watch tears fall in heavy drops. Her face flush with frustration. To some she was too dark. To others she was too light. Neither athletic nor graceful at the time, she was clueless about what it meant to be "feminine". Her lack of interest in makeup only reinforced her tomboyish image. And because she wasn't gregarious like her father, dealing with insults and slurs was never easy.

Her father saw things differently. He always did. "Of course, it isn't easy. We all have our own crosses to bear, regardless of race. Gender. Even religion. What is important is that you believe in yourself. Because if you believe that you can make it. And you give it all you've got. Working. Sweating. Trying... even beyond the point where you're ready to cry out 'Lord, I can't go on any further,' then mon ange, you will have understood everything there is to know about life. It is then that you will truly become an adult. For the thoughts of others will no longer be of such significance. It is at this moment, when the dust has settled, that all things are revealed to you. And you clearly see your purpose in life."

Close to reaching that point several times early on, no wisdom or purpose ever came of such trials. A blow to her faith and all she believed in came when the oldest of her two younger brothers, Franky, died from a stabbing while she was still in high school. It was the first time she ever witnessed her father emotionally broken.

A second blow to her faith came when her father passed away two years ago.

And while Sarah always lived as her father preached, working hard to cultivate those skills that God gave her, she did this despite her faith. No longer a regular attendant of Mass, she wasn't much different than her husband. Like him, she no longer possessed the faith in the divine she did when her father was alive. To Sarah, her father *was* God. When her father died, so did God.

Still, she furthered her education after high school, taking courses in marketing and business. In her initial interviews she was one of only a few women familiar with the large IBM computer terminals — with green screens that hummed and beeped — used in some of the offices. Sarah was also good with numbers. A consummate worker, she was keenly aware of what people wanted and expected. Her skills and talents for getting people on the phone, and her personable nature, impressed clients and employer alike. Though female, she was rising in the company she worked at; her work ethic and impressive results giving her the edge over all others. Male *and* female. Like her father, she began making a life for herself built on principals of moral character and skill, not on gaining acceptance of her color. Or, in her case, gender.

The flak taken after her hire was minimal. There were some stares. But she soon struck up friendships with co-workers and others in the building; that she was a little darker than everyone else no longer made a difference. She lucked out with her employer, too. A rather young, forty-something manager, she oversaw several seasoned professionals under her — all males with only one other female.

Sarah's employer was married with two kids.

Her husband was in often enough. And though they made a nice couple, it was her husband who would sometimes make her uncomfortable. With his stares. Sarah was sure these stares were more about her being a young woman who finally — post high school — developed a figure other than as a woman of color. Even so, the office was a pleasant place to work. And her boss was all for women advancing themselves.

For this, Sarah's father would have been proud. For her lack of faith, though, she knew he would be sorely disappointed.

Sarah never shared with her father Simon's view of religion and faith; never shared with Simon how lost she was when her father died. Her father's death left her clinging to Simon. And she never wanted to be that dependent on anyone. Much less a man. Simon's own issues with those close to him only complicated matters, which is why she chose to remain resolute in her pursuits. Be it education, employment, or family.

With the birth of their baby near, her tactful approach to all facets of her life left her exhausted. Her pain ran just as deep as Simon's. Something she feared might be misunderstood. Furthermore, she didn't want the burden of introducing yet another layer of conflict and instability. In the years since her father's passing, she made some progress in her healing. Not much. But more than Simon, whose own situation was only worsening, straining their relationship whether he was aware of it or not.

In the absence of her father, and no one to truly confide in, such issues weighed heavily on her mind. They weighed even heavier on her soul.

26

Simon collected the dishes from the table and brought them to the sink. They had finished a rather easily prepared meal of spaghetti and salad. He returned to the table to remove their glasses and a jar of shredded cheese.

Sarah carefully searched her husband's eyes. "You really want a boy, huh?"

Busy at the counter, he met her question with a neutral reply. "It doesn't matter to me what we have, so long as he's... um, *she's* healthy."

"I see what you did there."

"You did?"

Sarah giggled. "That last part was definitely for my benefit, huh?"

"Maybe. Hey, depending on how many boys you plan on having, I could always start my own baseball team. Isn't that every father's dream?"

This time Sarah's giggle came out as a snort. "Oh, and why not a softball team, Coach Free? Be nice to have our *daughters* play for the Women's Professional Softball League?"

He winked at her. "Got me there."

"Mmm," came the reply as she rubbed her belly.

"Seriously, whatever sex is fine so long as the baby is healthy."

Waiting until after Simon finished washing the glasses and turned off the faucet, she brought up a subject recently tabled. "We haven't really settled on any names yet."

"Yeah, we never did finish that conversation."

"I know you'd like to have your uncle's middle

name if the baby's a boy. I haven't forgotten that."

"Well, other than that, I'm open to anything. You know, like Rocky if it's a boy. Adrian if it's a girl."

Sarah smiled out of politeness. "Cute. But no."

"What about you? You've been pretty indecisive the last few weeks."

Sarah's response wasn't what he expected. Instead, her demeanor turned serious. "You really think we'll be able to handle it?"

"Handle what? Boy or girl, I can't imagine it being any worse raising one over the other."

"You know what I mean?"

Apprehensive about broaching the subject before, today she was especially uneasy. She didn't want to spoil the wonderful day they shared together.

Simon exhaled deeply as he squatted on the floor before her. "Is it the color thing you're worried about?"

Her silence answered his question.

"Let's get this straight, beautiful," he said as he caressed her thighs soothingly, "with my Italian blood, I'd be almost as dark as you if there was any more olive oil in me."

Sarah smiled reflexively before lowering her head.

"Hey, it'll be fine," Simon assured. "We just need to be involved parents and love him — *or her* — with everything we have. Our child will learn to not only survive, but thrive despite whatever skin pigment he or she happens to have. Society is changing. It will be all right! I promise."

He placed his hands over hers.

But Sarah removed her hands from Simon's before putting them over her belly. "That's not exactly what I mean..."

The baby was kicking.

"What is it then, sweety?"

"I love you," Sarah said, suddenly throwing her arms over Simon's neck, drawing him close.

Tight.

"I love you, too," he returned, awkwardly standing to embrace her in the chair.

"My cousin Dee called the other day."

And just like that she changed the subject before handing Simon her balled up napkin and some tissues.

Mood swings were par for the course these last few weeks. He was used to it. Throwing her trash away, he decided to humor her. When she was ready, she would clue him in about what she was thinking.

"Oh, what is she up to?"

"She's going to be holding an art exhibit in Hartford. In June. Other than that, she's doing well. She wants to know when we're going to get together."

Simon returned to the table. "We could go see her sometime this weekend. But you are about due." Lifting the bread plate, he wiped clean the tabletop. "She's more than welcome to come here, you know. I don't mind. It's probably best we stay close to home."

Changing the subject, he asked: "Hey, how's your brother, Monty?"

Of her two younger brothers, the youngest, Monty, short for Montgomery, was working in construction. He graduated from high school last June. He and Sarah's mom lived up in New Hampshire with Sarah's mother's sister. This was so Sarah's mom could care for her. But Sarah's mother was also playing the doting grandmother, caring for Montgomery Jr.'s baby, Jevonne. He came into the world about the time Monty graduated from high school. The baby was one of the reasons why Monty didn't go on to college. He had a girlfriend and baby to support now. And there was only so much Sarah's mom could juggle at one time. Especially at her age.

"Monty's okay," Sarah responded. "Aunt Barbara is not doing too well, though. Mom says her cancer has returned."

Sarah's relationship with her mother was always strained. Something she prayed would not be the case if she herself were to have a daughter. Already feeling shunned by her peers during her awkward teen years, Sarah felt further ostracized by her mother — a French Canadian with alabaster skin. More than jealousy over Sarah's closeness with her father, she feared her mother's feelings towards her were race related. Yet her mother was close to her brothers. Darker than Sarah's warm mocha skin tone, they were still not nearly as dark as their father.

That wasn't to say her father wasn't close to his sons. It was a different relationship. He was much more protective of his daughter. She was much more receptive to his affection. Sarah's brothers, perhaps because they were males or perhaps a result of looking so dissimilar from their sister and mother, had personalities far different from hers. Often impetuous, it was Franky's impulsiveness that was partly responsible for his premature death.

In the wrong place at the wrong time is how her parents broke the news to her and her younger brother. Sarah believed, however, that neither of her parents ever came to terms with what happened.

Following Franky's violent death, Sarah's mom changed. Perhaps to his detriment, she began babying Monty. And it was clear that she blamed Sarah's father for what happened.

Very much aware of how young black men are viewed by society — by police — Sarah's mother knew their show of emotion was most always seen as an act of aggression. Because of this, Franky and Monty needed a more involved male figure. One who didn't always rely on academics. One who didn't betray his own heritage and what it meant to be black in a white society. The boys needed to acquire street smarts and street cred. To learn how to navigate the world about them. Perhaps most importantly, they needed a male figurehead to validate their fears. Their frustrations.

As one who had long learned how to survive in a white society, it was primarily through education that Sarah's father had attained his respected status. But his sons did not know that. At their young age they couldn't understand because their experiences were different. They needed guidance until they were old enough to realize they could live up to their father's expectations. Until that point, a chasm would always exist.

At the time, they viewed him as weak. Certain that he had long forgotten the black man's struggle, they viewed him as one who compromised his integrity in order to be successful in a white society.

On the other hand, Sarah's father never understood why his sons couldn't focus on education. Why they couldn't rise above the distractions. He tried imparting on them that by acting on negative impulses fueled by misunderstanding and miscommunication, they risked feeding right into the very narrative they sought to escape. To protest. To change.

Frank Burnett knew very well the pressure that came with unrealistic expectations for young males was often overlooked by society. Especially in high school. And much more so for black males. The rage young black males like his sons harbored may have been justified, but his boys had opportunities before them. Frank Burnett saw to that. Worked hard his entire life to provide such opportunities to his children.

Sarah wondered if there was something in her father's own experience as a young man that may have impacted his ability — *or was it inability ?*— to reach beyond the divide to be more present for his sons. He was so close to her and had so much to share.

Did he see himself in his sons? If so, did he not like what he saw? Did it invoke memories he fought so hard to rise above? *Or forget?*

Complicating matters was the relationship between Sarah's mom and Simon. Rather, her cool and unwelcoming reception. She never liked him. Hence the reason he asked about her brother and not her mother. Again, Sarah couldn't help but wonder if it was due to race. She didn't understand how race could be a factor when she, herself, was a child of a mixed marriage. And if anyone should have been suspicious of Simon, it should have been her overprotective father.

She tried rising from her chair.

Simon moved in quickly to assist. "Oh, baby, no way. You sit right there, young lady."

"Young lady? I *am* two years older than you."

"Yes. Yes, you are," Simon replied, trying not to let on how much her ribbing about his age bothered him.

"Pissing you off, aren't I?" Her question, though spot on, was playful in its intention.

"No." Flashing an impatient *lets-move-on* smile, he added, "You like to always remind me about our age difference. Like it's a gulf!"

"Guess it's a good thing you're catching up then,"

she said in reference to his upcoming birthday.

Ignoring her last statement, he was intent on keeping her comfortable. They would be leaving shortly for Lamaze class. "Tell me what you want and I'll get it for you. I'm taking care of everything. It's bad enough I haven't been around. And you've been relying on Julie from downstairs to bring you to the doctors. The least I can do is make sure you stay off your feet."

"Thank you, Doctor Spock. And just what was I doing today?"

"That's what I'm saying," Simon replied, carrying the bread plate to the counter to wrap it in saran wrap before attending to a forgotten item on the stove. "You've had enough excitement for one day."

"Actually, I have to pee. Again! With the baby sitting on my bladder, I feel like I *always* have to pee." Angling around her bulging belly, Sarah managed to stand unaided.

Waddling over to the sink, she wrapped her arms around her husband who was busy washing the last pot. "How about you? Have you had enough excitement for one day?"

He felt a tingling sensation from her lips on the back of his neck. Though he thought it odd, he was also aroused by her large belly pressing against his lower back.

Simon regulated his breathing. "Are you sure it's safe to, um, engage in this type of activity while washing dishes?"

"Yum... very safe," she said, nibbling his earlobe.

Tossing the sponge into the sink, he turned round to give her a big kiss. He caressed her back with wet soapy hands. Drawing her near, his hands slipped lower.

Simon missed being this close to her for a long

time. Because of her pregnancy and his weird dreams, there hadn't been much intimacy. "Oh, how I've missed you," he whispered into her ear.

Things had gone well today between the two of them. Very much like the old days. Before the dreams. Before the dreams got weird.

"I've missed you." Sarah leaned into him as best as she could, considering the enormity of her belly. "Kinda sucks that we have to get ready for tonight's class."

Sarah ran her hands over his chest before sliding them down past her belly. Out of sight. To unbutton his pants. "Then again, I've missed something else, too." She felt his stomach tighten to her touch.

He smiled, grabbing her hands. Walking backwards, he was about to lead her to the bedroom when the phone rang.

Good Friday

APRIL 04, 1980

27

A yellow 1976 Subaru Station Wagon pulled up to the large green multi-family apartment building at 7:19 AM. Dressed in blue denim over a gray hooded sweatshirt, Simon ran briskly to the car. It was overcast and cold enough for his breath to trail visibly behind him. Nothing like the day before. And all too appropriate for the way Simon was feeling. New England was not about to see the sun again for a while.

"Sorry I'm late," Father Tomassi said as Simon climbed into the passenger side of the car. "Arrangements for Father Gordon's funeral have kept me hopping. And I was finally able to reach Gordon's niece."

Reaching out to Simon the night before with an unexpected phone call, the priest was interested in finishing the conversation begun on Wednesday. Hours prior to Father Gordon's passing. An event that was lost on Simon because he didn't remember anything after their time in the sitting room. Except for the dream. And even then, he wasn't putting the two together.

Simon replied to Tomassi's words with a nod, preoccupied with catching a glimpse of Sarah in the window before they drove off. When she didn't appear at any of the apartment windows, his earlier suspicions were confirmed: she wasn't at all happy with him.

Something was bothering her. But right when he thought she was going to come clean about what was on her mind, she chose to change the conversation rather than let him know the truth. Up until Tomassi's call, the day was happily spent together — the first in a very long time. The strange events of the past week temporarily forgotten. Of course, life lately was awfully fast paced. There was always something to do. Whether it was school or, up until recently for Sarah, work. And soon there would be the baby. Further exacerbating things was Simon's worsening strange dreams. He was certain it was slowly damaging their relationship.

"Dude, you're still in the honeymoon years," Larry's older brother told Simon a couple of months ago. "Try being married like me for almost ten years. It ain't easy ya know. My wife is a bossy lady. She'll go all Tasmanian devil if I give her any trouble. Once I learned, then I was all set and there was peace at our pad."

Simon smirked at the thought. Luckily that hadn't been his experience. In fact, their time together yesterday felt strangely therapeutic. Getting much of the baby's room completed and trying to clear their minds of the strange, unimportant things that were occurring in their lives was a welcome diversion.

He reflected on how fast time flies and how often the small things are overlooked. One of the many reasons they married so early was not just to consummate their relationship, but to keep their relationship intact. What with work and school, not living together all but guaranteed they would never have seen each other.

Sarah was very cool to him during Lamaze class. Her annoyance with Tomassi's call was evident in her evening demeanor. But Simon knew there was a lot on her mind. Finances. Simon's schooling. His future employment. And, of course, the baby.

Then there was Sarah's father. Simon was certain his wife was keeping from him how difficult it was for her that her father would never be able to share in this event.

Simon unconsciously sighed as Father Tomassi continued talking in the background. He had no idea why the priest was sharing this information about another's upcoming funeral.

"... is preparing to be one of the co-celebrators at Monday's funeral for Father Gordon. And there will be many more priests from around the area there as well." Father Tomassi glanced time-to-time from the road to Simon to his rear-view mirror. "It is going to be held at the bishop's church in New Galilee. We'll be there in a couple of hours."

Did he say hours? A row of houses flashed by in quick succession. "You know, I could have driven. Or we could have waited to talk. After all, you're still in the middle of organizing everything for the funeral."

Simon couldn't stop thinking of Sarah. Maybe he was reading too much into everything lately. After all, while he was sure he felt a headache come on in the morning, he spent the day relatively free of any migraines. He even slept well last night, given his dreams and the events of the past week.

He so very much enjoyed yesterday. And he wanted it back. If only he could convince himself recent events were all a by-product of stress. Fatigue. And one hell of an imagination, he resolved.

"Simon, I know I told you that I wanted some company today, seeing the bishop and paying my final respects to Father Gordon and all. And I know that I said I wanted us to finish our talk. But that's not entirely why I've asked you to join me."

Simon noticed they were heading south on Route

9 and out of town. Within an hour, they would pick up Route 95 north to New Galilee. Once a large, booming town, the invention of synthetic oils crippled the whaling industry that was a primary source of Galilee's economy. This, along with an emerging industrial society no longer as dependent on naval commerce, transformed the area into a town of antiquity. Vintage shops lined the coast and many of the original historic buildings built in the 1800s that were still intact either became tourist attractions or private homes for the affluent.

"Okay, I'll bite. Why did you ask me to join you?" Simon inquired, looking over at the priest. "And how did you get my number?"

"You know, I really love this state. We're close to Massachusetts and Rhode Island. And what a coastline. It's quiet. Out of the way."

"Seriously? You can't answer *any* of my questions? I have a wife that I should be home with because she's pregnant and has another doctor's appointment today. Instead, I'm here with you. I don't even know you. Now, why did you ask me to join you? And where are you taking me?"

Simon exhaled heavily, returning his focus to the window and passing scenery. Biting his lower lip out of embarrassment, he didn't mean for his words to come out as harshly as they did.

The priest stole small glances in Simon's direction while still trying to focus on the road. "Telephone directory."

"Huh?"

"Your number. It was in the telephone book."

Simon said nothing in response. But for a nod, he continued to look out the window.

"I know this is difficult. But hear me out. Remember one of the last things I said to you before

I went upstairs the other night? I said that there was something... something special about you. I had trouble placing you in the proper context because it's been so long. I thought it was because I was distracted. Tired. But considering the circumstances at the time..."

The priest paused, checking his side view mirror before edging the car into the passing lane. "There is a reason why this is all happening, just as there is a reason why you came to my church that night."

Simon shuddered, unsure if it was from the cold. Or from something else.

"Let's not forget your experience with Brother Stanley Iris," Father Tomassi said.

Simon reluctantly looked over at the priest. "Who?"

"Why, the man in the restaurant."

Simon's head filled with questions. More questions. Nothing *but* questions. And yet, no answers. "How do *you* know about the man at the restaurant?"

"The same way I know of the boy you saved at the tracks," Father Tomassi said with a broad grin. He held within his grasp a secret that intrigued Simon.

It also frightened him.

"My son," the priest said excitedly, "you are a miracle waiting to happen. The signs were there but I have been blind to them."

"I don't understand."

"You will," Father Tomassi said quietly, a smile on his lips and water in those blue eyes of his. "God willing, we all will."

The rest of the car ride to New Galilee was driven in silence.

28

Removing his black, thick-framed reading glasses, the Most Reverend Bishop Peter Reibold could only shake his head and say, "it certainly does appear to be plausible, Dave."

Bishop Peter Reibold was a large, commanding man. His presence was enough to make one submit to a bow when meeting him. It was an awkward contrast to his genteel and personable nature that left most humble in his presence. One sensed he was uncomfortable with this. Though a respected member within his Roman Catholic community and responsible for a rather large regional diocese, he never considered himself better or above anyone else. As he saw it, he would always be one of God's lambs. And as a human being, imperfect. Capable of sin. Fallible.

Though only fifty-seven, Bishop Reibold, up until a few years ago, always looked much younger than his real age. The last five years, however, were tough. And the bishop now looked older than Father Tomassi remembered. The death of close friends and diocesan duties were taking their toll, leaving him looking increasingly worn.

It was a little after noon when Tomassi and Simon settled in with the bishop at his residence. They had arrived at Saint Catherine's Cathedral in New Galilee earlier in the morning, shortly after the bishop finished a meeting with local clergy regarding final preparations for Sunday's Easter Mass. A tribute was also planned to honor Father Gordon's more than fifty years of service to the Church and parishioners of Connecticut.

The two gentlemen then accompanied a few other priests who knew Tomassi and the bishop — and were longtime friends with Gordon — to Pavellemano's Funeral Home. Calling hours for the public were later in the afternoon. When Father Daniel was scheduled to meet with Gordon's niece and the few remaining family members.

Simon retreated to the back of the room away from where Jonathan Gordon's body lay resting. Out of consideration, he wanted to allow Tomassi and the others privacy to pay final respects. Since Gordon's casket was open, Simon made a point to strategically sit where, even when he looked forward, Father Gordon's body could not be seen.

When Tomassi made way to the back of the room to join Simon, Simon tried to hold back his personal distaste for the funeral scene. Simon always deemed such rituals as primitive.

"I beg to differ," the elder priest replied. "Think of it more as a proper sendoff. This is why the Roman Catholic funeral service consists of three parts: a vigil, the funeral Mass, and then the Rite of Committal."

"Sorry, but who wants to be remembered lifeless? Stone dead. Face shrunken in with make-up plastered all over. I don't." Simon remembered the funerals held for his parents and his uncle all too well. Perhaps that is where his feelings originated.

"Life... living... is difficult for many people. At these functions, people can share their experiences with surviving friends and strangers alike. They offer comfort and understanding to family members because they get to share in the good spirit the deceased embodied while alive. I never understood it myself at first. But that is why there are also celebrations afterwards. The one we're planning will celebrate all the joy Jon brought us and his parishioners. All those selfless years helping others.

"When you think of the timing, too, it's quite fitting since it's the time of the Easter celebration. Christ rose on the third day, restoring faith and hope that He would come again. Surely Jonathan shall rise again to join our creator. And we with Him when we leave our mortal shells behind."

Tomassi wiped his nose with a white handkerchief he removed from his rear pocket. Death was always a difficult subject for him. Reminiscing about Father Jon Gordon made his heart ache.

"His guidance will be sorely missed. There was a time," he paused, the kerchief balled in his hand. Resting on his knee. "There was a time I couldn't see past my own pain. I was also very afraid of death. But the Lord, Simon..."

The priest sighed heavily, attempting to heed his own words so often passed on to others. "It's through our faith that we truly find strength." He was fully aware that his own was quite shaky for a man who wore a collar. "Even if we need reminders from time to time.

"For when we are released from this world, it's into the arms of Mary and Jesus that we'll ascend. Truly, the funeral ritual is only as primitive as you perceive it to be. The morbidity of it remains in the eyes of the beholder."

Simon wanted to refute the priest. To explain how he really didn't fear death, but felt more time should be allowed for mourning. Not celebrating. He then thought better of it. His own loss was a pain he was sure others wouldn't understand. Besides, if it was a matter of faith, he was out of luck. He lost his long ago. God saw to that by taking his parents. And his uncle.

Returning to Saint Catherine's Cathedral, the bishop gave the two a short tour of the grounds and grottos — shrines of rock near the water dedicated to Saint Catherine of Siena and Mother Mary. This was primarily for Simon's benefit. Now, finally alone in the bishop's study on the third floor of the rectory, Father Tomassi and the bishop relaxed in leather wingback chairs of Georgian style gathered around a walnut conference table exchanging pleasantries about each other's work at their respective parishes. Simon sat in silence, observing the men dressed in their standard occupational attire. The only contrast to the black suit jacket, shirt, dress pants, and dress shoes: the white tab in the collar.

Asked to briefly relay his most recent experiences, Simon easily complied. At once he oddly felt at ease with these men, even if he did have a nagging feeling of being watched.

A priest Simon had yet to meet — looking to be in his thirties, with dark hair and dark beady eyes — entered the room. He carried in his hands a tray of coffee and tea. It was, after all, a holy day of fasting and abstinence. Bishop Reibold thanked the younger priest as he placed the tray on the table.

Noticing Simon shift uncomfortably in his chair, the bishop realized introductions were in order. "I'm sorry, gentlemen. Where are my manners?" Standing, he gestured to the young priest positioned behind the seated Tomassi who also rose.

"David Tomassi," Tomassi said, extending his hand.

"David. Simon," the bishop began, "meet the newest member of Saint Catherine's and our new accountant, Father Jacob Dawz."

"Gentlemen," the younger priest acknowledged,

shaking Tomassi's hand before nodding at Simon. Simon remained seated, scrutinizing the newly introduced visitor.

"I've only arrived Wednesday and already I'm a bit overwhelmed. What with the finances, the funeral, and the Easter celebrations."

"You've done a fine job of not showing it," the bishop said, falling back into his chair. Addressing the others, he added: "He's been damn near working day and night since arriving. So far as I've seen."

"Well, there's much to be done."

Simon crossed his arms over his chest, continuing to study the priest before him. "You look awfully familiar," he said cocking his head. "Have we met before?"

"I don't... I don't think so." Something in Jacob's countenance changed for a fraction of a second as he looked to Tomassi. And then to Simon again.

Father Tomassi saw it, but it was the bishop who gave Jacob an out.

"Jacob here has already garnered quite the reputation," he said without a hint of resentment. "Already published several papers on Demonology, Exorcisms, Ancient Rituals and the effects societies undergo without religion. He's a foremost authority. Even recognized by the Vatican."

Enjoying the attention, Father Jacob was unable to conceal a growing smile. "Perhaps, Simon, that's where you know me from."

"Nah, don't think so. I don't follow the *Vatican Gazette.*"

"Simon," the bishop said sharply. "Was that necessary?"

Shrugging, Simon did little to withhold his disdain. Flicking a dead fly from the tray of beverages, he defended himself. "What! I don't! Is there a *Vatican Gazette*?"

"It's quite all right," Jacob said turning his focus to the bishop. "Anyway, I figured you and your guests could use something to drink. Gladys seemed busy. I'll be working on the finances in Sister Anita's office if you need me."

"Yes. Thank you, Jacob. Very thoughtful of you."

The priest excused himself. But not before casting one last glance at Simon. Meeting his glare, Simon could swear the eyes he saw were anything but human.

29

The bishop, having excused himself some twenty minutes earlier, left Simon and Father Tomassi to their own thoughts. Simon still wondered how any of his problems were the concern of a couple of old priests. Yet, he could not deny the company of these men to be oddly comforting.

Father Tomassi struggled in the foggy haze of memories to remember that which was forgotten. In what seemed a fruitless exercise, there were things he knew he should be remembering. But thoughts of Father Jonathan Gordon's funeral, and his own Mass schedule for the Easter weekend, were on the forefront of his mind. These thoughts distracted him from the task at hand.

The two were discussing Simon's upcoming role of fatherhood when the bishop returned, a black leather scrapbook under his left arm. Discolored news clippings stuck out from all sides. Some were curled with age or water damage. Others were folded.

"You both will have to excuse me. I didn't mean to be gone for so long."

Tomassi was surprised. "You found it!"

"Ahh, yes. But that is not what took so long." Pausing, the bishop held the book in both hands. "'Fraid I needed to take care of some business."

It took a moment for Tomassi to catch the hint that went right over Simon's head. "You okay, Peter?"

"Quite," the bishop replied. "It's that..." On his face there appeared an expression of such incredulity that it was difficult for him to finish the line.

"I know," Tomassi replied quietly. "I know."

Then the bishop tossed the scrapbook onto the large table where it landed with a loud thud. "Found it last night after your call, David. So many years ago. Isn't that something? I forgot I had this. I mean, I vaguely remembered. Like it was somewhere back here." The bishop gestured to the back of his head.

Only after retrieving the book from the basement did the memories, nearly as dusty as the book, begin slowly resurfacing.

"Could barely remember where I put it. At one point early on, I kept much of what's in here in a large box. Can't quite recall when I finally got around to organizing it. In fact, it was only after our conversation on the phone that I... I don't know."

Father Tomassi nodded, knowing full well where the bishop was coming from. Recalling the other night — the night of Gordon's passing — put it all in perspective for him.

Bishop Reibold sat, and placing his glasses back onto the tip of his nose, opened the book to look over the wrinkled documents before him.

"What exactly are you looking for?" Simon asked.

"We'll know shortly," was all the bishop would say.

Squinting his eyes, he leafed through the pages of notes and articles — many of them bookmarked with index cards or other slips of paper — until he rested on one passage dating back over twenty years to April of 1958. He read it aloud: "And Mary said unto David, Matt, and myself, 'Ignored have the harbingers been. Satan hath declared war against thee. Let thy eyes and ears be opened to what ye portends.'"

The two older men in the room trembled as the words took hold. Awakening the past. Simon, however, merely looked on with curiosity, having heard, what he thought, was his uncle's name.

"'Woe unto all them unaware of... the year of His second rising, twenty before the End Times. This is my son. Hear Him. Woe them who shan't behold the day of His new resurrection in place of time immemorial. For He only is incorruptible, Himself the Almighty, the judge of mortal men whose lack of supplications shall bring forth darkness thus covering the boundless world. There, in the Great Battle, will the souls of men be moved and arise to be judged by the one who is seated aside of God, the Immortal. But not before all the elements of the world are laid waste, and the stars fall from Heaven into the sea.'"

"Whoa, that's pretty heady stuff," Simon said watching the ashen face of Father Tomassi in response to the bishop's reading. "Scary, too. If you believe that stuff."

Regardless of the older men's response, Simon didn't buy much into words that were most likely written to strike fear in the hearts of the faithless. How else to keep everyone in line? Scare the hell out of 'em.

"Are we at the end of times, Peter?" Tomassi asked the bishop, ignoring Simon's comment.

The bishop continued reading before addressing Tomassi's question. "'Unheeded thy warnings hath gone. Dark hath become the halls of thy son's house. Prepare, then, for that which will bring about the beginning of the end...'"

"Seriously? You guys really buy into this? What is this book? Where did you get it?"

Both men appeared pale even in the brightly lit room. Peter let the book slip from his hands.

Tomassi searched the deep recesses of his memory trying to recall the finer details. Like an overflowing file cabinet his aged brain was cluttered with so many memories. It was a dreadful thing getting old.

Simon knew was at the heart of the miracle. To them. That he was sure of. But for them to have forgotten what was most important? He couldn't believe it.

Rising, Father Tomassi pulled the book forward to finish reading the passage. "'So shall if ye fail, forget all things in lack of preparedness. The hour of the Christ Lord is nigh; the power of the Anti-Christ grows. The greatness and wonder will soon be revealed to all, but not before the sun rises to the Weeping Age and sets on the Great Battle of the Twentieth Generation from which the Christ Lord was first revealed.'"

Seeking strength and guidance to recall the distant and forgotten past, the two priests immersed themselves in prayer.

Simon, whose questions still weren't even addressed, impatiently reached for the book himself. Looking over the scribbled words on the pages before him, he found the last line of the passage the bishop was reading. "'Pray for thyselves and for thy brothers and sisters. In time, when the disciple, born of the Weeping Age confronts the darkness, will the coming be known.'"

Simon thought he heard one of the men gasp.

"Shouldn't we perhaps explain to Simon what this all involves, or..." Father Tomassi remarked while the bishop looked beyond him. Recollections — visual, emotional, spiritual — of his time in Adánia came back to him in foggy, fragmented bits.

"David, are we that late? Could it be we have forgotten so much since Matt passed away?" Using one of his big hands, he rubbed his red, watery eyes. "I'm not even sure how much I remember. Or how much is part of my nightmares."

Looking over to the young man in their company, the bishop inhaled sharply with trembling lips. "I'm so sorry, Simon."

30

A wintry mix of precipitation fell from the gray afternoon sky. Though raw outside, the room the men occupied on the third floor grew stuffy with heat. A by-product of the antiquated steam heating system. The clanging of the radiator was difficult to ignore. The bishop cracked open a window.

Conversation came slowly, as it was a revelation of sorts to the elder priests as much as it was to Simon. Each of the older men struggled to remember. To understand their purpose. The more they talked with Simon, the more they talked about his uncle. And the more the past came back to them.

Returning from the window, the bishop leaned on the top back of his chair. "It's something. Your uncle. Dead some five years now."

Simon nodded in agreement.

"As unbelievable as it may seem that we both knew your uncle, it's even more incredible that we have been awaiting your arrival for quite some time now. We just didn't know when you'd arrive."

"Me? You've been waiting for me?"

"We didn't exactly know it would be *you*," Tomassi noted. "At least... well... it seems we have forgotten some details."

"Well, I don't even understand how you came to know my uncle. I don't understand any of this really."

The bishop forced a polite smile. "Of course you don't." Reaching out, he placed his hand on the young man's shoulder. "But as much as you don't understand, you must realize at least this much: all that has happened to you, and what you will go on to do, has been anticipated. Or, if you want to look at it another way: prophesied."

Simon looked to Father Tomassi. "Is this what you meant by calling me a miracle?"

Tomassi compressed his lips and nodded.

"What is it that I am supposed to do? I haven't even said a prayer or gone to church in years! I don't even—"

"Do you not remember the other night in the rectory?"

Simon wasn't sure what Tomassi was getting at.

"Father Gordon?"

"You've been talking about this Father Gordon since the car ride. I don't know who he is. Am I supposed to?"

The priests looked at each other before Tomassi answered. "If I had to guess, I'd say it was probably very much like your other experiences this week."

Again, Simon was lost on the implication.

"What do you remember about the other night?"

"Other than us talking? And you having to go upstairs? Nothing."

"What do you remember *after* that?"

"I was home."

Father Tomassi's features softened as he recalled Simon's actions that night. "My son, you ushered Father Gordon into the afterlife. You helped him cross over."

Both pastors stole glances at each other while Simon digested the seemingly absurd story.

"Some scholars believe Christ was not even aware of the mark He was about to make on mankind until He was preparing to sacrifice Himself. Even if He did have an idea about what was to happen, all was still not revealed to Him until His father felt it was time."

"Wait? Sacrifice?"

"That's not exactly what David's getting at, Simon."

"It's that something special I told you about. If you search within yourself and allow yourself to be graced by the Holy Spirit, you will know that all of this... all that I am saying... is true."

Simon hadn't shared with the priest his dreams. Not specifically. It was the one thing they hadn't gotten around to talking about the other night. "You truly believe all that is happening to me has something to do with Jesus Christ?"

Tomassi and the bishop nodded.

"And my uncle?"

"Simon, many things occurring each day in all of our lives have much to do with the Trinity," the bishop said. "As for your uncle, he was responsible for putting the more recent things into motion. He, more so than any of us, had a better inkling of what was going to happen."

"How? How did my uncle know these things would happen? He's been dead for five years!" With eyes closed, Simon shook his head in disbelief.

"My boy," the bishop said, gently placing his hand on the table before Simon as he sat again. "It's okay. Quite honestly, there are also many things we're not even sure of."

"What none of us knew in the beginning," Father Tomassi attempted to explain, "was that something drew us — the bishop, your uncle, me — to Adánia. Our experiences there bind us. The Lady of the Immaculate Conception visited us in visions there, just as she probably has with you."

"I've never been to Adánia."

"You needn't have been. Wait, you mean you've

never been visited by Mother Mary? She reached out to us there because... well, surely due to our service at the time. Your uncle, too. But can you deny she hasn't reached out to you in some way?"

Simon was silent. But his pursed lips and clenched jaw spoke volumes for him.

"If you allow yourself time to process this, her message will come back to you. It may have already. You may not realize it yet, that's all."

Tomassi rose and stretched before continuing. His joints and muscles sore. Stiff. Reminders of his aging body.

"Your uncle experienced his first vision at about the age of fifteen during his first visit to a little town in Columbia called Adánia. He was visiting Adánia with a youth ministry group that spent almost two years raising enough money to go. So moved by the experience he even requested to go after he was ordained, pushing for ministries in the surrounding areas. People in these areas lived in abject poverty. They faced starvation and sickness on a scale that was unimaginable to a young man from the states. The conditions there were awful. They still are.

"Bishop, here," Tomassi continued, motioning to the bishop with a nod of his head, "was sent there to organize the small Christian communities of the tierra de la pia." Making quotation marks with his fingers, he translated the Spanish for Simon: "'The land of the devout' — an area near the holy town of Adánia."

The bishop shared a glance with his friend before returning his focus to Simon. "The significance, of course, is lost," said the bishop, "unless you are aware of the religious history behind the town. You see, Simon, your uncle wasn't the only one to experience visions there. Hence, the reason for its moniker."

Simon searched his childhood memories for anything relevant. "I think I remember hearing or reading something about it. Wasn't there a girl or a boy who saw the Virgin Mary there?"

"Yes, a boy *and* a girl. But the girl, who grew up to become Sister Maria de Jesus, is the one most associated with—"

"Wait," Simon interrupted. "Wasn't that in France?"

Tomassi snickered. So few young people knew of the saints and mystery that make the Church the institution it is today. "Our Lady of Lourdes appeared several times before Bernadette Soubirous in Lourdes, France in 1858. Yes," he pointed out. "Mother Mary — Lady of Fatima — also appeared before Lucia de Jesus dos Santos in Portugal around..."

"I think it was 1917." The bishop filled in the date when Tomassi turned to him with a questioning glance.

"Yes, thank you. And, this is important, *both* have been recognized by the Church. But the one in Adánia didn't become enshrined and officially recognized by the Church until Pope Pius Paul pushed for it in April of 1970. Some seventy years after Maria saw the Blessed Mother.

"Bishop Reibold, myself, and your uncle have all been in contact for some time. Well, we *were* in contact since our visitation of the Blessed Mother some twenty years now, but..." Tomassi trailed off, remembering the emotional blow the death of their old friend, Matthew Free, had on them all. "I came into the picture later in the year after your uncle was already there. Together we worked on setting up ministries and the Holy Shrine, now adjacent to the church built to honor Mary in the hills of Adánia. We were so naïve at the time about the things that were happening in the world."

"Tell me about it," Bishop Reibold commented, his glasses back on the table in front of him. He was rubbing his swollen red eyes. A feeling of nausea struck him as he remembered his experience with Pope Pontius only days earlier. It was an experience that defined one of the two evils he felt existed in the world. The first, an evil brought on by power and hubris; the other by the evil one himself. Since the first of the two was difficult enough to deal with, he prayed he would never have to deal with the latter.

"As one would imagine, Simon, there exists, or have existed, men far greater than we. But then the Bible does quote our Lord Jesus... well, there's the part about the meek inheriting the earth. I'm afraid we all fit that description."

The men sat in silence until Simon asked about his uncle. I thought I knew him. But I guess I didn't."

"You knew him," the bishop said. "Don't misinterpret this rather secret part of your uncle's life as anything against you."

Memories of a young Simon returned to him. Forgotten blurred memories. Like what happens when one tries remembering a fading dream. But there was no denying the love Matthew had for his nephew. The willingness to do whatever necessary to raise the boy in a protective environment.

"He loved you as his own son and fought like hell to get you to stay with him at the rectory. Those types of things were really frowned upon. If I remember correctly, some of the clergy at the rectory were also very much against it. So either he had some great pull or there was some serious divine intervention going on."

Simon was apologetic. "Forgive me, I wasn't

trying to suggest..."

"Do you remember how your uncle would have retreats several times a year?" Father Tomassi asked.

"Sure, he went on a lot of them. But I remember him being away the most shortly before he was killed. I never understood why he worked himself so hard. I never saw the others work anywhere near as much as he did."

"Now you know," Father Tomassi said, hints of sadness in his voice. "It was all for — and about — you. He was entrusted with this, this secret even before you were born. Did you know when your uncle was ordained?"

"No, I...wait! Yes, of course. 1958. The year I was born." Simon wasn't shocked by the coincidence until Tomassi revealed another coincidence.

"Yes, he *was* ordained the same year you were born. Are you ready to hear something else? I also underwent the Rite of Ordination that same year, having found religion a little late in my life," Tomassi said.

"And I was consecrated to the office of bishop. Same year," the bishop noted. "There was a great connection we all came to share beginning that year."

"The entries you heard the bishop read, Simon, all occurred around your birth."

Simon felt an emotional jab to his solar plexus as his eyes suddenly welled up.

"The last one, Mary's last appearance to Peter and I, occurred on the very day you were born." Father Tomassi allowed it to sink in before rationalizing his statement. "These things are not simply matters of coincidence. Certain events have been occurring for a very long time. Nearly a thousand years. To ensure that the plan, this prophecy I guess we can call it, is fulfilled."

"Yeah, this forgotten prophecy," the bishop mumbled.

"Your uncle, however, always seemed to..."

"Know more," the bishop said.

"...be one more step ahead of us. Yes," Tomassi explained.

Matt was a dear friend to them both. But here, as they fought to recall musty details, they bemoaned the many years gone by. They blamed themselves for the lack of preparation. Felt shame for their lack of belief.

"Thinking about it now, Mother Mary must have visited him additional times. It's the only explanation that makes the most sense."

"That or he knew whatever he was involved in endangered those around him — those he loved —as much as it did him," the bishop proposed. "He may have been visited again. Maybe he was better at reading the signs. Your parents, after all, were pretty consumed with..."

"Samael," Simon whispered.

"...your brother."

"Odd that this didn't come back to me the night you came to All Hallows. That I didn't immediately recognize the name. I believe I met you once when you were a child. You were with your uncle. And I now seem to recall your uncle pushed for your parents to have a will. To have them list him as your caregiver should anything happen to them. It was always understood that you'd go to him." Then looking to the bishop, he shrugged. "Presumably to minimize the risks involved."

"Did he know when he was going to die?"

"He wrote me not long before he died, certain that his time was short. But it really was unexpected," the bishop explained, bobbing his head in recognition as an old memory resurfaced and became clear. "That is why we forgot the signs. He kept them alive. Kept us prepared. I'm afraid we've come close to letting him down."

"He did indeed keep us prepared. Since his death, I'm ashamed to say things have gone all foggy," Father Tomassi admitted more to himself than to the others in the room.

The coffee and tea long since consumed, it was now late afternoon. A cool breeze stole in from the open window chilling the once warm room. The mixed precipitation outside was forecasted to change over to snow farther north as the evening drew near. Darkening the outside.

The bishop leaned back in his chair and crossed his legs. "Let's run through your experiences a bit more and see if we can spark any more memories. It can't hurt to discuss more about what brought us here."

Simon shrugged his shoulders. "Well, somehow Father Tomassi knew about a boy and a man I dreamt about."

"You didn't dream that. It happened. It was real," Tomassi confirmed.

"And it appears I also dreamt about Father Gordon."

"Ah, but I was one of three witnesses to that one."

Simon smiled as he nodded.

"You're remembering?"

"Seems Father Gordon communicated something to me in my dream."

"And?" the bishop asked.

"That Father Tomassi's intuition was correct." As unbelievable as it sounded coming from his lips, Simon couldn't help but join the other men who responded with a soft laugh. Perhaps it was relief. Maybe it was confirmation they weren't all crazy.

"But how?" Simon asked after a few silent minutes passed.

"In the scrapbook," the bishop pointed out. "Came across it last evening. There is a passage about a disciple of the Weeping Age confronting the darkness. Both are to have equal powers."

"What exactly does that mean?"

Tomassi: "The boy at the tracks lived, no?"

"Yes, but—"

Bishop: "The gentleman, our Brother Stanley Iris, did not."

"Okay, but that doesn't explain... Wait, what? Brother Iris?"

"Simon." Tomassi leaned back in his chair and made a steeple with his fingers.

"No, allow me, David," the bishop asserted. "I realize you're trying to digest vast amounts of information in such a short amount of time, questioning and wondering how it fits into your life. How it affects your future."

"As are we, I suppose," Tomassi admitted.

"Indeed," the bishop acknowledged. "The thing is, we, Simon, are nothing in the grand scheme of things. The Great Mystery that makes up the Church began two-thousand years ago with the birth of Jesus Christ."

He leaned forward to begin once more leafing through the large, dusty scrapbook. "You've heard of the Second Coming, right?" he asked Simon, peering from over his glasses while looking through the book.

"Sure. The Apocalypse. End Times. What about it?"

"You say it so... casually." Tomassi was slightly taken aback by Simon's indifference.

Simon met Tomassi's eyes shrugging his shoulders. With palms upward, he mouthed the word *What!*

"Many scholars have theories about End Times." Poring through the pages of the scrapbook, the bishop continued to talk as he searched. "Among the most popular theories surrounding the Second Coming is Christ's return in fire from the heavens. Others postulate His coming as the Man King last seen ascending to the heavens following His resurrection. In either case, there's debate as to whether His return after a two-thousand-year absence will be *just* to reclaim His faithful..."

"The Rapture," Tomassi clarified before the bishop continued.

"Yes, before a thousand years of rule under Satan's hand. At which time He will return to usher in the *next* thousand years of peace. Still another theory posits His return to *face* — to take on — whatever evil has gestated here, the outcome of which will determine the future thousand years of life here on earth?"

Simon shuddered.

"You can look at the same sources, books by the Apostles or Books of Revelation, and adopt your own theory."

"But?" Simon asked, wishing the bishop would get to the point. They were, after all, supposed to be the experts.

"But they're wrong." It was Tomassi who answered Simon's question. "Adánia became sacred ground because of the Blessed Mother's appearance to Sister Maria. But between the death of Christ and the first recorded apparition of Mary, there is a very significant — but overlooked — footnote."

"It is spoken of only in the most private of circles.

Even there it's kept hush-hush."

"And that would be?"

Losing interest in the details, Simon longed for the truth. He suddenly thought of Sarah. She had another doctor's appointment today. Privately, he was ashamed for not being there tending to his husbandly duties. It shouldn't be Julie, a mom herself with two kids in the apartment downstairs, once again chauffeuring his wife all over the place.

"Even before young peasant girl, Maria Valencia, spoke of an apparition in the form of the Immaculate Mary who touched her soul in April of 1896, a battle was waged with one of the Church's very own."

The bishop looked up at Simon from his notes. "Gerbert d' Aurillac, leader of the Church from AD 999 to AD 1003." He turned the scrapbook around and slid it over to the young man. "Meet Pope Silvestre II."

Wind rattled the French doors leading to the outside balcony as sleet pelted the windows.

Catching a draft of cool wind, Simon shivered. He stood for the first time all afternoon to stretch. He also needed to use the bathroom. Looking around the room, he noticed Father Jacob watching him. Startled, Simon smacked the table with the back of his hand, nearly knocking his coffee cup over. The other priests followed the commotion with their eyes to find Jacob standing in the doorway. Consumed in their conversation they, too, weren't aware of his presence.

"Gentlemen, my apologies for disturbing you. Bishop, the visiting Bishop Umgumbwe is tending to tonight's Mass. And I sent Gladys home earlier because of the poor weather. I was about to prepare some food. Would you gentlemen like something to eat?"

The bishop returned his attention to the other two men in the room. "There's still more to go over. You might as well stay for supper."

"What do you think, Simon?" Tomassi asked, stifling a yawn and stretching his arms in front of himself.

"It's really no matter to me," Simon lied. "I really don't have an appetite, though. I do need to find a john."

"Nevertheless," the bishop resolved, "a bite to eat would be wonderful and much appreciated, Jacob."

"Very well. Simon, I can show you where you can go."

Avoiding Jacob's eyes, Simon hesitantly left the room to follow Jacob.

31

If it were any other day besides Good Friday, Father Jacob would have prepared a meal using food left over from a luncheon provided the day before in the church hall for a group of teachers who agreed to take on catechumenal duties beginning in late August. As part of an initiative to get more young people involved with the Church, the bishop successfully recruited a group of lay people to join the program in addition to the sisters and priests from the three local parochial schools. While awful in matters of finance and budgeting, he was much better when it came to young people and their religious education.

Getting commitments this early meant there would be plenty of time for preparing. There would also be the matter of coordinating the youth group and choir.

The meal Jacob was putting together on this day of fasting and abstinence, in accordance with Lenten tradition, was a light meal of rice and fried fish. Having already breaded the bass fillets, he set on gas burners a frying pan with too generous an amount of oil and a pot of water for the rice. Then he went about quickly tearing apart some lettuce, placing the leaves into a bowl. From the cutlery block on the counter, he removed an eight-inch all-purpose knife. Selecting the best tomato he could find from the fridge, he rinsed both the tomato and the cutting utensil.

Engrossed in his thoughts as he ran down his *to-do* list, Father Jacob was oblivious to the sizzling oil in the pan. No sooner did he slice off the ends of the tomato did there come an angry pop from the pan, followed by a succession of others. The pop pop pop sounded eerily familiar. Too much like something he tried very hard to forget over the years.

But those days in the foreign jungle still haunted him. They would always haunt him.

Shrugging off the thoughts, he picked up the pace so he could finish slicing the tomato before turning his attention to adding the fish.

Another pop burst from the pan. This time followed by a dab of pain. Before Jacob realized he hadn't lowered the flame under the frying pan, the grease let loose a battery of splatters. Drops of grease showered the stove. And his hand.

Jacob reflexively reacted. Flinching, with knife in hand, he recoiled from the onslaught.

The pan on the stove momentarily forgotten, Jacob was drawn to the intense throbbing beginning to emerge in waves from his hand. In his haste, he sliced into his fingers when he flinched. Slowly, rivulets of blood flowed from the cuts. They joined with beads of splattered grease at the edge of the counter before succumbing to gravity.

Jacob watched the fluid gather from his fingers. So much blood!

The grease spit from the pan with an angry intensity. Jacob, too preoccupied for the moment, attempted to use his free, uninjured hand to wipe up the mess. He succeeded only in smearing it with the grease all over the green Formica counter.

So much... blood!

Trembling, he brought his bloodied hands up to his face. Copious amounts of red fluid relentlessly streamed from his lacerations, dripping all over the counter and floor as he clenched his fists. It was all he could do to repress the memories of the past that stirred from deep within. Memories almost as angry and scorching as the popping hot grease.

My God! So much blood!

The words echoed in his mind. Though he wasn't sure if they were his or not.

What have I done?

Blood dripped onto the journal, leaving little dark red dots as he finished his most recent entry by writing in the date: March 30, 1975. He placed the pen on to the desk with a shaky hand.

What have I done?

What have we done?

But it felt so...

Good! a weaker voice in his head said against the other.

He turned off the lamplight.

What have I done?

Wiping his crimson-stained hands on his shirt, he rose unsteadily. The pen and the lamp, everything he touched, would have to be washed or wiped down. The clothes he wore, however, would have to be destroyed. And the letter... he would have to write another letter and send it. Right now, though, he needed to cleanse himself of his awful deed.

If not spiritually, then physically.

Jacob knew something was amiss.

But it felt good!

It was that voice again. One. Of many.

Oh Lord, Jacob pleaded, I thought once I served you, I would be rid of my pain.

He knew now that any promises of a family, of a normal life, were never going to be fulfilled.

Leaning heavily against the wall, it held him up as he made his way in the dark to the water closet. Entering, he pulled the chain to the overhead bulb. Lit, it swung from side to side, causing the shadows to dance along the walls.

Gazing at himself in the mirror, he wasn't all that surprised that he barely recognized the face staring back. The face was too dark and ghastly for someone in his late twenties. Glistening a pale yellow, his skin was covered with a thick layer of sweat. The eyes, wet with tears, were dark holes with eyeballs set too far back in its sockets.

A noise outside distracted him from the mirror. The others would be wondering where he was. He would have to get back soon. And while everything went smoother than he thought it would, he was still nervous.

But it felt good, the voice in his head purred seductively.

Nervous or...

So good, the internal voice beguiled louder and stronger than his own thoughts.

Nervous or excited.

Why did they have to taunt him so much?

Yes! It felt so good...

He reflected on the words. There was indeed a feeling of accomplishment now that the deed was done. He couldn't deny that.

Slowly and deliberately, he washed his bloody hands in the filthy sink. The foul-smelling cold water sputtering from the faucet stung his skin. But he splashed some of the water onto his face anyway. Surprisingly, he found the act quite refreshing. Soon the feeling of nervousness washed away to cautious optimism. By the time he was done washing up, there welled up from within him a feeling of sheer jubilance.

Lucidity returning, he couldn't help but smile. Amused by his own half-human expression in the mirror's reflection. Befuddled by eyes that were not his own looking back at him from the glass, his smile grew into a wide, toothy grin.

All the while, behind him in the dark shadows, where even the light refused to go, he could feel another presence.

A presence that was always with him.

It did feel good, the presence whispered into the grinning madman's ears.

It was the robed stranger from his dreams. The robed man who was with him ever since Vietnam.

"You have done well, Jacob. And for that, you shall be rewarded."

32

The bishop finished chewing the wad of fish in his mouth before speaking. As the afternoon transitioned into early evening, he and Father Tomassi were remembering more details of their lost days. "As I said before, those of Mother Church were quietly nervous that either this entire thing was an elaborate hoax conspired by children or by someone else intentionally manipulating the children. The other scary scenario was that it was the work of the devil himself. Understand, superstition runs wild when certain events cannot be substantiated. In small villages like Adánia, experiences like these can go one of two ways depending on the belief system in place. They can be seen either as a blessing or proof of a curse."

Swallowing down the remainder of his wine, he wiped his hands and mouth with an embroidered napkin before throwing the cloth onto his plate.

He pushed it aside before speaking again. "Mary singled out these children, Bernadette, Lucia, and our Maria on purpose, you see. Why them? We'll never truly know, but we can speculate they were all part of a master plan since they all share some commonalities. What needs to be stressed here is that after the children explained Mary's wishes for world peace and greater faith, they also issued from Mary a warning of a growing evil.

"Now, this could have been — can be — easily applied to any number of things that have happened in the world since these experiences. These events. At the turn of the twentieth century, for example, the world was in the midst of new technology what with the second Industrial Revolution. And then the world wars. They weren't too far off. Columbia, already having long suffered as a troubled country, was fighting for its independence from other countries and among political factions within its own borders. In fact, the same year that brought Mary's second visit to Adánia, Columbia was engulfed in a bloody four-year civil war that lasted until 1903. It was in this war, as a matter of fact, that Maria lost her cousin, Eduardo Cerves.

"The Church had already established a presence there for many, many years... decades, in fact, when your uncle, David, and I arrived in the country in '58. We were there to rebuild the churches and communities that saw the deaths of nearly two hundred and fifty thousand people in a war lasting nearly a decade. Even now, the country has been tied to terrorism. Guerrilla movements. One wonders what the '80s will bring."

"Much like Israel and the Arab world, I suppose," Tomassi speculated, swirling the last of his wine in the glass before gulping it down. "So much strife. So much bloodshed. Even in God's land where He once walked. And you have to wonder why?"

"In any case," the bishop continued, sucking a piece of fish from his teeth, "there was another secret that apparently only Maria knew. Let me see if I remember this correctly. If I recall, she revealed it to the Archbishop of the Santa Vienta Church. Stories suggest that he truly believed her and refused to tell anyone *but* the pope. Directly and in person. But the pope of the time never received him. And Maria's visions were disregarded.

"Maria grew up and joined the Holy Sisters of Advent, serving her community through the bloodshed that her country endured. A devout woman, some ecclesiastical scholars say that she could certainly be compared to Mother Theresa. But because of her association with the events in Adánia, her life of servitude and devotion was always understated. Undervalued, even.

"Throughout her life she kept sending letters to each of the popes in the hopes of gaining an audience. She was finally received when the events taken down, recorded, by the priests of her village years earlier were collected by a reporter. This journalist then published his findings through a European press. Suddenly the Vatican was interested in these accounts. And then in her."

Asked Simon: "That's good then, no?"

Tomassi chuckled. "If only there wasn't a cover up."

Simon's eyes widened.

"Yes, well, David is correct," the bishop said. "The Vatican suppressed these published documents once they got their hands on them. Furthermore, they only allowed Maria to meet the pope through an intermediary. Not in person. In truth, they were furious about the commotion being made over the anything-but-subtle messages that were leaked and exposed to the general public regarding Church Dogma and the mystery, long held exactly that — a mystery. Pope Pius Paul was only the second pope to learn the details of her secret. But the first to hear it firsthand. I shudder to think how Pope Pontius would handle something like that."

"Why?" Simon inquired.

The bishop ignored the question. "To wrap up this history lesson, your uncle somehow got a hold of these documents long since buried. He became very involved with them — consumed and even obsessed over them, really. And his determination landed him a brief opportunity to speak with Maria before she disappeared. The visions he experienced as a youth, and with us as an adult, led him to devote his life to the Church. To him, it was as if the events in his life led him to this juncture. That all his questions might be answered by meeting with this woman.

"So he met with Maria to validate everything. Maria, however, had grown old. All those many years — a lifetime — trying to get someone to hear her out... Specific details of the visitations that took place over sixty years earlier were slipping away. Some of her accounts contradicted what was written; she sometimes remembered things that didn't occur anywhere near her. In the end, it was her notes, hidden to avoid confiscation by the Church in those early days, and those that somehow survived through an underground group of religious villagers in the Santa Vienta Valley, that became *key* pieces to the puzzle. The secret, then revealed, wasn't a hoax as the Church led the world to believe."

"And what secret was that?"

"Why, that Christ was — *IS* — actually coming!"

Simon snapped to a standing position. His head about to explode. This really was too much. And his questions were STILL unanswered. Damn them!

"Simon," Tomassi said softly, acknowledging Simon's body language and facial expressions. He then slowly proceeded. "The secret Maria held was of a prophecy heralding the return of Christ. In order for that to occur, she warned, the Church must prepare itself. We believe... Rather, we are remembering... that somehow, someway, you are connected to it."

"That's preposterous! What am I supposed to do?" Simon asked. They had already been through this, hadn't they? It was an apt question that none seemed to know the answer to. If they did, they weren't coming clean.

"Your uncle was killed, I'm afraid, before the rest of his research could be completed. And... well, we believe that when your uncle was killed someone else may have also become aware of his work. We do know that Brother Stan, the missionary priest from the diner, worked with your uncle briefly in '74 and '75. Your uncle entrusted him with some of his work, though Stan did not realize the scope of the research he was doing. We believe he risked coming out of hiding to deliver what remained of your uncle's notes when he died the other day."

"How do you know this Stan guy didn't kill my uncle?" Simon accused, placing both hands on the table and meeting Tomassi's eyes.

"You know in your heart that to be untrue. Besides, your uncle saved Stan's life years before. And the bishop received a letter a while back regarding Brother Stan's return to the states. It was postmarked from Italy but already several weeks old," Tomassi replied.

"We know he had nothing to do with your uncle's death," the bishop said. He winced suddenly feeling ill. A quiet belch brought temporary relief as he rose to clear the rising tension in the air. Getting the circulation going again in his legs, he walked to the walnut liquor cabinet located at the far wall across from the table. After finding the bottle of cognac he was looking for, he pulled the cork and poured himself a bit into a snifter. Because this was a day of abstinence, no alcohol besides wine was to be consumed. But the bishop found the current circumstances warranted a slight deviation from such sacred traditions. "What we didn't know was what happened to the remainder of the documents and any other research completed over the years."

Before continuing, the bishop took a generous sip, grimacing as the cognac warmed his throat. "Damn it. If only I didn't overlook the letter from Stan. Inattentive we have become in our old age.

"As you can tell, we've only begun putting things together over the last couple of days, having forgotten so much in so few years. We thought it was solely related to the preparation for Christ's return. Your experiences this week with Stan and Jonathan... They reveal otherwise. Unless they're all actors in a greater story we're unaware of."

Father Tomassi pushed aside his plate and pulled the old scrapbook closer. Leafing through the pages, he came to one and paused, reading it slowly. "'Behold the Guardian who shall glorify from the darkness those seeking the light.'"

He looked up at Simon. But the bishop spoke before Tomassi could.

"For all we know, even the boy you saved from the tracks could fit a piece here translated from our earlier notes. Perhaps that's where it begins. Where we need to shift our focus."

Simon couldn't see the connection. He sat back down feeling somewhat defeated. He was never going to understand what it was they saw in him. Or how the series of weird events fit into what they were telling him. He'd just as soon return to his own life. Forget any of this happened. Maybe he could score some medication to deal with the dreams.

"On the other hand," Bishop Reibold then said, "all three occurrences most likely apply to the entries."

"'Alas, the darkness declares the souls of the weak. Sacrifice shall be in His name, the name of the

Most Holy.'" Tomassi paused again after his reading. This time Simon didn't wait for any translation.

"Let me guess. The guy in the diner?"

"Perhaps," the bishop said from across the room, adding a bit more of the cognac to what was already in his glass.

"'Affirmed shall the Herald of the Weeping Age be, and in whose manifest shall the light expose the darkness.'"

"Not a clue," Simon said, his renewed interest waning once more. Listening to the religious fantasy spelled out by the two before him, he couldn't help but presuppose their sensibilities were warped by the very dogma they ascribed to.

"Peter and I... we've forgotten so much. After you came to visit me. After what you did to... with Father Gordon. The cobwebs... they began clearing. Little by little, memories flooded back. Simon, we are trying desperately to pick up the lost pieces. We truly believe the Weeping Age is upon us. Now. And we fear there is something called the Great Battle coming."

"How could my uncle have translated these things way back when to match up with recent events? And how exactly does anyone know the Weeping Age, or whatever you call it, is really here? Where is the irrefutable evidence?"

Tomassi clicked his tongue. "When Mary spoke to us..."

Simon pursed his lips. "Spoke to you? Mary *spoke* to you?"

"When she appeared to us..."

"Years ago, as we explained earlier," the bishop clarified. "It was then that she spoke of something happening in the twentieth generation of the age at which the Christ Lord was first revealed. Therefore,

I don't think we have much time."

"You really believe this battle is coming? Now?" Simon asked skeptically. "There's still twenty years until the end of the millennium!"

"It just may be, Simon," the bishop said, drawing closer to the table. "Look, we're as much in the dark. Some of the stuff in this scrapbook I recorded after the visions we all received. My notes. They're... Matthew was the one who put his life into researching parts of Maria's visions. He deciphered clues. Translated cryptic messages. Kept it fresh. I mean I kept articles and things that appeared connected, but..."

"We got old," Tomassi said. "And time got away from us."

"It sure did. And dammit all, if things didn't suddenly get foggier after... after his death." He paused to brush his thumb across his nose. "The passages we read earlier were some of the ones Matt was sure would play out somehow. We've sort of attached the events that you've experienced to the other parts ourselves."

"Bishop, is this right?" Tomassi was looking at another passage with a bunch of scribbles near it. It looked as if the bishop had reflected on the passage at some point earlier in time.

Grabbing his reading glasses from the table, the bishop read aloud the selection. "'Heed thy own convocation, for thy just Shepherd must make ready thy sheep.'"

"Simon," the bishop said, looking up after reading the passage, "if you could remember any more about your dreams, it might give you a clue as to your role in this. We seem more convinced than you about the series of events that have occurred. But I thought you would have some idea. Some hindsight. You know, maybe from talking." The bishop swallowed hard, unconsciously rubbing his belly.

"It's alright, Peter," Tomassi said, noticing his friend wasn't looking too well. Truth is, he hadn't been looking well for most of the afternoon. He stacked their dirty dishes. "You know what, I think we'll be getting back. Besides, the roads are probably worsening."

Peter nodded. "I thought this was it, David," he confessed quietly. "I am sorry. Weeping Jesus, he may even be the Savior, himself. Perhaps this Pahana boy he saved is. We need to remember. I don't know how much time we have to keep going round and round in circles."

Simon, taking a cue from Tomassi, also stood. It was late. Certain his wife was growing anxious with each hour of his absence, he needed to get home. He couldn't bear the thought of her going into labor without him there. If she did, he'd never live it down. Never forgive himself. Besides, they needed to continue their own conversation from the night before so he could learn what was truly worrying her. Aside from the fate of the world, Simon did have his own problems to deal with.

While the two older gentlemen continued to speak of their prophecy, Simon randomly went through the books on the shelves near the table. The walls of the room were lined with various tomes and leather-bound books. Classical literature was intermixed with books on faith and doctrine, theology, Church canon. Simon was drawn to one book in particular. He picked up the book on *Popes and Prophecy*, trying to ignore what his role in all of this was.

Tomassi leaned into the bishop. "His coming wasn't all," he whispered. "There was more, wasn't there?"

The bishop's face grimaced in pain. "This was good. Today. Us talking. Jogging the memory. But, oh, David, as I said earlier, we are nothing in the scope of plans the Lord has for mankind. I can't believe all has been lost."

He felt the color run from his face. All that he believed... the hope he held for the children he spent his life dedicated to... everything wasted and in vain because he let them down.

Because he let mankind down.

The thought buckled his knees from under him, forcing him to sit down.

33

Father Tomassi was straightening up the conference table when he heard Simon mention Pope Silvestre.

"What about him, Simon?"

"You guys mentioned him earlier. But never explained why the bishop has him in his scrapbook."

The bishop was sitting with his head in his hands. He carried the weight of the world on his shoulders. His joints ached and his stomach was a churning sea of acid that kept threatening to creep up on him. "Some scholars believe," he said raising his head, "that he thwarted Satan's attempts at claiming the world for his own for another thousand years."

Simon combed through the book in his hand.

"He paid a dear price, my boy," the bishop said. Elbows on the table, he rested his chin on cupped hands and looked over at the young man. "A hefty price for what he believed in."

Tomassi collected the stack of dishes and was about to bring them into the kitchen. "In the quietest of circles within the Church, it is believed that Silvestre was able to trick the devil into allowing mankind another thousand years before showing himself. This herculean accomplishment was to allow the followers of Christ a chance to rise up and, in a sense, redeem themselves. Thus, in turn, they'd be better prepared for The Battle. Silvestre believed in the good of Man. Even if that belief failed him."

With that, he left to bring the dishes to the kitchen.

"I'm not sure I..."

"You're not sure," the bishop remarked, his voice deep with rancor, "because you're a kid and you're not one of faith. You are not living in the times of old when people revered the Church and feared God. Your generation thinks Christmas is for presents and religious holidays are for days off from school.

"Aurillac — Pope Silvestre — lived during a time when people devoutly respected Church laws and doctrine. A time when they feared the Almighty. Would you believe he was even there performing Mass on the eve of the new millennium, side-by-side with the peasants and poor? That was unheard of at that time in history. Each of the classes giving of themselves to the Lord as equals. Readying for the thousand-year reign of Christ to come to an end followed by the Judgment and a new beginning.

"The years 999 and 1000 came and went, though. And still the world continued as before. However, and here's where it gets interesting, Pope Silvestre was without a tongue and one of his hands when he died in 1003. He removed both himself as penance for consorting with the devil. It is written that the devil then blinded him. But not before he forced Silvestre to witness the demons of Hell playing with his eyeballs."

"That can't be," Simon said, red and embarrassed by the bishop's mislabeling of his generation. As with the rest of the afternoon's news, he was finding the stories more fascinating than scary.

"It's true," Tomassi said, returning. "Whatever he did, though, seemingly worked to buy mankind the additional thousand years. But what has the Church done to repay him? Why they've kept everything a secret and allowed avarice and hubris — human weaknesses — sully the papal seat. Look around. We've all failed, son. Key members of the

Church have failed. Mankind has failed."

"Isaiah 65:17: 'For behold, I create new heavens and a new Earth; And the former things shall not be remembered or come to mind,'" the bishop recited from memory.

"Satan is coming back, Simon. Hell, he's already here. But there is to be a huge battle. The souls of everyone on this planet are at stake," Tomassi warned. "Literally." He reached for his coat draped over the back of his chair.

"Okay, suppose I take this in. You have yet to articulate where I fit into this supposedly big battle." Simon wondered if other church leaders experienced similar delusions. Perhaps an effect of old age and their belief system.

"Do you even know why we have a pope?" Tomassi asked.

The bishop snorted at the question.

"He leads the Church," Simon replied.

"Yes and no. Historically, do you know the papal's place in the hierarchy of God's Church?"

"No, I guess I don't."

"My son, the pope is the *rock* of the Church." Having only put on his scarf, Tomassi returned his coat to the back of the chair before approaching Simon and placing his hands on the young man's shoulders. "Jesus entrusted the Church to one of his Apostles, Simon Peter. It was Simon Peter who was supposed to keep faithful the Church until His return."

Simon was as much suspicious as he was speechless. Looking into the watery eyes of Father David Tomassi, he really wanted to believe them. To believe *in* them. At a loss for words, he could only blink in response.

The bishop's groan broke their eye contact

before Tomassi dropped his hands to return to his friend.

"Peter, are you okay? We're going to leave now. I think it's best you get some rest."

Simon, about to put the book he was thumbing through back on the shelf, looked down at the page where he left off. There, on the page, was a painting of Saint Peter.

Simon Peter. Apostle. Fisherman. Disclaimer.

The one who would come to inherit the throne of the Church. There he was. The Leader of Christ's lambs. Rock of the Church.

Something ruptured in Simon's head without warning. Unsteady, he was overwhelmed by sudden flashes surging inside his head. He knocked over a chair as he struggled to keep from falling over.

Father Tomassi and the bishop ran to Simon as he lay on the floor thrashing about.

Memories in a series of flashes came to Simon in rapid succession. Each invoking immensely powerful sensations.

Flash.

His parents in a casket. Faces sunken-in under a thick layer of beige paste. "I'm sorry, Simon, but your parents have gone on to a better place," someone was telling him as strangers gathered around to comfort him.

Flash.

"You wicked cur," Father Boucher angrily charged. "Little boys don't belong here." Simon was being roughly ushered down worn wooden stairs into the dank darkness of the rectory's stone cellar. Forced into isolation while his uncle was away. Where strange statues stared down at him. Punished for overhearing muffled moans and funny sounds Father Boucher made with a woman Simon never saw.

More memories flooded Simon's consciousness.

"Hi. Simon, right? My name is Sarah Burnett," a shy, pretty girl said from her stool next to him in Art class.

Another flash.

"Your parents are dead. How does that make you feel?" Doctor Samuels was asking him.

Flash.

"I'm pregnant!" Sarah's eyes were bright and full of anticipation. Simon's heart was instantly in his throat with joy. And pride.

They came and went even faster now.

"I'm sorry. It appears your uncle was murdered..."

"There is still time..." Gordon said to him before dissolving.

Tomassi in the rectory. "There is something special about you..."

Simon talking with Sarah. "I don't think it was a dream..."

Tomassi in the car. "You are what has been prophesied..."

Simon talking to himself. "What if I had something to do with...?"

Simon in his dreams. "Uncle Matthew?"

A voice cried out in his head. "YOU ARE KEFA!"

Simon and Sarah talking about her pregnancy. "Dammit, Sarah, can't you understand? Color doesn't matter to me..."

Father Gordon. "THERE IS STILL TIME..."

Sarah's mother. Disappointed. "I don't want you seeing my daughter."

Jackie's breasts up against him. Her mouth on his.

His friend, Larry. Angry.

Sarah's father. Cautious. Hopeful. "I know you'll never do anything to hurt her."

Father Francis. "He's no Christ..."

Simon felt something in his head pop. His body

convulsed in response.

The two elder priests watched helplessly as Simon's mouth opened to a silent scream.

Hurling now through space and time, Simon's journey was one of madness. The two collared strangers who stood by trying to comfort him as he twitched and convulsed melted away to a handful of friends celebrating the return of the One they worshipped. They wore robes and sat on mats of wool placed over a dirt floor surrounding a table slightly above the ground.

"Do you love me?" the bearded man sitting at the center of the table asked. His eyes seemed to peer into the soul.

"You know I do, Lord," came Simon Peter's weak, unconvincing response.

"Then care for my sheep."

Simon blinked at the request.

Blinking again, he found himself near a small fire aside a large wall. Wailing and screaming could be heard from the surrounding shadows. He kept himself covered to shield from the chill. And to shield his identity.

"Hey! Aren't you with the one they call Jesus?" a guard in gold and red asked. His sword gleamed in the light of the fire.

Simon rejected the insinuation. "I don't even know the man."

Flash.

"Simon, Satan has asked for you," the figure at the center of the table warned. This time, it was from an earlier feast they shared... Their last supper.

Flash.

"I don't even..."

Flash.

"He wants to manipulate you into doing his

bidding. But I have prayed so that your faith will never be completely destroyed..."

"Lord, please! Satan will never..."

Flash.

"I don't even know..."

Flash.

"So that when you fail..."

"Lord, how can you say that? I... I love you."

"You will have the strength to repent. To turn once again to me."

Flash.

"I don't even know the man."

Flash.

"I'm ready to die for you now." Words spoken unconvincingly.

Flash.

"You will deny me."

"I'll never... deny you."

Spinning.

"Aren't you with the one they call Jesus?" A man in gold and red was asking.

Spinning.

"I'll never deny you."

Spinning.

"THERE IS STILL TIME."

Falling.

"I don't even know the man," Simon said, rejecting the implication.

Falling.

"I'll never deny you."

Time and space rushed in on Simon branching two lifetimes into one.

"You are the rock, Simon Peter. Feed my sheep." Words from the man with eyes so beautiful they touched — no, embraced — the soul. He held out His arms to Simon. Visible were the holes in his palms from His *suffering. His sacrifice.*

Falling.

Surrounded in white light the statue of the Immaculate and Blessed Mother rose into the air, becoming flesh as it did so. This time it wasn't in his back yard that she appeared. It was Adánia, Columbia. Her words clearly audible.

"Simon, *atta kefa*... you are the rock."

34

The bishop hung up the phone when the line crackled and went dead. It was then that the French doors to the balcony of the bishop's study broke open from the sudden force of wind. Lights flickered as the sheer drapes blew about under the assault of driving sleet. Running to close the doors, he used all his strength to shut them against the furious gusts.

Simon's sudden convulsing abated. But left him unresponsive. Eyes fluttering wildly, only the whites of his eyes were currently visible when Father Tomassi peered behind a lid.

He held the young man's head in his lap. Simon's clenched, white-knuckled fists, protectively placed before his face, were stiff. Immovable. Like his twisted and semi-fetal position. Saliva streamed at intervals onto Tomassi's leg and carpet.

"Peter, this is madness. We have to get him to a hospital."

"Let me try the emergency number again. If I can't get through, then we'll drive there ourselves."

"W-wait..." A faint voice rose from the semi-supine body.

Tomassi drew his arms around the young man and pulled him up to a sitting position.

Simon's words came with great difficulty. His tongue a giant rubber ball in his mouth. All he could manage was: "I... I think I know now."

The bishop, his face sweaty despite the chilly air, walked over to where Tomassi was holding Simon. "My God! You are the Savior. Aren't you?"

"Sir," Father Jacob interrupted from the doorway.

Startled, the bishop nearly stepped on Tomassi and Simon. Sidestepping in front of the two men between the table and bookshelves, he moved to obscure Jacob's view.

"Oh, my," Jacob said apologetically. "The lights went out and I heard some noise."

The bishop jerked his hand up. "Everything here is fine. Thank you."

The other priest nodded with acknowledgement and left quietly without question. But not before a quick peek to see what the bishop was attempting to conceal.

Waiting until he heard the door shut, Simon addressed the bishop's earlier question. "The Savior I am not. The Blessed Mother. She appeared to me. Called me *Kefa*. Father Gordon called me that, too. I didn't know. Didn't know what it meant."

Simon's mouth was dry. His words came slowly. He was trying to regain control of his body. "Gordon said it wasn't too late."

The bishop shakily poured water into one of the tumblers still on the table from dinner and handed it to Tomassi. Tomassi was about to bring it to Simon's lips when Simon weakly took the tumbler into his own hands.

"*Kefa*," the bishop said, placing one hand on Tomassi's shoulder to steady himself as he knelt. His face flushed from the effort. "Aramaic for rock. Could it be you are the next rock of the Church?"

"Well," Tomassi acknowledged, taking Simon's empty cup, "his name *is* Simon Peter."

The bishop hauled his heavy frame up, inwardly cursing his decision to kneel. He advanced a few difficult steps to the table to browse through the scrapbook once more as Tomassi helped Simon up.

With reading glasses in hand, the bishop held them to some of the pages. "'Heed thine own calling to convocation, for thy just Shepherd must make ready thy sheep.' Hmm." He put his glasses on.

Tomassi eased Simon into one of the chairs before coming to stand beside the bishop.

"Damn!" the bishop sighed, jerking his glasses from his nose. Simon may have been deemed the rock of the Church, but he wasn't even a priest. Moreover, he was still a kid!

Tomassi sensed the bishop's frustration and looked over at Simon. "You remember anything else? Any other messages? Timetables? Directions?"

Simon could only shake his head. Completely drained, he sat half-slumped in the chair. With great effort, he continued to open and close his hands to reduce the stiffness. Right now, aside from regaining mobility, he wanted to rest. As it was, he was finding it difficult keeping his eyes open.

The bishop struggled to remember that which he still could not. Finally, he called it a day. "I think what is best now for all of us, considering what has happened to Simon, is to be on our guard. If we're not too late, as Father Gordon implied, perhaps we have a small window yet to go... to go through this more thoroughly. To find out how Simon fits into all of this."

Father Tomassi and Simon headed back home shortly after. But not before a prayer with the bishop.

With notes exhaustively examined, and as many memories as they could recall for the day dissected, the two older gentlemen made plans to talk further tomorrow. Their immediate concern: Simon's condition. Considering the immense pressure he was under, his seizure could be a result of a number of things.

For the sake of Simon's health and his young, pregnant wife, they thought it best to get Simon back home posthaste. After all, a two-hour trip in wintry weather still awaited them.

Holy Saturday
APRIL 05, 1980

35

S imon pivoted, and although the surrounding mist initially obscured his vision, he recognized the figure emerging to be his uncle. A large bald man, his uncle had a reddish-brown patch of hair that ran the bottom-back and sides of his head. Once over the ears, it became one with his sideburns. Together they merged into a full but neatly trimmed, wiry beard. He was as Simon remembered him.

"There's something else you need to know," his uncle said.

"What is it?"

"There is danger, nephew."

"Danger? What kind of danger could I possi...?" His uncle was no longer there as a shifting mist encircled Simon. "Uncle Matt?"

Standing outside the restroom of Big Ed's Diner, it was his uncle this time who was on the floor surrounded by curious onlookers.

Simon felt something urge him forward. Clearly reliving the dream from days earlier, the other man, once Stanley Iris, was nowhere to be seen.

"Uncle Matt?"

"Come. Bless me," his uncle said as a dark shadow passed over his features.

"What? I don't know why you're..."

"You're supposed to be the one, right? Now c'mon and bless me with your blessed holy water."

Simon brought up his hands. They were wet like he remembered.

From the floor, the body that now looked like Simon's uncle grew agitated. Simon held his breath as the face beneath him reddened with strain. With rage. The skin of his temples pulsed as a raised pattern of grotesque veins became visible. Never had he ever seen his uncle this irate. And it greatly frightened him.

"Bless me," his uncle spit. "BLESS me. BLESS ME, YOU WICKED CUR!"

The words thundered about him. As if his uncle's mouth were right up against his ears. Attempting to shut out this abomination, Simon was about to cover his ears when he noticed his hands were no longer wet with water. But with blood.

"I will not die by your hands. Do you hear!" the person on the floor accused. All around people crowded about. Blocking his view. Pushing and shoving against each other. Angry faces gnawed and snapped their jaws as if they were anything but human.

Then Simon saw. It was Sarah now. Not his uncle. Her eyes seethed with such hatred that it made Simon's blood run cold. "DO YOU HEAR ME?"

Simon eyed the scene before him. His breath shallow. Blood covered his wife's swollen torso. It poured freely from between her legs. She vomited the angry words as blood oozed from her nose and ears. "*WE* will not die by your hands."

Frozen in horror as little hands tried freeing themselves from the womb, stretching her swollen stomach, Simon closed his eyes and screamed back as loud as he could.

This isn't real, he kept telling himself until something grabbed him and spun him around. "Hey, kiddo. It's me."

It was his uncle. This time with Father Gordon. They were in the backyard of Simon's infancy once more. Where he saw the Blessed Mother in his dreams.

Still trying to shake off the hideous images of his uncle and Sarah, he cautiously extended his hand to touch the man before him. He needed proof it was really him. "Uncle Matt?"

"C'mere," his uncle said, giving Simon one of those big bear hugs he loved so much.

Comforted by the embrace, Simon sighed. "It's really you."

"Yes. And so was the warning you were sent."

Simon sensed what he experienced wasn't a good omen. But it was only a dream, wasn't it? Wasn't it?

"Not even your dreams are safe anymore," Father Gordon said, seeming to answer Simon's unspoken question. "The power of evil grows stronger as the time grows near."

Simon couldn't help but notice that both men were dressed in their standard clergy attire.

"That is why we are here," Simon's uncle explained. "And there is still more you need to know. The prophecy must be fulfilled if mankind is to have a chance at salvation."

"There is more at work here than the Lord. The balances of nature do not work by God's hands alone."

Simon was frustrated. More cryptic talk. Just like Tomassi and the bishop. "What time is growing near?" Simon entreated. "Why do I have to be a part of it? I want my regular life back. I'm tired of this religious mumbo jumbo stuff. At first I was intrigued. Honored even. But now you're all scaring the hell out of me. Why can't anyone give me a straight answer about anything? I'm still not sure what it is I'm supposed to do. Moreover, who am I? Uncle Matt, I'm a nobody."

His uncle answered carefully. Simon was much

too vulnerable right now. They needed to keep close should anything else happen. "Simon, your feelings are very understandable."

Because they were late, the evil they would encounter would be stronger than they anticipated. If Matthew was better prepared, even his death wouldn't have put the prophecy in jeopardy. Now, five years later, nearly everything was forgotten. Lost.

Matthew didn't fault them, though. If it was the fault of anyone, he felt it was his. And his alone.

"Simon, Father Tomassi and the bishop haven't been able to tell you much because they don't remember everything anymore. And I didn't complete my research before I died. I failed them. I have possibly failed you. Only time will tell. But the signs have revealed that you are the one. You... are the rock."

Matthew lowered his voice as he cupped the young man's face in his hands. "You have no idea how much power you have. Always remember your faith is the key to your destiny."

"The other side can be misleading and that's what we have to carefully watch out for. They have been testing you... testing your strength and your faith," Gordon added.

"Rock? That doesn't mean anything to me. What am I supposed to do? What is coming?"

Father Gordon looked over at Matthew then back to Simon. "A miracle is going to occur tomorrow and you are to see it through."

"But there is still a chance that won't happen," said a voice emerging from the surrounding haze. Following the voice to his left, Simon watched the bishop emerge with Father Tomassi in tow.

"True. Everything hangs delicately in the balance

for the next twenty-four hours," Father Gordon explained.

The bishop smiled when he saw Simon's expression. "Don't worry, Simon. Father Tomassi and I are still alive. Like you, we're having the same experience. The same dream."

The priests acknowledged one another. And the many years that passed between them. They also reaffirmed their commitment. To each other. To Simon. To seeing the prophecy through.

"We're very sorry, Matthew. Our memories of what we must do and how we must prepare for the Great Battle are coming back to us. However gradual and fragmented, they *are* coming back," Father Tomassi confessed.

Simon's uncle put a hand on Tomassi's shoulder. Giving it a light squeeze, he turned to address the others before him. "Our time grows short, gentlemen. We must act quickly."

Then he addressed his nephew. "Me and Father Gordon are here for you and will be watching over you on the celestial plane. Father Tomassi and Bishop Reibold are the two people you can count on if you need anything on the terrestrial plane."

"David, Peter," Father Gordon warned, "we sense the evil is growing. It is the strongest, yet. Dark forces sense and know the time is near. Legion will do whatever it can to prevent the miracle."

"What would you have us do, Matt?" Tomassi asked, the mist about them beginning to thicken into a fog shrouding their view of the yard and the foliage beyond.

"You two realize more of the prophecy here than you do when you are awake. The research from Brother Stanley's investigation to connect the dots was as complete as it could be."

"There were problems with that," the bishop interjected. He wondered why Matt wasn't aware of it himself.

"Even so, there is nothing more I can give you now. A number of signs were to occur to bring the *kefa* to us. And you two have done well enough deciphering them. The rest is up to the Lord. He will reveal to Simon what he must do at the proper time. Is anything preventing that? Sure there is. But how we stop it is as much a question to me as it is to you. Keep Simon in your prayers. If anything happens to prevent the miracle, the prophecy will not be fulfilled. Our greatest strength lies in our faith. And our unity."

Simon's uncle paused. His expression one of great concern. Again he turned to Simon, repeating himself. "Your faith, dear nephew, must be strong. Accept all that has happened in your past. Accept it as part of God's plan. I know you are still in pain. Still grieving. That you still carry with you much anger and guilt. But you must acknowledge the Lord in your heart."

Simon opened his mouth to respond when a memory of words spoken a lifetime ago flashed in his head. *I don't even know the man.* Simon violently shivered at the thought.

To the bishop and Tomassi, Matthew stressed caution. "Beware, gentlemen. There is a Judas among you. His heart was once pure. But he has been misled. Corrupted, he is now inhabited by many."

A sudden swirl erupted between the five men. It howled loudly, forcing Matthew to shout over the tumult. "Lucifer has manipulated him long. I doubt he can be saved. His mission is not only to stop you. It is to destroy you."

"Destroy us?" Simon shouted.

"How will we know who he is?" Tomassi asked before anyone could answer Simon.

"The Betrayer is someone whose evil goes unnoticed because he..."

With the wind picking up and raging so fiercely, the rest of what Matthew said was drowned out.

Tomassi shouted against the turbulent wind. "What did you say?"

"I know you still don't understand everything," Matthew said, suddenly closer to Simon now. "In time, you will. Be aware that you will be tested in ways unimagined. The love and devotion others have for you, as well as your own faith, will be what keeps you safe. It is time for you to turn back to Him."

"But..."

"Remember your faith. Hold dear those things you already have. That you've always had. He's pleading in prayer for you."

"What do you mean, 'turn back to'," Simon pressed.

It was getting harder to see, much less hear, against the wind's fury. Even with his uncle so close now, Simon fought against it to keep his eyes on him.

"What's supposed to happen if I succeed? What exactly is the miracle?"

"They already told you," his uncle said joyfully. "It's the second..."

But even that much Simon didn't hear. Instead, he saw his uncle's lips move in between big smiles when suddenly the mist eclipsed everyone.

Weightless, Simon floated.

He was alone. Or so he thought.

"SIMON!"

Opening his eyes, he was 12-years old again. In his uncle's rectory. The rickety staircase he feared as a child creaked and moaned under his weight as he cautiously made circles in place.

A familiar musty odor stung his nostrils, making him cough each time he inhaled. Except for the steps, the basement was hidden in shadows dark, deep, and alive. The dull light of the paint-chipped stairwell unable to penetrate the living and breathing Cimmerian shade. Young Simon would have to brave the remaining stairs, pivot left, then sprint to the end of the cobwebbed room. There, tethered to the only bulb in the entire nineteenth century stone walled basement, was a tattered string Simon could barely reach.

That is, if there *was* a working bulb present. Lately Father Boucher took to removing the bulb from the socket before imprisoning Simon while his uncle was away.

Luckily young Simon remembered with precision the most direct route necessary to avoid the frightening statues. Especially the larger-than-life stone cast crucified Christ with a head nearly half the size of Simon's body. Its strangely disfigured expression haunted the young boy. Seeing it was almost always a sign something bad would surely follow.

Readying to make his run down the stairs and past the statue, a thought occurred to Simon.

I don't even know the man.

Focused on his course, he dismissed the thought. If he could only move from his safe spot on the steps.

I'll never deny you.

Above him, the pasty yellow bulb illuminating the staircase seemed to dim with every nervous exhale.

Faint movements drew his attention. First to the left.

Then to the right.

All at once the paint-chipped walls came to life. Bleeding from its many cracks and crevices centipedes and other arachnids emerged by the hundreds. Thousands. Over and around the stairs, multiple life forms of various sizes skittered about. Creepy crawlers of all sorts were everywhere.

Someone — or something — once more took to screaming his name from atop the stairs.

Father Boucher was on his way with the strap. Simon had been bad. Yes, he did hear Father Boucher and the woman. But he didn't mean to. He didn't!

But Simon didn't come face-to-face with Father Boucher. It was a mirror image of himself soaked with blood cackling and waving a leather strap in its hand.

Transfixed with terror, Simon couldn't take his eyes off his evil twin. As its grin broadened, the dull yellow glow of light above them turned crimson.

Then the basement door slammed shut with a force hard enough to send the creepy crawlers scattering.

Left alone in the scariest place in the world, young Simon remained paralyzed with fear as creatures of the basement crawled over him.

Bathed in the dark glow of the light above him, he slowly began to feel a presence reaching out to him. Another. Then another. Soon a dozen. A hundred. A thousand souls reached out for him from what was supposed to be the basement floor.

The lamentations grew louder until, ever so quietly, Simon heard the faint scraping of something heavy against the stone floor. He trembled in fright, curling himself into a fetal position.

More distinct now, the scraping sound rose over the cries of the souls reaching out to him. Twelve-year-old Simon's greatest fear was about to be realized: the statues were coming for him.

Numb with fear, he dared a look. The thin ray of light from the basement window revealed one of the statues to Simon. Squinting, he went against his better judgment. Leaned forward.

His eyes widened at the sight once concealed in shadows. From within the pitch, and bathed in burgundy, Simon discerned the stone-cast Christ. With hands still fastened to the wood, the attached cross scraped loudly behind.

Christ raised His head. "Your turn," it growled in a low raspy voice before a wicked grin spread across its face.

Simon shrieked as the shadows of the basement fought to conceal what little light shined. All the while his thoughts betrayed him as they always did.

I don't even know the man.

The darkness swirled about. Shadow upon shadow. Alive. Devouring first the basement, it now encroached the stairs.

The bulb above Simon burst, sending shards of glass everywhere. Simon raised his hands to shield himself, crying out in agony as he felt the fragments pierce his skin.

Petrified, there was nowhere to go as his footing gave way. He fell back as the other statues crowded him. Souls reached for him.

All around him the endless gloom crept up from the floor, overtaking him and the stairs. Soon Simon would be lost to the souls of the abyss whose hands now tore at him.

Pulling him apart in a million directions. Pulling him apart into a million pieces.

Young Simon knew he was going to die. Tortured souls beckoned him by name. Welcomed his descent.

Dragged into the very pits of Hell, his last thought betrayed Him yet again.

But I don't even know the man.

36

I t was difficult to hear over the siren.

"Lost a lot of blood," the mustachioed paramedic repeated.

"He'll make it," Father David Tomassi stated firmly between prayers.

En route to Bethlehem General Hospital, the priest tried maintaining his balance on the bench inside the Nazara Fire Department's 1978 Dodge ambulance. Across from him, an emergency medical technician sat in a jumper seat.

Father Joseph followed behind with Sarah, doing everything in his power to comfort a very hysterical and very pregnant wife.

The tech was checking the EKG cables and IV bags when Tomassi once again yelled over to him. "He's a lot stronger than you think."

"Hope you're right, Father, cuz he's comatose. Breathing. But comatose."

As Simon lay before them on the stretcher, Tomassi bit down hard on his lip to stave back tears. Unable to remain still, he repeatedly folded his hands over one another. An act that betrayed his assured words and calm demeanor.

It was 3:33 when Tomassi awoke from his dream. Knowing there was something weird about the way the dream ended, he immediately set out for Simon's place with Father Joseph. Sure enough, he arrived to find Simon's wife beside herself in a state of shock.

Though details were sketchy, Sarah discovered her husband about the time Tomassi started off towards Nazara. Even in her distress, she wasted no time calling 911.

Thankfully the paramedics were quick, arriving before he and Joseph. Time was a luxury they didn't have.

Tomassi was unprepared for what he saw. And it nearly stopped his heart. Blood was everywhere. Simon a pale lifeless corpse.

With precious few minutes to spare, temporary gauze dressings covered Simon's hands. Split open, his blood-soaked tee was bunched up at his sides so the EMT could prep his chest with electrode patches and wires for an EKG.

The line on the monitor currently a horizontal green. Methodically, the emergency personnel continued diagnosing and treating the dying *kefa* with cool, detached efficiency.

Pupils examined. Pulse palpated at the carotid and radial arteries. Then the infusions: a treatment of dopamine before an infusion of epinephrine.

When no response registered on the monitor, out came the paddles as Simon was defibrillated.

For an old priest who experienced war, seeing Simon so vulnerable — his body heaving in response to the electric shocks to the chest — was still jarring to watch.

The prophecy, deciphered by Father Matthew Free after a series of visions and incomplete research, told of dangers and obstacles. But this?

One thing was for sure, Tomassi may have begun recalling more of the prophecy, especially while awake, but he worried about what was ahead. How blind where he and the bishop without *any* of Matthew's final notes?

Tomassi recollected a line recorded from one of the priests at the Santa Vienta Church in Columbia: *A battle shall rage, for the powers of darkness grow in wrath. And upon the last hour of the last stand, so shall it be fought.*

He trembled at the remembrance. Words shook him to a low not experienced since his sister's passing when he first heard them. As life continued, however, nothing around him ever seemed to resemble the evil that was foretold. Surely as priest and veteran he would have witnessed something that would prepare him for the day. Something to set the moment apart from all others. To help him believe. To make him believe. That's it, he realized. As always, it comes down to what makes us believe.

But wasn't the taking of another life enough to believe in the existence of evil? Wouldn't such callousness indicate the presence — or influence — of evil to commit acts so vile?

Was war to blame? Movies? Television? Desensitizing viewers by repeatedly exposing them to abhorrent actions and behaviors, however fictitious?

Perhaps that is the devil's greatest trick. Convincing man he doesn't exist. That true evil resides in the very heart of the Lord's prized creation: man.

Father Tomassi brought a hand to his mouth as he quietly began to weep at the thought. Wept for letting his sister down. For failing to remain strong.

Feeling emotionally and spiritually unprepared, he wished he had Peter Reibold's strength and conviction. A man of detail and used to taking charge, the bishop's only show of frustration seemed to come from his inability to remember the past as it related to the prophecy. As it related to Matthew. Simon.

Tomassi, unlike the bishop, was worried about everything at this point. Especially Matthew's ominous warning of a "betrayer in brethren's skin who would go unnoticed." Someone close to them *was going to* or *had already* gone against them.

The ambulance came to an abrupt halt. Having called in ahead, hospital staff was ready to receive the non-responsive Simon. In the dash to the emergency room, the EMT gave an expectant doctor the run down on Simon's vitals.

Already a long night, it was going to be an even longer morning. Tomassi, thinking it best to update the bishop, exited to find a phone.

37

A young doctor looking very haggard walked into the waiting room and put out his hand. "Mrs. Free? Doctor Bill Goldstein."

Sarah stood with Father Joseph's assistance. She rubbed her belly to calm the life inside as much as she did to calm herself. "My husband?"

"We're still evaluating. Wounds are quite severe. He's lost a lot of blood. The heart is very weak."

Sarah faltered slightly. Her face contorting in response. Father Joseph steadied her until she could stand upright again.

"Maybe you should have a seat before we continue," the doctor offered.

"I'm fine. The baby just kicked is all. Now, what about my husband?"

"If you don't mind my asking, when are you due? You look close to term."

"Never mind me," Sarah said, gritting her teeth. "What about my husband?"

Catching the pregnant lady's tone, the doctor decided against pushing it. He instead went about answering her question. "He remains extremely critical and in a state of prolonged unconsciousness."

Sarah's moist eyes widened. "What does that even mean?"

The doctor pursed his lips. "He's in a coma."

"Oh, my God."

"It's a situation we are monitoring very carefully. While we believe all foreign objects to be removed at this time, his heart, a muscle, has been severely compromised. Weakened due to multiple strokes."

"Foreign objects?" she cried. "What foreign objects?"

"Your husband arrived with multiple lacerations to his upper extremities. Surgery was performed to remove and address penetrating trauma to those areas. Most specifically his..." Here the doctor paused to address concerns raised while administering care to her husband. "Mrs. Free, your husband... Do you know if he was under the influence of anything last night? Earlier this morning?"

Sarah looked down and rubbed her belly. "No."

"Has he been overly stressed? Emotional? Acting out of character? Depressed?"

"I don't... I'm not..." was all Sarah could manage. She knew what was coming next.

"Do you know of any reason why your husband would want to kill himself?"

Sarah sobbed into Father Joseph's coat as he eased her back into one of the pastel-colored chairs.

"Jesus, Mary, and Joseph," a voice bellowed from behind the doctor. It was Father Tomassi. "Are you deliberately trying to get her to lose the baby?"

"Of course not."

"This is what's come of care at hospitals these days!" Tomassi's voice was as elevated as his temper.

"Sir, if you would kindly lower your voice."

"It's Father! Father David Tomassi, son." He further opened his coat. "I wear a collar. And having dedicated over twenty years to ministry, I think I have earned the respect and title of Father."

"I don't think yelling... I d-didn't mean to—"

But Father Tomassi wasn't done. "I've made a call to Doctor Victor Samuels. When he gets here, he will be the one running the show."

Waiting for the ambulance with Sarah, Tomassi saw the name and number on the fridge. Remembering the conversation with Simon a few days back, he asked Sarah if this Samuels guy was his doctor. When she briefly hinted at their history, Tomassi snagged the card on the way out. Though Samuels was more of a counselor, Tomassi felt he should be apprised of the current situation.

A shadow passed over the doctor's face in response to Father Tomassi's threat.

Tomassi crossed his arms. "Is there a problem with that?" The priest knew full well Samuels wouldn't be able to do much. But by watching and listening to Goldstein, he also recognized signs of exhaustion. Perhaps even indifference. This doctor was on the tail-end of a double-shift. And right now Simon's condition was of the utmost importance.

"N-No," the young doctor said, acquiescing. "I'll have a report prepared for Doctor Samuels. In the meantime, I will..."

"Whoa, now. You'll do nothing except prepare that report," the priest demanded, suddenly all over the doctor. He clutched the doctor by the arm in mid-stride. "Because if anything happens to that young man, I swear to God, the Almighty Father in Heaven..."

Father Joseph gently placed his hand onto Father Tomassi's arm. Tomassi released his grip, allowing the frightened doctor to continue making his way down the hall to prepare for Doctor Samuels' arrival.

"Thought it was Sarah you were concerned about?"

Father Tomassi shook his head. His expression grim. "The stakes, Joseph... so high. For both."

The younger priest had no clue to what Tomassi was referring. With his back to Sarah, Father Joseph whispered to his peer. "You do know they already prepare reports at the end of their shift?"

Tomassi patted Joseph's arm in response. His ire already subsiding.

"Mrs. Free," Father Tomassi said before taking a seat nearby.

Sarah was alternating between wiping her nose and wiping the streaming tears. "Please, call me Sarah." To soothe her protruding belly, she rubbed it while absentmindedly rocking back and forth.

"Certainly. Sarah..."

"Do you mind if I smoke? I desperately need a cigarette right now," she said, withdrawing a pack of Vantage 100s from her purse. Hands shaking badly, she could barely lift the cigarette to her quivering lips.

"I don't mind," Father Tomassi answered. "But.. but what about your baby?"

Exhausted. Sarah lacked the strength to even address the priest's question of concern. She let the cigarette hang from her lips.

Tomassi continued, changing the subject. "Simon's doctor will be arriving shortly, and he will look in on Simon. Help coordinate the medical response. Things will begin looking up. Rest assured. I also recently got off the phone with a friend. Bishop Reibold. He'll be saying some extra prayers today.

"Besides," Tomassi added with one of his exaggerated smiles, "it's Easter. There'll be even more parishioners to help him pray."

Sarah searched the old man's eyes. Searched them for sincerity. Honesty. Truth. "Thank you. You've been very kind. Spending a lot of time with Simon lately?"

"Yes, I guess I have," he replied. Sitting back, he crossed his legs, feigning comfort in this early hour.

He noted how puffy Sarah's eyes were from crying. The redness of her nose.

Removing the still unlit cigarette from her lips, Sarah addressed the priest. "Tell me, Father, have you noticed anything different about my husband's behavior?"

Father Tomassi dodged the question with a question. "How do you mean?"

Sarah scoffed at his blatant deflection. "Oh, come on. Please don't patronize me. I'm not ten. And if there is anything you don't do well, it is lie." Sarah wiped her nose again.

"You'll have to forgive me, but I know of nothing that would have caused..." He wasn't exactly lying. While he could easily come clean about Simon's role in a prophecy that may — or may not — exist, Tomassi had no clue why Simon would have tried to...

Sarah was studying him closely. "Caused what, Father?"

Unless, Tomassi wondered, the evil one somehow already got to him.

Sarah shook her head after scrutinizing the priest. She didn't mince words. "You can't even say it to my face, can you?"

"Now, now. Simon will be okay."

Once more Sarah studied the face of the collared man before her. But his subterfuge implicated him in his complicity.

There was only one man she ever trusted. One man who never hid the truth from her. That man was her father. Father Tomassi's disingenuous demeanor only angered her the more she looked at his fake face. She damned him for conveniently hiding behind the collar.

The elder priest cocked his head to one side, nearly struck by one of Sarah's blows. No longer in control of her emotions, Sarah's voice was thick with animosity. She lashed out at the priest, pounding clenched fists against Tomassi's chest. "Damn you! Damn you!"

With that, she buried her face in her hands. Worried. Exasperated. She sobbed hysterically.

Father Tomassi remained still. Silent. He definitely had that coming. While no words could express his sorrow, he *needed* to keep her in the dark. There was no telling who the evil prince would go through to get to Simon. And there was no way Tomassi wanted to see Simon's wife caught in the middle of this. Least of all Simon's child. It was bad enough that the boy would be fatherless should Simon have to sacrifice himself in the Great Battle.

The priest put his hand on the young woman's back and tried to soothe her in place of his silence.

"I... I know my husband has not been well. But I also know that's not all. There's something else, too. And I know you know damn well what it is." Wiping fresh tears from her eyes with the back of her hands, she clenched her teeth as a contraction ripped through her insides.

When the priest still offered nothing, Sarah baited what little she did know. "He thinks he's been having visions."

Father Tomassi continued his reticence, even as Sarah's eyes pleaded for something — anything — that would help her to understand.

"It's connected, isn't it? Dammit, Father. If it was an affair, I might be able to handle it. But this? This I can't... Why would he try to kill himself? He tore apart the bathroom. Everything. Destroyed. Why would he try to slit his wrists? Haven't I given him enough space? Haven't I absolved him of enough responsibility with this... this damn baby?"

Tomassi reached out to her just as her eyes squeezed shut. She lunged forward. "Ugh!" Clutching the priest's arm, she twisted his coat in her hands as waves of pain passed through her. "Oh God! My water. I think it broke." Sarah began to sob again. "It's... It's too soon. This doesn't feel right."

Sarah inhaled sharply before looking up at Tomassi. Her wet swollen eyes full of worry and confusion.

While he may have appeared evasive to her questions, there was no questioning his motives when it came to her labor. Father Tomassi sprang into action. Standing, he motioned for Joseph. Joseph was discreetly far enough away to give them space but close enough to be of assistance. After whispering a few words into Joseph's ear, Joseph took off down the hall while Father Tomassi returned to his seat near Sarah.

It wouldn't be long now. He held her close. Comforting her as best as he could as she sobbed and shuddered.

After surveying the waiting room for those who may be eavesdropping, Tomassi came clean to Sarah. "Your husband did not slit his wrists."

It took a few breaths for the woman pressed up against his chest to process what he said. "Then why," she asked as quietly as the priest. Her breathing, no longer a series of sobs, came in gasps. "The cuts. All that blood. It was... It was all over him.

"I knew, Father. I did. I didn't want to believe it. But I knew he was heading in this direction. School. Us. The baby. His childhood. At some point, it comes to a head. I felt it when I lost my brother to gang violence. When my own father died. But why would he do this now? It's his birthday. He's about to be a father! Why?"

"The cuts he suffered were not all located on his wrists. Let me assure you, Mrs. Free, he did not try to commit suicide."

Sarah shifted. Sat up with difficulty. This priest, after only knowing Simon for a few days had the audacity to act like he knew more about her husband than she did. But he wasn't the one to find Simon lying on his back. His clothes drenched in his blood.

So many questions. How? Why? A seizure? A struggle? Sarah kept asking herself over and over why she didn't hear him.

Father Tomassi moved aside a few errant strands of hair from Sarah's swollen face. "How much has Simon told you?"

Sarah stiffened defensively at the insinuation. "I am young but that doesn't mean I'm some pathetic, dimwitted housewife who sits at home watching *Donahue* all day."

"That's not at all what I meant."

"I *am* a college graduate. Educated and independent."

"I'm sorry..."

"He told me about the dreams. Even the weird ones he's experienced lately. But he's always had dreams that were somehow... different."

The priest nodded.

"He also told me about going back to Samuels. And how he met you. Ugh!" Another contraction.

She slumped forward before using every ounce of strength to force herself back up. If something was going to happen to this baby, it was going to happen in the Emergency Room. Not in the lobby. She was going to make damn sure of that.

To steady herself, she again clutched the priest's coat. A layer of perspiration glossed her forehead. Her upper lip. "He even told me about the absurd possibility of having saved people. Strangers he doesn't even know."

"Do you believe him?"

Tomassi was supporting Sarah as she struggled to stand. She saw Father Joseph coming down the hall with a nurse pushing a wheelchair in front of her.

"I don't know what to believe." Sarah was more preoccupied with getting herself in the wheelchair than answering the priest's question.

But Tomassi pressed. "Do you believe him?"

"I don't quite know what..." Sarah's face again contorted. Labor was not far off. She grunted through a tightened jaw. Her breath a series of short huffs as the nurse arrived.

Tomassi eased her into the wheelchair before holding her shoulders firm. Determined that he get an answer before Sarah left the room.

The old man's breath was hot in her face when he asked a third time. "Mrs. Free, do you believe him?"

"NO, goddamn it. No." Sarah surprised herself as much as the priest. But she had had enough. And if this old asshole in front of her didn't get out of the way, she was going to lose her baby. Simon's baby. "There. You... heard me say it. Happy?"

Sarah tried to mask from Father Tomassi how much she despised these recent circumstances. How much she despised him. She didn't believe any of it. And as the last few weeks demonstrated, she was alone. Pregnant. And alone. Worse yet, she was about to give birth. Alone.

Things weren't going the way she planned. The way *they* planned. It angered her. Now that the truth was revealed. Exposed. The anger consumed her. She was angry with Simon. And very angry with his new friend who moonlighted behind a collar. The time her father always said would come had indeed arrived.

The pain rippled through her insides as the tears came. She silently screamed for her father. Questioned if she could go on. If she could take much more.

As far as Sarah was concerned, the Lord failed her. Again. That much she and Simon shared. But Simon and his own demons be damned. If all that was happening to Simon was somehow religious in origin, she cursed God for doing this to her. And her family.

Yes, Sarah gave the priest the confession he desperately sought. Acid churned in her stomach as she regarded the old priest before her with contempt.

Waving her arms in front of her, she dismissed him before hunching down in the seat. "Now leave me alone. I'm about to have a baby."

Tears that earlier streamed freely once more gushed. The nurse hurried the sobbing pregnant woman out of sight leaving a very stunned Father Joseph and a very worried Father Tomassi.

38

Ever since getting off the phone with David Tomassi, the bishop found himself too troubled to sleep. In less than a week, he and David saw their rather immovable world descend into one of utter chaos. The realization of Simon's role in the prophecy somewhat illuminated. But too late. And with a hefty price. Not only were they without all the facts, they still weren't remembering everything. It was quite possible they never would.

The bishop returned to his personal Bible, which lay before him on his lap. He read the following: *But he was wounded for our transgressions, he was bruised for our iniquities: the chastisement of our peace was upon him; and with his stripes we are healed. All we like sheep have gone astray; we have turned everyone to his own way; and the LORD hath laid on him the iniquity of us all.*

Bishop Reibold sighed heavily. "Dear Lord, forgive me. We lambs really have gone astray."

His eyes rested on the one line in the holy book that caused him to shiver most violently: *He is brought as a lamb to the slaughter.*

Removing his glasses, the bishop rubbed his swollen, leaky eyes. "My God, what have we done?"

Several fitful minutes later, he tossed the covers aside. He hated being idle. Still nauseous, he had been violently ill since David and Simon left Friday evening. Aching all over, his head continued to throb. Especially the more he tried to focus on Simon and the prophecy. Slowly rising from the bed, he got into his bathrobe while burying his feet into slippers.

There was so much to do. But he was so sick. So exhausted. So drained. Some twenty-four hours without much improvement, it looked like he would need more rest if there was any hope of presiding over tomorrow's Easter Mass.

In an act of foresight before retiring last evening, he set up the visiting bishop to cover the 7:00 AM Mass with the intention of at least participating in the one at 11:00.

The visiting South African bishop had been a godsend, already covering last evening's Stations of the Cross and offering to preside over tonight's service. Local parish priests and Father Jacob were also lending a hand.

With the Lenten season coming to an end, the Easter celebration — the resurrection of Jesus Christ — was among the most important within the Church.

The bishop ventured off into the shadowy hallway of the rectory's third floor, past paintings depicting significant moments of Jesus Christ's life. Christ in the Garden of Gethsemane. Christ crucified on Skull Mountain. Christ in the arms of Mary. Even one of Him risen before the Apostles shortly after His death.

"A death," the bishop recited unconsciously, "He freely accepted."

Once on the second floor, he made his way to his cluttered office. Fumbling with the keys in his robe, he unlocked the desk to remove the leather-bound scrapbook.

Running a hand over the binder's worn leather, he then patted it reassuringly while reciting the Hail Mary. His conscience fixated on one line that kept repeating in his mind over and over: *pray for us sinners now and at the hour of our death.*

It was crucial that they make sense of all of that

has happened. And all that *was going to* happen. Even in his state, grounded in mortal limitations, he was determined to do everything in his power to forge on. To remember.

With the scrapbook under his arm, he reached the top of the stairs with difficulty before detouring to the bathroom. He needed something for his upset stomach. And something to help him sleep.

He was so tired.

Recalling his brief conversation with Tomassi, the queer feeling when their dream-meeting last evening was abruptly interrupted was shared. Having dissipated so quickly, it was as if they were somehow cut-off. But if they were supposed to have protection from the inside, where did Jon and Matthew go?

Rummaging through the medicine cabinet, the bishop knocked over a box of straight edge razor blades. Watching the sharp steel strips scatter into the sink and onto the floor, he couldn't help but be reminded of Simon.

He uneasily collected them back up wondering if Simon's experience was a form of stigmata. The next time David calls, he'd have to mention it.

Whatever it is we're up against, the bishop deduced, stretching to relieve the kink in his lower back, it certainly exceeded even Matthew's expectations. Or fears.

The bishop joggled his head to clear his thoughts. Damned if he didn't think something was clouding his mind. His state of nausea and frequent episodes of diarrhea certainly weren't helping.

With a palm full of aspirin, sleeping pills, and his daily dose of Tenormin for his high blood pressure, he used a Dixie cup full of Pepto to wash them down before returning to bed chewing on six chalky Tums.

He would rest for a spell before once again going through the scrapbook.

Back in bed, he clicked off the light. Closing his eyes, he began a set of prayers an old nurse from the orphanage he grew up in taught him.

Frightened by the large rats that spilled from the walls at night, he was too young to realize what they were at the time. All he saw were beady red eyes reflected in the moonlight. He was certain at the time it was something evil.

The older kids mercilessly taunted the young small Peter Reibold that it was the boogieman coming to get him.

For a long time after that, and well into his teens, whenever he was afraid of the dark, or the boogieman with its evil red eyes, he would recite the nurse's prayer.

"For you, Simon," the bishop whispered as he drifted off to sleep. "For you."

39

Simon found himself on an altar of cedar. His vision, obstructed except for no more than two feet in front of him by a thick fog, was almost as cloudy as his head. Sitting up, everything in Simon's body hurt. Especially his throbbing hands. Palms up, he observed the still raw lacerations.

"Remind you of someone?" A voice veiled by the mist mocked him.

The white haze then cleared enough to reveal a large stone-cast Jesus Christ nailed to a wooden cross some several feet above Simon. Set before a mostly barren and twisted cypress tree atop a rocky knoll, it was an even larger version of the one from his uncle's rectory. The one in the basement. The one that he feared.

Simon observed thin streams of fresh blood slowly seep from Christ's spiked hands just as his own hands began to spasm.

Twitching, Christ's hands opened and closed around the spikes becoming flesh as they did so.

On the crucified man's head lay a crown of thorns. Its sharp spikes deeply embedded into the exposed skin of His skull. The now human Christ figure arched His back in a painful grimace.

Simon looked at his own wounds. Blood pulsated in spurts from the gashes in his hands. An unholy voice laughed in his ear.

"He boasted that He would suffer for mankind. So suffer He shall."

Horrified, Simon shut his eyes to force the image from his mind. Until the cackling subsided.

Eyes open once more, the lifeless figure he was taught was the Son of Man did not frighten him. It instead brought about an emotional response, filling Simon's eyes.

He approached the figure as it reared its bloodied head to face Simon, revealing not Jesus Christ, but Simon's uncle. His eyes bore into Simon's. The evil voice, however, belonged to neither. "It is finished. You are mine, Simon Peter. You always have been."

Simon's tears flowed more freely now as his thoughts shamed him.

I don't even know the man.

The wicked voice laughed. Further taunting Simon. "You failed Him once. And you have continued to do so. Even in this lifetime. Another thousand years and mankind remains as weak and easily corruptible as ever before."

Simon tried to block out the taunting voice. But he was alone. He cursed the priests who brought him into this. Cursed them for making him view his uncle differently from what he remembered. Cursed the dreams that claimed he was special when he felt anything but.

He was alone. He was always alone.

On the cross, Simon's uncle's lips formed silent words. But all Simon could do was focus on his uncle's hollowed out vacant eyes. Fight it! Simon urged his uncle silently from within. Fight it!

Then with a hoarse whisper, his uncle beckoned him closer. Compliant, Simon came within arm's reach of the crucified figure. His uncle's mouth, agape, suddenly spewed forth a torrent of insects and worms.

"Noooo!" Repulsed, Simon backed away from the abominable scene before him.

Alone. Always alone.

Then words and thoughts that were not his own came to Simon. Simon yielded to the feeling that overcame him, kneeling in the dirt at the altar to recite these words — *prayers?* — taught to scare away the boogieman.

From ghoulies and ghosties, and long-leggedy beasties, and things that go bump in the night, Good Lord, deliver us!

Over and over the words were recited until the fear that gripped him began to slowly give way to assurance.

And faith.

"It won't wor..." a vile voice threatened before stumbling angrily. "You are a fool, Bishop. Your lack of faith is of no match for me."

Bishop? Did Simon actually hear the voice refer to the bishop? Acknowledging in his heart that he may not be alone after all, Simon joined in the recitation of the boogieman prayer.

Something within urged him on. Putting his soul, and what little faith remained after all these years into the prayers that came to him, he cried out the words with growing conviction. Together he and the bishop repeated the prayers despite the evil one's taunts. "From ghoulies and ghosties..."

The still and quiet air around Simon erupted into a relentless gale that violently kicked about dirt and debris. Beyond the raging wall of wind, Simon thought he could make out deformed figures dancing about.

"Fight it, boy," the bishop's familiar voice encouraged Simon. "There is yet hope."

But then the cross before him ignited into flames. Flames that quickly worked their way up the wooden beam. Taking Simon's uncle with him.

The skeleton of charred flesh that was once his

uncle called out to him before becoming engulfed in the blaze. Simon pivoted, shielding his eyes as the intense inferno scorched his back. "You can prove your love to Him. This is your shot at redemption. You can do it! You have to!"

Simon opened his eyes to an orphanage bed once belonging to an infant Bishop Reibold. Oblivious to Simon's presence, the young bishop was reciting another prayer now. The words formed in Simon's head as he joined the child beside him.

The Light of God surrounds me. The Love of God enfolds me. The Power of God protects me. The Presence of God watches over me. Wherever I am, God is, and all is well.

In unison they prayed to the Lord. For their lives.

But the air, electrically charged and unsettled, came alive like it did at the altar. It rapidly encircled the bed. Picking up speed, it spiraled about them faster until, with a loud roar, the floor under the bed gave way. Taking Simon with it.

A frail seven-year-old bishop yelled for Simon as he grabbed the bedpost for support.

Foul and hoarse, a cacophony of laughter rose above the rushing wind. The hot breath of the damned seared the hairs on their necks.

Simon was fast descending into a hellish abyss. Flying amid the flames snapping at his heels, unholy supernatural creatures welcomed his descent. Great lamentations rose from the bowels of the abyss — a hole so deep Simon was left without any concept of space.

Or time.

Fight it, Simon. His uncle's words. They, too,

filled his head. *You can do it, nephew.*

In his endless free-fall into a sea of fire, Simon concentrated on the prayers he and the bishop recited. The young Bishop Peter Reibold caught on and began again, too.

The prayers of the two eventually drowned out the wicked laughter. Simon, exhausted and near ready to admit defeat, found himself no longer falling. Sprawled out on the floor, he was once again in a room near the young Peter. Sweat saturated his forehead and stung his eyes. his clothes stuck uncomfortably to his body.

Peter, still visibly shaken, held steadfast to the bedpost with one hand. He extended the other to Simon.

There was still an overwhelming feeling that something unholy was present. Watching. Waiting. Simon wondered where Father Gordon was. Or if the flames that claimed his uncle was a trick.

"Hurry, the boogie man ith coming." The little boy spoke with a lisp. "Gwab my hand, Thimon. There ith no time."

Simon beheld the fear in the child's eyes. Palpable and real. How he hoped it would be over soon. That this was another dream. Another test.

Reaching for the boy's hand, something from the emptiness ensnared Simon's torso. Forcing breath from his lungs, the feeling of a million sharp teeth bore into him before pulling him under the bed. Into the hole where light refused to go he was sucked once more.

Little Peter Reibold shrieked. Bawling, the little boy was hysterical as he called out to Simon. "Juth gwab my hand. Juth gwab my hand!"

Wails and moans erupted from the emptiness below the bed as the demons awaited their prey.

Their prize.

Acrid and foul, the dark chasm spewed forth a poisonous air. Held within the tightened grip of the unknown, Simon's breathing became a series of short wheezes. He clawed at the wooden floor. Up under his fingernails he scraped bits of wood in his struggle to reach the bishop's extended hand.

It was no use. Simon's body, traumatized by the excruciating pain, was fast losing sensation. He heard the crunching of bone from whatever demon devoured him. Its evil venom now fast coursing through his veins. Held suspended between life and death, he beheld his own hands with their bloodied hemorrhaging holes.

It was over.

Simon could barely breathe. "Forgive me, Lord." Losing consciousness, he admitted what he knew all along. "I'm just not strong enough."

40

Father Jacob Dawz removed the gauze covering Friday's accident in the kitchen to examine his still-swollen hand. Even now, some thirty hours later, it seeped gobs of red and yellow. Though he severed the tip of his thumb, boring a cut to the bone on the fore and middle fingers of his left hand, medical treatment for the wound wasn't an option. Thoughts of his time at the Veteran's Hospital brought back ill memories that he didn't wish to experience again. Besides, there was little time now.

Jacob squeezed his pus engorged thumb. With slurping sounds, the odd colored, foul-smelling seepage fell thickly into the sink. Massaging the stubby digit, his attempt to drain it only resulted in forcing the skin to fall away from his entire thumb in one heavily saturated flap.

Pulling at the skin, he pulled a raw line across his palm. Still attached and hung up in the fleshy area between his middle and ring finger, the flap of skin came free with one quick tug.

Rubbing it between the thumb and index finger of his right hand, he regarded the flap of skin with curiosity. Sliding the bloody patch of skin over his tongue, he took in the metallic taste of his own blood without much hesitation or thought. A jolt of ecstasy electrified him as he sucked the tiny pieces of flesh still clinging to the patch of skin.

It was only when his eyes found his reflection in the mirror, the flap of skin hanging partly free from his mouth, that the human side of Jacob registered the surreal moment. Sickened by what he saw, he retched. The heaves came violently. All over the mirror and porcelain basin he expelled the contents of his stomach to a chorus of laughter.

Shaking with fear and outrage Jacob made a fist with his mutilated left hand, splitting the skin free from his sliced fingers. In an act of defiance, he slammed it hard against the pedestal sink. This time there was pain — immediate and agonizing enough to cloud his vision. He passed out. A disfigured mound of flesh on the cold linoleum floor.

Jacob awoke with a start in the base of the tree, sweating profusely and itchy as all hell.

He was back where he didn't want to be. A place he thought he escaped years ago. Something was crawling all over him. Spreading into streams over his body.

They were on his hands. In his hair. All over his face. Biting and tearing at his flesh.

Scrambling out into the sunlight, he realized his body was under attack. Jacob threw himself onto the ground, violently rolling to dislodge the Vietnamese flesh-eating fire ants. Memories of the eviscerated village baby coming back to him.

Unloading his belt of mags, he stood to run. The pain in his leg momentarily forgotten, he fell hard where he stood. Smacking his face against an unseen rock.

Blood poured from his swollen nose into his mouth. With each exhale, he expelled the pooling blood gathering about his lips.

Using his rifle to hoist himself up, he hobbled through the woods. All about him lay the dismembered bodies of both American and Viet

Cong soldiers. Foul tasting bile made its way up his throat as he worked his way through the destruction. Over and again he tripped and fell over the obstacle course of death.

Limping deeper into the jungle, he was horrified by the surrealistic nightmare before him. Trees, bare from chemicals sprayed by American forces, littered the landscape like remnants of a Salvador Dali painting come to life.

The throbbing in his leg was overwhelmed by the pain of the ants continuing to feed on him. Blood from his nose drew them to his face. Soon they would encompass his entire head and he wouldn't be able to see where he was going.

He sought a waterhole — anything — to extract the ants and to escape the sickening sights before him.

Already in his hair. Under his shirt. In his pants. The ants bit deeply. Pierced his flesh.

There was nowhere to run. Nowhere to hide. To escape. No way to fully dislodge the ants as they gathered around his bloodied nose. One over the other fighting. Clawing. Biting. Chewing.

Jacob could hold silent no longer.

He cried out at the top of his lungs only to have his cries echoed back at him. Ridiculing him.

Multiplying, the tiny killers worked their way over his face and into his mouth. Into his nostrils. Up his nose. Gnawing. Feeding. Over his eyes.

Jacob stumbled blindly. Never seeing the Claymore mine's trip wire. He went down wailing in pain. Twisting his already injured leg. In sheer defiance of the pain, he forced himself up onto his knees to shout out to the skies above him as the ants tore at his tongue. His throat. At through his cheeks.

"Why? Why do you bring me *back* to this Hell?"

A mixture of anguish and anger filled his voice. "You promised..."

Did he ever truly escape the jungle or was his life nothing more than a dream as he lay with the rest of his platoon. Dead. Dying.

"Fail me," came the answer in the form of an icy whisper as the bomb went off, "and you will pay."

The robed man kept Jacob alive long enough for him to feel every part of his part of his body ripped apart.

41

Disoriented, Simon vaguely sensed he was still alive. If nothing else, he was conscious.

"Thimon?" It was the young bishop.

To Simon, his time had come to an end. It didn't matter, though. He was not strong enough for what God intended. He never was. He failed. More than that, perhaps they failed each other.

Moments from now all would be forgotten. And Simon, free of responsibilities forged in another lifetime, would spend an eternity a captive of the damned.

"Thimon. Thimon. Thimon." A demonic voice mocked young Peter Reibold. "Thimon. I'm tho thcared. Thave me."

As the evil entity taunted the bishop, Simon questioned the Blessed Mother's choice. Why? Why did she choose him? What reason could Jesus Christ have for choosing Simon as the rock?

"Th-Thimon!" This time it really was little Peter, reaching out to Simon from somewhere far away.

Then another voice could be heard. Though familiar, it was too far away to identify with any surety. "Though he fall, he shall not be utterly cast down. For the Lord upholds him with His hand."

Then the younger bishop once more. Pressing on. Drawing nearer. "Th-Th-S-Th-S-S-Ssimon."

The tenor of his voice deepened. Grew older. Stronger. More resolute.

"Nooo!" A throng of voices from the dark void clamored at this sudden development, sending forth flames from the hole that set the bed — and Simon — afire. "We are Pluton. Prince of Fire!"

Bishop Peter Reibold's large adult hand was suddenly over Simon's, pulling the young man upwards through the void.

It wasn't enough. Whatever held him in the flames only bore down even more. Unwilling to relent.

"Hold onto my hand," came the voice of the adult bishop Simon knew. "I am here, son. Do not be afraid. I'm not leaving you."

But it was little comfort as the flames continued furiously working their way up Simon's legs, burning the clothes from his body. His blistered skin slipped away from his legs. In seconds, he would not even be able to see the bishop's hand.

Nor would it matter. The bed was an inferno. The smell of burning flesh strong in their nostrils.

The bishop held steadfast. His voice boomed above everything. A spark of light in the encroaching void. "I am here. Do not be afraid. You hear? You hold on."

But like all previous tests, it was too late. Darkness enveloped Simon's lifeless body of scorched flesh as it was torn in two.

* * *

Simon's final thoughts before he was torn asunder were of his wife. And their unborn baby.

Then a voice reached out to Simon from across the endless void. "I have prayed so that your faith will never completely be destroyed. So that when you fail, you will have the strength to repent. To turn once again to me." Voices, past *and* present came to Simon as he floated in the timeless ether of death.

Lord, I would never deny you. Words spoken by Simon so very long ago.

He thought of their baby again as an image of Mary holding a baby Jesus illuminated the dark emptiness before him.

"Satan has asked for you," the image of Jesus said to Simon. "He wants to manipulate you into doing his bidding."

Floating in the abyss, the images gave way to a speck of light lost in a horizon of obsidian darkness. As Simon drifted towards it, the speck began to spread from the center. From it, a thin ray became visible.

"I have prayed," the voice of Jesus said to Simon as the ray of light became a prism of brightness.

Clean. Exact.

"The eyes of the Lord are on the righteous. And His ears are open to their cry."

Pure. Warm.

Simon, embraced by the growing undulating light, had the feeling of flight. Of speed. He was moving toward its center.

"I have prayed so that your faith will never completely be destroyed," Jesus said to Simon as the white light rushed in on him, illuminating the vast empty space. "You will have the strength to repent. To turn once again to me."

Simon was suddenly aware of the bishop's hand before him. Holding it, Simon squeezed with all his might. Over the devilish screams piercing the air, Christ's words echoed in his ears. And then those of his uncle. "Fight it, Simon. There is hope."

All around Simon and the bishop, deluged in the flames of the burning bed, were familiar voices reciting prayers. Amid the developing intensity, they gave Simon strength. They drowned out the demons seeking to claim his soul.

Still tightly gripped by the bishop, the skin of their hands melted away as the bed — and the room he and the bishop occupied — combusted.

Simon's thoughts as he became one with the flames were of his baby. And of Jesus Christ.

Set your mind on things above, not on things on the earth. For you die, and your life is hidden with Christ in God. When Christ who is our life appears, then you also will appear with Him in glory.

He at last completed the connection — the bridge of time — begun that day at the bishop's rectory. Surrounded by those whose faith exceeded his own. Whose belief remained steadfast even when he wavered.

The Lord, Simon realized, *is* my strength. My fortress. My deliverer. In whom I will trust.

"I am," Simon Peter Free, the rock, fully acknowledged, "ready to die for you."

42

I mmersed in murky water, Simon couldn't see the bishop. But he knew the bishop was with him somewhere in this liquid world. Had to be. Simon propelled himself upwards, feeling his lungs expand with each stroke of his arms. His legs, useless now, made his efforts to reach the surface that much more demanding on his faculties.

Through the surface ripples, Simon was certain he recognized the shapes standing above him. Trick or not, he was still willing to take that chance. A hand penetrated the water. It stretched out to him as his lungs were about to burst. Simon drove toward it, clutching the immovable hand tightly.

Fear not, Kefa. I'm not going to let you go. I will never let you go.

The hand pulled him through the water. Followed by another hand. Together they drew Simon up towards the fisherman's small wooden boat.

Breaking the surface, Simon inhaled deeply. Welcomed the much-needed oxygen into his lungs. To his surprise, the saving hand he tightly clung to was revealed to be the hand that always offered him salvation. Father Gordon's hand was the other helping him up into the boat.

Jesus smiled at Simon. Placed a hand on Simon's shoulder. At once, it released from Simon the pain he carried for all those centuries. Those lifetimes. His failure, his guilt, absolved with the simplest of gestures.

"I have prayed so that your faith will never

completely be destroyed." He then pulled Simon close and embraced him. "Yours, Simon Peter, the *kefa*, is the Kingdom of Heaven. You will walk with me once more when this is over."

Enveloped in pure love. Forgiven. Simon wept as he was held. Accepted. Welcomed. Relieved. Comforted.

He survived. Survived the trial. He now knew his mission. Knew what he was meant to do. Faith renewed, he was not about to let go no matter what happened next.

Easter Sunday

APRIL 06, 1980

43

Father Tomassi whispered into Simon's ear. "Don't be afraid. You hear, son? Hold on."

The elder priest was holding vigil with Simon since early Saturday morning, refusing to leave Simon's bedside. Delicately holding the young man's bandaged hand, he assuaged Simon by recounting how he, the bishop, and Simon's wife were pulling for him.

Yet the part about Sarah pulling for Simon was a lie. She had problems of her own. At the moment, she was in labor.

Distraught over Simon's hospitalization early yesterday morning, Sarah didn't realize the baby shifted its position. This shift applied increased pressure to her bladder. During one of her false contractions, she urinated over herself thinking her water broke.

"Lightening," the doctor tried explaining to the two priests. "The medical term for the baby lowering itself into the pelvis is called Light—"

Father Joseph, demonstrating a rare show of uncharacteristic impatience, cut the doctor off. In a very short time, he had grown very fond of the young Mrs. Free. "Her contractions? What about her contractions?"

Finding the situation amusingly odd, the doctor wryly smiled to the dismay of both Tomassi and Joseph. "Where, may I ask, is the father?"

"In ICU," Tomassi said with a wave of his hand. "It's a long story."

"Guess that would explain her rather fragile

emotional state."

Joseph persisted. "Her contractions?"

"Should I be expecting you, then, in the birthing ward in place of the father, Father?" the doctor flippantly asked.

Tomassi could tolerate no more. "You have a singular wit, Doctor. Now, what about the damn contractions?"

Doctor Ethan Whitmore — the only one amused — managed a smug grin even as he straightened himself. "Look, I assure you. She's fine. The contractions were simply false labor pains. They're known as Braxton Hicks contractions. Close to term, it's not unusual for the body to prepare itself for the real thing."

Beholding the elder priest's genuine look of concern, the doctor then softened a bit. "Relax. It really is going to be okay. I've given her a sedative to take the edge off. In the meantime, we'll be keeping an eye on her for a few hours to see how she progresses. But given the circumstances, I think it's probably a good idea that she's already here."

Sarah, thanks to the sedative, slept through Saturday morning. But the doctor, concerned with her hydration levels, decided to keep her under hospital care until evening. Father Joseph kept vigil at her side, while Tomassi spent his time with Simon. Sure enough, around dinnertime, Sarah's cervix dilated to ten centimeters. It was only a matter of time before she delivered the baby.

Simon remained unchanged. While downgraded to critical but stable, his situation was still serious. It was also why for most of the last twenty-four hours Father Tomassi was with him, leaving only to place calls to the bishop, Father Francis, and to check up on Sarah. While Tomassi planned to run home to get some rest, he realized that he wouldn't have been able to sleep anyway. Feeling increasingly discouraged with each passing hour, the thought of whatever pivotal event in the history of the Church and mankind happening without Simon deeply troubled the elder priest.

He was even more saddened over his and Bishop Reibold's failure to properly guide the young man. They acted like senile old men. Now, because of their feebleness, a father wouldn't live to see the birth of his own child.

Father David Tomassi's old fear tugged at him. The images of Simon's bloody and inert body difficult to forget. He wondered how God could allow this to happen. Feeling powerless, he felt his faith shaken by it.

A twitch of Simon's hand a little over an hour ago kept his faith from completely shattering. He hoped it wasn't simply a reflex, believing that somehow things would turn out the way they were supposed to. Whatever that way was.

Tomassi continued whispering into Simon's ear. "I'm here, son. I'm not going to let you go."

* * *

Head lowered in prayer, Tomassi floated in and out of a dreamless sleep when Simon's grip went tight. He awoke to find the young man sitting up in his bed. Soaked with perspiration, his eyes were as wide as half-dollars.

As Simon's vitals went off the charts, a commotion was underway at the Nurse's Station.

Simon's initial prognosis hadn't been good. In fact, as Tomassi only learned after Simon stabilized, the young man had already "expired" several times.

One of the last times was on the operating table during surgery. A loss of blood requiring transfusions, a series of strokes, and a cardiac arrest led his team of doctors to believe that any recovery would be limited. That is, if one occurred at all.

What Tomassi was witnessing was nothing short of a miracle. "You did it. You really did it," Father Tomassi whispered. His hand firm in Simon's tightly bandaged grip.

Simon said nothing. He only stared vacantly ahead.

Tomassi noticed for the first time how much Simon's youthful features had visibly aged since their time at the bishop's residence. Once brown hair was now peppered with white and gray. Unkept, it only amplified the drawn haggardness of his unshaven face.

Simon then spoke in the same tone of voice he used when Jon Gordon was on his deathbed. "It's Jacob, David."

This was not Simon, the young man talking. It was Simon, the kefa.

"What?"

A group of nurses entered wheeling something on a cart.

Turning to address Father Tomassi, Simon spoke only one word before his grip loosened and a staff of frantic nurses besieged him. "Judas!"

44

The bishop stirred but was unable to move. He was choking on his own vomit. Through the thick haze of an unnatural slumber that left him heavy lidded, he forced himself awake.

There was something about the room and his current state that aroused fear in him. His digital clock blinked 3:00 AM. And the bulb to his bedside lamp would not switch on.

An odd smell emanated from under the bedroom door. He yelled for Father Jacob.

Sick as he slept, his mess covered the blankets. The sheets and his bed clothes clung to his body. A body bathed in a thick, unnatural sweat.

Coughing, deep and prolonged, he rose out of bed without even bothering with his robe or slippers. Upright, his stomach turned almost as fast as his head spun. He felt even weaker than the day before. Figuring he could sleep most of his sickness off before tending to at least one Easter service, he realized this wasn't going to happen. Even Father Gordon's funeral was postponed, what with David tending to Simon and the bishop still ill.

Bishop Reibold then reminded himself to search the scrapbook. More bile worked its way up his throat. He expelled what little was left in his stomach on the floor at the foot of the bed.

A light flickered from under his door. Someone was home. He wondered who. He wondered what time it was.

The bishop groaned trying to remember if he discussed the arrangements for Sunday's services with Jacob yet.

There was no answer when he called for Jacob again.

"Time to call it like it is," he grumbled to himself. Once he was better and things calmed down, he was going to consider having some additional priests brought in. "I can't deal with everything myself anymore. Even having Jacob isn't enough. Damn it to hell. This getting old stuff sucks."

Either that or it was time to retire he admitted openly for the first time in his life.

Falling back on the bed, he wiped a layer of sweat from his face and neck. Pulling at the clothes clinging to his boiling skin, he vaguely recalled parts of his latest dream.

He breathed — with great difficulty — a sigh of relief recalling how he and Simon defeated the demons. Still, part of him wondered how much of his dream was reality and how much was metaphor.

He chuckled at the absurdity of the situation as a fly casually buzzed his ear. A situation that only Tomassi and Simon would understand.

"Yeah, no kidding, Doc," he said to himself waving away what he was sure was an imaginary fly, "I was traversing the celestial plane when I found myself becoming very ill." That would go over well. He'd be committed to a rubber room for sure.

Questioning the lucidity of these experiences only moved him that much more to phone the hospital. To check in on Simon. It had been some time since he last received an update from David. He just needed to get his bearings first.

Again, the bile rose in his throat. But before he could swallow it back, he was on his knees heaving a mess all over the floor.

Again the buzzing. This time in both — no

around — his ears.

Something was wrong. Very wrong. But he couldn't quite put his finger on it, much less maintain focus for long. He rolled over onto his back exhausted. Hot.

Damn hot!

Why do you even bother? A voice derided from somewhere in the room. Or was it inside his head.

He neither argued nor moved. By the grace of God, he so badly wanted to close his eyes and sleep.

Above him on the ceiling he noticed for the first time an amassing group of flies.

"Jacob?" The bishop called out weakly in response to an odd noise in the hall just beyond his bedroom door. Perplexed by the haze that fogged his thinking, he wasn't sure if he was again dreaming.

A thought occurred to the bishop as he watched the growing cluster of black flies. A thought of his time back in the archbishop's rectory in Massachusetts some days earlier.

Ben. He closed his eyes. Jacob.

"Oh, Jacob." The bishop spoke the name in what was barely a whisper.

Their demeanor. Yes, it was their demeanor. Like they already knew each other. He cursed himself for being so blind. For not recognizing the signs.

I know all about your precious prophecy.

Opening his bloodshot eyes he was once again aware of a strange smell saturating the room.

Someone — something — was in his head. No. In his room.

Then the flies above him dispersed. Flying about the room, the growing cloud of insects turned on one another. Clashing, they fought for dominance. For the flesh they were about to feast on.

"Oh, Jacob. Why didn't I see it?" Reibold began

to sob in gasps. Tears blending with a new layer of sweat covering his cheeks as the flies crawled over his face. Beginning their feast.

Invading his ears. Crawling over his lips and into his mouth. Venturing into his nostrils.

Did Jacob know about the prophecy? He was mistaken. He had to be.

Did Jacob overhear anything on Good Friday when David and Simon were over? Did this mean Ben also knew? Or was the bishop overreaching in his sickly condition?

With great difficulty, he brushed away a collection of flies. It was a wasted effort. They immediately took up residence once again over his face and neck.

He needed to call an ambulance. But the voice in his head worked against his own thoughts. Chiding him. Distracting him. Even above the buzzing of the many winged harbingers of evil.

Senile. Old. Weak. So stupid.

He fought to focus on the growing creaks from behind the door. Fought against the swarm of insects alive and moving over his face.

Against the nagging voice in his head threatening to push him over the edge.

You don't stand chance.

"What demon dares?" he shouted, slipping in his vomit as he struggled to rise.

We are Pluton!

The bishop strode across the room — through the buzzing black cloud — with a sudden rush of adrenaline. Convinced he was indeed still dreaming, he reached for the handle of the buckling door.

You lack faith. You are no match for me. For us, the voice inside his head roared as the bishop threw open the door.

"Weeping Jesus!"

This was no dream. It took but a heartbeat to register the intensity with which everything burned. For the bishop to feel the skin of his right-hand melt instantaneously onto the doorknob.

The opening of the door unleashed a conflagration that overtook the rectory while the bishop slept. In his sickened state, and further exacerbated by the gasses released from the burning carpets and furniture, the bishop did not have a chance.

Meeting his death in the arms of the Prince of Fire, Demon Pluton, he was kept alive long enough to register the pain.

Long enough to see his own self run in melted pools of boiling pus. Long enough to witness sizzling flesh slide from bones before his boiled brain imploded within his skull.

45

Father Jacob made his way to the elevator. Running late, he impatiently checked his watch. It was already nearly 8:00. No doubt Saint Catherine's Rectory had been discovered by now. Its frame probably the only thing standing.

Three hours earlier he made his first call to Pope Pontius. Even though it was around 1:00 PM in Rome, well after the pope presided over the annual Easter prayer, Jacob's call was not received.

Jacob patted his left breast. Beneath his coat were the documents of the prophecy he confiscated from the bishop's scrapbook. In his haste to reach the hospital, he had yet to thoroughly review them himself.

But he also carried what the pontiff passed along to him that day at Saint John's. What was it he heard the bishop say Friday night in the company of David Tomassi and Simon? Something about Simon being the Savior?

Jacob grinned. The pope's missive tied in with what the voices inside his head told him. What the Pontifex Maximus passed along to him was proof that while there were days he questioned his sanity, he truly was doing the Lord's work.

Wasn't he?

Brushing thoughts of doubt from his mind, he went about his task. Savior or not, after he finished killing Simon, like he killed the boy's uncle, he would see to it that the pope received what he retrieved from the bishop.

And for his allegiance he was sure a promotion

within Vatican City was all but assured after such a productive morning. Clearly the defining moment Pontius spoke of a week earlier.

From the bishop's study Father Jacob began his day by consuming some healthy portions of cognac for liquid strength before dispersing the remaining bottles of liquor over the floor. The table. The bookshelves.

After seizing the bishop's scrapbook while the old man slept, he then entered the guest room where Bishop Umgumbwe slept. As luck would have it, the South African bishop was awake. He had been on his knees praying.

How fitting! Jacob thought at the time.

Wasting no time, Jacob unsheathed his eighteen-inch jungle machete. A keepsake from his 'Nam days.

There was no hesitation. No second-guessing.

Bishop Umgumbwe's head was cleaved nearly clean off. With veins and arteries ruptured, blood sprayed freely in all directions. His severed esophagus and trachea produced raspy audible gasps as his autonomic functions kicked in. His expression — one of absolute horror and shock — remained unchanged but for the moving lips. Umgumbwe's head hung to one side, held fast by the few remaining strands of connective tissue and cartilage.

With the spine disconnected at the base of the skull, it took a moment before the rest of his body registered what happened. The South African bishop's body then buckled awkwardly into a rapidly expanding puddle of discharging fluids.

Though perhaps unnecessary, as it didn't affect his overall task, Jacob still went about dismembering the sixty-something year old bishop. It would take nearly forty minutes to hack him into pieces small enough for the priest to be satisfied. So saturated was the carpet by this time that the blood seeped through the floor and was already beginning to bleed from the ceiling of the room below.

Sweaty and drained, a bloodied Jacob showered and dressed in his clerical best before phoning the Vatican. Unable to get through to the pontiff, he descended the stairs to the basement to complete the next phase of his mission.

But the antiquated gas boiler system wasn't easy to mess with. He tried kicking one of the pipes loose to no avail. Too much physical exertion. It took a tire iron to disconnect the gas connections, releasing the hidden toxin into the air.

Prior to leaving, he ensured the windows of the residence were tightly closed before turning all four burners of the gas stove on high.

It didn't take long for the gas to build up from the basement. Soon the place was a burning maelstrom.

As Jacob accessed the ramp onto Route 9 towards Nazara, the multicolored tendrils of flame could be seen in the distance clawing out into the dark early morning sky.

He would make one stop on his way to Bethlehem General: to once more phone the Vatican and to comb through the bishop's scrapbook before discarding the evidence.

The elevator came to a halt. Closely monitored, Simon was still in ICU. His condition stabilized, he was listed as fair but still under close observation. At least for the next twenty-four hours.

Short of a miracle, the woman at the front desk relayed to Jacob.

Jacob walked through the open doors, turning left before proceeding to the Nurse's Station. Passing the waiting room, he glanced in to find the dark, unlit room empty.

"Yes, Father?" a stoutly nurse asked when Jacob approached the station. She was sitting behind the counter stuffing her face with an egg-biscuit sandwich. Jacob looked her over for a nametag.

"Miss... Ah, Bonnie. I was wondering if you could direct me to Simon Free's room?"

"403A. Just down the hall." She pointed towards the hall perpendicular to where the station was located. "Are you with the other priests? No wonder he came out of that coma!"

"Excuse me?" Jacob was momentarily taken aback. "Oh, yes," he acknowledged politely, quickly recovering with a smile. He cursed under his breath at his oversight — a by-product of his overconfidence. Naturally Father Tomassi would be here.

"Why, yes. I am with the others," he lied. "And I was wondering if you could tell me where I might find Father David Tomassi."

The nurse wiped a piece of egg from the corner of her mouth with a napkin. She called over her shoulder to another nurse Jacob could not see. "Diane," she said with a mouthful of biscuit, "any idea where that nice older priest went?" Turning back to Jacob she made an embarrassing admission. "He reminds me of my grandfather."

"I think he said something about going to the cafeteria to get a bite to eat," the other nurse replied from the back room.

"Oh? And when was that?" Jacob asked.

"Not too long ago, I guess," Diane replied, coming to stand in the doorway. "It's been quite a morning. Your friend's a celebrity."

"Is he now?"

"If you're looking for the cute one..."

"Father Joe?" Diane asked.

"Yes. I think that's his name," Nurse Bonnie said. "He's in the waiting room."

"Yes, Father Joe... good ol' Father Joe. Thank you." Though he saw no one in the waiting room, Jacob wondered where they might all be hiding.

"If the other one comes up, should we say you're looking for him?"

Jacob held up both hands. "No, that's quite all right. Thank you. I'll go sit with Simon for a while. He needs all the prayers we can give him, you know."

Bonnie watched the priest walk away. An odd fellow, despite his politeness. Tense. Judging by the veins unnaturally protruding from his neck. Or anxious about his friend, she guessed, finishing off her breakfast sandwich.

But something about his eyes made her jittery. Black wells. Dilated. Too large for his pupils.

Seconds later, she was preoccupied once more with paperwork, forgetting all about Father Jacob.

And his eyes.

"Diane," a skittish Bonnie said, reaching for the ringing phone.

"Yeah?"

"Remind me to lay off the caffeine."

46

The priest stood in the doorway. This was going to be easier than he thought. Simon lay resting. But far from comfortable with tubes up his nose and in his arms. Jacob even noticed the patches stuck to Simon's chest with wires running to the monitors.

The body on the bed was already aware, however, of his visitor's presence. "Hello, Father Jacob," Simon said weakly.

To Jacob's surprise, Simon opened his eyes to face the visitor at the door. "Hello, Savior."

Simon faintly smiled in response. Jacob wondered what was behind that smile. If he wanted, he *could* summon the power to find out.

Quietly closing the door, he sat in the chair beside the bed. "Everyone already knows, huh?"

Weakly, Simon humored the priest. "Knows what?"

"Oh, please. Such humbleness is quite unbecoming even for someone of your celebrity status. Seems everyone in the hospital knows how you 'miraculously' came out of your coma. As good as dead, too. Only one who is blessed, such as yourself, could ever hope to survive what you did."

It was true. Simon was here, having survived his trials, each more violent and gruesome. Like dying a thousand deaths only to be re-born again. And again.

Yes, he was alive and breathing. But his trials — his tests of faith — aged him lifetimes over. His aged features and paralyzed legs reminded him so.

Perhaps it was the bridging of his past life with his present; perhaps it was going to Hell and back.

"And just what did I survive?" Simon asked, interested how Jacob knew so much.

Jacob sneered at the sly smile that continued to play at the corners of Simon's lips. "Do you dare mock me?"

"Don't you mean *us*?"

The priest's expression revealed what Simon speculated: that he was unaware of how much he was being manipulated. And by whom. Or what.

Struck with wanting to appeal to the human within Jacob before he did something there was no coming back from, Simon reached out to the man before him.

"Jacob, you don't have to do this. Your soul hasn't been completely corrupted. God *will* accept you into his kingdom—"

"Lies!" Jacob charged. With an air of haughtiness, he then proclaimed: "I will have my own kingdom."

"At what price? Look at what it has already cost you."

Jacob stood, bruised by Simon's all-too-accurate assessment. "You've no right to judge me, Savior. Believe in your God and I'll believe in mine. Leave it at that. Our parts will play themselves out."

"But you doubt your evil allegiance. I sense it. Can see it in your eyes. I can see through you. A light still shines within you."

"Enough!" Jacob roared, jerking his hands upwards to extinguish the lights in the room in a show of power. "Disillusioned you are. Whom do you serve? Mankind? God's greatest creation? Come now. You protect beings that are inferior. Imperfect."

Simon did not respond. He instead focused on the slight twitch developing in Jacob's mannerisms.

"See, you agree. If man were so important to your God, why not be the one to protect him? The truth is no one knows your God anymore. They've been abandoned. Deep within their souls they know this to be true. How else to explain the events in the garden? Your God... He knew this. But still He chose to curse man with little meaning. Insignificant and with little substance. That is," Jacob grinned, "until my master broke free of your God's authority."

Simon tried to reason with Jacob. "We are instruments of higher powers that neither of us will ever fully understand. Perhaps we're even pawns. Do you really think you're going to change that?"

"It is not I who will—"

"Scriptures. Gnostic texts. All of them are wrong. Satan took the fall. But it's been Lucifer all along. Lucifer hid behind Satan and the other dark angels. He's been manipulating them from the very beginning."

"Regardless, there can be but one savior, Simon."

"Listen to what I am telling you. Lucifer's angry with God."

"And why shouldn't he be?"

"He's been jealous of God's reign and His influence since the beginning of time immemorial. He wants to destroy everything God created."

"Including mankind?"

"Especially mankind. He hates that God protects them. Favors them."

"And just what is mankind? An experiment? Farce? Inferior beings with choice is an experiment ripe for failure. And nearly everyone has failed. You see, human beings *must* sin to feel saved. How twisted is that? How ironic is it that your God created a race of sinners and then..."

"You were once human yourself."

"...punishes them for doing that which they have been programmed to do? Finest creation, oh please."

Father Joseph came rushing in, interrupting them before Simon could respond. "Father Tomassi! Simon! Sarah is having the baby!"

Turning to Joseph, Jacob's expression went from one of surprise to one of pure exasperation as he began connecting the dots to the master plan.

He had been so shortsighted. Why didn't his master know this?

His smoldering eyes now turned to the invalid. "You knew I didn't know. Didn't you?"

Joseph, shocked to see this strange priest before him, moved forward to protect Simon. "Father, can I help you?"

He was cut off when Jacob lifted his hand. Seizing Joseph's throat, Jacob effortlessly lifted him from the floor without touching him.

Simon weakly entreated the wicked priest. "Let him go."

As Joseph's throat tightened under Jacob's power, he peered into the assailant's vacuous eyes. Set within dark hollow sockets, yellow pupils proved the presence of something unholy. "Ever the faithful one. Do you really believe in this Christ of yours?"

"I... Ack! I..." was all Joseph could manage reaching for the Rosary Beads in his blazer.

Aware of the legion of demons making their way to the surface inside Jacob, Simon fought his infirmed frame. Pulling the tubes from his nose, he was determined to get out from behind the demon-priest. To help Joseph. "Joseph, get—"

"Silence," Jacob commanded.

Lifting his other hand, Jacob delighted in

watching Simon claw at his own throat. As his eyes rolled back to reveal only its whiteness, his tongue retreated under the force of his collapsing windpipe.

Jacob asked again, humored by the petty human before him who claimed to be a man of the cloth. Little did the men of today know what that meant. Soft. Weak. "Do you really think you know your Christ? This Jesus? Have you that much faith to wait a lifetime for Him never to return?"

A group of hospital staff was suddenly about them, tipped off by Simon's monitors.

Joseph continued to fumble for the beads while his own esophagus crushed beneath Jacob's power. Before him, he recognized the demon-priest for what it was: a cursed mortal manipulated to carry out the Dark Lord's evil bidding. Within the icy grasp of his attacker, Joseph's near-unconscious state gave him momentary powers of acute perceptiveness. He became aware of a merry band of evil disfigured spirits gathered round the dying Simon.

Gasping his last breaths, he bemoaned the brutal, undeserving death awaiting them all.

47

Father Tomassi finished his prayer and strained to stand. "But deliver us from evil. Amen." Closing his small prayer book, he made the sign of the cross on its cover reciting the words "Pray for me, my dear sister, Laura" before returning the book to the inside breast pocket of his blazer.

Earlier he retreated to the hospital chapel instead of the cafeteria to pray for Simon to continue his miraculous recovery. And to find even more answers to the questions he and the bishop had about the prophecy. But after some prayers and suffering through the flaring pain in his joints from idleness these past couple of days, he thought it best to stand for a while.

With heavy heart, he finally made the decision to head home. There was so much to do, the least of which was getting some rest, that he was concerned. He wanted to check in on the bishop, still gravely ill since they last saw each other. Then there was the matter of Father Francis and the postponed funeral arrangements for Father Gordon.

Unlike yesterday morning when everything appeared bleak, there *were* signs of hope. Simon was fully conscious. And he spoke!

It didn't mean Simon was in the clear yet. In fact, this was probably the beginning of a very long road to recovery. Nonetheless, it was a start. Even if Father Tomassi did not know how any of it figured into their plans.

Tomassi chided their latest actions. Damn dotards they were, thinking they possessed the power, the fealty, to see such a monumental task through.

Suddenly feeling ancient and useless, he resigned himself to the present. He would have Father Joseph stay with Simon for the few hours necessary until his return. But he made a mental note to check on the status of Sarah's labor before heading home.

He faced the tabernacle to make the sign of the cross. So much for Easter being the holiday of hope.

Tomassi then turned to exit as the candles in the little chapel were unexpectedly extinguished. Darkening the room.

"David."

At once, the whispering voice was recognized. He fell to his knees.

"David."

Tomassi cried out in the dark to his sister. Arms outstretched. "Oh, my dear Laura. I am here. Blessed be to God."

A tap on the shoulder shocked the kneeling clergyman. Losing his balance, Tomassi tumbled clumsily forward.

"Father Tomassi? David Tomassi?" A young female attendant peered down at him from an awkward upside-down angle.

From the floor, Tomassi saw the door to the hallway open behind her, illuminating the room with a sliver of light.

Embarrassed. Feeling old and silly, the priest rose unsteadily with the attendant's assistance. Brushing himself off, he apologized before speaking to the silhouette. "Yes, I am Father David Tomassi. What can I do for you, my dear?"

"Something's happened with Simon," she said urgently.

The words immediately refocused Father

Tomassi's attention.

"His monitors are off the charts. They really need you up there."

He couldn't help but reach out to hug the young girl. "My goodness! Thank you. Thank you."

Moments after rushing from the chapel, he forgot all about the female attendant who didn't follow behind. Had he looked back, he would have seen a bright flash of celestial light rekindle the votive candles. He would have also seen the angel — once Laura Angiola Tomassi — fade from her corporeal form to ascend back to Heaven. But not before raising her hands skyward in prayer for her dear brother.

48

Father Tomassi used the stairs, unwilling to wait for the elevator. Reaching the fourth floor, he was met with flies and a gruesome scene. Covering his nose and mouth with a handkerchief, he fought the urge to retch. To draw strength, he recited a verse from Psalms.

When the heavy fire door slammed shut behind him, he immediately knew he was in the presence of evil.

The elderly priest warily made his way around the mutilated bodies lying in pools of red. Reaching Simon's room, he found Father Joseph in the clutches of a demon once introduced as Father Jacob Dawz.

Cursing himself for being daft, Tomassi now understood Simon's uncle's "Judas in brethren's skin" reference. It was a fellow cleric all along.

Observing Jacob's swollen oddly colored neck and distorted features, Tomassi couldn't believe how much Jacob had changed — transformed — in such a short time.

An image from the other day flashed in his mind. It was of him on the floor holding the kefa while the bishop provided cover from Jacob who had walked in on them.

Father Tomassi sighed with a heavy heart. He suddenly realized why he'd been unable to reach the bishop since the one phone call early yesterday.

The demon-priest's distended face turned towards his elderly counterpart, his clergy accouterments torn and tattered with burgundy splotches.

A listless Father Joseph hung suspended above the floor, laboriously gasping for air. His eyes rolled wildly about in their sockets. Beyond them Simon lay lifeless. Covered in flies.

"Have you come to challenge us, too, old man?" Jacob growled.

"Wh-What have you done?"

Unable to contain the tears blurring his vision, Tomassi struggled to speak.

"Oh, that's right. You don't like death. Do you, David? Is this a little too much for you? We can remedy that." Touching fingers to lips, he blew Tomassi a kiss.

Tomassi let out a silent cry as his left hand spasmed. Then seized. Clutching his arm, Tomassi fought the cold tingling sensation snaking through his veins. A few short heartbeats later, his lifeless body slumped to the floor.

49

The doctor couldn't believe what he was seeing. He blinked several times. Why hadn't he identified this earlier? He was thankful for the mask covering his face because then the nurses would have seen his expression. Nervous. Worried. There was no more time to reflect on the situation. The monitors were all coming to life. He needed to act. "The baby's breeching!" he announced.

"Heart rate rapidly increasing," a nurse to his right warned.

"Blood pressure dropping," said another.

"She's tearing! Prepare for an episiotomy. We're going to have to cut her."

And then Doctor Ethan Whitmore did something he hadn't done in nearly twenty years. He hesitated.

* * *

Some twenty-four hours ago, surrounded by men of God, Sarah Free tried to rationalize her husband's apparent suicide attempt. Exhausted. Emotionally spent. Her feelings of abandonment left her overcome with grief.

She felt lost. Broken.

And the latest incident with Simon had taken a toll. The cost: quite possibly their baby.

Her baby.

Now, with the cervix 100% effaced, this was the real thing. And so was the intense pain she was feeling.

Relying on her Lamaze techniques, Sarah insisted

on being in complete control of her faculties. Refusing an epidural, she was still hooked up to an I.V. because of her hydration levels.

But the pain... Was this normal?

And she was certain she heard the doctor say something about a breech. How could this be? In between tears, she tried her best to focus despite the din surrounding her. Despite the large medical staff now involved in ushering her baby into the world.

She tried her best to breathe. To remain calm.

"My baby," she cried softly to herself, closing her eyes. "Please help my baby."

Suddenly she felt a sharp, searing pain from between her legs unlike anything ever felt before. Letting out a blood-curdling scream, she swam in and out of consciousness.

"Oh, my God! Something's not right," she tried to tell the doctors as darkness consumed her. "Something's not right!"

"Marie..."

Sarah opened her eyes to find herself in a small clearing near a large, sparkling river. Rising from a bed of flowers set against a background of lush green — soft as cotton — grass, she looked out across a river to see her husband, of all people, advancing in a small wooden boat.

"Sarah Marie."

"Simon?" She spoke his name with some surprise. Then spontaneously waved to him.

She ran to greet him at the shore. "What's going on? Am I dreaming? Am I dead?"

Into ankle-high water, Simon stepped out of the boat to pull it ashore. Though barefoot, Sarah noticed he was wearing her favorite tee shirt and jeans. She always thought he looked sexy in this specific outfit. Rugged even.

Embracing her, he held her tight. Close. Like in high school. When they first fell in love. He held her like he would never let her go. When he pulled back to face her, she marveled at his features. She knew it was Simon. But now, so close, the face before her wasn't as she remembered. Gone was the shadow of pain that was always a part of his countenance.

He looked older. Aged.

"Walk with me," he said, taking her by the hand.

They stopped to sit on a protruding boulder alongside the bank of the river. Simon cupped the side of her face, caressing her cheek with his thumb.

She moved into his hand, closing her eyes. Upon opening them, she found Simon intently studying her. His loving gaze melted her heart, reminding her of their courtship. She kissed his thumb before smiling adoringly.

"We are the chosen ones, Sarah," Simon said to her gently. "But it's only the beginning."

"Chosen ones?"

How she didn't want the idyllic moment to end. She realized she wasn't as afraid of the future as she was when they talked on Thursday. Nor was she as angry as when the priest pressed her for an answer about whether she believed her husband.

Even in this state, however, she was still far from understanding what it was Simon proposed.

But did it matter?

Somewhere in her, scratching to break free, doubt still existed. Threatening the truth. If she even knew what that was.

"It is true. All of it," Simon said to her surprise. "I didn't understand because there wasn't time to.

Uncle Matthew died too soon. And the others forgot."

"Forgot?" She reached out to touch her husband's face.

Tender were his expressions, free of the pain and sadness that had consumed him for so long. She was most astonished by how his face glowed before her now.

"This is my second chance."

"Whatever do you mean?"

Sarah watched his lips closely as he spoke. She wanted to run her fingers over them. She wanted to press hers against his.

"A long time ago, I denied Him when I told Him I wouldn't. I denied I knew Him. Too much of a coward. He entrusted me with something sacred and I let Him down. I have continued to let Him down, many lifetimes over, pushing myself farther and farther away from Him. Not this time. This is my second chance. My chance to prove my love. My worthiness."

"I still don't understand."

"Christ entrusted me with the Church — to tend to His lambs, the people — until His return. We, Sarah... you and I will see to that. He will return and we will be the ones responsible for making it possible. We shall bring about the prophecy. The sacrifices of those before us, like Pope Silvestre, will not have been in vain."

"Who?" Sarah searched his eyes. "Prophecy?"

"Someday you will understand the journey of those before us."

"What can we possibly do, Simon? You don't even have a job and I'm about to have a baby. *Our* baby."

"Sarah, this may be mankind's last chance."

"We don't even pray." Thoughts of Simon shunning the Church because of what happened to his uncle came back to her. Then there were her own feelings of betrayal. Of abandonment. Anger. She never forgave the Lord for taking her father away from her.

Simon embraced her hands in his and brought them up to his lips. Kissing them, he then revealed what he came to know as the true prophecy: "You are to be the mother of the next Christ. The beginning of the Second Coming is upon us."

"I am to be the mother of..." A tidal wave of emotions rushed in on her, spilling tears from blinking eyes. "The *next* Christ?"

Shame as much as pride at the honor overwhelmed her. She was just as guilty of abandoning the Church as Simon was. Even if Simon wasn't aware of it.

"Who am I to be the mother of the next Christ? Simon, I..."

"I know," Simon said soothingly. "I know."

He wiped at her tears as she mouthed an apology before lowering her head.

"We are the only ones who can usher in the next Savior. It is He who will walk among mankind once more. And it is He who will meet the Antichrist.

"See, Lucifer hoped to return after Christ gave mankind a thousand years to freely choose their own path. But Pope Silvestre II tricked him into delaying his coming for an additional thousand years. Given a chance to prove itself during this time, mankind failed. Mankind failed in the first thousand years and is failing miserably now. Because of this failure, Lucifer's power has grown more than the Lord God anticipated. And darkness has entered the halls of His Church. The Great Battle, the Battle of

Armageddon, is not far off."

"Battle? Armageddon?" Sarah trembled at what sounded inconceivable. And then, looking to her husband, she asked, "What am I supposed to do if these are truly the End Times?"

"Everything rests on the baby. You will need to keep the baby safe until his destiny is revealed."

"But Simon, who am I? I'm not worthy. I didn't even believe you."

"Sarah..."

"I, too, was angry at God for so many things."

"Sarah..."

"And if he's born of color, he'll be persecuted."

"Our child's fate rests with the will of God. It is time to believe once again. To have faith."

Simon smiled reassuringly.

Mesmerized by his strength and resolve, Sarah was stirred by the very qualities she knew him to possess. That attracted him to her. "What are you going to do?" she asked.

"My job is not finished. And there isn't much time. My faith has already been tested. But now that Lucifer knows who *you* are. *You*, Sarah, will face the next test. That's why I have come to you. I have come to you so that you will know how much I love you — have always loved you — and so that you will know your key role in all of this."

"Lucifer? The angel cast from Heaven?"

"The very one. He hid behind Satan and the Dark Angels throughout time. But he is the architect set on bringing about the Apocalypse and the end of the world as we know it."

"How will I be tested?" Sarah put her hands onto her husband's chest. "And where will you be?"

"About that. There is something I must confess to you now."

Sarah felt his chest rise and fall with each breath. Leaning in, she lay her head to his chest as his arms embraced her tightly.

But then she felt him hold his breath. The words that followed struck her hard. "I won't be returning."

Sarah jerked her head up, eyes wide and moist once again. "What do you mean? Who will help me raise our child?"

Taking her fingers, he ran them over the scars set within his palms. "I am no longer alive." Then he brought her soft hands up to his lips to kiss them. "My time on earth is nearly over."

"But..."

Sarah was not ready to accept this. How was she to be the mother of the next Christ, a Biblical figure almost two thousand years old? And without Simon? Questions came to her that demanded answers.

"Simon, who did this to you? Why me? And what is this impending battle?"

Simon stood before once more holding her face in his hands. He heard her questions. Felt her fear.

"I love you. In time, everything will be revealed." He kissed her forehead.

She could still clearly hear his voice as he pulled away from her, returning —no, floating— back to the river. "I have always loved you, Sarah Burnett. I always will," he said pushing the boat into the water before climbing in.

No longer in shirt and jeans, she noticed he was rowing to the other side of the river wearing a robe of some kind. "I will be with you forever in spirit, Sarah. Until you join me."

On the bank beyond the shore across from her, she saw a crowd of people waiting for Simon. Among them were his parents. And her own father, flanked by her brother, Franky.

From the water and into the crowd that immediately surrounded him, Simon's uncle emerged. He had survived Lucifer's army. He would not be the only one.

The group of people he stood with turned to wait for Simon.

Sarah watched closely as her husband paused halfway to his destination to reach into the water. There she observed Simon pull a large man with white hair up out of the river and into the boat. The word *bishop* was carried to her by way of the wind.

Searching the crowd of people beyond Simon and the bishop in the boat, she again caught sight of her father. This time her father also saw Sarah. And he raised his hand to her.

Sarah waved back. Unsure of the future.

50

In the hallway the demon-priest cast aside Father Joseph with little effort. No longer interested in the dead mortal, his thoughts were now on the soon-to-be-born Savior. Closing his demonic eyes, he listened for the heartbeat of a newborn. Head tilted, his nostrils flared at the scent of newborn flesh. A few floors up, in the west end of the hospital, is where he would find the child in the Maternity Wing.

With great effort, he composed his swollen features. Removing his bloody rags, he replaced them with Father Tomassi's clergyman dress. Shaking Tomassi's blazer, he was careful to avoid contact with the older priest's little black book. The missal fell out of the pocket and onto the floor. After some deep breaths, Jacob continued to relax himself back to his more humanly form before setting off to find the baby.

* * *

"Joseph. Rise."

Father Joseph opened his eyes before reflexively drawing his hands to his throat expecting the worst. But after several gasps and some hard swallows, his breathing leveled. He was relieved to discover his throat intact.

Sitting up, the first sight to hit him was the incredible amount of blood everywhere. The second: Father Tomassi lying nearly naked in the middle of the hall.

Seeing Father David Tomassi down — and in

such a humiliating way — greatly distressed Joseph. After all, this was his mentor. A man who seemed immortal. Try as he might, he couldn't stifle the cry that came to his lips. "Oh, David."

The young priest was summoned. Heard his name. Joseph did a one eighty, but saw nothing. Or no one. Remembering Simon, he ran to the doorway of Simon's room to find him lifeless on his hospital bed covered with dead flies. Visible from a half-open mouth was a swollen blue tongue. Blood present in the openings of his nose and ears.

Stumbling over to him, he lowered Simon's eyelids out of respect while inwardly cursing the evil responsible for such a heinous act.

"Joseph."

A clean wind stirred above the stench of death. Joseph swore he smelled something pure over the bloodshed. Hearing his name again, he pivoted. This time his eyes fell on Simon. A standing Simon.

"Y-You're alive!" Joseph exclaimed joyfully. He moved in to embrace Simon only to realize it was a projection. An apparition. A spirit. "B-But how?"

"My mortal body lies as you see it."

Joseph looked away from Simon to the lifeless form still on the bed.

"There is little time to explain. Jacob is going after the baby."

"The baby! Oh, no. You don't mean *your* baby?"

Simon nodded.

"What should I do? What would you have me do?"

"Father Tomassi."

"I'm sorry, Simon. He's... dead."

A smile appeared on Simon's lips. "They said that of Lazarus, too. Please go kneel near David."

Joseph returned to the hall to carry out Simon's

request.

"Put your hand on his heart and pray with me."

Behind the priest, Simon joined in prayer.

A soft wind stirred more of the same clean, fresh air around the men amid the bloody chaos. Then Father Joseph heard Simon. "His is the light and the resurrection. The eyes of the Lord are on the righteous and His ears are open to their cry. The steps of a good man are ordered by the Lord and He delights in his way. Though he fall, he shall not be utterly cast down. For the Lord upholds him with His hand."

Joseph looked nervously at Simon.

"Dear Jesus, my faith restored in you once more. In fulfillment of the prophecy that you have overseen, I ask you to hear my prayers. For you are the resurrection and the life. He that believeth in you, though he were dead, yet shall he live. And whosoever liveth and believeth in you shall never die. Like Matthew and Peter, whom you released from the grip of darkness, I ask that you release David Tomassi. Let him sleep no more."

Joseph held his breath as his hand glowed. He didn't think it was possible but from his hand radiated warmth as well as light.

Simon then voiced a more resounding command. "From your slumber, David Tomassi, I command you to rise."

Deep within the expanse that held fast the elder priest, a light suddenly pulled him away. From the pain and suffering gripping him, he was suddenly flooded with waves of euphoria.

He accepted his passage. Anything to be free of this bleak void of uncertainty. But he prayed Heaven was his journey's destination from this purgatory.

"David?" Joseph asked.

The elder priest stirred. His first sight since being revived was an aged Father Joseph Carpenter whose usual cinnamon-brown hair was now tinged with wisps of white. His hand found Joseph's cheek wet with tears. "Joseph? Joseph, my son. Is that you?"

"God is here." Joseph wept hugging his mentor.

Yet while the younger priest appeared older to Tomassi, Tomassi appeared younger to Joseph. Much of the silver, having left his hair, returned to its earlier honey blond shade. Even those aged lines carved from a lifetime of painful experiences were absent.

"Indeed he is." Tomassi was suddenly aware of Simon's celestial presence glowing behind Joseph. He gazed at the young man with awe. This child he met briefly long ago in the presence of his uncle. Then, not more than a few days ago, all grown up sitting in the rectory talking about a wife. School. A baby.

"What happens now?" Joseph inquired of Simon as he helped Tomassi up.

"Only part of what has been prophesied has occurred. Goodness will overcome the evil. Light will overtake the darkness. The Lord has foreseen this. Some of the small battles may have been lost. But the war must be won. It begins with the Second Coming. The birth of the next Christ. That child, gentlemen, is my son. What is to follow will truly mark His return."

Joseph knew nothing of this. He almost couldn't believe what he was hearing. He couldn't recall anything in the Bible about a newborn Christ?

Father Tomassi nodded. He and Peter remembered nothing beyond Simon's involvement. Nor did they know that Simon's baby was to be the next savior. Mankind's hope. They only knew their faith and prayers were to keep Simon safe.

Their mortal shortcomings cost the lives of Simon's uncle. Tomassi suddenly sensed it also cost the life of the bishop. He wasn't sure how he knew. He just did.

Bowing his head in silent prayer, death would not consume him as it had in the past. He witnessed miracles this past week. The weakened faith of an old priest was newly restored. With a deep breath, he looked up at Simon.

"I know you have questions. Many of the answers you seek can be found in the Scriptures both revealed and hidden. Keep close the ones that have held you believers all these years and seek out the ones that have been hidden from the world. While the future is being rewritten as we speak, I can tell you this: you, Joseph, are to be his protector and you have been designated as the chosen one to watch over Sarah. Together, you both will nurture him and guide him in his youth. Vulnerable he will be to things he will not understand. Love him like your own son and keep strong his faith.

"David, you will take over Matthew's responsibilities long since dormant and abandoned. Record everything. Serve as witness to it all. Testify to the miraculous. To the mystery. Never let any of this be forgotten again. Mankind cannot afford to have darkness come this close to succeeding in the future."

"I will do my best, Simon. But how will..."

"Joseph, be prepared for your second calling. Events will lead your life away from direct involvement with Mother Church and a church you will no longer be responsible for."

Joseph, dumbfounded by the revelation, sat

silent before the shimmering image of Simon.

"David," Simon said, turning once more to face the older priest. "You will carry on the Church now. There is much to be done. Many obstacles to overcome. You will soon be promoted. Power and authority within the Church will you have. Stay true to your faith. And to yourself. The world must be prepared for the Great Battle. For the End Times."

"The end?" Father Joseph asked. "This isn't it?"

"Many changes will take place over the next twenty years. This is only the beginning. The Weeping Age is upon mankind. Anguish and tribulations, the likes mankind has never witnessed, will lay waste the elements of this world. The Deceiver has been delivered unto the house Christ entrusted to me.

"Be prepared, gentlemen, to question everything you have always held steadfast in the years to come. Whatever happens, try to see beyond your human emotions. Do not allow them to deter you of your duties. Of your faith. Beware of false prophets and religious teachers who thrive on power. Greed. Earthly riches. Abundant are the Lord's riches, but so tempting the evil one's. Remember..."

"Simon!" The two men called out for Simon as he abruptly faded from their sights.

51

The female doctor was seated in front of Sarah who was prepped for a natural birth.

"I thought you said there was a problem, Ethan," the female doctor whispered with alarm to her male colleague beside her. She was keeping her voice low because she didn't want to embarrass him in front of the nurses.

"Blood pressure stabilizing," one of the nurses said.

"Heart rate stable, Doctor," another one added.

"I... I thought that's what I saw. I thought there was a breech. No, I swear there was a breech."

"Jesus, Ethan. Other than some normal discharge, the mother appears to be progressing as expected. Baby vitals are within normal limits and... Nope, I don't detect any tearing, either."

The male doctor could feel the eyes of the nurses on him. "There was a fluctuation with the vitals, Gabs. We all witnessed it."

"It happens to the best of us, I guess. Right? Anyway, look, the baby's crowning. How about we deliver this thing?" Doctor Gabrielle Blume asked with a hint of attitude.

She had reason to be upset. She was about ready to join her family for Easter dinner. This is after already spending the morning at the hospital prepping for tomorrow's Board of Directors meeting. A meeting regarding fundraising for the cancer wing's expansion. But as Head Obstetrician, she was called into surgery because of a supposed emergency. It also didn't help that she lived close by. Her family was not happy with her right now.

"Of course," Doctor Ethan Whitmore said, feeling like a first-year med-student. "You want me to...?"

"Nah, I'm here and prepped. I'll let you take over once we're cleared." Blume made a mental note, however, to have the equipment thoroughly examined just in case. After all, her colleague was a competent doctor who braved complications with remarkable success before.

But Doctor Whitmore's account of events were authentic. Even if denied by his colleague and everyone in the room, he knew they witnessed it.

Furthermore, his patient experienced it. But now, having recovered from whatever it was they experienced, Sarah was present. She tried to relax. Pushing. Breathing as practiced in Lamaze class.

Exhausted, but aware, she was no longer fading in and out of consciousness; she also wasn't experiencing pain as intense as earlier. No sooner did she wonder if the nurses gave her something to quell the sensation did the baby spill out into the world.

"Stats?" the female doctor asked, wiping the excess amniotic fluid from the baby's nose and mouth before handing him over to the nurse who stood beside her.

In practiced, effortless motions, one nurse sucked the fluid from the baby's mouth with a suction bulb while another held the baby for the doctor to clamp and cut the umbilical cord near the navel.

The baby's first breaths brought with it a loud sustained wail followed by short gasping cries to test out the new set of lungs.

"Mrs. Free's vitals are all normal and within limits," the nurse to the doctor's right announced.

"Fantastic! Prep the baby. And let's get Mom

cleaned up," the female doctor ordered. "All yours, Ethan," Doctor Blume declared, beginning to remove her gloves. "If you'd like, I can go out to the waiting room and inform the father while you finish with the mother."

"That'd be great if he were here," Whitmore replied to his colleague. The doctors then exchanged a knowing glance requiring no other explanation or words. Such were the times they were living in.

"Baby?" Sarah whispered, trying to focus on the crying bundle the nurses were tending to.

The female doctor came around and placed her hand in Sarah's. Such a shame, these young people. No father around. No family. She smoothed back curls from Sarah's eyes. Wet to the touch, Sarah's forehead was dotted with perspiration from the delivery. "The nurse is running an Apgar test, sweety. You'll be able to hold your baby in a sec."

Getting the nod from Doctor Whitmore, who was overseeing the nurses cleaning up the mother and administering the tests, Doctor Blume added: "Congratulations, darlin'. You have yourself a healthy baby boy."

"Would you like something for the pain, Mrs. Free?" one of the nurses asked, handing the oddly colored bundle wrapped in a blanket to his mother. She was surprised the young mother handled the birthing as well as she did. "Thirteen hours. Not bad for the first one."

"No, thank you. I'll do," Sarah responded as she regarded her son for the first time. The baby's cries subsided when he opened his eyes to look at Sarah. And then to the fly unexpectedly on her nose before an explosion rocked the room.

"What the hell?" Doctor Whitmore yelled.

"Great! I'll never get out of here!" Doctor Blume

quipped, unaware of how right she was when a disfigured Jacob slammed open the doors to the delivery room.

"I WANT THAT BABY!"

52

voice from within the demon-priest's head annoyingly teased. "You've already lost, Jacob."

Jacob searched the room, ignoring the voice — merely another among many anyway.

Two doctors and three of the nurses still in the room scattered about. Unsure of what this deranged, disfigured priest was about to do. Cornered, it was nearly impossible to escape.

Shaking his head wildly trying to shrug the voice off, Jacob made his way to the nurse holding a bundle of bloodied towels. "Pardon me," Jacob said, exposing a rotted, toothy grin, "but I must bless the baby."

"But..." the nurse protested.

When Jacob realized the baby wasn't in the bundle, he swiped at the nurse. Sent across the room, she crashed into a set of cabinets.

Scanning the area, his nostrils flared with the intoxicating scent of the newborn still fresh in the air. Noticing the absence of mother *and* child, he let out a frenzied growl and tossed the stirrup bed aside as if it were scrap metal.

"Everyone out," was all Doctor Blume could manage. Her words were cut short by another explosion rocking the room. Crashing and igniting sparks, the debris trapped some of the hospital staff.

Jacob stepped out past the receptionist's office, taking part of a wall with him. Through a waiting room of screaming people and out into a hallway, it was irrelevant who stood in his way. Or who suffered from the path he tore in his search to find the newborn.

Holding out his arms, he turned his palms upwards. It was a simple gesture that commanded him into the air. Staff and visitors scurried away from the vertical form floating down the hallway. Those unable to flee suffered agonizing deaths. With little or no faith to protect them, their bodies violently convulsed when the possessed priest passed them. Though somewhere within the floating mortal shell there still existed remnants of Jacob's true self, he was now the physical embodiment of evil.

He was Legion.

And the faithless who came in contact collapsed into nearly unrecognizable heaps of bloodied flesh.

Sarah ducked off to the right as the demon-priest floated by. Opening the metal fire door to the stairwell, she made her way up the stairs for the roof, fighting the cramping pain in her abdomen.

And unaware of the trail she left behind.

Catching the scent, Jacob backtracked. He hovered before the closed doorway Sarah used. With but a look through hollow eyes, he blew it open.

He didn't need to climb stairs. That was an exercise for mortals. With a wave of his hand, he effortlessly levitated himself up the stairwell.

He was in no hurry. The female was no match for his power.

53

Father Joseph followed the carnage leading to the Maternity Wing. Unlike the bodies Jacob left in his wake, most of those in the delivery room were alive. Visibly traumatized. But alive. Momentarily unable to comprehend their supernatural experience, they staggered about like zombies.

Outside the delivery area, black flies buzzed about the bodies littering the hallway. Blood was everywhere. Joseph feared for Sarah's safety. He focused on a trail of blood separate from the carnage, praying he was not too late.

For Sarah. For her baby.

Reaching the damaged archway to the stairwell, he felt somewhat relieved when he heard a baby's cry. Looking up as he ascended the stairs several at a time, he saw a form rising in the center of the stairwell.

The figure had to be Jacob.

Joseph rubbed his bruised neck. He wasn't looking forward to coming face-to-face with him again.

Sarah reached the roof to find the door padlocked. She beat at it with her fists. Frustrated, and sensing Jacob drawing nearer, she slammed into it with her shoulder. Knowing it was no use, her anguish erupted in the form of heaving sobs.

"JACOB," a voice echoed from the bottom of the stairwell.

Sarah didn't recognize the voice. Nor did Joseph. But it distracted Jacob. Before continuing his climb,

Joseph withdrew into the corner shadows as Jacob passed him in his descent.

"Do not waste our time," Jacob remarked to whomever called for him.

"Jacob, you let me down," the voice said.

Following the voice to the basement floor, the demon-priest was surprised to find it was the bishop who summoned him. The old man stood before Jacob in his nightclothes. His skin burned and charred. One side of his face hung free from his cheekbones. The sliding flesh slowly submitted itself to gravity's pull. "I wanted you to see what you did to me. I wanted you to see how you let me down."

Jacob's human side struggled to surface. To attest that he was rarely ever in control these days.

Fighting to respond to the bishop, he was overruled by the demons inside. Demons who were all-powerful. They overtook him, filling out the clothes that once belonged to Tomassi.

Bishop Peter Reibold was dead. His seraphic presence ephemeral. Therefore, this was only a ploy. The demon-priest was being toyed with. His suspicions were validated when it only took one strong rotting huff to blow the bishop's body apart.

Preparing to again ascend, he gestured upwards when another voice summoned him.

With crushed, paralyzed legs turned inwards and blue, a dead-eyed Simon confronted the demon-priest.

"Aaarrrggghhh." The demon-priest let out a frustrated snarl as he struck Simon's lifeless body. The bloodless corpse dropped to the ground.

Another trick. No more! This was taking too long. Anxious to demonstrate his — *their* — powers before all, he began to rise. There'd be no more tricks. No more deceptions. He would crush the newborn while it lay in his mother's arms if he must.

His body continued its contorted transformation, tearing the clothes that covered him as he once more took flight. He would accomplish his task unimpeded.

That's when something seized what was left of his soul.

54

J oseph reached the top of the stairwell, relieved to find Sarah with the baby.

"It's going to be..." he began, out of breath, before realizing the futility of it all. Words at this point were unnecessary. Irrelevant.

She understood what Joseph meant to say. Nodding ever so slightly, she even managed a faint smile.

"The door. It's locked," Sarah said, trying to wipe at her eyes while holding the baby close. Wrapped in a blanket, the baby cried in short spurts.

"You're bleeding an awful lot."

She was shaking, too. Joseph thought she looked weak. But there was no mistaking her resolve.

"I'm fine," was all she managed before shuddering hard. Though appearances were deceiving, the cramping was subsiding.

Joseph pulled the remainder of his black clergy shirt from under his belt. After unbuttoning buttons still fastened, he took the baby from the reluctant mother as he handed over the shirt. She was still only dressed in her nondescript birthing gown. Saturated with discharge. As Sarah accepted it, she noted the gold cross attached to a gold chain against his white crew neck tee.

It reminded her of Simon. Of his uncle. It reminded her of her father.

Sarah shed her gown to put on Joseph 's shirt. Even though her placenta had been expelled while straining to climbing the stairs, blood and mucus still flowed freely. Running down her legs, it left wide puddles at her bare feet each time she stood in place for too long.

The priest looked away to give her privacy, walking down a few steps to the tenth floor to try the door. It wouldn't budge. Banging on the door he wondered if anyone was still alive since no one seemed to hear or respond to the commotion.

Hearing footsteps ascending the stairs, Joseph returned to Sarah's side as she anxiously welcomed back her baby.

"Father Tomassi," Sarah said, startled and relieved at the same time.

Out of his clergy standard, he was dressed in gunmetal sweatpants and a Black Sabbath *Sabbath Bloody Sabbath* tee. Though clearly out of breath, Sarah inwardly noted Tomassi's youthful transformation. In his hands, he held a small prayer book and crowbar.

"Seriously?" Joseph asked after seeing Tomassi's shirt.

"Not a word," the elder priest said between breaths. "Though it is fitting. Don't you think?"

Set against Tomassi's black tee was the front cover image from Sabbath's 1973 album cover. With hues of red and yellow, it depicted a dying man lying in anguish with a serpent wrapped around his neck. Watching over him, aside from a skull-headed bedpost prominently displaying the Number of the Beast below it, were six evil humanoid spirits.

Joseph shook his head frowning. "No, really. You couldn't have picked a worse shirt."

Returning to the matter at hand, Tomassi caught his breath. "Yes, well, figured you'd head for higher ground, and I thought you might need this." He handed the crowbar to Joseph who was still giving him the stink-eye.

Wedging the crowbar through the shackle part of the padlock, Joseph tried to find an angle from which to break it free of the locking bar. Each time was met with frustration as the crowbar slipped from the lock. The angle made the execution of the task that much more difficult.

Tomassi looked over at Sarah. At the blood all over her legs. He was nearly heartbroken when he came upon the afterbirth on the stairwell. Unsure of what the bloody organ mass was at first, he feared the worst. The thought still hadn't left him.

Sarah put a hand on his arm, regarding him with an expression of regret over their last conversation. Patting her hand, he nodded. But he was still alarmed. He was about to ask if she was in any pain when the lock gave way, one end of the crowbar slamming against the metal door with a loud bang that reverberated throughout the stairwell.

Together the three of them burst onto the roof into a cold driving shower of sleet and snow.

"What now, Joseph?" the elder priest asked of the younger one, fighting to ignore the cold daggers hitting his skin. This was no place for them to be. Especially Sarah. With a newborn.

"I was just following Sarah. I'm not sure what she's doing."

Sarah addressed the two priests as she backed away towards one end of the roof. The look on her face determined and extremely grave. "Since the devil wants a fucking miracle so badly, he's about to get one."

"Wh-Whatever do you mean?" Tomassi spoke watching Sarah's head of curls blow about her face from the wind.

"If I remember what I learned in my CCD classes, Christ denied the devil a miracle to prove to mankind that He was the Son of God. Well, I'm about to give him that miracle."

The elder priest figured out what she meant. If He ever dared put himself in harm's way, the Prince of Darkness was certain the skies would open and angels would spill forth to save Him from a mortal's earthly death.

Christ refused. He reasoned that the Lord should not be put to such foolish tests. That the Lord was not a puppet whose strings could be easily manipulated.

Though he understood this from his training and religious education, Father Tomassi also knew the action was debatable in some circles. By denying mankind the miraculous — the ingredients with which to believe in the divine — the choice to believe would be left up to mankind.

But weren't the exorcisms, the cures, and feedings of the masses enough to satisfy mankind's thirst for the miraculous? Wasn't that enough to believe?

Sarah unwavering in her decision, clutched the baby closer to her bosom. "Everyone will now believe as I should have."

Turning towards the roof's edge, she pushed headlong into the punishing freezing rain.

55

This time it wasn't an illusion. Simon stood before Jacob. His celestial form turned flesh. "Jacob, release yourself from the evil one's grip. I know you can do it."

The priest's split and swollen face, with eyes a thick mucus yellow sucked within black endless pits, looked at Simon. "Jacob is no more," the vile thing inside Jacob breathed with a raspy unnatural voice. "We. Are. Legion." With a lift of his palm, he sent Simon through the wall leading to the laundry section in the hospital's basement.

Simon dusted himself off as the demon settled back onto solid ground before him. Drawing both arms back, Simon then snapped them forward. The action let loose an array of celestial light propelling the demon-priest through the basement stairs and three other supporting walls.

Though his shirt was afire and his skin scorched, Jacob rose unfazed. "Your powers are no match for ours. This game ends now." His hands motioned to the floor directly underneath Simon. "Hell welcomes you home. Only this time, there shall you remain."

The concrete directly beneath Simon gave way. Simon scraped the cement with his fingernails, clawing at what remained of the floor before losing his grip and falling into the chasm.

Jacob, now satisfied, rose into the air determined more than ever to accomplish his task.

56

The greyness outside matched the situation and their ambivalent feelings.

"Sarah," the younger priest implored, "maybe this isn't such a good idea."

"You mean 'what if,' don't you, Joseph?" Sarah countered from the edge of the rooftop.

He paused, unsure how to answer because he was afraid it would show weakness on his part. That he lacked faith. Tomassi spoke up before there was a chance to answer.

"None of us know if this is part of the prophecy. How can you go through with it if you're at all unsure? We're not supposed to put Him up to such a test."

"It's not so much a test as a way to *make* you believe. You still doubt. I know you do. You *both* do. I did. I am sure that this is right," she said. Her conviction unshakable. "And if I truly am the mother of the next Christ, then I..."

The building shook as Sarah attempted to finish her sentence. Falling against the parapet wall, the raised edge surrounding the rooftop, she caught sight of people running about through the parking lot slush below. In the distance, she also noticed flashing lightbars of several emergency vehicles.

From her perspective, it looked as if no one could enter the building. She wondered if anyone had gotten out or if all the floors were somehow sealed off by the demented priest.

The sirens of the approaching law enforcement and emergency service vehicles from all over the city finally reached them. Watching everyone scatter about, it was clear no one was aware of what was happening above on the rooftop.

"Building's going to collapse, isn't it," Joseph sighed, flashing a worried look in Tomassi's direction. They both stood frozen and terrified as the building shook again.

"Joseph! Sarah! Look!"

Tomassi was pointing upwards. The overcast sky was parting in a circular motion.

Spinning.

A glow, faint at first, beamed through the dark gray clouds. Even as the freezing rain continued its driving force, pelting their faces, the light traveled through the opening in the sky.

Traveled *towards* them.

"It's not stopping," Joseph yelled.

The blazing beam of light glowed brighter as it rushed towards them, slicing through the roof of the building with the roar of a freight train. Sarah tried to find something steady to hold onto as the force of the flare's impact blew Joseph and Tomassi back onto the graveled rooftop.

"The stairwell," Tomassi yelled over the hum of the radiance.

The light was intense; its force powerful.

Reaching into the dark cleft Jacob created, the light searched — and then seized — Simon from the clutches of the demon horde.

57

The demon-priest moved aside as the brilliant celestial light came rushing by. Mustering the strength of unholy powers, he ascended the rest of the stairwell hastily. Keeping a safe distance from the light, he passed through the concrete and metal, girders, and joints, without much effort using his back to shield and collapse each set of stairs.

Once on the roof, he found the woman he sought clutching the baby he'd been searching for. Fathers Tomassi and Joseph stood nearby.

He saw them for what they were: frightened weaklings.

Ignoring the beam of light behind him, Jacob advanced towards them on foot.

Sarah held her baby close, trying to keep him warm and dry despite the sleet and freezing rain. But like her hair and the shirt she wore, the baby's blanket was wet. Saturated. If she wasn't so wound up, she would be immobilized by the damp coldness.

The baby was a different story. So young and new, he was vulnerable to the elements.

Tomassi and Joseph reduced their distance from Sarah as Jacob made his way closer, pausing to seizure into a misshapen hellish form more distorted than anything earlier. As his skin expanded, his clothes stretched into ripped rags vaguely resembling shirt and pants. Visible through his translucent skin was the fluid in his veins. Great bloody fissures erupted all over his face and neck. They oozed a foul substance mixed with what looked to be his blood.

Copious amounts of blood.

"THE BABY, PETIT ANGE! IT'S MINE!" The demon-priest's guttural command intentionally recalled words once spoken by Sarah's father.

Sarah tightened her hold around her newborn as the demon drew near. Neither the sleet nor the frigid wind chilled her more than the monstrosity before her. But if this thing thought it had a chance of getting anywhere near her baby, it was sorely mistaken.

"Leave her be," Tomassi said, holding his pocket psalter up to the demon. He wondered which currently controlled the priest. Then reciting the prayer to St. Michael, he said: "St. Michael the Archangel, illustrious leader of the Heavenly Army, defend us in the battle against the rulers of darkness. Come to the rescue of mankind, whom God has made in His own image. Holy Church venerates you as her patron and guardian. Entreat the Lord of Peace to cast Satan down under our feet so as to keep him from further holding man captive and doing harm to the Church."

The demon-priest halted its advance.

"Carry our prayers up to God's throne so that He may quickly come and lay hold of the demon, casting him in chains into the abyss... so that he can no longer seduce the nations."

"David Tomassi? I thought you died," the demon-priest exclaimed in a throaty chuckle before igniting the religious artifact in Tomassi's hand with a glance.

Tomassi stumbled back, promptly dropping the enkindled holy book.

"Perhaps your death wasn't as gruesome as it should have been. Too bad. I rather like the new shirt."

Joseph darted in front of Tomassi as Jacob let fly a ball of flame from his hands. It hit Joseph with such force that he flew into Tomassi. Falling hard, they slid in the icy rooftop gravel.

Jacob knew he should have finished Joseph off earlier. It was a weak gesture he would not allow to happen again. Reaching the young priest before he could recover, Jacob seized him by the throat. He effortlessly lifted him into the air with one hand.

"I ask you for a third time. Do you really believe in your pathetic Christ?"

"HEY!" Sarah screamed, standing against the parapet wall. Though frightened and cold, she knew she needed to do something — anything — to help Simon's friends. "Over here you bastard!"

Jacob leered at the petty female. With a serpent's tongue beset with rows of rotted teeth of black, he ran it over his cracked lips salaciously. Does she really think she'll be saved?

Christ throughout the centuries became predictable. If the angels weren't going to save Him *then*, why would they *now*?

Right where he wanted her, he discharged a spark of lightning from the fingertips of his free hand. Seconds later the building beneath Sarah gave way.

Falling back, she let go of her swaddled baby. She hadn't meant to. Flailing her arms, she lost her balance.

And her baby.

Unable to intervene, the two priests watched in abject horror as Sarah disappeared over the edge. Then the baby.

As Sarah descended, the three figures became smaller in her line of vision — three silhouettes against the beam of light that still burrowed deep into the hospital. Arms outstretched, she prayed she'd be the one to hit the pavement first. Prayed that would increase the chances her baby would live.

That is, if the baby landed on her.

Or was saved by God.

No matter, in her actions she would once and for all prove her love.

And affirm her faith.

58

Clutching his tarnished cross, he held it in front of the demon's face. "I... BELIEVE... AACH... IN... HIM."

Tomassi was up at once. "Goddamn you, you murderer," he cried.

Nearly all hope was lost now. This would be the end. Everything up to this point in vain.

Gathering his inner strength, Father Tomassi was going to do the only thing he could do. The only thing *left* to do. He was going to save his friend.

Though not an expert on exorcism rites, from spiritual, liturgical, and pastoral teachings Tomassi searched deep to recall sacred prayers used in exorcism rituals: "In the name of Jesus Christ, our Lord, Mary, Mother of God, Saint Michael the Archangel, and of all the saints, we steadfastly proceed to combat the onslaught of the wily enemy."

The demon's hold buckled, relaxing Joseph's throat enough for him to desperately suck in a mouthful of air again.

"God arises; His enemies are scattered, and those who hate Him flee before Him," Tomassi yelled against what was becoming a tempest of wind and frozen precipitation.

Joseph, short of breath, joined his colleague. "As smoke... is driven away, so are... they driven; as wax melts... before the fire, so the wicked... perish before God."

Unsteadily, Jacob took a step back. But he was not deterred. All was not lost. The Christ child was dead. He and his mother were surely nothing more than splattered remnants having hit the pavement below. Let these men of the cloth show off their trinkets and trust their empty words.

A jagged series of lines lit up the sky. Followed by a strike nearby. Shaking the building in its wake, a sudden clap of thunder. The priests struggled to steady themselves.

Joseph did what he could to put some distance between him and Jacob, moving closer to Tomassi when the beam of light that earlier penetrated the gray skies to strike the hospital roof withdrew to the heavens. Rolling clouds moved in accompanied by a series of echoing rumbles. It was then the driving precipitation and strong winds fell away.

But then day became night. Marked by a deafening silence. Nothing moved but the soundless clouds above eclipsing all evidence of light.

Jacob's sinister laughter sliced through the stillness. With the newborn Christ dead, there would be no Second Coming. He joyously lifted his hands skyward.

Tomassi, unable to distinguish in the pitch-black where Jacob or Joseph stood, made ready his final stand. With Rosary Beads in one hand, his waterlogged book of scripture, tattered and singed in the other, he issued the following command: "See the cross of the Lord. Be gone, you hostile powers!"

Holding his own cross steadfast, Joseph brought it forward. He joined Tomassi, hoping he was facing in the proper direction. "May your mercy, Lord, remain with us always."

"FOOLS!" Jacob yelled. "WE ARE UNTOUCHABLE!"

"For we put our whole trust in you," the two priests continued in unison.

"MASTER," Jacob testified, thrusting his arms

upward. "IT IS TRULY YOURS THAT IS GLORIOUSLY EVERLASTING!"

Lightning zigzagged across the sky. What followed was an earsplitting thunder with a clap so loud and with such force that it shook the hospital structure beneath their feet.

"We're gonna die up here. Aren't we?" Joseph asked Tomassi, visible only from the intermittent forked flashes in the sky.

Lightning from above — and behind — the angry swirling clouds flickered like explosive ordinance from some kind of space war. Pockets of nebulous sky lit up in random intervals.

Tomassi couldn't help but be reminded of *Close Encounters of the Third Kind*.

As streaks of electricity crackled, illuminating the racing firmament and the city below it, a figure advanced with every flash.

Dear Jesus, did Jacob summon the Prince of Darkness himself? Tomassi wasn't sure if it was the charge in the air or his palpable fear that raised the hairs on the back of his neck.

Jacob registered a different kind of fright on the lit faces of the men before him. He turned as a large streak coursed through the sky directly overhead to reveal the one figure who could challenge him.

"NOT YOU!" Jacob bellowed in a chorus of voices.

Simon brought up his foot and kicked the demon-priest in the abdomen. Jacob tottered backward as tendrils of lightning exposed the sky.

"More than any power, Jacob: Sheer. Human. Will. Because you see He gives power to the weak..." Simon said, rushing Jacob to connect his fist in an uppercut with the demon's jaw as the sky exploded. "And to those who have no might," Simon added with a left hook. "He increases strength."

Right hook. "I will not fail..." Right cross. "...the Lord... again."

Jacob faltered. But he could not be felled.

Another zigzagging pattern formed across the sky. A cacophonous thunder followed it.

Seizing Jacob by the shirt, Simon pulled the demon-priest close, smelling the putridity that oozed from him. This was going to end.

And now.

"The Lord said whatever Simon Peter says on earth, so shall it be done in Heaven." Looking to the fiery skies above him, Simon commanded: "Hear me as I beseech you one last time, Lord. By the power vested in me, I call on the communion of saints and *ALL* the angels..."

"...TO DELIVER US FROM EVIL," the priests joined. As if on cue.

But when nothing happened. When the world around them lay still in blanketed murkiness, Jacob took the opportunity to chastise their faith.

"You've been abandoned. As has mankind." He would teach them all. And in the process, lay waste to everything. And everyone. "Behold the seraph Leviathan!"

Squirming from Simon's hold, Jacob brought his hands together in a booming clap. His action released an explosive shock wave.

Thrown by the powerful force that sent flying debris from the rooftop, Fathers Tomassi and Joseph clung as much to each other as they did the barrier at the edge of the roof.

Simon skidded back but remained standing. Raising his hands in the air as shields.

From the evil incarnate's hands exploded a red and orange fireball. As quickly as it expanded it retracted. Collapsing in on itself, it left each hand encased in glowing, rippling energy. Against the surrounding darkness, the four figures were cast in its crimson radiance.

Simon moved forward. Reaching for Jacob, he was unaware of the demon Leviathan's history.

As one of Lucifer's First Order, he was one of Apostle Saint Peter's greatest enemies. And he was not about to let Jacob be caught off guard again. He deflected Simon's hand, burning it in the process.

Recoiling, Simon was visibly pained. But then he raised his arms. Snapping his hands open, he ignited a radiant white energy before making another attempt at Jacob.

With a sizzle and POP! Simon was launched across the graveled rooftop leaving a fiery trail in his wake.

Voice triumphant, the demon-priest was boastful. "SEE. There will be no mira..."

There was no mistaking the sound of flapping wings. Jacob was interrupted by the flapping of what must have been great wings for it produced a sudden discharge of incredibly strong wind. Wind that drew the men on the roof forward. Then back.

The demon-priest shielded his eyes from the blinding release of energy as a massive bolt of lightning struck at his feet.

"My God, they must be seven feet tall..." Joseph cried in wonderment and reverence.

The priests tried to comprehend what was visible in their periphery. In awe, they immediately got up on their knees to pray.

"Indeed," Tomassi replied.

"Archangels?"

"No," Tomassi whispered. "Seraphim." Tomassi wondered how many of the giant six-winged angels were present in the shadows. And if Simon knew they were here all along.

Then another encouraging thought occurred to him: Perhaps Sarah and the newborn Christ child lived yet.

What happened next confirmed his hopes. Like the still surface of a pond ripples when breeched by a leaf, the skies rippled as the center opened revealing scores of angels. Silhouettes against a white holy light, they descended from the heavens in rapid succession to a deafening clamor of flapping wings.

Some flew by Fathers Tomassi and Joseph as they sought out the larger seraphim. Others flew about the sky and hovered near Simon. What they were doing, the priests couldn't be certain. Their focus was drawn to the many battling the demon-priest.

The demon-priest under the control of Leviathan.

Flames of energy flew from his hands as he struck down the advancing angels.

The priests watched in alarm as angel after angel tumbled from the sky. Some fell on the roof near them. Others to the ground below.

Grouping up for an attack, they then began encircling the damned creature on the roof. Bearing down, the angels closed in.

Hundreds. Then thousands. Maybe even more.

"I don't understand," Joseph cried out to Tomassi. "Why don't they fight him?"

"They are," Tomassi replied.

"B-But where are their weapons? Why are they sacrificing themselves?"

"I'm not sure. This may be their first line of offense." Tomassi silently wondered if the angels misjudged the demon-priest's power. Only now discovering they were not immune to the energy that came from his hands.

But their numbers, nearly blotting out the light emitted from the aperture of their entrance, besieged Jacob. Through sheer bombardment, the angels assailed him with their wings. Little opportunity was left to pick them all off.

As Joseph stood, he watched the army of angels pounce the flailing malignant spirit while thousands more flew about.

"So, it is done? It is over?"

Beyond the flapping wings, Tomassi caught sight of a seraph standing close to Simon. "I'm not so sure," he confessed.

Sure enough, from under the pile of angels, there appeared beams of energy. First a few. Then multiple rays escaping from various angles. From within, a reddish hue grew in intensity.

* * *

It was the sound that Tomassi remembers most when he first came to. A loud FWOOM! FWOOM! FWOOM! Through the protective wings of the four giant seraphim now shielding them, Tomassi saw what could only be described as Biblical carnage. As bad as what he saw in the halls of the hospital, he was moved beyond tears by what he now witnessed on the rooftop. After all, these were the remains of celestial beings.

Feathers and blood sullied the scene before them all.

The latest demon to emerge — a seraph itself — overtook Jacob's body. Too great for the human shell it inhabited, the evil coursing through its veins irreparably altered its appearance. Head swelling, the skin covering his skull split and tore, freeing wet bloody flaps of hair that hung in parts off his head. He moved his arms in futility. Tried to break free of the mortal restraints.

In revulsion and pity, the priests looked away as the skin around Jacob's spine split from the base of his neck, running a line of torn, raw flesh to his lower back. The unholy sound forced them to cover their ears.

Fresh pools of blood and fluid saturated shreds of what were once his clothes. Large wings struggled to release against the skin trapping them. The demon Leviathan fought not only to control Jacob's body, he was going to physically emerge from the mortal casing.

At the ready, two seraphs stood on either side of Simon, adorned in armor and brandishing swords.

"The Christ child lives, demon. Your power was not enough to stop the prophecy," Simon said against the backdrop of angels hovering overhead. Many were encircling the sky in their ascendance back into the heavens. But not before recovering the bodies of their slain brothers.

It was at that point Tomassi understood. The angels sacrificed themselves so that Sarah and the baby could live. They distracted Jacob so that she could be saved. So that she could live.

He was sure of it. It was the only explanation that made sense.

"You know this is only the beginning, Kefa," the creature snarled malevolently. "Only but a part of the true prophecy has been fulfilled. We shall see what lies ahead at the time of the Great Battle at Megiddo."

Empowered by his own words, the demon once more advanced towards Simon. His body underwent an evil metamorphosis with each deliberate stride forward.

The seraph on Simon's far right advanced to protect the kefa. But Jacob disregarded him using the dark powers Leviathan commanded as the angel from the farthest left moved with unearthly speed. His Sword of Holy Light cut a swath through the monster's hide.

Speaking in multiple voices and languages, the demon-priest wailed in pain. Yet the pain only seemed to heighten their powers.

Commanding supernatural power over the sword with the power of Leviathan, he turned the blade on the holy seraph before Simon's other two protectors could act. Plunging the Sword of Holy Light deep, it sliced through the angel's armor and exited the other side.

"No!" Simon shouted.

Arresting Jacob's decaying expansion appeared moot at this point. Fluids of all kinds gushed over the rupturing body. Sopping hunks of hairy scalp fell in clumps onto the graveled rooftop. An ear hung suspended off the side of his peeling face, slowly journeying south with every twitch of the demon's body.

Maybe, just maybe, there's still a chance to reach the human side, Simon prayed. The alternative would be even more costly. So many lives, angel and human, already lost. How many more before the looming battle?

Simon begrudgingly met the advancing demon. Like two Greco-Roman wrestlers in combat, they locked hands over their heads in a struggle to determine mankind's survival.

"Come back with me, Jacob," Simon pleaded. Face-to-face with the beast before him, he tried transferring the energy from his hands to the lost human. Initially losing footing, he then slightly advanced forward.

Wrestling to surface one last time, Jacob's monstrous features relaxed. Unobstructed by evil intervention, he spoke his final words as a human. "I can't. I've lost. In the beginning I thought... I hoped it was... divine intervention. I didn't kn..."

Then Leviathan overtook what was left of Jacob's human soul with the help of Legion, thrusting his barely recognizable form upward so violently that his feet left the ground taking Simon with him. From Jacob's back, six large black wings tore free from Jacob's thinning flesh.

Fathers Tomassi and Joseph were repulsed by the sound. The sickening sound resembling the sound of tearing fabric.

Convulsing in mid-air, Jacob's hands glowed with the intensity of a mini exploding sun.

Locked in the demon's death grip, Simon was powerless. The demon bore down on him. Breaking his wrists.

"Did you really think you had a chance? Against all of us? Against me?"

Simon felt the demon's poisonous energy infect him. All hope would have been lost were it not for his protectors.

Already wounded by one attack, Jacob was vulnerable. Simon's other two protectors took up positions alongside the demon. Jacob tried to deflect the advance but Simon used what was left of his strength and power to hold captive Jacob's hands.

Flapping the not-yet-fully formed wings wildly, Leviathan screamed. "Let. Me. Go!"

Simultaneously the holy seraphim plunged their Swords of Holy Light into the demon.

"Noooooooooooo!"

The priests covered their ears to the unholy cries

coming from the possessed Jacob as he plummeted from the sky to land near the cavity that was once a stairwell.

Weak from battle, Simon was guided by the few remaining angels to safely stand nearby.

"Is it over?" Father Joseph asked.

Tomassi didn't answer. He wondered if it would ever be over so long as Jacob lived. All eyes were on Jacob's body. Accursed. Abhorrent. Lifeless.

Simon's protectors stood poised for action.

The demon-priest stirred. He struggled to rise, falling and floundering. Straining with what little humanity remained, Jacob faced his adversary. His features so altered that his expression vaguely resembled anything human.

It was the eyes that Simon was drawn to. They were not the pits that Simon recalled from the day at the rectory. Revealing a different message than the one conveyed by his unholy appearance, the eyes seemed to display remorse. Behind those eyes was what was left of the real Jacob.

Then came the bloody, decomposed smile. A smile of victory. Finding truth in Jacob's eyes, Simon understood.

Unable to control the demons that had come to possess him, Jacob knew what had to be done. It was time to succumb to the inner confrontation over his soul.

Leviathan defeated, Jacob could feel the other demons emerging to fill the vacuum of power. Ravaging him from inside. It was at that moment Jacob, the human, in his final breaths of life, leapt to his death.

59

Father Joseph joined David Tomassi and the two peered over the edge of the building to find Sarah under the care of paramedics.

The doors to the hospital burst open as Jacob's remains splattered all over the basement floor. But not before Jacob's sacrifice ignited a large fiery explosion that shattered windows and billowed smoke throughout the building.

People rushed about in panic. Many were unable to comprehend what they were witnesses to.

Those who witnessed flying celestial beings were already forgetting them. Some of the truly faithful would remember, seeing them again in their dreams. But the others would be too preoccupied with what they thought was a terrible freak storm that, from out of nowhere, ravaged the hospital the same time a killer dressed as a priest seemingly went on a rampage.

Looking out to the horizon Simon — flanked by seraphs on his left and right — watched the other six return to the heavens. One carried the angel injured in the exchange with Jacob.

Taking in the sun, low in the sky, Simon marveled at its beauty. Of its setting against the surrounding clouds ablaze with colors of deep orange. Though the Weeping Age was upon them, mankind would now have the chance to see the rest of the prophecy through.

But it wouldn't be long until the Great Battle — a battle fought at the peril of nonbelievers who threatened to push the world and its civilizations to war the likes of which mankind has never seen. It is then that the powers of Heaven and Hell will be revealed to lay claim to what remains.

An extension ladder from a Bethlehem fire engine hit the edge of the parapet, drawing Simon's attention. Firemen had apparently spotted Tomassi and Joseph.

Tomassi wondered if they saw the seraphim.

The priests fell before Simon as the two large remaining beings guarding Simon took flight. Coming to stand beside Simon in their place was the most exquisite angel Father Tomassi had ever seen. No painting or statue of the Renaissance could have better portrayed him with oils or stone. With curled hair that flowed past his chiseled face and thick neck, it fell about his massively broad shoulders. Not nearly as wide as the seraphs, he was about as tall. And solid. Stately.

Resting his left hand on the hilt of a sheathed sword hung about his waist, he, too, was dressed in some kind of armor. Surrounding him was a radiating light of warmth that reminded Tomassi of his visits from Mary back in Adánia.

The handsome angel said something to Simon the priests could not hear. But the news was positive judging by Simon's expression. Extending his wings, he lifted himself up into the air. He then hung suspended as if waiting for something. Or someone.

"Rise, David. Joseph."

"Simon?" Tomassi asked as Simon outstretched his hands to them. He was rising into the air with his back to the setting sun.

"All is well, my friends. Archangel Michael has informed me Sarah and the baby are safe and well."

Archangel Michael! Father Tomassi strained to once more catch sight of the beautiful winged celestial spirit, but the being was now obscured by the setting sun's glare. The glare would soon encompass Simon as well.

"There will come a time, gentlemen, when we shall meet again. Together we will all rejoice in the loving faith of Jesus Christ and His blessed mother, Mary."

Two angels, escorts having descended from the heavens, emerged from the bright hazy circle of setting sunlight. Blinding in its brightness, the priests were forced to shield their eyes with their hands.

"My friends," they heard Simon say, "my time has come. Remember our holy covenant. Hold fast the profession of your faith without wavering."

"But Simon," Joseph implored as Simon receded into the light with the angels.

"God's love for you is great; your faith now is strong. Remember all that you have witnessed."

"Simon?" they both called out into the empty air before them.

Joseph and Tomassi searched the skies. But Simon could no longer be seen. He was gone.

And they were alone.

"Hey, you two awright?" someone asked from behind.

The two priests jumped, grabbing onto the other one's arms.

It was only a fireman.

"Odd. The setting sun is mighty bright. Because of the glare off of those heating ducts, I almost couldn't make you two out."

Tomassi and Joseph looked from the fireman to each other.

And smiled.

60

A young female reporter with auburn hair dressed in a winter parka was one of the first on the scene. She and her cameraman set up for their shot in front of the hospital.

"Once again, this is unconfirmed. But our source indicates the deceased individual, after having jumped to his death from some ten floors up, is — *was* — a priest. Police are, for the moment, ruling his death a suicide. Though a thorough investigation will need to take place, this apparently ends a killing spree that seems to have begun this Easter morning with a fire set at Saint Catherine's Rectory. Among those who perished in that blaze: a beloved diocesan leader and a visiting South African bishop.

"I have been told the hospital is littered with multiple victims — a gruesome scene, one witness put it. Several other patients and staff suffered injuries after the individual then continued his spree here at Bethlehem General Hospital. In a community stunned by today's events, local police tell us it may take weeks before they know a motive and are ready to reveal the killer's identity. For KLF-NEWS, I'm..."

Tomassi turned away from the news in the waiting room. Standing, he stretched and yawned. This week had been a long one. The events over the last forty-eight hours were slowly becoming a blur. He'd have to begin writing soon or else risk forgetting everything. Something he didn't want to happen again.

This time the stakes were even higher. If that was even possible.

Exiting the makeshift waiting room, he headed to the restrooms to wait for Joseph. Only one part of the hospital was operational. And with minimal staff. Much of the structural damage forced the evacuation of nearly all patients to neighboring hospitals in other towns like Bristol. A decision to move all others would be made in the next day or two. For now, Sarah was put up in one of the open rooms. At least for tonight.

Father Joseph, having washed his face, neck, and arms, exited feeling refreshed. Exhausted. But refreshed.

Both pretty banged up, they both had changed.

Undergone a transformation is more like it, Tomassi marveled.

His esteemed colleague, for example, was no longer the insecure young man he once was. Nor was he in need of a mentor.

Tomassi, already aged and a victim of his own insecurities with death, felt resurrected by the experience. He was no longer sixty-three years *old*. He was sixty-three years *young*.

Silently the two walked the hall to Sarah's room.

61

Though it would be several days before his name was released, Jacob would, over the course of the next year, come to be correctly identified as the one behind several bizarre and previously unsolved murders. He would go on to be linked to the deaths of Aberthol North, Matthew Free, Stanley John Iris, Bishop Peter Reibold, and Simon Peter Free. This, in addition to several of the Bethlehem General's staff and patients. And South African bishop, Tandie Umgumbwe.

Jacob's wicked reach would span three states, with key evidence coming from forensics performed on skin tissue obtained from the remains of his splattered body.

The match would also eventually link him to the unsuccessful attacks on little Johnny Pahana, Sarah Marie Free, her newborn baby, and Fathers David Tomassi and Joseph Carpenter.

The fire at the bishop's residence — eventually ruled as arson — was said to have burned so intensely that the Fire Marshal, when interviewed by the lady reporter from KLF News, couldn't help but exclaim the fire to be "hotter than Hell!" He went on to add with sadness and frustration: "There was no way to put it out! My guys worked damn hard to contain it, too. We lost a couple of good guys that day. Several others were hurt battling that freak inferno. I swear, it's as if the clergy stored drums of gasoline in there or something."

Intense as it was, the fire mysteriously was limited only to the rectory of Saint Catherine's. It spread no further. Something no one could explain. And after some time, stopped trying to.

Firemen battled the blaze in frigid temperatures and high winds for nearly eight hours trying to wrest it under control. Though no one made the connection, the fire only began slowly extinguishing itself about the same time Jacob hit the concrete floor.

As for Jacob, the police discovered what remained of him in a saturated rancid splatter of blood and innards wearing what was left of Tomassi's tattered clothes. His skin, nothing more than a gelatinous membrane at the end, burst upon impact when it met the solid surface. No mention was made about the skeletal remains of what looked to be wings or blood-soaked feathers found near the body.

Long gone were any traces of the chasm beneath the hospital that hours earlier swallowed Simon. It was sealed when the heavenly beam of light completed its rescue.

News worldwide, the investigation into the murders reached as far as Rome. Especially since Jacob was a man of the cloth. A representative of the Roman Catholic Church. What nearly became a scandal involving the pontiff because of a phone call traced from New Galilee, Connecticut to the Vatican prior to the bishop's time of death, would be a stain upon his leadership for some years to come.

When asked what connection the pope might possibly have with Father Jacob Dawz, the pope denied having ever known Jacob personally. He claimed it was the bishop who reached out to him. The bishop, he said, was despondent when he saw him days earlier. He further argued it wasn't Jacob who set the fire. But Bishop Reibold. Exhibiting characteristics of psychotic depression, Pope Pontius claimed an act of suicide would be consistent with suicidal tendencies associated with such a diagnosis.

"It is obvious," the pope relayed with theatrical sorrow before the cameras, tears spilling down his cheek, "that the bishop, afflicted by an illness too great to bear, decided to take his life. After all, I should know... he and I were friends since seminary over thirty years ago."

62

Tomassi and Joseph reached the tiny makeshift room that was Sarah's and quietly entered. In their absence, Sarah fed the baby and now lay with her newborn cradled in her arms.

The doctors were baffled she incurred no significant injuries since she was up and around so soon after giving birth. Nor could they fully explain how she and the baby ended up unharmed since some people reported seeing a female fall from the roof. Some two hundred feet up.

Both priests declined to offer any kind of explanation, sticking instead to the story that they were up on the roof trying to escape Jacob. But the stories from witnesses became sketchier with time. Memories faded quickly. Before long, it was eventually forgotten. And dropped.

Sarah, for her part, never said a word. Aside from confessing her fear for the baby's safety prompted refuge at higher ground, she claimed the trauma left her bereft of any recollection. She told investigators she recalled making it to the rooftop one minute, then being administered to on the ground by the Fire Department the next.

The truth: Sarah remembered everything. Especially when Archangel Michael, accompanied by colossal angels with massive wings, caught her and the baby. And while she was a little banged up and weak, she felt better than she had in a very long time. She was at peace with herself. And for once, the world around her.

Still in his Black Sabbath tee, torn in multiple

places making it a better rag than shirt, Father
Tomassi took a seat beside her on the right. Father
Joseph, his singed and blackened cross dangling
against a charred dirty white tee, sat to her left.
Except to wash up, he hadn't left Sarah's side since
the fire department rescued him and Tomassi from
the rooftop.

Earlier he hardly recognized the face staring back
at him. Just as he barely recognized his mentor,
colleague, and dear friend. They were that roughed
up. Still, they looked much worse than they felt.

Sarah regarded the two men at her side, failing
miserably to articulate her gratitude for what they
did. For all they sacrificed.

Clutching Joseph's finger, the baby held tight
even as Joseph wagged it side-to-side. Appointed
with the enormous task of seeing that the baby grew
up properly, Tomassi's task was to prepare the
Church for the child's destiny. What all that would
involve, the two men could only speculate. But
Simon Peter had fulfilled his destiny as the kefa. The
rock.

Rock. A title Jesus aptly bestowed. And because
of the rock, a new dawn was cast on Mother Church.

And mankind.

Joseph picked the baby up and gently cradled its
head in his hand.

A thought of Simon flashed through Sarah's
mind. Earlier, while she slept, he appeared to her.
Waving to her from across the river, she also saw
among him so many other friends.

She believed now. Her father *was* right. A point
in her life had been reached. A point when she
couldn't take any more. But the Lord revealed to her
what was truly important.

In her dream, she strained her eyes as another

figure approached from behind Simon and his uncle. For a brief instant, she thought she could see Jesus Christ beyond the river. With open arms, welcoming Simon.

She wished she could have seen Mary. But she *felt* her nearby.

As Joseph gently placed the baby back into Sarah's arms, she remembered it was Simon's birthday.

Their baby was born on Simon's birthday. *Happy birthday, my love*, she said silently to Simon, caressing the baby's forehead. *Happy birthday!*

"Well," Joseph said, bringing Sarah back from her thoughts, "what did you end up naming him?"

"Christopher," she said, feeling Simon with her. Strong in faith and more certain of the future, she was unafraid to face whatever lie ahead. "Jason Christopher Free."

EPILOGUE I
MONDAY
April 14, 1980

THE VATICAN
ROME, ITALY

Scenes of what American journalists called a "massacre" on the holiest of days continued to dominate the local news on Italy's new RAI3 cable news channel. Across the large screen television in the dining area of the Vatican apartment were ongoing reports intercutting coverage from U.S. stations. Currently airing was a repeat report from earlier given by an American ABC reporter standing beside a hospital whose façade lay in rubble.

"It was here at Bethlehem Hospital one week ago that Jacob Uzziel Dawz, Vietnam veteran and New Galilee, Connecticut Saint Catherine's Roman Catholic priest, leapt to his death following a bizarre spree of murders. As of right now..." the reporter paused to look down at his notepad, "police are still trying to identify the more than eighty-seven hospital staff and patients who were brutally slain throughout this bizarre and heinous event. And it still remains a mystery to investigators what interest Mr. Dawz had in the Maternity Wing."

Though he should have been asleep, the pontiff found it difficult considering recent events. Events that cast a negative pall on the Church and threatened to connect him to Jacob.

Unable to conceal his simmering fury, he stood before the screen scowling. Bemoaning the advent of twenty-four-hour news coverage, he threw the remote against the wall in a fit of rage. Stepping over the shattered pieces of plastic and batteries, he made for the phone.

The Most Reverend Ferdinand Masselli, the pontiff's second prefect in under a year, was slowly getting accustomed to the pontiff's moods. In recent days, however, nothing could have prepared him for the wild swings in his boss' personality. The moods were understandable, he supposed, given the scandal and scrutiny Mother Church was currently under. It was the connection to the pontiff he didn't understand. The acts of one person surely did not reflect an entire world-wide parish.

"Yes, Holy Father..."

Even though it was early yet, Pope Pontius' prefect answered the phone on the second ring.

"I need you to phone America for me."

"Your Eminence? What time is it?"

"Dammit, Ferdinand? Why do you insist on questioning me?" the pope asked, his temper short. Flaring.

The camerlengo had forgotten himself. His boss was a man who tolerated very little dissension. He reminded himself not to slip like that again. "Forgive me, Holy Father." Fully awake now, he sat up, turned on the light, and reached for pen and paper. "Tell me what I must do."

II

SUNDAY
MAY 18, 1980

The prefect inquired, quietly entering the pontiff's private office. Except for the bleached white collar around his neck, the figure entering the room was dressed in a robe of black, highlighted with red trim. Around his waist was a red sash matching his red skullcap. "Sanctissimus Pater?"

The room smelled slightly of strong incense. And tobacco.

Leather furniture and matching tables shined, having earlier been polished. They were placed over waxed wooden antique floors. Gone were the plush carpets favored by those who came before Pontius.

Adorning the walls: two oil paintings mounted within Victorian frames. One painting a recent portrait of Pope Pontius I, the other a Renaissance piece of Jesus Christ.

The only statue in the room: one of Saint Peter. No other.

A large globe made by the most talented craftsman in Italy stood on a nearby mahogany stand.

Everything on the twentieth century desk was meticulously placed, though the pontiff's personal computer took up nearly half the available room.

Near it were volumes of ecumenical works for quick reference.

The pontiff stood before the window overlooking Saint Peter's Square puffing away on a cigar, hands resting behind him as he toyed with his rosary. Loathingly, he watched the reporters — vultures still hungry for a connection between the Vatican and Jacob's grizzly murder spree — desecrate holy ground.

Enough time had passed. He would soon issue a decree restricting their access.

Inwardly acknowledging his latest prefect's breathing, the pontiff anxiously anticipated the information he knew had been procured. But he remained steadfast in place, choosing to speak without turning around to address Ferdinand.

"Leave the list on my desk and go."

"Of course, your Eminence," Ferdinand returned, placing a list of names onto the Holy Father's desk before retreating.

It was only then that the pontiff pivoted, turning in time to watch the prefect leave.

He took in the circumference of the room. Noticed an insect flying about. Heard its buzzing.

Taking a puff from his cigar, he patiently waited. Assessed the room. If anything was out of place, he would see to it that those responsible for not doing their jobs would be reprimanded.

Discipline, he stressed inwardly as the invading pest made a pass close to his face. Catching the fly, Ben held it between the thumb and forefinger of his left hand.

Order. Turning the tiny, winged bug over, he regarded it curiously while exhaling a mouth full of smoke.

Unwavering obedience. Tenets by which he ruled.

Trapped, the fly's head jerked and spasmed as it assessed its options. Ben watched the legs rapidly move about. As if on an invisible treadmill. He observed its wings flapping so fast they were tiny blurs attached to a little hairy body. After a brief pause, the fly was at it again in the hopes the action would set it free.

Plucking the wings from the defenseless insect, Ben made sure that would not be the case. It was defenseless but it was not innocent.

"Consider this punishment for invading my space," he said to the fly.

Yes, if there was a problem, let those unwilling to submit to Pontius and Mother Church suffer the consequences. It made no difference to him.

As head of the most powerful institution in the world, Ben regarded all other things as insignificant. His destiny was far too important.

Ben placed the wingless fly on the windowsill. There it would spend the remainder of its short existence reminded of its crime. Its sin.

Unyielding in his approach, Pope Pontius was prepared to do unto others what he did to the fly should anyone stand in his way. Cross him.

Sitting in the large Italian leather chair behind the desk he began perusing the list of unpublished names faxed to his prefect. Compiled by the Federal Bureau of Investigations in the United States of America, the incomplete list identified many of the deceased victims of what would become known as the Connecticut Easter Massacre of 1980.

The pontiff's breathing quickened as he glanced through the alphabetized names. Searching. Scanning.

He knew he'd recognize it once he saw it. The name was sure to stand out—

"Simon. Peter. Fucking. Free!" He repeated the name again. This time louder. "Simon Peter Free!"

Tossing the papers up over his head, the unattached pages took flight. They scattered in all directions.

An excitable fit of laughter erupted from his stomach and worked its way up his throat. "So much for the Savior," he said to no one in the room, still laughing when he slammed his fist onto the desk. "Dead! Dead! Dead!"

Standing, he walked around the room reflecting on what spurred Jacob Dawz on. In the beginning, when he intercepted Jacob's first letter meant for his superior, he rarely gave it much consideration beyond its possible connection to the crazy nun's words. But there were things that Jacob knew. Things that could not be dismissed.

And he was driven. Unnaturally so.

But it was as if Jacob suffered from dissociative identity disorder. It wasn't only the letters — letters that appeared to be written by different people. Jacob was a priest. One who made a name for himself. Becoming an ardent scholar on Christology. Yet he moonlighted in the shadows. Held secrets that even Ben wasn't privy to. It was as if he was living multiple lives.

Jacob was a curiosity Ben needed to tread carefully. But more than a curiosity. More than a degree of foresight, when it came to a man in Ben's position, he needed to rely on instinct. Just as he did in his life before entering the church. Just as he did when he served as prefect dealing with Maria or Helmutt. Just as he had been doing as pope.

Instinct prompted him to hold on to the letters Jacob sent. To forge a relationship with him through intermediaries. To use Jacob's zealotry to further his agenda. To set up the chess pieces.

It was also instinct that prompted him to act when he realized someone had gotten too close to the truth. To Sister Maria's prophetic vision. So close they could possibly see the prophecy through. He knew the day would come. Knew it was possible. How fitting that another Free should factor so prominently in the prophecy.

Pontius wondered if it was like Sister Maria said. That the evil one manipulates people into doing things most when they are unaware. Relishing the thought, he wondered what others would say about *him* since he was guilty of doing the same.

Yet politicians manipulated in the name of patriotism. Church leaders in the name of faith. It was all relative.

Ben knew better. It wasn't demons and devils that were the scariest or the worst of all detestations. Mortal men had that category covered.

As one man's patriotism is another's terrorism, so too is one man's religion another man's cult.

Thoughts of Sister Maria de Jesus brought back recollections of her two meetings with Helmutt. And Helmutt's fear of the future.

Or was it fear FOR the future?

Ben wasn't fearful of or for the future. Not with the knowledge he possessed. Some of what Maria foretold *did* come to pass. Proof of that was found in Father Matthew Free's confiscated notes. But parts also failed to execute themselves. And if the old woman's visions were so threatening to Mother Church, to mankind, why was the Savior killed now? Why twenty years before the end of the millennium?

Once more before the window overlooking Saint Peter's Square, he deplored the reporters and non-faithful visitors mulling about. Detested their presence. Soon the whole square would be considered sacred ground. And he would dispense with them. It would be one of many sweeping changes he planned on implementing. His time was coming.

Eventually all would come to see his edicts as necessary. Then there would be no stopping him.

There was never any such thing as a Savior anyway. He knew it was all a farce. Coincidence. And now that the one seemly prophesied was out of the picture, it was time to get serious. Soon people would learn to not only revere the leader of the Roman Catholic Church, but they would also learn to worship him.

At the window, he relit the foot of his Cohiba Gordo. A gift from Cuban leader Fidel Castro.

He savored each deep puff slowly. Deliberately.

"Second Coming," he snorted, turning to face the Renaissance painting of Christ. One of only two paintings in the room. It depicted Jesus standing before His executioner — the one who judged him in Rome some nineteen hundred years ago.

"I'll give everyone their Savior. Their Messiah."

Seething with disdain. Eyes narrowed. Pope Pontius' lips curled as he extinguished his cigar directly on the painted image of the Christ King.

Q&A
WITH THE AUTHOR

STORY IDEAS AND INSPIRATIONS?

It would be inauthentic of me to suggest that growing up in a Roman Catholic household and attending a parochial school during my formative years didn't have an impact. They did. The only way I could make sense of what I saw, what I felt... things that couldn't be explained and blatant contradictions to religious teachings, was to write a story. My first, it took 15 years. As any writer will tell you, unless you're able to consistently spend time planning, researching, and writing, the process can take years. And it did. The ideas are based on personal experiences, dreams, and an exhausting amount of research. Research made easier as technology improved. The narrative truly came together when I realized what I wanted to accomplish with the story. And that was to explore which is more frightening and more dangerous: supernatural evil or human evil.

STRANGE EXPERIENCES WHILE WRITING OR THAT LED TO WRITING THE STORY?

Many dreams as a child and some very perplexing personal experiences made it into the story. Though not explicitly in the story, one late night while writing I heard voices, as in several people having a conversation I couldn't quite understand. Yet the house was dark. My wife was sound asleep. No TVs or lights were on. The time, however, was 3 AM.

SIMILAR EVENTS/PEOPLE IN THE STORY?

As the saying goes, truth *is* stranger than fiction. Do enough research and one begins to see a pattern. The trouble is, it's like pulling on a thread. Once pulled... well, you get the idea. I'll leave it at that. While this is a work of fiction, there is some fascinating thread pulling waiting to happen if you're willing to go there. Be warned. Once you do, there's no coming back.

OTHER BOOKS
BY THIS AUTHOR

Future Destiny

When Worlds Collide

*Of Space & Time: A Collection
of Science Fiction Short Stories*

*From Where I Sit: A
Collection of Short Fiction*

*Dark Awakenings: A Collection
of Haunting Short Stories*